Note on the author

Mary O'Sullivan lives in Carrigaline, Co Cork, with her husband Seán. Her bestselling novels *Parting Company*, *As Easy As That* and *Ebb & Flow* were also published by Poolbeg.

You can visit her website at www.maryosullivanauthor.ie

Also published by Poolbeg

Ebb & Flow
As Easy As That
Parting Company

Acknowledgements

The journey between the first hazy idea for a story and the final publication of a novel is a long one. Luckily, it's not a journey an author takes alone. I'd like to give my sincere thanks to everyone who has helped me along the way, especially the following people:

Paula, Niamh, Sarah, David and all the staff in Poolbeg – for your support, encouragement and faith in my work.

Editor, Gaye Shortland, for her generosity with her literary skills, her advice and patience.

Susan and Paul in the Feldstein Literary Agency – for support, encouragement and heart-warming optimism.

Karen O'Connor and Melissa Scully – who generously helped me with research.

Mary Lynsky and Karen Kinsella – for reading my embryo manuscripts and for their much appreciated advice and support.

A great big thank you to all who have bought my books and those who have taken the time to write, email and visit my website at www.maryosullivanauthor.ie. Your vote of confidence is very much appreciated.

And finally my family – Seán, Owen and Vera in Carrigaline, Paul and Craig in New Zealand, Annie and Emmett in Germany and my in-laws in Cork. Thank you all for your endless patience, understanding and support.

For Annie and Emmett

Ní neart go cur le chéile

CHAPTER 1

The thump, thump from upstairs was incessant. Meg felt as if the ceiling, the whole room, was vibrating to the rhythm of the awful noise her son called music. But at least she knew where Tommy was tonight. A headache was a small price to pay for that peace of mind.

Pressing the volume on the remote control, she turned up the sound and sat back to watch the TV news. War, drought, floods, poverty, wealth, power and powerlessness. Not what she needed now. Flicking through the channels she found a reality show.

When she heard the front door open she checked her watch. Nine thirty. John was home early tonight. He came into the lounge and threw himself into an armchair.

"How are you?" Meg asked.

"I'm whacked." He glanced at the screen. "Why are you watching this rubbish?"

She stood and handed the remote control to him, too tired to take up the challenge he was offering.

"Are you hungry? There's some cooked salmon in the fridge."

1

"I've eaten. Just a cup of coffee, please. And tell Tommy turn that racket down."

Kettle on, she went upstairs, tapped on Tommy's door and opened it. Her son was sitting in front of his computer, jiggling around in time to the music which was rocking the whole room.

"Your father's home!" she shouted over the noise. "Put on your earphones, please!"

Tommy turned around to stare at her. She looked back at her seventeen-year-old son and tried to see the child he had been up to a year ago. He was in there somewhere behind the studs and piercings. Somewhere underneath his mop of orange-streaked hair.

"So, the Fuehrer's here."

"Just do as you're asked," she said and closed his door before he could answer.

By the time she brought coffee into the lounge, John was asleep in his chair. He seemed vulnerable in sleep, the normally stubborn line of his jaw relaxed. She put the cup on the coffee table and went to wake him. Her hand on his shoulder, she hesitated. Maybe he needed rest more than coffee. But then she didn't really know what her driven husband needed. Success? Money? Promotion? He had all that but his ambition was still as honed as it had been when he'd started out as a handyman in the storage company he now managed and part-owned. He continued to drive himself forward, working impossibly long hours, fretting over contracts, second-guessing competitors. She touched his hair, silver-streaked but yet thick and strong.

Her hand slid from his hair onto his shoulder. She must talk to him about Carrie. She shook him gently.

2

"John. Your coffee."

For an instant he looked at her sleepily without any recognition in his eyes. Meg had to consciously control her resentment.

"Tough day?" she asked quietly, not really wanting to know. According to her husband his working life was a series of tough days, tough decisions, tough deals. A tough man. Strong, decisive.

He rubbed his hands over his eyes, then reached for his coffee and swallowed a long draught.

"Anything that could've gone wrong today, did. And we've got problems with the CCTV again."

Sitting across from him, Meg nodded and waited for the litany to start. Competitors were ruthless, tax prohibitive, profit margins dwindling. He never asked for her opinion. All he needed was an attentive audience and the odd nod of agreement. Meg had perfected the art of appearing to listen. It would be pointless trying to talk to him about his daughter until he had gone through his complaining routine.

Then Meg noticed the silence. There were no complaints from John. In fact, he had not said another word. She glanced across at him and saw that he looked drawn. Weary. His tie was loosened and his normally healthy colour had a tinge of grey.

"Are you feeling alright?"

Draining off the last of his coffee, he stood up. "Just exhausted," he said. "I'm off to bed. Tell Tommy I want him in my office at nine o'clock tomorrow morning. We're clearing out Bay 6 and I need extra manpower for a few days."

Instructions issued, he turned and left the room. No

goodnight kiss. Not even the peck on the cheek which had lately become their only form of physical contact. And no chance to talk about Carrie. Meg looked at her watch and did some quick subtraction. What time would it be in Maine now?

Going into the hall, Meg picked up the phone and tapped in the international dialling code. She knew the whole sequence of numbers off by heart at this stage. She listened as the line crackled and hissed. Eventually Carrie's phone rang on the east coast of the USA. Across the tumbling breadth and dark depths of the North Atlantic. It rang and rang. The voicemail greeting clicked in. Meg's hands began to shake as she listened to her daughter's familiar voice. Sweet and serious. A deep voice for such a young girl. 'Please leave a message after the tone and I will get back to you as soon as possible.' Meg tried and failed to keep the panic out of her voice when she spoke: "Carrie, this is Mom again. Please send me a text or call. It's a week since I last heard from you. You know I fuss. Love you."

When she put down the phone Meg just stood where she was, eyes shut, watching a stream of horrific images flash past. Her daughter lying in some back street, throat slashed. Carrie bound and gagged, kidnapped by gangsters, crying out for help, calling for her mother.

"Is this one of your new fads, Mom? Transcendental Meditation or something?"

Meg opened her eyes to a sight almost as frightening as her mental images. Tommy was dressed to go out, a silly little black bowler hat perched on top of his orange-streaked hair and eyeliner around his eyes.

"Where do you think you're going? It's after ten o'clock."

4

"Out."

"No! You're not. Come into the lounge. We need to talk."

"What about? I haven't time. I'm meeting Breeze in five minutes."

"Breeze! That says it all. What kind of a person would call himself Breeze?"

Tommy moved towards the front door but Meg got there before him. She stood with her back against the door, blocking his path.

"I'm serious, Tommy. You're not going out now. It's too late."

"For Christ's sake! I'm nearly eighteen. Stop treating me like a child!"

"Stop acting like one!" Meg shot back but that wasn't what she meant to say. God! How she wished with all her heart that he would act like the child he had been. Funny, co-operative, kind, bright and intelligent. A little stubborn but then he would have got that from John. Except that in Tommy the stubbornness had been tempered by a willingness to listen not very apparent in his father's make-up. The pre-Breeze Tommy.

"You're not eighteen yet. You'll do as I say until you learn to behave responsibly."

"You mean until I become the nerd you and the Fuehrer want me to be. Degrees pouring out my ears. Big deal!"

Meg had to clasp her hands tightly together. She wanted to slap her son's face, to see his defiance turn to shock. But the shock was hers. How could she ever want to hurt her child? What was happening to her? To the family.

"We really need to talk, Tommy. I don't want to argue. Please don't go out now."

5

Maybe it was the despair in her tone or maybe it was just the innate decency in him. For whatever reason Tommy lifted his hand and took off his silly hat. A capitulation. Taking out his mobile he began his impossibly fast texting. Meg guessed that he was cancelling his arrangement with Breeze.

"Do you want a cup of coffee?" she asked.

"Too late."

"Hot milk?"

When he nodded agreement Meg went into the kitchen and put milk for two into a saucepan. Tommy followed her in and sat on one of the high stools at the breakfast counter. His eyeliner looked even weirder in the bright kitchen light.

"If you're going to wear that stuff around your eyes you should learn to put it on properly," she said and instantly regretted making yet another criticism.

"Is that what you wanted to talk about? All-important appearances?"

"As a matter of fact I wanted to talk about Carrie. When did you last hear from her?"

Meg caught a hesitation, a beat of fear, before Tommy replied.

"It's odd," he said quietly. "I haven't heard from her for over a week. She's not answering her phone and she hasn't picked up any of her emails either. I wonder what she's up to that she doesn't want us to know."

Standing at the cooker watching the milk start to bubble, Meg felt her heart pound. Turning around, she caught the concern on Tommy's face. Her heart beat even faster. Tommy and Carrie were close. The strongest bond in the Enright household. Carrie was the caring older sister and Tommy her

6

adored young brother. Meg had often noticed them share a silent communication. Just like twins even though Carrie was the elder by four years. One always knew when the other was feeling down or sick.

"Is she alright, Tommy? I haven't heard from her either. I'm worried."

He shrugged his shoulders. "She's twenty-one, Mom. She doesn't have to report in to you every day. Anyway, she's not on her own in Portland. You'd have heard if anything bad had happened."

The sudden hiss of milk boiling over onto the hob brought Meg's attention back to the cooker. By the time she had mopped up the spill and poured out the two mugs of milk the closed look was back on Tommy's face. But Meg felt better able to cope with it now. He was right. If Carrie was missing or if her mutilated body had been recovered, either the Maine police or one of Carrie's friends would have contacted home. Her friends were a nice group. All second-year university students on a working summer holiday in America. Nice people. Just like Carrie. They would look out for each other. Especially Trina. Carrie and Trina Farrell were best friends. Meg smiled at Tommy.

"You're a sensible lad, Tom. You're right. I worry too much. Carrie will be home next week anyway. Which reminds me, you're back to school then too."

"I don't want to talk about it!"

"It's your last year in secondary. You've done so well up to now it's not worth throwing it all away. Remember our agreement?"

"Agreement? Is that what you call it? You and the Fuehrer laid down the law and left me no choice."

"Stop calling your father by that awful name!"

"It's a description, not a name."

Ignoring that comment, Meg lifted her mug and swallowed a mouthful of hot milk. She had put some nutmeg and vanilla into it. The flavours melded at the back of her tongue. While she savoured the warm tang Tommy stared at her defiantly. More relaxed now, she tried to reason with him.

"The deal was you wore whatever you liked for the summer holidays but you know well you won't be allowed back to St Martin's looking as you do now."

"Whatever," Tommy said, shrugging his shoulders.

All Meg's frustration and resentment rushed at her in an unstoppable wave. Banging her mug onto the counter she got up from her seat and stood in front of her defiant son, her face flushed and her throat almost choked with a flood of angry words.

"How dare you! Do you think it's easy for your father and me? We've worked hard to give you a good education. St Martin's isn't cheap. We've paid your fees there for the past four years and you're going back next week whether you like it or not. And that means complying with their dress code. No studs or piercings, no outrageous hairstyles and definitely no orange streaks! Understood?"

"You can't make me. And what is it with you? You're beginning to sound like the Fuehrer."

Meg knew she was handling this situation badly. Of course they couldn't make him go if he really didn't want to. The fact was, he did. Carrie had told her. By next week his studs and hoops would be removed and his orange streaks would be covered by a dark dye until they grew out. No

8

point in arguing about it now. This was just his way of asserting himself. Looking for attention. And her way of expressing her worry. Looking for reassurance. She took a few steps back from him and let out a long sigh.

"Suit yourself," she said. "You'd better go to bed now. You must be up early in the morning. Your father wants you in EFAS. Some bay or other needs clearing out."

"More slave labour."

"He pays you."

"Not the going rate."

Meg managed to keep her mouth shut. Tommy was telling the truth. John paid his own son less and worked him harder than anyone else. 'Character building', he called it and refused to budge from that position. Everyone was refusing to budge from their entrenched positions. John was determined to work endless hours for EFAS. Tommy seemed equally determined to go down a ruinous path. Even Carrie, gentle Carrie, was doggedly refusing to answer her phone.

"I'm going next year."

Meg looked at her son. What was he threatening now?

"Going where?"

"To America to work next summer. I'm not spending another holiday slaving in EFAS. Or maybe I'll just backpack around Europe. Anyway I'll be eighteen then. I can do what I like."

He picked up his hat and walked out of the kitchen. Meg listened. When she heard him climb the stairs she sighed with relief and picked up the mug he had left for her to clear away.

Kitchen tidied, Meg locked doors, closed windows and put on the alarm. She waited until the 'alarm on' sign flashed.

9

The Enrights were protected from the outside world for tonight.

But as she climbed the stairs Meg had to fight the feeling that she had locked the threats to her peaceful existence in rather than out. Guilty at such a thought, she leaned over and kissed her sleeping husband on the forehead. He muttered in his sleep and turned, taking most of the duvet with him.

Snuggling into his back, she slipped her arm around him. She listened to his breathing for a little while and thought about Tommy and what he might become, about Carrie and what she might be doing. Meg drifted uneasily from drowsiness to restless sleep.

CHAPTER 2

EFAS Storage Ltd was situated in an industrial estate on the western outskirts of Cork city. John Enright slowed down as he approached the complex. From here he could see the EFAS building dominating all the other units. It was bigger, brighter, cleaner. He remembered now, as he did every morning at this point, how small and insignificant the original unit had been. Not much more than a lock-up garage. For a fleeting moment he felt satisfied. Even happy. Seeing a truck looming in his mirror, he changed up gears and quickly headed towards EFAS.

The night-security guard was sitting in his van at the perimeter gates. As soon as he saw his boss approaching, he got out and opened up the gates for him. John rolled down the driver's window of his car.

"Morning, Ollie. Quiet night, I hope?"

"Not a whisper."

John waved and drove towards the main doors of the building. Having parked and locked his car, he stood and looked carefully around. He scanned everything – the car park, the fencing, the bulding itself – knowing that he could detect the smallest change, the slightest evidence of an attempted break-in. It wasn't that he distrusted Ollie. He was a solid, reliable night-watchman. It was just that John had learned by experience to trust his own judgement above all others. Besides, Ollie was getting on now. He might not be as sharp as he once had been.

Satisfied, John punched in his code, opened the front door and headed for his own office. The first thing he did was to put on the kettle. It was tradition that he and Ollie shared an early morning cup of coffee. By the time John had emptied out his briefcase and booted up his computer, Ollie had come in and made the coffee.

"D'you know, boss, number five camera's still out of action? I thought 'twas to be fixed yesterday?"

"It should've been. I'll put a bomb under that crowd today."

Ollie nodded his agreement. He was worried about that camera. It was trained on the west side of the building where it overlooked the Jacuzzi and Hot Tub company next door. The most vulnerable spot on the whole site. "I keep a good eye on it but I don't like the trees there. Too much cover for anyone who wanted to hide out."

"Pointless asking that prick next door to cut the bloody trees," said John. "He just won't listen. What about extra lighting?"

Ollie was silent, the mug of coffee in his hand and a glazed expression in his eyes. John recognised that look. It was the same expression Meg wore whenever EFAS was mentioned. He felt a flash of anger. It would be nice to have the luxury of being bored by the day-to-day problems of running this business. What did any of them care about the millions of euro worth of goods that EFAS had pledged to store securely? The responsibility for insurance, temperature control, humidity, security, marketing and payroll all lay on his shoulders. None of them gave a damn. Not Meg and certainly not Tommy. Carrie used to be a good listener but she had her own life nowadays: a carefree student life paid for out of EFAS profits. And even Ollie seemed to be joining the ranks of the bored this morning. He was still staring vacantly ahead, mug in hand.

"Ollie?"

The older man focussed his eyes and looked straight at John. He appeared unsure, uncharacteristically nervous.

"You seem a bit on edge, Ollie."

Ollie put down his mug of coffee and leaned forward. He cleared his throat.

More than edgy, thought John. The man was really nervous. "Spit it out."

"There's something I feel I should say to you, boss."

"We're friends, Ollie. Go ahead. Say whatever's on your mind."

"It's your son."

"Tommy?"

"Well, about his friend really. Jason Goodall. The punk who calls himself Breeze. He's bad news, boss. I know of his family. His older brother's a drug dealer. He's not fit company for your lad."

For an instant John had an image of his son. Orange-streaked hair, studs and hoops, ridiculous clothes and a permanently defiant expression. It seemed par for the course that Tommy should have an undesirable friend. Meg had mentioned something about this Breeze character. Something about tolerating him until Tommy grew away from him. He hadn't really been listening. But drugs? Jesus!

"Are you saying Tommy's on drugs?"

"God, no, I'm not! I'm not even saying that Jason Goodall has anything to do with them. It's just that his brother has form. His father has done time too for burglary and assault. Not the kind of people your son should be mixing with. I'm sorry if you think I'm interfering. I just thought you should know."

John stood up from behind his desk and walked over to Ollie. He put his hand on the older man's shoulder.

"Thanks for telling me, Ollie. I'll have a word with Tommy. As a matter of fact he's coming in here this morning. I want him to clear out Bay 6. A bit of hard work will be good for him."

Long after Ollie had left the office to go home for his day's sleep, John sat at his desk. Fuming. He'd have a word with Tommy alright. More than a word. The spoiled brat needed a good kick up the backside. He'd had all the advantages. No night school for Tommy Enright. No slaving all day and studying into the early hours of the morning. Not for him the struggle his father had in order to make something of himself. He was an ungrateful pup. And most of it was Meg's fault. Her 'let him be his own person' nonsense was showing results now.

Guilt began to niggle at John. He had been too busy, too preoccupied with EFAS to notice his son changing from being a well-balanced teenager to the surly freakish person he now was. When had it happened?

The door to his office opened and Francine entered the

14

room on a waft of perfume. She smiled at John and for an instant he forgot all his problems.

* * *

Meg pulled the blinds across and glanced out into the garden. It looked cold outside. She could sense the drop of temperature in the watery light and the morning mist which was slow to burn off. It would be a sweater day. Sliding back the wardrobe doors, she rifled through her stock of knitwear until she found her favourite cream angora sweater. That choice made, the rest was easy. Meg was a creature of habit. She always wore her brown suede skirt and boots with her cream sweater. She always arrived into work at nine o'clock and had pasta for her lunch. She always did the window-dressing and buying for the soft furnishings shop which she and her oldest and closest friend, Lynn, co-owned. She always cooked and shopped and did the myriad domestic chores while John ran his little empire ...

Meg's meandering thoughts suddenly took a sharp turn and focussed on EFAS. She glanced at her watch. It was almost eight thirty and there was no sound from Tommy. Grabbing her beige jacket, she went quickly to his bedroom and rapped on the door.

"Tommy! Come on! It's half past eight and you're supposed to be in EFAS for nine."

"I'm nearly ready," Tommy's muffled voice replied. He was obviously still in bed.

"I'm going in ten minutes!" she called. "Get up if you want a lift. I won't wait."

She stood outside the door until she heard the rustle of

the duvet being thrown back. Then she went downstairs to have her orange juice and muesli because that's what she always had. Tommy pounded down the stairs five minutes later, looking even more dishevelled than usual. He grabbed a banana from the fruit bowl and shrugged on his long black coat. Meg glanced at him and for a moment saw him through John's eyes. He probably felt embarrassed by his son. Maybe even a little ashamed of him.

The drive from the suburb where they lived to EFAS took only ten minutes. As they pulled up outside the gleaming white premises dotted with lines of Ferrari-red roller-shutter doors, Meg turned to Tommy.

"Try to be civil to your father today, would you? Let's keep our family business private."

"Too late. Everyone knows he looks on me as a loser and I think he's a —"

"Tommy! You've said too much already. Anyway you'll be late. Go on."

To Meg's surprise, Tommy leaned across and gave her a hug. "Cheer up, Mom. Carrie'll be back soon."

He jumped out, walking smartly towards the entrance until he remembered to slouch. With his long coat trailing the ground and his orange-streaked hair he had certainly achieved the rebellious look he seemed to want so much. Meg smiled as she watched him. Her last born. Her baby. A boy floundering his way towards manhood. John would never understand that. His own rite of passage had been powered by ambition and hard work. And a hard-faced mother who had reared him alone after the early death of his father. Meg shivered. She hadn't thought about Hannah Enright for a long time. She had barely remembered her since the funeral. Hopefully it would be a long time before she recalled the surly woman again. Meg was not surprised when a black cloud passed over the watery sun. It was probably Hannah floating by. Letting her know that she was watching, monitoring her every thought and still disapproving.

Glancing at her watch, Meg realised that for once she wouldn't make the shop for nine o'clock. Neither would Lynn but then she never did. She normally launched herself breathlessly in the door at half past nine. Not that it would make much difference. On impulse, Meg took out her phone and dialled Lynn's number. The phone had almost rung out before it was answered by a breathless Lynn.

"I'll be a little late this morning," Meg told her. "I have something to do before I come in."

"Are you alright, Meg? Has something happened?"

"No, I'm fine. Just someone I need to see and now is the best time. I won't be long."

"Take all the time you need. It won't be that busy anyway. See you later."

Meg switched off her phone, knowing that Lynn would still go through her usual make-up routine. The shop would not be opened on time this morning. So what? To hell with the shop. Cushions and curtains were hardly matters of life and death. Her daughter's welfare could be.

As she got to the front door of EFAS she thought she heard John's raised voice but then she knew he would be far too professional to shout in the hallowed temple of his precious storage business. Opening the door, Meg discovered that the loud voice belonged to the forklift driver who was issuing orders to Tommy. A changed Tommy. Already in overalls, his hair tied back in a pony-tail, he was busily stacking boxes at the far end of one of the aisles.

Worried that her son would think she was spying on him, she quickly turned towards the reception area. A very attractive blonde girl sat at the semi-circular beech counter, a bank of screens on the wall behind her. Meg's eyes flicked from the girl's perfect make-up to her pristine white blouse. This must be the new receptionist John had mentioned. Francine. Yes. A very efficient worker according to John. He had forgotten to mention that she had super-model looks. Maybe he hadn't noticed.

"Good morning. May I help you?"

Her voice was soft and slightly husky. Welcoming. Meg smiled at her.

"I'd like to see John Enright for a moment."

"Could you give me your name, please, and I'll see if he's available."

She was efficient alright. Very protective of her boss. No wonder John thought she was good at her job.

"I'm his wife. Meg Enright. You must be Francine."

The girl hesitated for a moment before taking Meg's outstretched hand. Up close Meg noticed minute lines at the corners of the beautiful blue eyes. Francine was not as young as she appeared at first glance. The handshake too was assured. The touch of a confident woman.

"Follow me please, Mrs Enright," she said, leading the way towards John's office, obliging Meg to trail behind her. Francine tapped on the door of the office and opened it. Meg was close enough to see John's face as he looked up and saw the receptionist. He smiled. That lovely smile Meg had not seen for so long. The one that sparked lights in his brown eyes.

18

"Mrs Enright is here to see you, John. Don't forget your nine thirty appointment."

The lights faded instantly in John's eyes. Meg was struck by his guarded expression as he watched her step past Francine and walk into his office. Behind her she heard the door click as Francine left.

John waved his hand towards a chair. Meg waited for him to ask what he could do for her, just as he would any client. Instead he seemed as dumbstruck as she. Waiting for her to make the first move. Like a game of chess. Or poker. Hiding all the real feelings. Feigning a winning hand. Gamesmanship. Knickers to this!

"I want to talk about Carrie. I'm worried about her."

"Why are you worried? It's Tommy you should be concerned with. Did you see the way he turned up for work this morning? If he wasn't my son, I wouldn't let him set foot on the premises."

"Have you heard from Carrie recently?"

The angry glint which had flashed in his eyes at the mention of his son's name faded. He frowned and then became more thoughtful. Taking out his mobile he flipped it open and scrolled through recent messages. When he looked up at Meg again, puzzlement had replaced anger.

"That's funny. It's well over a week since the last message. Not like her at all. Why? Has she been in contact with you?"

Meg shook her head. In fact Meg shook – from the tips of her toes to the top of her head, she shook. She had pegged John's reaction as her litmus test. She always fussed and worried. Most of the time without justification. John never did. He had an inner core of calm logic which allowed him to examine a situation clinically. The concern on his face now sent her own fears for her daughter's safety into overdrive.

"What can we do?" she said. "Should we contact the police?"

"Stop! Panicking isn't going to help the situation. Did you check with Tommy?"

"Of course. He said she hasn't been to an Internet café for the past week. No email from her. She hasn't texted him either. Her phone is just going to message minder. I know something terrible has happened."

Despite her best efforts at self-control, tears began to well. Uncapped now, the well gushed in hot, salty streams down her face. Opening her bag, Meg poked inside for a tissue. By the time her shaking fingers had freed one from the packet John was standing beside her, his hand on her shoulder.

"Come on now, Meg. There's no need for hysterics. She's probably just having a last knees-up before coming home. She's due back next week, right?"

Meg nodded agreement but she didn't feel it. Wasn't that the problem? Would Carrie ever be home again? Would they ever get another chance to hear her infectious laugh or see the magnificent dark brown eyes she had inherited from her father? The longing to see her beautiful daughter was so strong it pressed onto Meg's chest in a band of searing physical pain. She folded her arms protectively across the pain as if it was the embodiment of Carrie. Closing her eyes she watched as images of Carrie's first steps, her first day at school, her debs ball flashed past. Suddenly John was kneeling in front of her, his arms around her, holding her tightly, stroking her hair, comforting her. She laid her head on his shoulder and drew from his strength.

"It'll be alright, Meg. She's an adult now. You've got to learn to let her go."

"But …"

A tap sounded on the door and it immediately opened. John's arms dropped quickly to his sides. Francine stood there, looking from the kneeling John to the tearstained Meg. "I'm sorry to interrupt, John," she said, "but your appointment's here."

John stood and nodded to Francine. She turned and closed the door softly behind her.

"It's Patrick Morgan," John explained, walking back to his chair behind the desk. "I don't know what he wants. It's unusual for him to look for a meeting. I meant to go to see him at his house or take him out for a drink but I've been so busy. I'm sorry, Meg, but I'll have to see him now."

Meg nodded her understanding. Patrick Morgan was the man who had given John his chance in life. The man who had initially employed him, had encouraged him to study and who had eventually sold 40 percent of EFAS shares to him. They had built up the storage business together but more importantly Patrick Morgan had become the father John never had. Of course she understood.

"I'm sorry for disturbing you at work."

As soon as she had uttered the words, Meg knew the moment of closeness they had just shared was over. Everything fell back into place. EFAS was John's priority, his achievement, his reason for getting up every morning. Knowing that she was being unfair, even petty, she gave her eyes one last dab of the tissue and stood up.

"We'll talk to-night," John said. "And don't worry. If we haven't heard from Carrie by then, we'll make a few calls. If there was anything wrong, we would have heard."

Exactly as Tommy had said. Like father, like son. Maybe

that was the problem between Tommy and John. They were too alike but neither of them could see that.

John was already busy at his computer, his focus on the screen. Meg closed the door of the office behind her and walked into reception. Francine was sitting beside Patrick Morgan on the couch reserved for clients, her long legs elegantly crossed.

Meg was shocked at what she saw. Patrick was well into his seventies but he had always been a fit man. Burly yet never unhealthily heavy. He had retired three years ago but not because of ill-health. Meg recalled now that she had thought him a little feeble, a bit shaky as he had shared dinner with them last Christmas. But nothing out of the ordinary for a man of his years. That was only eight months ago. He looked thin and drawn this morning, his face wrinkled with folds of loose skin. A walking stick lay propped against the couch He offered his hand to Meg without standing.

"Meg. How are you?"

"Well, Patrick, thank you. And you?"

"Surviving. I must have a chat with that husband of yours. Excuse me."

Picking up the walking stick, he leant heavily on it and heaved himself off the couch. Meg just stood there, not sure if she should offer assistance or not. The proud tilt of his head as he shuffled across reception did not invite help. For the first time Meg realised that Patrick Morgan was an old man, a sick man. But more than that, she had a glimpse of where she and John were headed. They were so quickly racing towards stiff joints, grey hair and forgetfulness.

"Mrs Enright, I hope you don't mind me saying but I

think you may want to visit the Ladies before you go. Your mascara has run a little."

Meg should have been grateful. Instead she resented Francine's patronising tone. She glanced at the other woman's flawless make-up, muttered her thanks and went to the bathroom. When she saw her mascara-streaked image in the mirror, her resentment turned to hot embarrassment. How could John have let her out like that and what must Patrick Morgan have thought?

She did some quick repairs, brushed her hair and looked closely in the mirror again. The image reflected was that of a cool, sophisticated woman. Dark-haired, hazel-eyed, small nose and a wide, full-lipped mouth. Not classically beautiful but attractive none the less. Respectable for a woman of thirty-nine. For a woman who feared her daughter was dead and her son set to ruin his life. A woman whose husband did not even notice that her mascara had run. As she watched, the image in the mirror changed. The eyes began to fill with tears and the full lips puckered.

Hating the self-pitying image, Meg straightened up her shoulders and took a deep breath. She went out to reception and strode past Francine. She had no idea what she was going to do but she would not be waiting until John found time in his busy schedule to look for his daughter. Carrie was in some kind of trouble. Meg knew it with every cell in her body. Knowing was not enough. The time for doing had come.

CHAPTER 3

Murphy's Law came into force in all its perverse glory. Town was unusually busy. Every traffic light flicked on to red just as Meg approached and it was impossible to get a parking space. She would have to go to the multi-storey car park now. That was a good ten minutes' walk away from Bridge Street where Curtain Call, the shop she and Lynn co-owned, traded — the small soft furnishings store they sometimes jokingly referred to, very privately, as their Inferior Design business.

As she walked through the centre of town Meg glanced at the window display of their main opposition. It was part of a multi-national chain, with huge buying power behind it. Curtain Call stock would fit into a corner of this chain store. Yet they lacked one ingredient which Lynn and Meg supplied to their customers: the personal touch. Meg went to people's homes, measured their windows, advised on colour schemes, designed custom-made curtains and blinds which Lynn then made up. Or she used to in the early years. Most of the machining was outsourced now.

Satisfied that the opposition's window display was mediocre, Meg walked quickly past Cork Opera House which had inspired the name for their shop, over Patrick's Bridge and then onto Bridge Street. Waiting for a green light at the pedestrian crossing, she looked across at the building which housed Curtain Call. Sandwiched between two similar three-storey buildings which had once been home to merchant princes, it had the sad appearance of a place occupied by many but cared for by none. The gutters needed clearing and the stonework cleaning. The different styles in blinds and curtains on the upper windows were a telltale sign of transient occupants. Sometimes the landlord rented out to private individuals and at others he let the upper stories as office space. The building was nothing more than an investment to him. Meg and Lynn on the ground floor were his anchor tenants. Turning her head this way and that, Meg examined the large display window of Curtain Call. She had just decided that it was attractive enough to entice custom when the crossing lights turned to green.

As she reached the door of the shop she realised she had not thought of Carrie since she had parked the car. A rush of guilt and panic flooded through her. It felt as if Carrie was floundering in deep waters and Meg was standing on shore, hands in pockets, ignoring her daughter's cries for help. What in the name of God was she to do? Just as panic was climbing towards hysteria, the shop door opened and a customer came out carrying two huge bags. Through the semi-transparent bags Meg noticed the intricate handsewn design of the ethnic cushions which were selling so well. Somewhere inside herself she found the strength to smile at the customer and make a mental note to order more of the cushions.

The shop was packed with browsers. Lynn was in her element. She would be playing her favourite game, having bets with herself as to how many she could entice to buy. She had a great record. Her charisma was a huge part of Curtain Call's success. Meg waved to her, slipped past the furore, went into the kitchenette and took off her jacket. She had calls to make, orders to write, stocktaking to do but her mind refused to click into work mode. Besides, Lynn probably needed a hand with the browsers.

An hour later the shop was cleared. Their business was successful enough for both of them to be glad of a quiet spell. Lynn parked herself on her high stool and chatted away endlessly while Meg made coffee in the kitchenette. It had become their habit over the many years they had known each other that Lynn talked and Meg listened. Meg handed Lynn her mug and then sat down herself. Lynn instantly stood and took the two long strides needed to cross the space between them.

"Do you realise you forgot to put coffee in the mugs? Sugar – yes. Milk – yes. Coffee – no! What in the name of God is wrong with you? I can see that you've been crying."

"I'm sorry. I'll put the kettle on again."

"Sit! You've been in a fog the last week. Talk, Meg. "

It happened again. The tears came out of their hiding place. Meg sniffled as she told Lynn about Carrie.

"I know there's something wrong. Carrie would never forget to contact home. Or decide freely not to. She's not that sort of person. You know her. She's considerate and kind. Either she can't because …"

"What does John say?"

"That we'd have heard if something terrible had

26

happened. That she's just having a last fling before she comes home."

"Well, he's definitely right about one thing. Somebody would have told you by now if she was missing or had an accident. I don't think Carrie is the type to be having a last boozy splurge though."

"I know. For some reason she can't contact home. Not even an email to Tommy. You know how close that pair are. She's in terrible trouble. I can feel it. She may even be dead." Meg began to shiver as the 'dead' word echoed around the little kitchenette. Saying it had brought it from the realm of secret dread to real possibility.

Lynn tore off a wad of kitchen roll and handed it to her. "Dry your eyes and pull yourself together. Yes, I think you're right to be worried but from what I can gather that's all you're doing. Have you tried to contact any of her friends? A big group of them travelled together, didn't they?"

"Six. All from her college year. I don't have numbers for them."

"You know their parents, don't you? Wasn't Siobhán Farrell's daughter one of the group?"

Meg nodded. Of course! Trina Farrell. Carrie's best friend. Why hadn't she thought of that? Probably because she had been too busy trying to convince herself there was nothing to worry about.

Lynn got up and headed for the shop. She came back with the phone book in her hand. Flicking through the pages, she pointed to a number and handed the book to Meg.

"There's Siobhán Farrell's number. Go ring her. Now!"

Meg blew her nose and wiped her eyes on the coarse

kitchen paper. Going out to the shop, she stood looking at the phone in dread. Suppose Trina was missing too. Or suppose Carrie had left to come home and they thought she had arrived safely. Suppose ...

"Dial the number!"

There was no disputing the authority in Lynn's voice. Fingers shaking, Meg dialled. She almost stopped halfway through. She wanted to know. God, how she needed to hear any news about Carrie! But she still had hope. Something in the deep dark depths of her psyche told her the knowing would destroy the last vestiges of her hope.

"Stop dithering!"

Meg dialled the remaining digits and waited for Siobhán Farrell to answer her phone.

* * *

John was trying not to stare. Unsuccessfully. Patrick Morgan looked like a very sick man. A shadow of the person he had been. It must be, it could only be, cancer. John could not bring himself to ask and obviously Patrick was finding the telling as difficult. The past fifteen minutes had been spent talking over EFAS profit and loss accounts and projections. Not a mention of the loss of Patrick's bodyweight or the pallor of his skin.

Francine pushed the door open with her elbow and came in carrying a tray. When she had laid out their cups for them, she smiled at both men and left again. Not needing to ask, John put two sugars and a dash of milk into Patrick's tea.

"She's seems like a nice girl," Patrick said, nodding his head in the direction of reception. "What about her work?"

"Excellent."

"Where did she work before? Did you check out her references?"

"She's been with a few high-profile firms. Francine comes here well recommended."

They were silent then, the sounds of distant voices from the warehouse and the muffled whirr of the forklift making their silence seem deeper. Patrick's fingers twitched when he lifted the cup to his mouth. The sight of the trembling fingers angered John. He wanted to see Patrick's steady hand. The strong hand which had guided EFAS from start-up to profitability. The hand which had lifted John from hopelessness to achievement.

"What in the hell is wrong with you, Patrick? You're not well."

John's words were an accusation. He had not meant to sound so harsh. He tried to take the edge off the harshness by smiling but his facial muscles refused to move. Patrick's cup clattered noisily against the saucer as he put it down.

"I have a terminal illness, John. That's why I asked to see you today. It's time for me to tidy up my affairs."

John sat staring at the man he had come to regard as father. His guide. His mentor. His inspiration. This was not supposed to happen. Where was the strength, the determination which had marked Patrick Morgan's character? The man sitting here was beaten. A disease in clothing.

"Is it cancer?" John heard himself ask even though he knew he did not want to hear the answer.

"No. Motor neuron disease. Incurable and advanced."

"Surely there's something, somewhere, a clinic maybe …"

Patrick raised his hand and there was a shadow of his old

29

authority in the gesture. "I'm past that stage, John. I've been lucky. The progress has been relatively slow these past few years. But palliative care is my only option now. I've come to terms with it."

John dropped his head. For the first time since his mother's funeral he felt sadness. He wanted to cry. Swallowing hard, he raised his head and looked at the sick old man across from him.

"What can I do? Do you need help in any way?"

"Yes. We have decisions to make. About the business."

Of course. Patrick was majority shareholder in EFAS. By a big margin. He owned 60 percent to John's 40 percent. And he was unmarried. Childless. What was going to happen to his shares? John felt a blush of shame begin to creep from underneath his collar as a thought, a hope, a greedy ambition he had always harboured pushed its way into his conscious thoughts. He willed Patrick to say the words, to pat him on the hand and say: 'You deserve to own the company, son. You earned it.' And he had. By Christ, he had worked for those shares! He had certainly earned the right to be Patrick Morgan's successor. John Enright was EFAS. For the past three years anyway.

Leaning on the desk for support, Patrick levered himself up and began a stiff and feeble walk around the office. John cursed himself for not visiting the old man more often. He had been alright last Christmas, hadn't he? A bit thinner maybe, a bit paler, but not a shivering wreck. There had been no obvious trembling as Patrick had sat at Enright's table for Christmas dinner. Nor had there been any hint of wasting muscle and feebleness in their frequent phone calls. If only he had taken the time to go see Patrick he would not be so shocked now. Maybe he could have done something about it earlier, found a cure. There were always new drugs, weren't there?

"What type of motor neuron do you have?"

"ALS. Amyotrophic Lateral Sclerosis. I'm well aware of what lies ahead."

John nodded. It was so sad that Patrick had no companionship in his dying days except this lethal disease. EFAS had been his life. There had been no space in his mind or heart for a wife or family.

"Is that why you left here three years ago? You weren't just going for a well-earned retirement, were you? Did you know then? "

"I knew from the first stumble. I didn't know then of course exactly what was wrong but something told me I was starting down a slippery slope. And here I am at the bottom. I can no longer fight the inevitable. I'm managing at the moment with a housekeeper. A great woman. But the day is coming when her help will not be enough. One of my problems is that the nursing home is expensive so I wanted to stay out of it for as long as possible."

"We could increase your pension to cover the cost," John offered immediately.

Patrick eased himself onto the chair and smiled at John. A wan shadow of his characteristic broad grin.

"Thanks for the offer, John, but no. Now, the reason for my visit here. The future of the company must be decided."

"Indeed," John muttered but for once his mind was not on EFAS. He was trying to cope with the idea of a life without Patrick Morgan, without his encouragement, his wisdom. The past few years must have been horrific for the old man. Alone and sick. And dying. John looked down at the desk, unable to meet the eyes of the man he had so badly let down.

"I could sell. That's one option."

Jesus! Sell! The reality of the situation hit John. He could have a new boss, maybe an active man who would want to impose his own ideas on the running of the company. A 60 percent man who would belittle John Enright and his insignificant 40 percent share. A domineering, authoritarian prick. A bully. Illogically, John hated the mythical new owner already.

Raising his head, he stared at Patrick. A drool of saliva had begun to snake from the corner of the old man's mouth. He didn't seem to notice. John was riveted by the slow progress of the trail as it approached the point of the chin. He waited for a drop to form, to swell and then plummet onto the desk. Instead the silvery trail curved underneath the chin and into the craggy folds of neck skin.

"Well, John? What do you think of that as an option?"

With a conscious effort John lifted his gaze from the wasted neck and looked into the eyes of his mentor. They still shone with all the intelligence and alertness which had made Patrick Morgan such a successful businessman.

"I-I don't know. I …" John lapsed into silence.

The realisation of his carelessness, his stupidity, suddenly hit him. He should have had a plan in place. Now, not some dim and distant time in the future. He should have anticipated this day. Had he thought Patrick was going to go on forever? The truth made John turn his face away from Patrick's sharp gaze. He had believed, in the most secret part of his mind, that Patrick would hand EFAS to him, his protégé, on a plate. To whom else could he leave it?

That was why for the past three years John had not thought beyond being in sole charge of EFAS. It was his apprenticeship, his training period until Patrick died and left it all to John Enright. His dream realised. Yes, Patrick Morgan was somewhere there in the background, on the other end of the phone, but it was John, John Enright, the widow's son, who ran the business. It was he who had taken all the responsibility. His deference to Patrick had only been out of respect and maybe a need for the old man's approval. They both knew the continuing success was down to John's astute management, his dedication. His obsession.

But the sick old man sitting across from him this morning was showing no signs of gratitude. His stare was cold, calculating. John straightened up his shoulders and took a deep breath. No fucking way was a crippling disease going to steal it all away from him.

"I'll buy your shares," he offered.

Patrick laughed and the saliva danced out of the corner of his mouth. "We've shot ourselves in the foot, John. We've been too successful. You know what the business is worth now. Could you afford it?"

How in the fuck could he afford it? Patrick Morgan knew that. They had taken nothing but a basic wage out of EFAS for the first ten years. Then John had the cost of his 40 percent shares, the house, the kids, school fees and college fees had come along. And setting Meg up in her business with Lynn. Curtain Call was paying its own way now but the profits were small. For all his success John had not managed to accumulate any significant wealth.

"I could borrow."

John knew he sounded like a petulant child. 'I want, I want!' The company was valued at six million now. Storage was big business and EFAS had been ready and waiting for the boom. Borrowing that amount of money at this stage in his life was not viable and he knew it. It could be risking everything. Patrick was looking steadily at him, his mouth curled in what would have been a quizzical smile but for the drool. And what could he offer as collateral against the loan? The shares, his house, Meg's business? He'd be owned lock, stock and barrel by the bank and when would he get out from under that debt?

"Maybe not. Too risky," John admitted. "If only I was younger, but at forty I don't think it's feasible to draw all that debt on myself. So what do you suggest, Patrick? Put your shares on the open market?"

"I have a nephew. My sister's son. He lives in New Zealand."

John thought he had misheard. That he was the one losing his mental capacity.

"You have a what? A nephew? But I thought ... I thought ..."

"You thought I had no one, is that it? That my sister was dead and the Morgan line was at an end. Well, John, I'm sorry to tell you – you took your eye off the ball."

If John had any lingering notions that the disease was affecting Patrick's intellect they were quickly banished now. The old man was staring at him with eyes as alert and keenly perceptive as they had ever been.

"My nephew, Yan Gilmore, will be taking over my shares and playing an active role in the day-to-day running of the company. As soon as all the immigration requirements are sorted, he'll be here. Within the next few weeks, I'd say. So you don't have to worry about borrowing or taking on debt. Not for EFAS anyway. My shares are not for sale. Your only concern now is preparing yourself to share the running of this company with Yan Gilmore. "

John felt as shaky and weak as the old man looked. Too late now, he saw that he had been foolish. Neglecting Patrick had not alone been unkind and ungrateful. It had been a very bad business decision. It was obvious that Patrick had long ago mapped out the whole future of EFAS. And this never-before-mentioned nephew in New Zealand had a central role to play.

* * *

Meg knew instantly from Siobhán Farrell's cheery greeting that she had no worries about her daughter Trina. There was no hint of fear or any sign that Siobhán had been waiting anxiously for the phone to ring.

"Can you believe how quickly the summer has passed?" Siobhán asked. "I thought they were daft to go all the way over to Maine but it turned out to be the right thing, didn't it?"

"Maybe. Carrie certainly seemed to enjoy working in the café. She loved the scenery too. The mountains and lakes, the beaches ..."

"It wasn't just the scenery she fell in love with, was it? Your Carrie seems to have found the man of her dreams."

The phone suddenly became a dead weight in Meg's hand. Little prickles of fear raced along her spine. She opened her mouth to ask Siobhán what in the hell she was talking about but the words stuck somewhere between shock and hurt. This couldn't be true! No way would Carrie have met someone and not said a word. Not told her mother. They were close, weren't they? They were mother and daughter. They were friends for God's sake!

"Meg? Are you still there?"

Meg realised her hands were sweating when the phone began to slip. She quickly wedged it between her head and shoulder and wiped her palms on her brown suede skirt, leaving dark streaks on the fabric.

"Are you alright?" Lynn mouthed.

Meg nodded and firmly grasped the phone again in her right hand.

"Meg? Are you there?"

"Yes, Siobhán. I'm here. Just a glitch on the line. What were we talking about? Carrie's boyfriend I think, wasn't it?"

"Oh, Garth, yes. A 'fine thing' in Trina's words. How much better could you do than the boss's son? I thought the others should have gone to the cabin with Carrie and Garth but they were hell-bent on New York. Spending every cent they earned during the summer on rubbish, no doubt. Your Carrie's a sensible girl."

"The cabin? What cabin? Carrie isn't with her friends?"

There was a pause on the other end of the line. Siobhán Farrell knew now that Meg didn't have a clue where her daughter was but Meg was gone beyond caring what anyone thought. Carrie was not with her friends. She was alone in some godforsaken cabin in Maine with this person named Garth.

"Have the girls heard from Carrie since they left her?"

36

"They didn't leave her. She left them."

"Whatever. Has she been in contact with them?"

"I don't know, Meg. You sound worried. Have you not heard from her?"

"Not for over a week."

"Oh!"

'Oh' indeed. The softly spoken exclamation said it all. The nightmare had woken up and was shaking its darkest threats in Meg's face. Mocking her. Accusing. Maybe Carrie had been alive up to yesterday. Maybe she could have saved her daughter if only she had acted sooner. Tears gathered in a hot knot and lay, unshed, in that place where her fear for her daughter's life ached. Lynn took the phone from her hand.

"Siobhán, Lynn Rooney here. I've only heard half this conversation but I gather Carrie is not with her friends."

"Hi, Lynn. No. As I told Meg they went their separate ways for the last part of the trip. Carrie and Garth have been inseparable for the whole summer. I'm surprised she didn't tell her mother she was going to the cabin."

"Could you contact Trina? Find out if Carrie has been in touch with her. Or if there's a contact number for the place where Carrie is supposed to be."

"Of course. Give me Meg's mobile number and I'll ring back as soon as I have any news."

Lynn reeled off Meg's mobile number and then put down the phone. Meg was shaking now, the unshed tears almost choking her. Lynn grabbed her arm firmly and sat her on the high stool.

"Things are no worse than what they were, Meg. You would have heard if anything bad had happened to her. You must keep believing that. Now, I'm going to shut this shop and drive you home."

Meg imagined the emptiness of her house. Carrie's bedroom with its collection of soft toys. Albums full of baby pictures. Firsts. First tooth, first step, first day at school. First lock of her black silky hair. First trip to the States. Instantly every first became a last. Carrie's last day at college, her last day at home. Her last days.

"I don't want to go home, Lynn. It's too lonely there."

"What about John? Will I drive you to EFAS? You're in no fit state to drive yourself."

"He's busy."

Lynn nodded. John Enright was always busy according to Meg. Not that Meg ever complained but the tacit implication was that John Enright was a less than devoted husband. Which made Lynn wonder how happy their marriage really was. Knowing that her thoughts were straying into an area which was none of her business, Lynn did the only thing she could think of to help the friend she loved like a sister. She shoved a drawing pad and a bunch of pencils in front of her.

"Draw, Meg. Sketch your heart out. Before you've finished Siobhán Farrell will be back on to you with news."

The shop door opened and a blast of cold air came in from the street with the customer.

"Oh, shit!" Lynn said, peeping into the shop. "It's Eileen Corkery for her awful floral drapes and they're not ready yet. I just couldn't get myself to work on all those swirls and trailing leaves."

"Thread," Meg reminded her.

Lynn laughed. Of course. The stock excuse. Waiting on

exactly the right shade of thread. Special delivery. In one energetic sweep Lynn had left the kitchenette and was greeting Eileen Corkery in the shop.

When Lynn came back, Meg was staring into space, her sketch pad untouched.

"C'mon, Meg! Do some drawing. The phone will ring before you know it."

"I don't expect to hear from Siobhán Farrell for a while yet. New York is five hours behind us. They won't even be up yet."

"Well then, get sketching."

Meg pulled the sketch pad towards her. Lynn knew her so well. Better than anyone else. The only way she could ever really express her feelings was on paper.

Her sketch emerged from the terrified depths of her soul, dark and twisted and full of shadows.

CHAPTER 4

Meg looked up from her sketch pad to see Lynn checking her watch.

"What about lunch?" said Lynn. "You'll have your mobile with you so you needn't worry about missing the call."

The thought of food made Meg's stomach churn. How could she eat when Carrie might at this very minute be fighting for her life? Or maybe she had already lost the battle.

"No. You go on. Enjoy lunch. I'll keep the shop open and then I might slip away early this evening. Okay?"

Agreeing reluctantly, Lynn left to go to the pub a few doors down the street where they usually lunched. Meg had known she would. Lynn was fighting an ongoing campaign. She was on nodding and smiling terms with a man who had begun to lunch there too in the past month. He was tall and dark-haired and always wore an immaculately pressed suit and shirt. So immaculate was his dress that they had christened him 'The Suit'. Just Lynn's type of man. She had set her sights on him so he hadn't a chance of escape. Maybe she would make her move today when she was alone.

40

There were times when Meg envied Lynn. No, envy was too strong a word. More she wondered what it would be like to be Lynn, to have her freedom and lack of responsibility. She always seemed so happy, so optimistic about life. She made things happen because she believed they would. Perhaps that was easier when you had nobody to worry about but yourself. Which brought Meg back to worrying about her daughter again. Trina and the rest of the gang must be waking up in New York by now. They might be hung over and broke but at least they were together and alive.

Glancing down at her dark sketch of gnarled branches and thorny stems, Meg ripped the page from her pad and tore it into shreds. As she was dumping the pieces into the bin she heard the shop door opening. She welcomed the sound. A stranger, or someone she was acquainted with as a client. Someone who knew nothing about her missing daughter or her defiant son. Someone who thought Meg Enright had no worries beyond the fall of a curtain.

Squaring her shoulders, Meg walked into the shop. She stood still when she saw Siobhán Farrell.

Why was she here? Why hadn't she just rung? The questions tumbled around in her head but she didn't want to hear any of the answers. Siobhán looked uncomfortable, opening her mouth to speak and then closing it again without saying a word.

"They haven't heard from her, have they?"

As Meg heard herself say the words she prayed with every ounce of strength in her body that Siobhán Farrell's face would break into a smile, that she would say it had all been a misunderstanding and that Carrie was in New York with her friends, drinking and spending and having a wonderful time. Instead Siobhán walked towards her and caught her shaking hand.

"No, Meg. I'm sorry but the gang have not had any contact at all with her for the past week."

"But why …?"

"There's an explanation. You look terrible. You'd better sit down."

"Tell me, Siobhán. For God's sake, just tell me! What's happened to my daughter and why wasn't I told?"

Over Siobhán's shoulder Meg caught a glimpse of a passer-by looking in the window. The woman had that acquisitive look in her eye which meant she had spotted something to buy. The window-shopper's expression changed from interested to angry as she saw Meg walk to the door, turn the sign to 'Closed' and lock the door from the inside. The woman tossed her head and turned on her heel with an energy that said she wouldn't be back to Curtain Call ever again.

Standing with her back to the now locked door, Meg leaned against it for support.

"Well, Siobhán? What's happened to Carrie?"

"Nothing – nothing at all as far as I know," said Siobhán hurriedly.

"Then why has nobody heard from her? Why isn't she answering my calls?"

"Carrie left her phone in Portland when she went north. They don't like phones. Not when they're in the cabin anyway. It's a sort of retreat."

"What in the name of God are you talking about, Siobhán? Who are *they* and *what* cabin?"

"Is there some place we could sit down? You look like you're going to faint and my feet are killing me."

Meg's first thought was to dash over to Siobhán and shake the information out of her. With iron self-control she eased away from the door and led the way into the kitchenette. She filled the kettle and then sat opposite Siobhán.

"Now speak."

"Has Carrie told you much about where they were working?"

"The Haven Café. Yes. She loved it there. She's into this organic food and fair trade tea and coffee business. She liked the people who own it too."

"The Hemmings."

Something about the way Siobhán's mouth tightened around the word 'Hemmings' sent shivers of fear through Meg. She waited for Siobhán to go on, to explain her implied disapproval but the only sound in the room was the kettle coming to boiling point, spluttering and then clicking off. The tiny space was hot with steam yet cold with tension. Were these Hemmings criminals of some sort? Maybe they were smugglers. Or murderers.

Siobhán was staring at her hands, twisting her wedding ring round and round as if she was trying to screw it off her finger.

Fear sparked Meg's anger. "Do you know where my daughter is?"

Siobhán started at the fury in Meg's voice. Her hands were suddenly still and she lifted her head. "She's gone to Mount Desert Island with Garth. The Hemmings have a cabin there. A getting-back-to-nature hideout. It's somewhere off the east coast of Maine. Up in the direction of the Canadian border."

That name again. Garth. The boyfriend Carrie had failed to mention. Why? And why did Siobhán Farrell seem so reluctant to talk now when she had been so chatty on the phone earlier?

"Carrie's boyfriend, Garth," said Meg. "His surname is Hemmings, isn't it? He's the café owners' son?"

Siobhán nodded.

"And what's wrong with the Hemmings? Will you tell me for Christ's sake! You're holding something back. What is it? Is Carrie in danger?"

"I only know what Trina told me today. This is the first I've heard of it too. And I'm sure Garth is really a nice boy but ..." Siobhán was twisting her ring again, her eyes darting about, her lips pursed.

"But *what*, for heaven's sake?"

"The Hemmings family are founders of a cult. "

Noticing that Meg's eyes grew huge and terrified at the mention of the word 'cult', Siobhán went on quickly. "They run these cafés all over Maine and they recruit new members through their clientele. Trina said that Carrie seemed to get very involved, that she was very influenced by Garth and his father."

"A cult? What kind of cult? Black Magic, Satanism? What is it?"

"Nothing like that. It's New Agey, I think. A sort of getting-in-touch-with-your-spiritual-side thing. Not so much religion really as self-awareness."

Meg hadn't realised how tensed up her shoulder muscles had been until she felt them relax a little. So Carrie's boyfriend was involved in some soul-searching movement. That would appeal to Carrie, so deep, so questioning. But it still didn't explain why she had not mentioned Garth and why she was completely out of contact now.

As if Siobhán had read her thoughts, she volunteered the next bit of information without having it dragged painfully from her.

"Trina said the gang tried to talk her out of the trip. They weren't too happy about her going to such an isolated place but Carrie insisted. And she made them promise … well … she made them promise not to say anything to her family."

Meg's relief of a minute ago was replaced now by hurt. And resentment. Could her daughter have changed so much in three short months? Carrie, who had never given her parents a minute's worry, Carrie who always put other people's feelings first. Maybe Garth was a nice boy but his influence on Carrie was not nice.

"Tea? Coffee?"

Meg was by now convinced that Siobhán was hiding something else. As she made the tea and a coffee for herself, Meg wondered too how much Tommy knew. It would be inconceivable that Carrie would not have told him about a new man in her life or about this movement which seemed so important to her. Tommy would have known if she had been hiding something from him.

"I'm sorry I haven't better news for you, Meg. But I'm sure she'll be fine."

"Would you be worried if the positions were reversed and it was Trina gone north with a boy you never met to a place you never heard of?"

Siobhán did not answer. She looked down at her hands again and started the incessant twisting of her ring. Meg handed her the cup of tea just to stop her fidgeting. Siobhán took a sip and then, putting the cup down, opened her bag.

"Here's the phone number for the café in Portland – that's the Hemmings headquarters. Carrie is due back there next Friday. Then she's heading to New York to meet up with Trina. If you spoke to Karl Hemmings I'm sure he could put your mind at rest. And don't forget to put in the 207 prefix for Portland."

Exhausted from worry and the effort of trying to get information from Siobhán, Meg leaned her arms on the counter and dropped her head onto them.

"My mind will be at rest when Carrie is home and when you tell me what it is you're holding back," she said, the words muffled in the fluffy wool of her angora jumper.

"She'll be home, don't you worry," said Siobhán. "And I'm not saying anything else. Trina did have some negative things to say about ILM but …"

"ILM?"

"Inner Light Movement. That's what they call their group. Their cult. But you know what Trina's like. She's a little atheist. She'd condemn anything that smacks of religion. I wouldn't set too much store by what she says about it. Just you phone Karl Hemmings to put your mind at ease and then try to get some rest. You look exhausted."

With great effort Meg lifted her head up and smiled at Siobhán Farrell. Her mouth curved, she felt the corners of her eyes crinkle but she knew the smile did not reach her eyes. It was the best she could do. The half-smile lasted long after the other woman had left the shop. Meg clung onto it for comfort. Pretence was the only protection she had left.

* * *

Tommy was sorry now that he had not got up on time this morning. He was starving and he faced ten minutes' walk to the nearest shop to buy sandwiches for his lunch. If he chanced sneaking off to the shop early that snitch of a forklift driver would grass on him. Dan Shorten was an arse-lick. They were all arse-lickers here. They thought the sun shone out of John Enright's backside. If only they had to live with the bloody Fuehrer they wouldn't be long changing their minds. As soon as he thought of his father Tommy remembered Breeze. He would have to ask today. He had promised. There was no convincing Breeze that John Enright would be a prick to work for and that anyway there were no jobs going in EFAS. What was there to do here except lock up the stuff people wanted to store and then make sure it wasn't stolen? The Fuehrer made such a big deal of it.

At last the forklift was switched off.

"Lunchtime!" Dan Shorten shouted as loudly as if the engine was still running.

Tommy dropped the box he had been just about to lift and went for his coat. With no thought in his head beside a ham and cheese roll, he made his way out of the building and walked through the front gate. He almost tripped over the hem of his coat when Breeze seemed to appear out of nowhere.

"What in the fuck are you doing here? You nearly made me fall, jumping out like that!"

"Did you ask?"

"I've been working my bollocks off all morning. I didn't have a chance to pee let alone have a conference with my old man."

47

"You said you would. You're not going to let me down, are you?"

Tommy stood and looked at his friend. Breeze was cool. Cool as a breeze. Number one razor around the back and sides and a really thick mop of glossy black hair on top. He was big for seventeen, already with man-sized biceps. But it wasn't his hair or his physique or even his sharp clothes that made Breeze stand out. It was the energy in him. Not the rushing and racing type of energy. Breeze wouldn't waste effort like that. It was a power you could sense inside him, coiled, waiting, ready to spring into action when need arose. And yet he was gentle too. Even a wimp sometimes. Like the way he cared for his mother.

"Look, Breeze, I hope you don't have the wrong idea here. I said I'd ask him but I'm not promising anything. There are very few jobs in EFAS, you know. Just six really. My dad and his partner, the forklift driver, the security man, the receptionist and a maintenance man. He just needs someone every so often for doing some donkey work. That's usually me."

"Who's the security man?"

"An old geezer. Ollie. He only works nights. The place is riddled with cameras. It's like Fort Knox. My old man is paranoid."

They began walking again. Tommy was conscious of his lunchtime slipping by. If he didn't get something to eat soon he would probably conk out.

"What's he storing in there? Cash or something? Why all the security?"

"People's furniture and stuff when they move house, and businesses store documents and pieces of machines and every kind of shit you could imagine. Boring stuff. Why are you so interested in it anyway?"

Breeze shrugged and quickened his pace but not before Tommy had caught a very angry expression flash across his face. Tommy had to trot to keep up with him.

"I get the message," Breeze said. "You don't want me anywhere near your old man's business. That's why you haven't asked him to take me on."

"Don't be such a girl's blouse! I told you I'll ask when I get the chance. But I wouldn't hold out any hope."

They had almost reached the shop now. As unceremoniously as he had appeared, Breeze left. From quick walking pace he accelerated into a run and was already as far as the main road before Tommy had got to the shop door. Tommy looked after him and saw anger in every graceful stride. Breeze had a lot to be angry about.

* * *

John had tried to be sociable all through lunch. It had helped that Francine was there. She and Patrick Morgan seemed at ease in each other's company. Almost like old friends. She kept the conversation flowing lightly – the weather, the looming general election, even golf.

John allowed all the chat to go over his head. He had only one thing on his mind. Yan Gilmore. The rabbit out of the hat. The son of a sister Patrick had not seen for twenty years. A sister he admitted never having had much closeness to anyway. In fact he hadn't even gone to New Zealand for her funeral ten years ago. And now he was bringing this Yan from the other side of the world to work in EFAS. No –

49

fuck! He would *own* EFAS. Sixty per cent. A stranger who had never as much as laid eyes on the place.

"Would that be okay with you, John?"

John started. They were in the car park of the restaurant and he had not even noticed that they had finished lunch and walked outside. Francine was staring at him, a worried frown on her forehead. The little puckers suited her. Gave her gravitas. John smiled at her.

"Sorry, Francine. I'm a little preoccupied. What did you say?"

"I asked if it was okay with you if I drove Patrick home. He's a bit tired now."

"I'll get a taxi, just like I did to get myself here this morning," Patrick muttered.

John nodded to Francine to go ahead. He hadn't noticed that Patrick was no longer driving. How could he have noticed such a little detail when he hadn't even seen that Patrick was preparing to sell him out, to go over his head, to put him in a position where the only way forward would be to cripple himself with debt. In fact he had even closed off that option. The old bollocks had scuppered him.

"On second thoughts, I'd appreciate that, Francine," Patrick said. "I do feel very tired."

John looked at his partner's grey face with the dark circles underneath the eyes and guilt tore through him. This shrunken little man was the once great Patrick Morgan. Mentor, friend, father figure. On impulse John ignored Patrick's outstretched hand and enveloped the old man in an embrace. He held him tightly as if through sheer willpower he could transfer some of his own strength into the frail body.

When Patrick stood back and looked up, there was no sickness or frailty in his sharp eyes.

"If you're willing, we'll set up a video-conference with Yan sometime this week. How's that with you?"

John nodded agreement, knowing it was probably already arranged. He watched as Francine gently led Patrick towards her car and helped him get in. Then she walked around to the driver's door, opened it and stood looking back at John for a micro-second. It was long enough for John to realise that she had overheard the conversation about Yan and that she was probably wondering what in the hell was going on. He would talk to her when she came back. Just about Patrick's condition of course. Patrick's replacement was none of her business. She wouldn't pry anyway. Francine was a good listener.

Feeling slightly better, John drove back to EFAS. His improved mood lasted until he scanned the monitors in reception and saw Tommy sitting on a stack of pallets outside the back of the unit, happily puffing away on a cigarette. Jesus! Glad to have a concrete focus for his anger, John strode through the unit. Inside the back door he slowed his steps and began to walk softly. To creep. Quietly, noiselessly, he opened the door a slit and pressed his face against the opening. He was only about six feet from where his son was sitting, oblivious to being watched. John glanced out at the waving tops of the firs. They were bending towards EFAS. He was downwind of Tommy. A curl of smoke blew towards him. John sniffed deeply and then, despite his anger, he smiled. All he got was the acrid whiff of tobacco. Nicotine. Not wacky baccy or any of that druggy shit. He suddenly remembered himself, twelve years old, no backside in his trousers but a cigarette in his hand, crouching down for a furtive puff behind the school shed. Maybe there was yet hope for Tommy. John silently closed the door and went back to his office to wait for Francine's return.

* * *

Francine was in no hurry to get back to the office. Good information-gathering was never rushed. She had learned the value of knowing a long time ago. Knowledge was power and more than anything else Francine Keyes wanted power. It was just a matter of finding the right time and of course the right information.

As she settled the sick old man into his favourite armchair in his own home, she saw the gratitude in his eyes. He didn't want sex. That card was off the table because he was gone past that particular vulnerability. But he did need companionship.

Francine would give it to him. She would sit and listen and bide her time. Her task now was to find out every detail about Patrick Morgan and get as much influence as she could over John Enright.

CHAPTER 5

Meg forgot to change the 'Closed' sign on the door. It wasn't until she saw Lynn flip the sign on her way back in that she realised she had been sending customers away. Anyway, she would not have been able to cope with people. Not with so many questions spinning around in her head. She did not wait for Lynn to ask. She told her about Garth and Mount Desert Island and Carrie's trip to a cabin in the middle of nowhere. Without her phone. She told her everything Siobhán Farrell had been willing to pass on.

"Are they hippies?"

"The Hemmings? I doubt it. They own a whole string of cafés across Maine. A bit too capitalist for love-and-peace people. But then what in the hell do I really know about any of it?"

"So what're you waiting for? Find out. Ring this Hemmings man. The Messiah."

Meg looked down at the crumpled piece of paper in her hand. What could she say to Karl Hemmings? Accuse him of abducting her daughter, of changing her personality?

"Just tell him you need to contact her urgently," Lynn said. "Lie if you have to. He'll probably be lying too."

"Maybe it's a bit too early yet. I'll wait until it's around their lunch-time."

"You mean you want to put off the confrontation. Why don't you get John to ring? He might be – mmm – more assertive. What did he say about this Mount Desert Island business?"

"I didn't tell him."

Without saying anything further, Lynn went to the storeroom and began to sort through stock. Meg could hear her shifting heavy bolts of fabric around and then loud clatters as thick pattern books from the top shelf hit the floor. Lynn did spring-cleaning whenever she was upset. It didn't happen very often but it was always very loud and usually meant that everything had to be put back when the bad mood passed. Of course she was worried about Carrie too. Lynn was her godmother and had spoiled her godchild since the day she'd been born. But that was only part of the story. For some reason, the fact that Meg had not told John the latest news seemed to have been the trigger for this particular fit of spring-cleaning.

Meg put the piece of paper with the Portland number written on it onto the counter and began to smooth it out. The creases flattened under the heat of her hand. The noises from the storeroom were getting louder. Meg continued to smooth the paper, trying to imagine her conversation with Karl Hemmings. Maybe he would be very kind. An understanding man who would sympathise with her worry and offer to contact Carrie immediately. Then maybe he would ...

A really loud bang followed by a yelp of pain cut into Meg's thoughts. She raced into the storeroom to find Lynn sprawled on the floor, the stepladder lying across her.

"Lynn! My God! What's happened? Are you hurt?"

"I'm alright."

Meg caught the ladder and lifted it out of the way. She looked first at Lynn's limbs. They seemed to be alright. No awkward angles or obvious broken bones.

"Can you move?"

Fingers and toes wiggled. With Meg's supporting arm around her, Lynn pulled herself into a sitting position. Bending her knees, she lowered her head and allowed her auburn curls to fall around her face.

"My pride is hurt," she muttered.

"Don't be daft. Everyone has accidents. Nothing to be ashamed of. Just so long as you're not injured."

"But I am! Meg, I made a terrible fool of myself at lunch today. I really let myself down."

Slowly Lynn lifted her head and a wan face that Meg did not recognise peeped from behind the curls. A vulnerable Lynn with tears in her green eyes. Meg lowered herself to the floor and, sitting close to her friend, reached for her hand.

"Was it The Suit?"

Lynn nodded. "He's a prick! It turns out he's married anyway but his wife is welcome to him. Do you know he implied that I was on the game? A prostitute!"

"No! How could he!"

"Well, I did come on a bit strong, I'll admit that. But he knew I was vulnerable, not depraved. He just wanted to humiliate me. Pervert! Control freak. And loud too.

Everyone in the whole pub heard what he thought of me. I was so ashamed, Meg. He stood there haranguing me while people sniggered behind their hands. I can't ever go back there again."

"We're both going there tomorrow," Meg said with the strength she always had in dealing with other people's problems.

Lynn shook her head. "I can't. He was right in some of the things he said. I did flirt outrageously. I'm lonely. For the first time in my life I feel incomplete. A failure. Yes, I have a nice apartment, a flash car, a business and loads of friends. But nobody special. Nobody to share with like John does with you. That's why I was so mad at you when you casually admitted you hadn't even bothered telling him about Mount Desert Island."

Meg put her arms around Lynn and held her close. Words were in her head. Treacherous words. About how she too felt alone, about how John was never there for her, how EFAS was his passion, the great love of his life. Even Lynn, who knew her so well, did not guess her feeling of isolation. Now was not the time to tell. Not when Lynn was hurting so much and Carrie was God knows where. But as she sat on the floor of the storeroom, holding her friend, Meg knew that she was harbouring words in her head that must, sometime soon, be spoken aloud.

* * *

John was pacing. He had no control over his rhythmic walking around the office. It was something his body had decided to do while his mind tried to reason a way out of the Yan Gilmore dilemma.

Buying Patrick's shares was a non-runner. It would be a risk too far. John was not built for risk-taking. His achievements to date had been gained through prudence and hard work, not speculation. Besides, Patrick seemed to have removed that option very neatly. His shares were not for sale.

So what then? Was he supposed to sit here while this blow-in arrived with all his new ideas? Patrick said his nephew was in the tourism business. What in the hell could he know about storage, about Ireland and doing business here? And why would a man his age be willing to travel this far to ...

John suddenly stopped pacing. Maybe he had just found the answer! There was no need for Yan Gilmore to be here. He could just fulfil the same role Patrick had done for the past three years. A sleeping partner, quietly collecting his dividends at the other side of the world while John ran EFAS. Patrick should have thought of that before he had set this mad plan in motion. Now John had an uphill battle to persuade a man he had never even spoken to not to go along with his dying uncle's plans. But he could do it. He must do it.

Feeling better now that he had the germ of a strategy, John sat at his desk and picked up a pen. He would figure this out point by point. Point one must be the inconvenience of uprooting from your native country, your family and friends. Had Yan Gilmore family? Did he have a wife and children? John dropped the pen again. How in the fuck could he deal with this when he was working with one hand tied behind his back? Patrick had told him very little about Yan Gilmore other than that he was in effect about to hand EFAS over to him.

There was a soft tap on the door and Francine came in, carrying a cup of coffee.

"I thought you might need this, John. I noticed you were upset at seeing Mr Morgan so unwell today."

Her perfume wafted over John as she placed the cup in front of him. He smiled at her and waved her to the chair on the other side of the desk.

"I don't have my notepad. I'll get it now."

"No, Francine. I don't want you to take dictation. Just sit down and tell me about Patrick. How was he when you left him?"

"Exhausted. I was a bit worried about leaving him but he insisted he was fine. Anyway, his housekeeper was there."

"That's Patrick for you! He's hidden his illness well for the past few years. I had no idea he was so sick until this morning."

John bowed his head. In shame. He had just glibly admitted that he had been neglecting the man to whom he owed everything. What must Francine think? That John Enright was an ungrateful and cruel man, ignoring his dying colleague?

Then another feeling, more puzzling than shame, began to push all John's other thoughts aside. It was an urge, a need for Francine's approval. Suddenly he realised that he did not want this girl to think badly of him. Why? In the name of God, why? She had been here only three months. He barely knew her. Unless of course he counted all the dreams he'd had of her. The ones where they walked hand in hand through woods, along the banks of rivers, into hotel rooms. The dreams where he gently removed her clothes until she was lying naked ...

John heard a rustle and the clink of the silver bracelets with the swirly blue stones Francine always wore. Her hand reached across the desk and lay on top of his. Her skin felt smooth and cool, just as he had known it would.

"There was nothing you could have done for him, John. He's a proud man. He needs to keep his dignity."

John raised his head slowly. He looked into Francine's eyes. He noticed how deeply blue they were, how blonde her hair, how creamy her skin. He drew his hand away, but not because he didn't like the touch. He loved the gentle contact too much. He began to sweat now and struggle for mature, business-like control. He failed.

"Francine," he heard himself blurt, "would you like to go for a drink some evening?" Francine smiled then and he gloried in the whiteness and evenness of her teeth. It was as if his dreams had come to life.

"I'd love to, thank you. I'm free tonight. Would that suit you?"

"Yes, yes. Great, Francine. What time? Where?"

The phone rang. Francine picked up it. "EFAS Storage. How may I help you?" She listened to the caller and then answered calmly. "One moment please, Mrs Enright. I'll put you through."

She handed the phone to John, pushed back her chair and stood. He took the receiver and indicated to her to sit. He must talk to her. Finalise arrangements. He couldn't let her go now.

"Hi, Meg. I'm sorry about this but I'm in a meeting. I'll call you back."

Without waiting for Meg's reply he put down the phone. He leaned towards Francine and then immediately sat back in order to put distance between them. She was watching. Waiting, glancing at the beads of sweat on his forehead.

"So will I pick you up, Francine? Where would you like to meet?"

She bowed her head and her mane of blonde hair shimmered like a silken veil. John's heart sank. She was changing her mind. And why not? Why should a beautiful young woman like this want to spend time with him? She raised her head again and turned the full power of her blue gaze on him.

"I'll meet you anywhere, John. It doesn't matter to me. But you may need to be more discreet."

"It's only a drink! I'm not suggesting – I'm not …"

"I know. It's just that people talk."

John nodded agreement. She was right of course. He was a married man and this town could be very small. For a moment he imagined Meg's hazel eyes, tear-filled because someone told her John was seen in town with a stunning young blonde. He began to realise how stupid the whole idea was. How undignified. His heartbeat slowed and his jagged breathing steadied.

"I'm sorry, Francine. This was not a good idea. My mistake."

"I was going to suggest my apartment. It's more private there. I could cook for us and we could chat in peace. What do you think?"

John couldn't think at all. His mind was too full of Francine images – intimate, candle-lit scenes where hand-holding eventually led to a full embrace and …

"You're in Waterside Apartments, aren't you?" he managed to say at last.

"Number 8. You know where they are?"

Everybody knew where Waterside Apartments were. They were the most elegant development on the quayside, a glass-fronted tower overlooking the River Lee. She must have independent means. She certainly couldn't afford it on her EFAS pay. He smiled at her.

"I'll see you around eight then. Thank you."

"I'll get my notebook now," she said, as coolly as if the arrangement they had made had been just another piece of business.

John smiled. Getting to know Francine Keyes was going to be an interesting experience. The doubts, the thoughts of deceit and hurting Meg were somewhere in the back of his head. He left them there and did his best to concentrate on work.

* * *

Meg felt humiliated as she put down the phone.

"He's busy. At a meeting," she muttered.

Recovered now from her fall, Lynn seemed to be back to her energetic, take-charge self.

"Never mind. You'll just have to ring Hemmings yourself."

Meg looked around the shop. It was busy again. There were people rifling though sample books, others touching fabrics as if their fingers could decide which curtains would suit their homes, some just browsing. She had an appointment with Rhona Sheehan this afternoon. A consultation on new drapes for her big house with lots of windows. A good client.

The customers, the shop, even the bolts of fabric, seemed to close in on Meg. She had to get out of here.

"Lynn, would you mind cancelling my consultation with Rhona Sheehan? I've got to go. Will you be okay here on your own?"

"Well, of course I can manage. But what about you? Are you going to see John? He'll want to talk to Karl Hemmings too, won't he?"

"Must go." Meg collected her coat and bag and dashed out the door. She covered the distance to the multi-storey car park in record time, drove at speed and was in the driveway of her home before she even had time to wonder what she was doing rushing about in such a frenzy. Coffee was what she needed now, strong and black.

As the kettle boiled Meg got out the scrap of paper with Karl Hemmings' number on it. She stared at it as if the figures held the answer to Carrie's whereabouts. A secret code. She made her coffee, sat at the table and took a long swallow. The caffeine rushed through her system, bolstering her energy. And her resolve. She got the phone and brought it back to the table. It sat there, staring at her. Accusing her of cowardice. She picked it up and keyed in the number. While it rang on another continent, Meg gulped her coffee. She had to fight the urge to clap the phone down. Her thoughts were not organised. What was she going to say to this man? How was she going to find out where her daughter was without sounding hysterical? How do you ask calmly if your daughter has been murdered?

"Hi! Haven Café. Jilly speaking. How may I help?"

Thrown by the female voice, Meg just sat there, unable to utter a word. What had she thought? That Karl Hemmings was standing by waiting for her call?

"Hello! Hello! Who's on the line, please?"

An image of Carrie flashed before Meg. The dark brown eyes had a hurt, lost expression. Meg almost reached out to touch her, to hold her in her arms and never let her go. She took a deep breath.

"May I speak to Mr Karl Hemmings, please?"

"I'm sorry, ma'am. Mr Hemmings is busy. Would you like to leave a message?"

"It's urgent that I speak with him. Is there any possibility he could take my call? I'm ringing from Ireland."

"Who will I say is calling?"

"Meg Enright. Carrie's mother. I must speak with Karl Hemmings. It's really important."

The desperation in Meg's voice must have come across to the girl. She agreed to see if she could bring Mr Hemmings to the phone. Meg kept the phone pressed to her ear, listening to background chatter as if she could by some miracle pick up the sound of Carrie's deep voice in the babble. She heard the clatter of ware and the ring of a till so she knew the phone must be in the café. The line squeaked and buzzed. Meg held her breath, fearing that the connection was going to be cut.

"Karl Hemmings here. Can I help you?"

The voice was strong and musical. A deep bass. A confident voice.

"Hello, Mr Hemmings. My name is Meg Enright."

"Yes, Carrie's mother. She's spoken a lot about you. How artistic you are and beautiful. Do please call me Karl."

"Where is she? I haven't heard from her for over a week."

Meg winced. She had not meant to be so brusque. To sound so out of control. But she had no interest in social chitchat now. She needed answers.

Karl Hemmings cleared his throat. "You sound worried, Meg. I can assure you there's no need to be. Carrie and Garth, my son, are gone Down East to our cabin there. They're sharing a little quiet time together."

"So do you have a contact number for her?"

"I said they went for some quiet time. That means no phones, no TV, no computer. None of the distractions of our age. Electronic noise is deafening this generation. That's why nobody can hear their inner voice any more."

Jesus! He was preaching to her. Trying to distract her with his proselytising. He'd better learn that she would not be sidetracked.

"I have an urgent message for Carrie. I need to speak with her. I must."

"They're due back Friday. Isn't that soon enough? They need some time and space."

Except that Meg was sitting she would have fallen. Her legs began to tremble uncontrollably as she finally realised that Karl Hemmings had no intention of putting her in contact with Carrie. Why? What was he hiding? Was Carrie even alive? Gripping the phone so hard that her knuckles were white, she spoke with a quiet anger so much fiercer than any blustering tantrum.

"Mr Hemmings, I know my daughter and your son went to Mount Desert Island. I know she left her mobile phone behind in Portland. Now if you don't give me a contact number for her in Mount Desert Island, I'll ask the local police to initiate a search. I haven't heard from her in over a week and I'm not willing to wait any longer."

Karl Hemmings began to make some soothing sounds. Sonorous now-now-nows. He was prevaricating.

"The number," said Meg. "There must be a phone in this cabin."

"No, there's not. That's the whole point in it."

"And what about if they got sick or had an accident? Do they have neighbours?"

"Not for quite a way. But there is a radio. They contact us over the radio in the evenings and we all pray together."

"So will you ask, no, *tell* Carrie to get to a phone and ring home. We'll be waiting for her call."

"You're so anxious, Meg. You must feel tired with all that stress. It's destroying your energy."

"Of course I'm anxious! I need to hear from my daughter! I need to speak with her. What time will you be in contact with the cabin?"

"We link up around seven in the evening. We like to sleep on a prayer."

Seven this evening in Maine. Around midnight here. She glanced at her watch. Just four in the afternoon now. Another eight hours to go before she knew whether Karl Hemmings passed her message on or not. Before she knew if Carrie was really in this cabin, if there really was a radio link, if Carrie was really alive.

"I'll be waiting to hear from you, Mr Hemmings. I'll give you until eight o'clock your time, one a.m. here. If I haven't heard from you by then, I'm going to contact the police and file a missing person's report on my daughter. Do you understand?"

"You're very angry, Meg. Let me pray with you."

Meg slammed down the phone. Her legs were so weak she had to drag herself up the stairs on hands and knees. She crawled along the landing and pushed open the door of

Carrie's bedroom. The sweet flowery smell of Carrie engulfed her. Pulling herself up, she shoved the collection of soft toys aside and threw herself across the bed. Then she howled with grief for the beautiful daughter she believed she had lost forever.

CHAPTER 6

From the locker room Tommy watched the forklift driver
head towards the reception area. Dan Shorten had a furtive
look about him as he crept up to the desk and spoke quietly
to the receptionist. Shorty was furtive. A sneaky bollocks.
He would be complaining about Tommy now, asking to see
the boss, telling how "the kid" was late back from lunch and
took three minutes extra for his tea break. Dan's words
always hissed out the side of his mouth so that from one
aspect he was silent while from the other he was spilling his
guts. Well, shag him! And shag the old man too. Tommy had
worked his balls off today.

With all that shagging on his mind, Tommy looked with
interest at the receptionist. Francine. She was nodding her
head as Shorty dribbled out his words, her long blonde hair
shimmering. Dan's barrel chest puffed up when she smiled at
him. She was old. Maybe twenty-six or seven. Even so,
Tommy's eyes went from her shining hair to her breasts
which pushed against the fabric of her white blouse. She had
a big pair of knockers for such a slim woman. They were

high and pert and Tommy wondered if they were silicone. He'd have to feel them to find out, wouldn't he? Or if she ran he'd know. Maybe he could chase her to see if her boobs bounced. Shorty must know. He was leaning so close to her that his nose was practically in her cleavage.

Suddenly Shorty straightened up, turned from the desk and began to walk away, a swagger in his stride. Tommy moved in from the door of the locker room and began to take off his overalls. It was going-home time anyway.

Shorty came in and without glancing at Tommy went straight to his locker. The smell of sweat filled the poky little room as the forklift driver wriggled out of his overall.

"Chatting up Francine, were you?"

Dan Shorten turned to glare at the person he called "the kid". It was obvious he resented the boss's son being foisted on him. Tough!

"I saw you, Shorty. Your face was down her blouse. Dirty old man."

The lips twisted and the small bright blue eyes narrowed to a slit. "Watch your mouth! You might be the boss's son but I don't take no crap from no one."

His long black coat now on, Tommy tired of this game. "I'll see you whenever, Dan. I'm not sure if I'll be back tomorrow. Try not to miss me."

He left Shorty muttering inaudible words out of the side of his mouth and headed towards reception. To his disappointment, Francine was not there. She must have gone home. Going to his father's office, he tapped on the door and opened it.

He got no further than the spot where the parquet flooring of reception gave way to the royal blue carpet of the

manager's office. He stood still, his hand on the door and his
eyes on the two people in the room. His father was sitting at
his desk with Francine standing at his right-hand side. They
were separated from each other by two feet of physical
distance but the intense gaze they were sharing breached
that distance. His father, pale-faced, was looking up at
Francine as if begging a favour. Francine, cool, a slight smile
on her lips, seemed to be the one in control. She had a jacket
on now over her white blouse but her breasts still pressed
against the thicker fabric as if the jacket had been moulded
to her body. She held herself with pride and confidence
while John Enright seemed to grovel. Tommy felt like an
intruder. A Peeping Tom. As if he was spying on a very
private moment.

Francine was the first to break the intense silence. She
turned her eyes on Tommy and smiled. "Come on in – I was
just leaving," she invited as if it was her office.

Tommy's hand dropped from the door and he walked
slowly towards his father.

Francine tucked her bag under her arm and strode across
the room in that long-legged, hip-swaying gait she had. Both
men followed her with their eyes and she knew it. She
paused in the doorway.

"Tommy, I think you should know I've been passing on
tales." Then she shrugged. "Just doing my job."

Turning gracefully on her heel, she closed the door
behind her. Tommy sat. His father, head bowed, was rubbing
his temples.

"What tales? It was Shorty, wasn't it?"

John stopped massaging his forehead and looked at his
son. Tommy felt for an instant that his father wasn't seeing

him. He had a bewildered, haunted quality which had never been part of what John Enright was. With a shock Tommy realised his father was vulnerable. What in the fuck had Francine said to him?

"Dad? What's wrong? What did she say?"

John smiled. An ironic smile. Not in response to anything Francine had said. The irony lay in his uncharacteristic reaction to her blonde beauty, her sexuality, her gentleness. He had discovered an urgent need which had lain dormant for years and Francine now seemed to be the only person to fulfil that need for excitement and, yes, danger.

He saw the puzzlement on his son's face and wished he could talk to him. Explain. Admit he was being stupid, naïve, short-sighted, swayed by his emotions and not common sense. All the weaknesses of which he accused Tommy. But that would be a humiliation too far.

"Jason Goodall," he said at last.

"Breeze? What about him?"

"Dan Shorten complained that Goodall was hanging around waiting for you at lunch-time. He said Goodall's a hoodlum and that your friend was sizing up the security here. 'Casing the joint' I think it's called."

"For fuck's sake!"

"Watch your mouth!"

"You can talk! What's going on between you and Francine? I saw the way you were gawping at each other!"

John sat back suddenly. Denials, explanations sprang to mind but the words stuck in his throat. He was angry. At himself for being vulnerable. At Francine for being irresistible. Mostly at Tommy for his perspicacity.

"How dare you! Keep your filthy mind to yourself. And

don't you ever, *ever*, bring that piece of garbage you call Breeze around here again. Do you understand?"

Tommy understood alright. He understood that his father had not denied he was having it off with Francine Keyes. Dirty old git! Cheat! How could he do it? It would destroy Mom if she knew. She was so sensitive. So airy fairy, or artistic as the family preferred to say. But then anyone who underestimated his mother's intelligence would be making a mistake. She might seem at times to be a bit spaced out but she had an underlying strength and a very sharp mind. She was worth ten of Francine Keyes.

"You'd better not upset Mom. I'm watching out for her, even if you're not. And as for Breeze. He's my friend. I know about his family. I know his dad is a criminal. A thief and a drunkard. I know his brother is a drug dealer. Breeze has nothing to do with them. "

"Jesus Christ! Has everything we tried to teach you gone completely over your head? Do you honestly think any other boy in St Martin's would be seen with the likes of Jason Goodall? It seems to me all the money we spent on your education is gone to waste."

"Money! That's all you think about, isn't it? That and screwing the receptionist!"

"Get out!"

"No! Not before you listen to me for a change."

Father and son stared at each other, each knowing that their relationship had reached a new stage. The rules were changed. Tommy was no longer willing to see himself as the boy to be moulded and John could not now believe himself to be a man deserving of respect and blind obedience. He had already cheated on his wife by arranging to meet

71

Francine. The new rules meant that when Tommy talked, John would have to listen.

"Breeze is one of the most genuine people I've ever met. It's not his fault he's from the wrong side of town. You weren't born with a silver spoon in your mouth, were you? Don't you love to bullshit about how you worked your way up from poverty?"

Bullshit! John shook his head. The certainty of youth. The quick judgement and confidence in your own opinion. John remembered it well. How he never had a doubt that he would succeed. How he chose his own path in life and travelled along it with determination. Patrick Morgan had just been a stepping-stone along the way. He would have got there with or without him.

"Well, Dad? What have you got to say? It's not like you to listen without interrupting."

Jesus! More criticism. Today seemed to be a day of reckoning for John Enright.

"I admire your loyalty to your friend," he said slowly, even humbly. "But you and Breeze move in different worlds. You've been given great opportunities, Tommy. Don't throw them away."

"I've no intention of doing that. But I'm not going to live your life all over again for you. Doing things the way you want me to. This is my life and you might as well know now I'm not working here when I leave school."

"So what are you going to do? Hang around street corners?"

Tommy hesitated for a moment and then spat his words out. "I'm forming a group with Breeze. We're both good musicians. We're going to make it. I know it. We have the talent."

A headache which had been threatening all day suddenly came to life and tightened its sharp claws around John's head. He'd had enough of this day, facing his weaknesses, watching control slip out of his grasp. He needed a respite, an oasis of peace to lick his wounds. He needed to be in Waterside Apartments soothed by Francine's blue gaze and gentle touch.

"Go home, Tommy. I want you here again in the morning. Goodnight. Tell your mother I'll be late."

"What's new?"

Tommy stood. He wasn't sure what to do. He could hardly ask for a job for Breeze now. The old man looked knackered. Almost as if he'd keel over if he wasn't sitting. Maybe the prick was feeling guilty about fooling around with the receptionist or maybe he was afraid Tommy would tell his mother. That's how little his father knew him.

"Mom is very worried about Carrie," he said. "So am I. Try to get home at a decent hour."

Tommy went, the hem of the black coat he had bought in a charity shop picking up little flecks of blue fluff as it trailed along the carpet.

John dropped his head onto his hands and wished that he could be strong enough to follow his son home. An image of Francine flashed across his mind again. He knew he would follow where she led and he hoped with all his heart that it would be a wet and warm place.

* * *

Lynn checked everything again. Just to make sure. She was used to having Meg do the locking-up. On the street outside she waited until the beeping alarm went silent. That was it for today. The shop was locked up. Now what? Dinner for one, then salsa-dancing class. The class she had joined in the hope of finding a swarthy Latin-American partner. And indeed she had found swarthy partners in plenty. All female and all as needy as herself. They laughed and giggled, had a grand time, swaying and swooping to the blood-stirring music, taking turns to dance lead, pretending that some day, any day soon, they would be dancing in the arms of the man of their dreams.

Playing pretend was more than Lynn could cope with tonight. She felt tired. Not physically. Her energy had not failed her yet. But she was tired of her life. That prick in the pub today had focussed her attention on all the negatives. The shop was great. It kept her busy and provided a comfortable lifestyle. Her friends were many and very precious to her. She had several holidays and holiday romances every year. It was the life she had chosen for herself. No ties, no responsibilities. No depth or breadth. A shallow stream of meaningless affairs and lonely meals for one. Anyway, she wouldn't be missed from the class. One less spare part for whom to find a partner.

Lynn sat into her car and turned the key. She should veer left at the nearby traffic lights and head home. She would have except she could not get the image of Meg's troubled face out of her head. How did Meg cope with the phone call to Karl Hemmings? Had she been terrified, intimidated? Had John been there to support her? She could ring her of course to enquire if she was alright – but suppose John was at home, suppose they were having a family conference to discuss the situation? What would she be like then? The nosey unmarried friend, sticking her nose into private family business? On the other hand, judging by the number of times Meg had said John was always busy, maybe Meg was at this minute home alone, shrivelling under the weight of worry. Compromise seemed like the best option. Lynn decided to head towards Meg's house via the longer southern route. That would bring her past the Industrial Estate from which EFAS traded. All she had to do was drive to EFAS and see if John's car was still there. If it was she would call to Meg, if not she'd just go home and mind her own business.

Her mind made up, Lynn wasted no time in getting to the Industrial Estate. EFAS was easy to find. It was the biggest and brightest unit there, security cameras dotted along the roof of the building and high wrought-iron fencing all around. There a silver Ford Avensis in the car park. John's car. Now what? Head straight to Meg, talk to her, comfort her if that was what she needed?

The more Lynn thought about Meg alone and frantic with worry the angrier she became. How could John be here when Meg's world was falling apart? Lynn had witnessed the way he had cut short Meg's phone call today. He had only spoken to her for a matter of seconds. Just long enough to say he was too busy to take her call. Too busy to support his wife, too busy to be concerned about his daughter.

Knowing with certainty that she was overstepping the bounds of friendship, Lynn drove into EFAS and parked her car beside John's. Quickly, so that she couldn't change her mind, she walked to the entrance. The door was locked. She pressed the intercom.

"Hello?"

"John, Lynn here. Can I see you for a few minutes?"

"Hi, Lynn! Of course. C'mon in."

When the buzzer sounded she put her hand to the door and it swung in. The clack of her high heels echoed as she walked on the parquet floor of reception. She headed towards the beautifully finished semi-circular desk. Her eyes were instantly drawn to the image of her car on one of the bank of monitors behind the desk. Dimly lit corridors radiated out from reception, each lined with red-doored lock-up units. She started when a door to her right suddenly opened and John appeared.

"I had no idea you ran such a big operation here, John. No wonder it keeps you so busy."

"Too busy sometimes. If memory serves me right it's years since you were last here."

"Must be five or six, I suppose. Patrick Morgan was in charge and this place was about one third the size it is now."

"Ah! Patrick Morgan."

Lynn waited for John to go on but he was standing with a faraway look in his eyes. She took the opportunity to examine him more closely. It was some time since she had last met him. John, it seemed, lived his life in EFAS. He was maturing well. His dark hair was now strewn with silver, his tall frame more padded than it used to be. With a start she realised he was edging his way towards middle-age.

"Patrick's not well," he said, suddenly dragging his drifting attention back to Lynn. "He has motor neuron disease."

"I'm sorry to hear that. Is he at home or …"

"For now anyway. Would you like a tea or coffee, Lynn?

76

I was just about to make something for myself."

Lynn began to feel uncomfortable. John was edgy, continuously checking the time.

"Am I delaying you, John?"

"No, you're fine, Lynn. It's just I've an appointment in town at eight. A business thing. Plenty of time yet."

He must be wondering what she was doing here. She was wondering the same thing herself. Would she ever learn? She should probably go for damage limitation now. Just say goodnight and run.

Instead she said "Okay – coffee" and followed as he led the way into his office. She watched as he made coffee for them both and she remembered that night so many years ago when she had first seen John Enright. She and Meg both spotting him as he came in the door of the disco, elbowing each other, giggling, both hoping he would look in their direction.

"Do you remember the disco in The Grattan Club, John? The one where we first met?"

He placed a mug of coffee in front of her and sat down. "Of course I do. How could I forget? I couldn't decide whether to ask you or Meg to dance so I asked you both. That was the night we became the Three Amigos, wasn't it?"

Lynn looked away from his gaze. That's what she had thought then too. The Three Amigos: Meg, Lynn and John. Until one year later when the three had become two. Meg and John had fallen in love and Lynn had gone travelling. France, Germany, Italy, New York and once, on another impulse, India. She had come home for the wedding of course. She had been Meg's bridesmaid. When she had discovered that the bride was three months pregnant Lynn had travelled some more.

"We've changed, you and I, John. But Meg hasn't. She hasn't developed a protective shell."

"You're not that much different either, are you? You still rush in where angels fear to tread. I think you're going to wade in with both feet now. What's on your mind?"

"I'm worried about Meg."

There! She'd said it. What was she going to say next? John, you're neglecting your wife, not giving her the support she needs? Jesus! What had she been thinking barging in here with her half-baked ideas? More importantly, how was she going to worm her way out of it without spoiling the friendship?

John's expression had changed from warmth to wariness.

"What do you mean? Why are you worried about her? What's wrong?"

What's wrong? His daughter was missing, his wife crying her eyes out and John Enright asks what's wrong!

"Carrie, of course! Meg's frantic. Surely you know that! Meg is convinced Carrie has come to harm and she's cracking under the strain. She needs a lot of support until all this mess is sorted out."

"What mess? Carrie is having a few days' holiday for God's sake! She can't be tied to her mother's apron strings forever. She's twenty-one. Meg just doesn't know how to let go."

"I don't think going off to a remote cabin with some kind of Jesus freak is just having a few days' holiday, as you put it!"

"Jesus freak? Cabin? What are you talking about, Lynn?"

Lynn stared at John. What in the hell had she gone and done now? She'd opened her big mouth once too often this time. Stupid, impulsive Lynn! Lonely, parasite Lynn, sucking the life out of someone else's relationship.

"I–I'm sorry, John. I shouldn't have said that. I assumed Meg would have told you this afternoon about Carrie. And, Garth – her new boyfriend – he's not a freak of any kind. As far as I know, that is."

"It seems you know a lot more than I do. Why don't you tell me the rest of the story?"

"Ask your wife. It's not my place to tell you."

"A bit late for tact now, don't you think? You'd better talk."

Lynn lowered her head and stared at the desktop. For one usually so accommodating to the streams of words which flowed around her head and out of her mouth, she now found herself parched of any speech.

John stood and began to pace. Lynn noticed how tense he was. He ran his hands through his hair and didn't seem to notice that he had left it standing up in peaks. He came to a stop beside Lynn and sat on the corner of the desk, his long legs stretched out so that she could see the defined muscles of his thighs and calves. He was close enough for her to smell his aftershave. Spicy and warm.

"Well, Lynn. What was it you came here to tell me?"

"I told you. Meg is extremely upset."

"About Carrie? So she's got herself a boyfriend. Is that what Meg can't face?"

Looking up at John, Lynn noticed that his eyes had lost none of their soulful darkness. How could someone have eyes which promised such sensitivity and yet be so blind to the hurt of others? Like when he had blithely announced that he had taken a year to make up his mind but that Meg was his choice. No more Three Amigos. Just like that.

Lynn was angry with herself. Coming here had been a mistake. Yet another regretted impulse. The pseudo-gaiety of the salsa class would have been a better choice. Pushing away her coffee mug, Lynn picked up her bag.

"I'm sorry I bothered you, John. I was just concerned about Meg. None of my business really."

"Wait! You haven't told me ..."

The door opened and a white-haired man in a security uniform poked his head into the office.

"Everything alright, boss?" he asked, looking from one to the other.

"Fine, Ollie, thank you. Eh, this is Lynn. She's a friend of —"

Lynn stood abruptly, startling the two men. She didn't want to hear just how John Enright categorised her. A friend of his wife, his family, *his* friend? With a sort of half wave to John, she strode to the door and brushed past Ollie — aware that they were both looking at her as if she had lost her mind. She sped out of the building, across reception and into her car, not allowing herself to think until she had reached home, closed the door and drawn all the blinds.

Then, with the world safely locked out, she blushed with shame. She could no longer tell herself that she had been trying to help Meg. It was as if Carrie's disappearance had been the opportunity she had been waiting for all these years. She had convinced herself that she had long ago outrun her feelings, left them on top of the Eiffel Tower, under the Brandenburg Gate, at the Taj Mahal, thrown them in the Trevi Fountain. But she knew now they had travelled back with her and had flourished in their hiding place. Until tonight. Now she admitted why she had endured all her relationships and enjoyed none. He was still the one. *The* one. John Enright. Her best friend's husband.

Lynn went to the freezer, got out a large tub of ice cream and spooned half of it into a dish. Then she heated some, a huge some, of chocolate sauce. Armed with her comfort food and a box of tissues, she slipped her *Beaches* DVD into the player, sat back on the couch and promised herself she would not cry until the very end of the film. Then she could believe her tears were being shed for Barbara Hershey and Bette Midler.

Ten minutes and half a tub of ice-cream later, a searing pain flashed through Lynn. The cold-hot sugary mess had triggered a nerve in one of her back teeth. It was the reality check she needed. This was real pain, not imagined like the poor-lonely-me syndrome which had seemed to permeate today. She was behaving like the self-absorbed teenager she had never been. To hell with this!

Switching off the DVD, she glanced at her watch. Seven thirty. She'd be late for her class but that was nothing new. She was always late for everything.

As she grabbed her dancing shoes and car keys, Lynn knew she would shine in the class tonight. She would be at one with the passion and fury of the music. She would tap and stamp and twirl and glide. She would bend and sway and push her body to the limit. Until she no longer thought of things which were unthinkable.

CHAPTER 7

Like an over-anxious teenager on a first date, John arrived too early at Waterside Apartments. He had often seen this building from across the river but this was his first time being so close to the much-lauded flagship quayside development. Standing on the pavement outside, he glanced at his watch and saw it was only quarter to eight. It would be gauche to go in now but yet he didn't want to stay hanging around outside. Some passerby might recognise him. He'd have to lie to them as he had to Lynn. What in the hell was he getting himself into?

Deciding suddenly, John turned right and walked into the lobby. He was immediately enfolded in a wave of light and cool air. Marble-tiled floors and potted palms, tall and luxuriant, gave it the ambience of a five-star hotel.

A uniformed porter approached him.

"May I help you, sir?"

"I'm looking for Apartment 8, please."

The porter led John to the lifts and directed him to the first floor. Committed now, John rode the lift and got out on floor one, his feet sinking into thick carpet. Number 8 was to the left. He walked to the door and lifted his hand to the bell. Last chance. He could turn around and go home. Back to his wife and son. His very upset wife according to Lynn. The wife who sometimes didn't notice whether he was there or not. John pressed the bell.

Sharp little taps echoed from inside – someone walking on wooden flooring in high heels. The sound approached the door and suddenly Francine was standing before him, a silk robe wrapped around her slim body and spiky-heeled sandals on her feet.

"John, come in. You're a little early. I'm not quite ready yet."

He walked in but didn't see much of the apartment. It was huge and airy. He sensed the space but could not take his eyes off Francine. She was not wearing any clothes underneath her robe. No bra because he could see the outline of her nipples, no panties because he could see a dark triangle reflected through the thin fabric. Or maybe she was wearing a thong. Jesus! John was sweating and his heart was thumping. He remembered stories of old men dying of heart attacks in young girls' apartments. He had laughed at them. Suppose it happened to him? What a way to be found out!

Needing to calm himself, John walked to the huge picture window. He looked down at the river. The Lee was swirling and grey. Cars snaked along the street beneath, traffic busy, even at this hour. A visiting French naval ship was docked further up the quay, its pennants fluttering in a strong, unseasonable breeze. He hadn't noticed that it was so windy out but now the people scurrying past the City Hall and across Parnell Bridge were huddled into their coats.

Seagulls caught the air draughts and rose or swooped as the wind took them. He watched one bird land on the copper cupola of the City Hall and teeter on the dome before launching into the breeze again.

Francine walked up close behind him. He heard the click of her heels, smelt her perfume, sensed her body heat.

"My favourite view," she said. "The City Hall is beautiful when it's lit up. The limestone gleams. You'll see it later. Why don't you sit down, John?"

He turned to face her. She was standing close, so close her breasts were almost touching his chest. Over her shoulder John saw a red leather couch, strewn with white fluffy cushions. He stepped around her and walked towards it, hoping she wouldn't notice his shortness of breath and his shaking hands.

"What would you like a drink? A scotch, brandy, wine?"

"Water, please. I'm driving."

"Not thinking about going home already, are you?"

"Of course not," he laughed, trying to sound sophisticated, a man of the world, used to calling on beautiful young women. Just as it would appear by her casual and confident approach that Francine was used to entertaining men. How she'd laugh if she knew his sexual experience had started, and would lately appear to have finished, with his wife. He must stop thinking about Meg. About sex.

"How long have you lived here, Francine?"

"A while now," she answered vaguely, handing him his glass of water and sitting on the couch beside him. "I like it. I'll show you around later. After dinner. Do you like moussaka?"

"Yes, I do," John answered, not sure whether he did or not.

He had an idea it was some sort of Greek dish. Jesus, he was out of his depth here! Francine was so much more worldly and sophisticated in these surroundings than she seemed in the office of EFAS. Why in the hell was a woman like this working in a suburban storage company?

"How are you feeling now?" she asked. "You were quite upset today about Patrick Morgan."

"To be honest, I feel angry. It seems unfair that a man who worked so hard all his life can't enjoy the retirement he earned."

Her hand slid across the couch and rested on his thigh. He felt the fingers gently begin to massage his thigh muscles. "You're a very kind man, John. Sensitive and caring."

He put his hand on top of hers. He meant to gently lift her hand away, make his excuses and leave. He couldn't handle this. He wanted to fuck this beautiful woman but his conscience and his Catholic upbringing were battling his hormones.

Her cool fingers began to move slowly underneath his hand, gently massaging, re-assuring. His fingers curled around hers. Their hands were speaking a language which needed no words.

Somehow his hand lifted of its own volition and reached out to touch Francine's golden hair. As his fingers slid over the silky strands, he realised he already knew exactly what her hair would feel like. He had dreamt the silken texture. His fingers touched the soft skin of her neck. Her eyes were steady on him, not inviting or rejecting. Just questioning, as he was.

He allowed his hand to slip underneath her hair and touch the smooth skin of her nape. Trembling, with a will of their own, his fingers traced the cold track of the chain she wore until they reached the pendant nestling in her warm cleavage. His breathing was quicker now as he stared at the imprint of Francine's nipples against the fabric of her robe. As if to confirm the signals her body was giving them both, Francine slowly undid the belt which held her robe. John tried to still his heartbeat as her breasts were revealed, full, pert, their paleness emphasised by her dark, erect nipples. They were perfect breasts. He touched them. They were firmer than what he had imagined. With both her hands on his head, Francine guided his mouth towards her breasts.

The doorbell rang. John drew sharply away from Francine. His heart was still pounding but with shock now. Who in the fuck was at the door? Surely to Christ she wasn't going to answer it? Francine was coolly drawing the edges of her robe together and slipping her feet into the sandals John had not notice her slip off.

"Don't answer," he whispered, a desperate plea in his eyes.

Francine laughed. "I must. Or else we'll have nothing to eat. I'm not very good in the kitchen. I hope to convince you I have compensating talents though."

Leaning towards him, she swiftly but very passionately kissed him, pushing her tongue into his mouth which hung open with fear and shock. Then she stood and calmly walked to the door which opened directly into the lounge where John was sitting petrified on the red-leather couch.

He sank back against the fluffy cushions. What in the fuck was he thinking? What was he doing here? Idiot! Having a mid-life crisis. Jesus! He was forty. She was what, twenty-five or six. He was married, she was single. He was the boss, she the employee. On all fronts this was wrong. Foolish.

His back to the door, John was afraid to turn around in case he saw a familiar face peering in at him cowering on the couch. She had the door open now and was chatting easily with the delivery person. They appeared to know each other. Neither seemed bothered by the fact that Francine was obviously nude underneath her robe, that her lips showed the tenderness of a recent kiss. There was an aroma of food. A garlicy smell. His stomach, already in turmoil, almost jumped into his throat. He hated garlic. Hated the smell of it and the aftertaste which lingered long after the meal was digested.

The door closed and he heard Francine click-clack towards what he assumed was the kitchen. He stood up and called to her.

"Francine!"

"Easy, John, don't be too anxious. We'll eat first."

"I'm going," he said, walking towards the exit door. "I've just remembered something. Somewhere I must be. Urgently."

She came into the lounge, a serving spoon in her hand.

John hesitated. She was stunning, blonde hair tumbling down her back, her perfect body swathed in softest silk. Was he mad? How could he pass up an opportunity like this? She was obviously available. If the door bell hadn't rung they would probably be in bed by now, writhing, licking, sucking … Jesus! He'd better get out of here.

"Thanks for the drink. Bye, Francine. Sorry about the rush." He kept babbling as he fiddled with the door lock. He couldn't open it.

Francine strolled over to him, breasts thrust forward. She stood close, looking up at him, her two hands on his shoulders.

"You're sure about this, John? You really must go?"

"It's very, very, urgent that I go now. I don't know how I forgot."

She shrugged, causing her robe to slip down her left shoulder. John imagined kissing that smooth skin, licking the hollow in the curve of her neck.

"Suit yourself," she said, reaching up and opening the door with one swift turn of the lock. "See you tomorrow."

Outside on the corridor, John dashed towards the lift. It wasn't until he was back in the lobby that he began to breathe easily again and his heartbeat slowed. He had wanted her so much. That had been the frightening thing. For once in his life John Enright had really wanted to do the wrong thing, to be abandoned and downright dirty, to cheat on his wife. To live a little, for fuck's sake.

"Are you alright, sir? Did you find Apartment 8?"

It was the same porter who had spoken to him earlier. "Yes, I did, thank you."

John went out the door with as much eagerness as he had come in. What had he been hoping for? A fumble, a groping session, maybe some heavy petting. He most certainly hadn't been expecting the assault of Francine's full-on sexuality, nor the attack of guilt which had paralysed him.

Outside it was still windy and the traffic was heavy. John took the long route home. He had a lot to think about.

* * *

88

It was getting dark. Meg welcomed the fall of night. Only four or at most five more hours to go before she would know the truth about Carrie. Showered and in her dressing gown, she lay on the couch, cool slices of cucumber on her swollen eyelids. The television was turned low so that she could also hear the thump of Tommy's music from upstairs. He had been sensitive enough this evening to spend a little time with her and then to leave her alone. Tommy needed his alone time too. He had been very hurt and shocked to hear about Carrie's secret boyfriend.

None of the background noise blocked out Karl Hemmings' voice in her head. Over and over, she replayed their telephone conversation, searching for clues that her daughter was safe. Searching for evidence that she was alive or else …

Meg suddenly swung her legs onto the floor and sat up straight. The cucumber slithered down onto her dressing gown. She peered at the television through blurred but now less swollen eyes. Walking over to the TV, she raised the volume. She had vowed that she would not allow any more negative thoughts. She would not show tragedy the way by anticipating its path. Crossing her fingers, she touched the wood of the mantelpiece. Salt! She must get some and throw it over her shoulder. Not caring that she was behaving illogically, Meg dashed to the kitchen and grabbed the salt cellar. She poured a little heap onto the palm of her hand and tossed it over her shoulder.

"Mom?"

She spun around to look at Tommy. He was smiling but she could see the worry in his eyes, the hurt that Carrie had not confided in him. She opened her arms and he came to her. She hugged him close. Her son. The defiant boy with the potential to become a caring man. A man unafraid of his feelings.

Meg pulled away from Tommy and noticed that he had his coat on. For a moment she wondered if he had slept in it.

"You going out?"

"Yeah. I told Breeze I'd drop over. I won't be long. Will you be alright for a little while?"

"No problem. Off you go. Anyway, your dad will be home soon."

Tommy's expression hardened. Meg so desperately wanted to tell her son that his father was a good man even though, yes, he could be dogmatic and distant. If only Tom would listen, she could explain that John's way of showing how much he loved them all was to provide them with a lifestyle he had only dreamed about when he was young.

Tommy was as far as the front door now, waving his hand to her without looking back. Meg's eyes raked over him, from the top of his orange-streaked hair right down to the hem of his black coat. She stared at the fingers of the hand he was holding up in a silent goodbye. The strong square fingers. An image of those same fingers, miniature but still strong and square, flashed across her mind. She remembered cutting the nails when he was only a week old, remembered the solid little hand in hers as he toddled to kindergarten. She noticed and stored every detail about her son as he went out the front door.

Going back to the kitchen Meg realised she had forgotten to get something ready for John to eat. Needing something to occupy herself, she opened the fridge and peered in. A few slices of ham, eggs, cucumber and barely enough milk for breakfast. She hadn't done any shopping. Maybe if she hardboiled some eggs she could make him a ham and egg sandwich. One of his favourites. His mother used to make them for him. There she was again. Hannah Enright. Insinuating herself into their lives even though her own was spent.

"Go to hell, Hannah!" Meg shouted into the empty kitchen, then quickly grabbed eggs and a saucepan so that she wouldn't have to think about what she had just said.

It worked. Hannah Enright drifted away from her thoughts. But she couldn't stop thinking about Carrie, no matter how she tried. Why hadn't she realised that the morning in the airport three months ago could have been the last time she would ever lay eyes on her daughter? Why hadn't she seared the image on her memory as she had just now done with Tommy? What about Carrie's fingers? They were long and narrow, yes, but was she wearing nail varnish when she left? Were her nails French-polished, was her shiny black hair loose or tied back? That morning had been a blur of luggage and visas and passports and a group of young people excited about their trip. Carrie had been absorbed into the twittering, giggling group, lost in their collective excitement. Had she waved? Had she given a last glance back? Meg realised she wouldn't have seen her anyway. Her eyes had been blurred by tears.

The eggs were boiling, making a dull thud as the bubbling water pushed them against the saucepan. Meg watched as they bounced and toppled around. The vigorous rise of the stream of bubbles was hypnotic and soothing. There was also something profoundly sad in the flat pop of the bubbles as they hit the surface. Deflated in all their glistening glory. All that energy spent just to drift off into the extractor fan as wispy steam.

Knowing for sure that she was losing her battle for positivity, Meg sat at the kitchen table, the phone by her hand, and waited for somebody, anybody, to rescue her from the images of violent death which bubbled but refused to drift away.

* * *

Tommy walked quickly. It was not safe to stroll in this area. The streets were wide and well lit but everywhere little gangs seemed to have found dark corners in which to lurk. Hoods up, they lolled against walls, pushing and shoving each other, always keeping an eye out for an unsuspecting stranger. Someone they could bully and frighten. Someone who would make them feel strong and in control. He felt safe though. Everybody knew Breeze was his friend. Nobody around here messed with the Goodalls.

When he passed the house which had a fountain occupying most of the miniscule front garden, Tommy knew he would soon reach Breeze's place. He was used by now to the rows and rows of identical terraced houses. When he had come here first he wondered how people found their own homes. It was a while before he began to notice the wrought-iron fences on some, the porches built onto others. The huge water fountain. Attempts to personalise the impersonal.

Breeze lived in Number 232. The low gate was rusty and the tiny front garden clogged with weeds. Ignoring the bell, Tommy knocked on the door. The bell had not worked for a long time. Breeze must have been waiting for him because the door opened immediately, allowing a waft of hot and acrid air to escape. Tom took a deep breath of fresh air before going in. The little hallway smelled like a urinal. A sure sign Mrs Goodall had fallen into another of her depressions.

"My old lady's in the front room. Come into the kitchen," Breeze said, leading the way.

The kitchen was spotlessly clean but it was still permeated by the smell of urine. Tommy tried to decide whether Mrs Goodall pissed all over the house or whether she just pissed herself and didn't wash.

"Want a Coke?"

Tommy shook his head. "No, thanks. I can't stay. There's a bit of a crisis in our gaffe. Carrie hasn't rung home in over a week. Remember I told you she's in the States?"

Breeze raised a quizzical eyebrow, then went to the fridge and got himself a drink. Tommy understood. There wouldn't have been anyone to worry if Breeze hadn't rung home for a month, not to mention a week.

"How old is your sister? Didn't you say twenty-one?"

"Yeah, but my old lady fusses. She needs to know where we are all the time. Anyway I just wanted to tell you, no joy with the old man. There's no work going in EFAS. Sorry, Breeze."

Unscrewing the cap off his bottle of Coke, Breeze put it into the bin. He was fanatically tidy. Except of course for the messy front garden. Tommy could never understand how Breeze let dandelions, thistles and nettles run riot outside the front door when he would not allow as much as a speck of dust inside.

"Well, thanks for trying, man. Bet your old fella heard

about my family. He'd be afraid to let a Goodall set foot in his place."

"He did mention something about not wanting you hanging around. The old prick of a forklift driver complained about lunch-time. Fuck them!"

"Fuck them good!" Breeze answered, raising his Coke bottle in salute. "Anyway, I think I might've got something else for a few weeks. A guy near here, a half-arsed builder, wants a labourer for a job he's doing. I spoke to him this evening. He's to let me know tomorrow."

"Hope it works out."

"It will. He'll pay me shit and work the balls off me but at least he won't be taking any tax. And he doesn't care about my surname."

"Breeze, I …"

"No need to say any more, Tom. I know the score. Besides, the labouring job is local. An extension to a house. I'll be able to keep an eye on the old lady. She's heading for another one of her turns."

Tommy shivered. From the little Breeze had told him, Mrs Goodall's 'turns' involved overdoses and many hours of sitting in a chair rocking herself into oblivion. And pissing.

"Isn't there someone who could help? Her doctor or social services or someone?"

"We look after our own."

Not for the first time Tommy felt a distance between himself and Breeze. There was always the 'us' and 'them'. Yes, they shared a passion for music. Rock music. That's how they had met. Buying discs in a music store. The biggest one in town. That day there had been only one copy of Thin Lizzie's *Black Rose* album in the store. They had both reached for it at the same time. That was almost a year ago when Tommy's interest in Thin Lizzy was only starting. He had been so impressed by Breeze's encyclopaedic knowledge of the band in general and Phil Lynott in particular that he had insisted on Breeze taking the one copy available and was satisfied just to order one for himself. Then he had gone home and looked up the internet, bought books and studied Thin Lizzie until he knew almost as much about them as Breeze did. On the fourth of January, the anniversary of Lynott's death, they had played Thin Lizzy for hours on end and drunk cans of beer in this kitchen until it was time for Tommy to stagger home. He had somehow made it to his room that evening without his parents discovering how drunk he was. Carrie had known, of course. She had covered for him.

"So when do you go back to school? Next week?"

"Fuck, yes. I promised the old lady I'd do the Leaving. I'm off after that though."

"Where to?"

Tommy looked at his friend. The only real friend he had. The only person who understood his passion for music and his need to be free. And yet there was a gulf between them. Too wide to take that final step. Tommy had been inspired today when he had told the Fuehrer he was going to form a rock group with Breeze. It had the right effect. He had seen the disbelief and then rage on his father's face. For an instant John Enright's attention had been focussed solely on his son. But now, here in the quiet of the pokey kitchen, with the stench of Mrs Goodall's urine in his nostrils, Tommy could not tell Breeze of his idea. Not without talking to Carrie first. Not without finally deciding whether he himself was 'us' or 'them'. He stood.

"Don't know what I'm going to do. Maybe I'll go to the States. Or Germany. I don't know."

Breeze walked with him to the door, the sting of ammonia getting stronger as they passed the front room. Out of the corner of his eye, Tommy saw Mrs Goodall seated in an armchair, faced in the direction of the television, rocking herself backwards and forwards. He looked quickly away. Breeze opened the front door and Tommy took a gulp of air.

"I'll see you then, Breeze. Let me know about your job tomorrow."

"Yeah."

Tommy stepped outside and his eyes fell again on the tangled mass of weeds in the tiny front garden. They seemed even higher in the dusk.

"How about I come around tomorrow evening and give you a hand to cut the grass?"

"With what? A fucking nail scissors?"

Breeze closed the front door, leaving Tommy standing on the narrow path between the rampant overgrowth on either side. He had hurt Breeze's feelings. It hadn't dawned on him for a minute that Breeze might not have a lawnmower. He should have minded his own business. And for now that business was looking out for his mother, trying to find out if the Fuehrer was really knocking off the receptionist and discovering what in the fuck was going on with Carrie.

* * *

"God! The kitchen stinks!"

Meg jumped. She hadn't heard John come in.

"Hardboiled eggs. I made you some sandwiches."

"I couldn't eat now. A cup of coffee will do fine. Where's Tommy?"

"Gone to see Breeze."

"I should have known. I suppose he told you I warned him today to keep that criminal away from EFAS?"

Meg heard EFAS and her mind shut down. Carrie was missing, Tommy was upset, she herself was frantic and all John could still think of was blasted EFAS. He must have roller-shutter doors and CCTV cameras on his soul. If he had one. She tied the smelly egg sandwiches into a plastic bag, threw them in the bin and then got air freshener and sprayed it around. The kitchen still stank.

"Well, did he?" he demanded.

He was sitting at the table, his tie loosened and his jacket draped over the back of his chair. She noticed that he was getting heavy – not fat, but he seemed to be developing a slight paunch. A middle-aged spread. His colour was pasty too.

He stood suddenly and strode across to where she was standing, aerosol can in her hand. He parked himself in front of her and glared.

"What did he say?"

"What are you talking about, John? What did who say?"

"God, you never listen to a word I say! What did Tommy say about today?"

"He said he was worried about Carrie. I'm worried about Carrie. Lynn is worried about Carrie. And what about you? Are you in any way concerned about your daughter? Does it matter to you in the slightest that we can't contact her?"

John's shoulders slumped and he let out a long sigh. He

reached towards her and drew her into his arms. She leaned against his broad chest and closed her eyes as his hands rubbed the tensed-up muscles of her back.

"I'm sorry, Meg," he whispered into her hair.

She didn't know whether he was sorry for not worrying about Carrie, not taking her call today or not eating his smelly egg sandwiches. Whatever it was, Meg forgave him. She could forgive him anything when he held her in his warm and safe embrace. She listened to his heartbeat and breathed in the scent of him. He slid his hands up and gently stroked her hair.

"I do love you, Meg. I should have been there for you today. Lynn told me you were very upset."

"Lynn told you? When?"

"She called to EFAS on her way home from work. She was waffling on about cabins and Jesus freaks. What's all that about?"

Meg pulled away from him and went to put on the kettle. She felt cold and weak as soon as she stepped out of the protective circle of his arms but anger propelled her. Lynn should not have interfered. It wasn't her business. But it wasn't Lynn Meg felt angry with. It was the man who had held her so closely only minutes ago. If he had taken her call today, then Lynn wouldn't have gone to see him and he wouldn't be standing here now, ignorant of the fact that his daughter was in serious trouble.

Kettle on the boil, Meg turned to her husband and told him word for word what Siobhán Farrell and Karl Hemmings had said. He listened carefully, nodding occasionally.

"Well, do you still think I'm fussing?" she asked when she

had finished, one part of her hoping that he would say yes.

The frown on his face gave her the answer she didn't want.

"You told him we'd contact the police if we don't hear from Carrie tonight. Right?"

She nodded, then sat at the table and glanced at the clock. Half past nine. John came to sit beside her and took her hand. When Tommy came in, he joined them. The Enrights were together yet apart as they sat in their kitchen waiting for this stranger named Karl Hemmings to ring. Minutes dragged by, coffee was made and went cold.

As midnight approached, Meg prayed. Tentatively at first, then with more fervour as she remembered long-forgotten formulae. They all stared at the phone on the table as if wishing would make it ring. A sad little séance, they encircled the phone and listened to the silence as the clock moved inexorably on.

Tommy was the first to break the circle. Leaning back in his chair, he ran his hands through his hair, a habit learned from his father or else something genetic which made them both find comfort in dragging their fingers through their hair in times of stress.

"How long're we going to wait? Hemmings said twelve, didn't he?"

"I gave him until one our time," Meg said, surprised at the calmness of her own voice. In fact her serenity was a revelation to her. Maybe it was the rare bond between the three of them, maybe it was that Carrie was so much in their thoughts that she seemed like a physical presence or maybe it was just the comfort of rediscovering prayer. For whatever reason, her heart beat more slowly and her hands shook less.

"One on the dot," John said. "I'll give him until then but not a second longer."

"What'll you do, Dad? Get on to the Portland cops or try to contact this Mount Desert Island place?"

"I'll ring Willy Feeney. I went to school with him. He's a Super in the Gardaí now. He'll know what to do."

Meg noticed Tommy relax, reassured by his father. Just like it had always been before Tommy had become possessed by hormones. This might yet be a night for miracles.

They all jumped when the phone rang. Three hands reached out to grab it. John's long arm got there first. As he flicked the speaker, Karl Hemmings' rich voice boomed into the kitchen.

"Hi! Karl Hemmings here. May I speak with Meg?"

"John Enright speaking. Carrie's father. Where's my daughter, Karl? I want to speak to her."

"Oh, John! Nice to talk to you. Carrie has told us all about you and your storage business."

"Did you give Carrie her mother's message? Did you ask her to ring home?"

The line crackled. Meg's heart began the racing rhythm she thought she had banished. Her inhaled breath seemed to go only as far as her throat and sit there, leaving her lungs gasping for air. Karl Hemmings was stalling again. He was pausing only to make up excuses. Plausible, time-wasting excuses.

"Where's my daughter? What have you done to her?" she asked as loudly as her aching lungs would allow.

"Hi, Meg. Good to hear you again," Karl drawled. "I did explain the difficulties to you, didn't I? There's no phone in the cabin."

"Get my sister on the phone or the cops will have your ass in jail before you know where you are!" Tommy shouted, his voice cracking with emotion and a deep anger.

"Ah, that must be Tommy. The young brother. May the Light shine in you, son!"

The mugs on the table clattered as Tommy drew his fist down hard onto the timber surface. "I'm not your son, you pervert!"

Carrie's low sweet voice filled the air. Three pairs of eyes stared at the phone as her disembodied voice rang around the kitchen. There were some hisses and crackles but the words, the sounds, were unmistakably Carrie. Daughter and sister. Gentle, loving Carrie.

"Hi Mom, Dad, Tommy. Karl told me you've been talking to him and that you're anxious about me. I'm sorry to have upset you but there's no need for you to worry. I'm here at Mount Desert Island with Garth, Karl's son. It's the most beautiful place in the world. Lakes and forests and clean fresh air. I'd phone you tonight but the nearest phone is six miles away and there's yet another hurricane warning in force for this area. Nothing to worry about once you stay safely indoors. They're used to it here. I'll be back in Portland on Friday and I'll ring then. How's my brother? Hope you're ready for back to school, Tom. Don't worry, folks. I was never happier. I'll see you very soon. Looking forward to snuggling into my own bed with all my soft toys. May the Light protect you all!"

A soft click sounded and Carrie's voice was no more.

"Carrie! Speak to me, Carr!" Tommy shouted, grabbing the phone.

John gently caught his hand and took the phone from

him. "That was a recording, Tom." Tommy put his arms on the table and dropped his head onto them. Meg stared at his bowed head, the sound of Carrie's voice still echoing in her head.

"That's the best I could do for tonight," Karl Hemmings said. "Sorry about the quality but I taped from the radio link. I hope it puts your mind at rest."

"How in the hell could my mind be at rest when she's in the back of beyonds with a man I don't know and a hurricane threatening?" John's voice was low but full of fury.

"Did she sound distressed?"

"Well, no. But how do I know you didn't have a gun to her head?"

Meg gasped. She had never thought of that. And she banished the thought now. Carrie did sound happy. Serene.

Karl Hemmings was laughing, uttering soothing words.

"We don't carry arms. We rely on the power and strength of the Light. Trust your daughter, John, and trust in the Light to watch over her."

"I put my trust in the police. I want to hear from Carrie, to speak to her person to person. Friday is the deadline, Hemmings. Do you understand?"

"I do, John. Goodnight, Meg, Tommy. I'll pray for you all."

The line went dead, the tenuous link to Carrie cut off.

"That was Carrie alright," Tommy said. "But at the same time it wasn't. What's all this 'light' stuff about?"

"I told you Karl Hemmings is leader of some type of movement," said Meg. "Obviously a quasi-religious one by the sound of things."

"How can you be so cool, Mom? Aren't you afraid she'll join up this cult or whatever it is?"

102

Meg lifted her hand and smoothed her son's rumpled hair. She smiled at him. "No, Tom. I'm not. I don't care if she comes back with her head shaved and parades up and down the street in orange robes. I don't even care if she's pregnant or smoking pot. I just want her home and I believe now that no matter what, our Carrie will be back to us. Do you agree, John?"

John was frowning, looking down at his hands, carefully recalling the conversation with the slimy Karl Hemmings and the taped message from Carrie. Just enough to keep them from contacting the police. Enough to mollify them until … until what? But Hemmings was right in one thing. Whatever was going on, Carrie was a willing participant. John knew every nuance of her voice, each low, husky note. She had sounded calm and in control. He looked up at his wife and son.

"Yes. I agree. But I'll ring Willy Feeney tomorrow anyway. See what I can find out about Hemmings. And look at the time. It's already Wednesday. We'd better go to bed."

Tommy got up and stood between his parents. He hugged them close. A warm, loving hug and they hugged him back, not letting go even when his hoops and studs pushed coldly against their skin. Then, without another word, he turned and went to bed, a boy missing his older sister, a man supporting his parents.

John took Meg's hand and led her upstairs. They made love. A passionate, mind-numbing, worry-assuaging, guilt-ridding, all-absorbing union of wants and needs. It was as if their bodies were creating Carrie all over again.

Exhausted then, Meg slept. John lay on his back and tried to stem the tide of returning thoughts. They flowed out of the darkness, wearying his sated body, troubling his restless mind. Carrie and the Hemmings, Tommy and Jason Goodall, Francine Keyes and the promise of excitement she held, Patrick Morgan and the person named Yan Gilmore who was set to travel halfway around the world to take over EFAS. The never-before mentioned nephew.

Leaning on his elbow, John gently kissed Meg's sleeping face. He eased himself out of bed and went downstairs. He made tea and looked in the fridge for the egg sandwiches he had refused earlier. No sign of them. Meg must have thrown them out. He sat at the kitchen table, drumming his fingers, wishing that he had not given up cigarettes. Every nerve-end was tingling from the sex with Meg, fired by passion, rage, guilt. What would his mother say to him now? He knew as sure as if she was sitting beside him. 'EFAS is your business, son. You built it up. Don't let Patrick Morgan's upstart of a nephew take it from you.' And he would agree with her but how in the fuck was he going to stop Yan Gilmore? What would she say about Francine Keyes? Like she had always said. Never trust a smile that doesn't reach the eyes. And it was only now, in the dead of night that he realised Francine had steel in her beautiful blue eyes.

CHAPTER 8

It was still dark night in Maine when someone shook Carrie's shoulder. She was terrified at first, stuck as she was halfway between the comforting images of a dream and this sudden wakefulness.

Then she saw Garth hovering over her bed in the dimness of the log cabin, the cabin deep in the woods she shared with ditzy Joyanne who alleluiaed and giggled from dawn 'til dusk. He put his finger to her lips, warning her to be silent. They both glanced across the room to the other bed. There was no movement from Joyanne other than the rhythmic rise and fall of her breathing. Garth put his head close to Carrie's and whispered to her.

"Get dressed. Put on walking shoes and a jacket. It'll be cold where we're going."

Warm and sleepy and longing for closeness to Garth as she was, Carrie could see no good reason to go anywhere. Maybe she should drag him into the bed and make love to him accompanied by a chorus of alleluias from Joyanne. Smiling at her ridiculous fantasy, she nodded to Garth. He crept from the room to wait outside for her while she dressed.

Outside it was cold and velvety black. The darkness shimmered with unseen movements and whispering sounds. Carrie held Garth's hand as they walked the rough path past the other cabins. Sometimes their steps were loud as twigs snapped under their feet and then at others they were as silent and stealthy as the forest animals. Carrie's sense of adventure was dulled by uncomfortable guilt. What would her parents think if they could see her now, willingly being led through dense forest in the dead of night by a man she did not really and truly know? Easy. Her mom would be terrified and her dad outraged. Not wanting to face her mother's fear or her father's anger, Carrie tightened her grip on Garth's hand and banished all thoughts of home.

The night seemed less dark as the path eventually widened and led to the small clearing which served as a parking lot. Garth took the zapper out of his pocket and pointed it in the direction of his SUV. The sounds of doors unlocking and the glare of indicator lights flashing seemed incongruous in the peace and stillness. Carrie gladly jumped into the passenger seat. The dampness of the night was penetrating her bones. She rubbed her cold hands together as Garth drove along the now-familiar path and towards Park Loop Road.

"Okay. You can tell me now. Are you taking me somewhere special or am I being kidnapped?"

"No. You're not being kidnapped, although I did consider it. And yes, we're going somewhere very special. Just have patience."

Carrie sat back. The heater was on and she began to feel

sleepy again. And against all common sense and caution, she felt safe. Cliffs, hills and trees loomed dark on either side of the road as they drove along, enclosing them in their own warm space. She knew they were heading towards the town of Bar Harbor and she thought of the store she had seen there which specialised in tourmaline jewellery. She must buy a piece for Mom. Tourmaline was such a beautiful gem, so many colours and swirls in each stone. Mom would love it. The shopping would have to be done soon. Friday they would head back to Portland and to what? A sad goodbye followed by a few phone calls and emails until she and Garth finally forgot each other and this magic summer they had shared? Until they moved on with separate lives on different continents?

Carrie sat up straight. They were veering off Route 233 onto an unfamiliar road. The engine whined as the car began to climb. Up ahead the lights of another car seemed to be climbing skyward. She knew then where they were headed.

"Cadillac Mountain! You're taking me to Cadillac Mountain to see the sunrise! Oh, thank you! Thank you, Garth!"

Leaning across, she kissed him on the cheek. He smiled at her and for an instant she thought her own depth of feeling was reflected in his eyes.

She had read about Cadillac Mountain even before she had come to Maine. At 1530 feet it was the highest point along the North Atlantic seaboard. From early October to early March, when the sun rises south of due east, it was the first place in the United States to be struck by the sun's rays each morning. In a continent of superlatives, Carrie thought this one of the most awesome. It was late August now, almost

September. She would not be amongst the first in America to glimpse the rising sun today but she knew instinctively she would be the most impressed. Reaching down she poked in her backpack just to check that she had brought her camera with her. She had. It had been permanently with her since she arrived here. To go anywhere on Mount Desert Island without a camera would have been unthinkable.

Garth had barely parked before Carrie jumped out of the jeep. Looking around the lot, she was surprised and a bit disappointed to see so many other people. She had imagined this to be a private experience shared by only the two of them. Garth, as usual, read her thoughts.

"Don't worry. We'll find our own place. Just follow me."

They started out on the path which encircled the summit, Garth carrying a rug and lighting the way with a torch. The pink granite boulders of Cadillac Mountain glowed in the narrow beam of light. All along the way, despite the darkness, people seemed to have found nooks and crannies to settle into and wait. Some had tripods set up and others were just snuggled into their warm clothes enjoying the camaraderie of the vigil.

They seemed to be walking for a long time even though Carrie knew the summit path was only half a kilometre long. She glanced down at her wrist before remembering that she had decided to leave her watch off when she travelled Down East.

"What time is it now?" she asked.

"Just gone ten after four. No need to rush. Sunrise won't be for another hour. Do you want to rest?"

Carrie shook her head and they continued walking. There were fewer people now. Less whispers, giggles and laughs in the dark. Garth took a right turn off the path and immediately Carrie felt the softness of vegetation beneath her feet. An invigorating, fresh smell wafted upwards from the crushed alpine plants underfoot. A few yards on they came to a curved boulder. Centuries of wind had eroded it into a semi-circular shape.

"This is it, Carr. As near to the sky and the rising sun as we can get."

Garth spread the rug in the shelter of the curve. They both flopped to the ground and took a minute to get their breath back.

With the torch off and the arms of the boulder sheltering them it was obvious that Garth had done as promised. He had found them their own place. Other voices carried on the wind, torch lights flickered occasionally but nothing impinged on their fragrant, private space on Cadillac Mountain.

"How long to sunrise?" Carrie asked but she really didn't want to know. This was a moment she hoped would go on forever.

Garth didn't answer. Instead he reached towards her, put his arms around her and pulled her close to him. Carrie closed her eyes and leaned into his body. At last, she thought. She had been waiting and wondering for three months, wondering if he would ever make love to her, wondering what was wrong with him – with her – that he didn't even try ... His hands stroked her back, her hair, her face. He tilted her chin and kissed her as he had never kissed her before. This was the warm, passionate kiss of a man who wanted the woman in his arms. His lips crushed hers, his tongue probed, his hands slid towards her breasts.

Then he stopped. Pulled back, leaving her with thudding heart and bruised lips.

"What ..." she began, as disappointment swept over her. But then she could not think how to go on. Yet how could she get the answers she needed if she could not ask the questions? And suppose the answers he gave were not the ones she wanted to hear?

"We need to talk," he said and she just nodded.

She bit down on her now-tender lower lip. Whatever Garth's problem was, it couldn't be explained by an ILM ban on sex before marriage. They were quite liberal in their attitude towards sex, once it took place in a loving relationship. Was Trina right after all? Was he going to tell her he was gay? Shit! Shit!

He was silent beside her. She reached out for his hand.

"Tell me. Get it over with."

"I want to be with you, Carrie. More than anything else in the world. But you know what the movement means to me. Not just because my father founded ILM. I truly believe that the Light lives in each of us and blesses the lives of those who dedicate themselves to It."

"Yes. I know that and I respect your beliefs."

"Well, there's the problem. Don't you see? It's not enough just to tolerate my beliefs. ILM is a whole way of life."

Laughter sounded as a group of four passed by. Carrie moved back a little and leaned against the rock. She was puzzled. What was Garth trying to say? That he could not be with her because she was not a consecrated member of ILM? The laughing group of four had moved out of earshot and only the low rush of wind disturbed the silence. It was as if Cadillac Mountain was waiting to hear what Carrie had to say. Even Carrie was anxious to hear what she had to say. It seemed like it was time to make a decision, to finally settle the issue which had played on her mind ever since she first set foot in Haven Café. And yet she hesitated. She had found spirituality and comradeship in Inner Light Movement. They had welcomed her into the fold as Garth's friend. They had included her in prayer meetings and in their social life. But in a very subtle way she was not one of them, nor was she sure that she wanted to be.

"Why are all ILM members white and middle class?" she asked.

"They're not. Just the people you've met. The Light is the life force in every soul. Souls don't have colours or social status."

"But do you believe only ILM members can be saved for eternity?"

"You're Roman Catholic. Isn't it your belief that only Roman Catholics will get to heaven?"

"No! I don't believe that. I'm not sure if I even believe in an after-life."

Garth's sharp intake of breath told her she had said the wrong thing. He didn't move but yet they seemed to be farther apart. She shivered, suddenly cold, knowing that if she agreed with his views, agreed to become a member of ILM, then that distance between them would disappear. But yet she had to listen to the little voice inside telling her she was being manipulated, that if Garth wanted her as much as she did him, he wouldn't care what religious beliefs she held. Or even if she did not believe in any god at all. How many of these beliefs were truly Garth's? Was he so weak that he allowed Karl Hemmings to dictate?

Weary from all the questions Carrie leaned her head back against the rock and closed her eyes. She heard a distant hum, like a swarm of bees, rising and falling on the wind. As the noise got louder she realised it was the excited sound of people cheering. Opening her eyes she saw the eastern horizon begin to pulse with a golden light. It shimmered and deepened and spread as the sun rose. Garth put his arm around her shoulder and together they watched as orange and lilac and fiery red streaked the dark skies. They stood to welcome the dawn of a new day.

"Praise the Light!" he said and she answered "Amen!" with the same depth of fervour.

They smiled at each other in the radiance of the new morning and they both knew that they were sharing something far more intimate and profound than sex.

Standing closely together on the very top of Cadillac Mountain they watched in silent awe as low gnarled trees, wild blueberry barrens and crops of pink granite boulders emerged from darkness. Beneath them they saw the rising sun wash over the Cranberry Islands, touch Eagle Lake with shimmering red and pink and yellow, while in the distance they could make out Schoodic Peninsula on the mainland. Each way they turned, to the south, northwest, northeast they were regaled with splendour. They didn't speak. They didn't need to. They just stood and watched and felt very small as the massive drama of night and day played out all around them.

"I'll always remember this," Carrie whispered. "It's etched on my soul."

"So you definitely have a soul? Praise the Light!"

Carrie opened her mouth to explain. To convince him

112

that she had never truly doubted a spiritual dimension to her physical existence. The words remained unspoken as she saw the twinkle in his eye. He was teasing her!

"Brat," she muttered as she snuggled closer to him. She and Garth still needed to talk about their future. But she was more hopeful now than ever before that they did indeed have a future together. Wherever that would lead.

CHAPTER 9

John almost overslept. He woke suddenly and knew the bedroom was a lot brighter than it should be. Autumn sun was pouring in through the half drawn curtains, highlighting copper strands in Meg's dark hair. He looked at his watch and saw that it was nearly seven o'clock. He was normally driving into EFAS at this time. Careful not to disturb Meg, he eased out of bed, had a quick shower and headed for work.

On the approach road he saw that Ollie was pacing by the gate and checking his watch every few steps. John drew up beside him.

"Sorry, Ollie. I overslept. Anything to report?"

"Nothing, boss. I was beginning to think though you had an accident or something."

"I didn't hear my alarm. Sorry for delaying you. Do you want to go straight away now?"

"If it's okay with you, I'll go. Herself will be anxious."

John smiled and waved at the old man as he dashed to his van and drove off. He had met Ollie's wife, the woman he always referred to as 'herself'. It would take a very brave man to keep her waiting.

John was sitting at his desk, computer on, before he could consciously gather his thoughts together. Problems flooded over him. He stood and began to pace. The Francine problem came to the fore. It didn't really matter what had actually happened last night. Or nearly happened. The fact was that he had made a complete prat of himself by going to her apartment. He might as well have had sex with her. It was going to be a very awkward situation now anyway. God! How she must have laughed when he scurried away. She probably rang a few girlfriends to share the joke. How in the fuck was he going to face her this morning?

He made his coffee strong and swallowed a big mouthful. His head began to clear. Francine was a sophisticated woman, a twenty-first century woman. Sex was no big deal to her. She would probably shrug the whole pathetic incident off as a mistake on both their parts. And so should he.

Feeling trapped in his office, he went out to reception. Francine's sweet perfume hung in the air. As he stood staring at the space she had made her own, he noticed the flower arrangement she had put on the reception desk. Tasteful. That was one of the most attractive things about her. Francine was always impeccably groomed and she touched her surroundings with the same sense of style and class.

He remembered now the day he had first interviewed her. After a string of competent but uninteresting applicants for the job as receptionist, Francine had pulled into the car park in her BMW convertible and sashayed into the office on high heels. Her skin had been tanned then. She was just back from a holiday. A break, she had said, while she was deciding which direction she wanted her career to go.

Frowning, John turned and went back into his office. Opening the filing cabinet, he took out the employment records. He flicked through them until he came to Francine C Keyes. Twenty-six years old. Address: 8 Waterside Apartments. Glancing at her previous employment history, he noticed that she had not stayed with any one employer for longer than twelve months. And there were gaps. Just like the two months before she had started work here. She had good references. Efficient, competent, an asset. He hadn't checked out any of them, despite giving Patrick Morgan the impression that he had. From the minute Francine had walked into his office, John had known that he was going to give her the job.

The door opened and Dan Shorten stepped into the office. John jumped guiltily as if the forklift driver had caught him peering at Francine rather than her files.

"Is Tommy in today?" Shortie asked.

"Yes. He'll be here at nine."

"I'll make a start on unloading all that shelving from BargainBuy's unit. Their truck will be here around twelve to collect it."

"Fine, Dan. Good man."

Distracted as he was John failed to notice that Dan was still standing there until the forklift driver cleared his throat.

"Something wrong?" John asked, looking at Dan shuffling from one foot to the other.

"I don't want to be telling tales but you should know that your son is smoking at the back of the stores. He'll set the place on fire if he's not stopped. I wouldn't say anything otherwise."

John bit back the temptation to tell Shortie go fuck himself. The little prick was gloating, spitting his words out of the side of his mouth. For some reason, he hated Tommy. Maybe he felt Tommy didn't show him due respect, in which case John understood his resentment.

"Right, Dan. I'll have a word with him. Thank you. You'll be glad to know he's back to school next week."

"Ah, no, I didn't mean anything like that. He's a grand lad but ..."

"Thanks, Dan."

Shortie got the message and sidled out of the office, closing the door after him. John waited until he heard the footsteps head off in the direction of the storage area. He had suspicions, unproven, that Dan Shorten spent some of his time listening outside the door. Knowing that he had enough real problems without imagining more, John got out the phone book to look up Willy Feeney's number. It was a long time since they had last spoken. Willy had been just a sergeant in the Gardaí then. But they were both from Hyde Street and Hyde Street people had always stuck together. Willy would be able to find out about these Hemmings in Maine. The so-called Inner Light Movement.

But John did not ring Willy Feeney. Nor did he find the number. He just sat at his desk, worrying, waiting for Francine Keyes to come in. Until she did, he had no way of knowing if they could ever again have a viable working relationship. Could he give her dictation without imagining her naked breasts, could she take dictation without remembering his panicked escape from her apartment? What a stupid error of judgement his visit to Waterside Apartments had been!

As the morning ticked by in agonisingly slow beats of time, John began to believe that his error of judgement might yet prove to be a huge mistake.

* * *

Even though the leaves of the maple tree at the end of the garden were already tinged with brilliant autumn reds, this morning glowed with heat and light. It was in tune with Meg's mood. Hearing Carrie's voice last night had pushed most of the fear and darkness from her mind. Having John make such passionate love to her had dispelled the rest. It had been a long time since they had shown their need for each other. She sang while showering, an off-key version of "You Raise Me Up".

Tommy was in a peculiar mood. It was impossible to keep up with his changes in temperament. He was very quiet as Meg drove him to EFAS. Guessing that he was still upset by Carrie not telling him about her boyfriend, Meg broached the subject with him.

"So Carrie has found herself a boyfriend. I wonder why she didn't tell us about him earlier?"

When he didn't answer she glanced across at him. He had a closed, sulky look on his face. She knew then she had guessed correctly. He was hurt because his sister had not confided in him.

"She'll be home next week," she said. "You two can catch up then."

"What makes you think she'll be back? She sounds totally taken in by all this religion stuff. Not like our Carrie at all."

It was as if a cloud had scudded across the sun, blocking out the heat and light. Fears that Meg had thought allayed came rushing back. What else had Carrie not told them? Three months, three whole months she had kept her relationship with Garth secret. What other secrets was she keeping from them? The Carrie they knew would not have done that. They had reached EFAS now. As Tommy got out of the car he said he might go to see Breeze straight after work.

"Why don't you bring him to our house? I'd like to meet him."

"And have the Fuehrer insult him? No, thanks."

He slammed the car door. Meg had misjudged his mood. He wasn't sulking. He was angry. She watched him as, head bent, he strode towards the front door. She thought of going after him but then decided against it. He would have to work this one out with Carrie when she came home. Anyway, she couldn't be late for Curtain Call again this morning. It would be nice to see John though. Only for a minute. Maybe a quick cuddle. Just reassurance that last night's passion had not been merely a reaction to their worry about their daughter.

As she was deciding, a sports car drove through the gates. It was the receptionist. The roof-top of her BMW convertible was rolled back and her long blonde hair was blowing prettily around her. She lifted a hand and gave Meg a royal wave. Meg waved back and tried unsuccessfully to return the smile. Francine made her feel uncomfortable and not just because of the embarrassing mascara-streaked encounter with her yesterday. There was something cold about her.

The girl's long legs showed to advantage as she got out of her low-slung sports car. The cause of her own discomfort suddenly struck Meg. She was jealous. John worked with this beautiful young woman eight hours a day, five days a week. No wonder he hadn't mentioned her stunning good looks. Not something a wife needed to know.

Meg switched on the engine and put the car into gear. She could not go in to see John while Miss World was floating around reception on her cloud of perfume. Definitely Chanel too. Just how much was John paying her? Annoyed with herself for her pettiness, Meg jammed her foot on the accelerator and left EFAS behind her as quickly as possible.

* * *

Even though he was sitting in his office, John's senses were so heightened that he knew when Francine Keyes drove into the car park. He mentally tracked her movements: locking her car, walking to the entrance door, crossing to her desk, taking off her jacket and hanging it up in her locker, booting up her computer. Coming into his office. Her footsteps were loud on the parquet flooring as they approached his door. He held his breath, waiting for her knock. There was none. She just pushed the door open and walked in.

"Good morning, John. I hope you got home safely last night."

"Good morning, Francine. I did, thank you."

She was wearing a beige skirt, just above the knee, and a cream blouse. Her face was fresh, with the minimum of make-up. The epitome of the businesswoman. Not a trace of the vamp in the silk robe, sandals and nothing else.

"Sorry I had to leave your apartment so quickly. It was a very urgent appointment."

"You didn't leave quickly enough."

"What? What do you mean?"

Francine sat, smiled at him and then demurely lowered her eyelids. John tried to gauge her thoughts in the silence. He admitted to himself, with growing alarm, that the woman sitting opposite him was complex. Inscrutable. Sitting quietly in her halo of golden hair she appeared innocent and vulnerable. But there was something in the stillness around her which spoke of steely control. She lifted her head and looked directly at him.

"I feel traumatised. Used and abused. I'm very upset. You took advantage of your position as my boss. I offered you hospitality in my home but you wanted more than that, didn't you? I may have to go for counselling."

A jolt of fear ran through John. An animal instinct to protect himself, to prepare for attack. He sat up very straight in his chair and made a determined effort to keep his voice steady.

"What in the hell are you talking about? Counselling? For what? Because I didn't want your moussaka? Or anything else you were offering me for that matter."

"You assaulted me, John Enright. Sexually assaulted me. Ripped off my clothes and wouldn't stop even though I said no."

John's heart gave one violent thump in his chest and then seemed to stop. The words 'sexually assaulted' echoed so loudly in his head that he thought his ear drums would burst.

"Lying bitch!" he said in a vicious tone he didn't recognise as his own.

"We'll never work this out if you talk like that. I'd hate to get to a stage where it would be your word against mine. Even innocent gestures can sound so crass and vulgar in court, can't they? And Mrs Enright is such a nice lady."

John sat still, his mouth open as if to finish a sentence he had abandoned. But he had no words to speak. Shock and dawning realisation had robbed him of speech. Francine had laid a trap and he, fool that he was, had fallen into it. Too late he remembered the times she had accidentally brushed against him as she left things on his desk, the way she thrust her breasts towards him, almost inviting his touch, the way she crossed her long legs when she sat opposite him, even allowing a peep at her stocking tops. Jesus! Why had he not seen that she was playing him for a fool? How had he allowed himself dream his adolescent dreams and fantasies? She had been leading him on, building him up and he had gone along with her scheme, drooling and panting his way into the poison snare. Unless she was just angry at what she saw as rejection. Yes, maybe that was it. An abject apology, some flattery, even begging if necessary, might be the answer. He tried to smile at her but grim-faced was the best he could do.

"I apologise if you think my behaviour was − was − inappropriate," he stuttered. "You must understand I'm upset about Patrick …"

She stared coldly at him. A bead of sweat trickled onto his forehead. He took out his handkerchief and wiped it away. Fuck! What in the hell should he do now? Maybe he should fire her. And make himself vulnerable to an Unfair Dismissal charge as well as harassment? But she could not stay. Not now.

"I think it would be better for both us, Francine, if you found another job. I will, of course pay whatever overtime and holidays you're due and give you a reference."

Her bracelets rattled as Francine raised her hand to stop him saying any more. "I'm not going anywhere until I decide what best to do. I can't make any decisions now, can I? I'm traumatised."

"You threw yourself at me, for Christ's sake! I see it now, how you strutted about and invited contact at every opportunity. You were naked last night, flaunting yourself. You practically jumped on me when I went to your door. Jesus, you wouldn't be out of place in a brothel! You must have thought I was a soft touch. A middle-aged old fool."

"Was I wrong?"

Neither needed to hear the answer to that question.

John tried to slow his breathing before he spoke again. To sound more manager than managed.

"What do you want? That's what this is about, isn't it? You're not upset or traumatised. You're smug because your plan worked. I don't have much spare cash. You should have found that out before you started your little scheme."

"What makes you think I'd want anything you have?"

She was staring at him – calm, cold, the blue eyes he had so recently thought beautiful full of ugly disdain.

"I could consider giving you severance pay. A reasonable sum. Say one thousand euro. That should help your trauma."

As soon as the words had left his mouth, John knew he had made yet another foolish decision. He had just admitted guilt by offering to pay her off. She sneered and John knew she had won this round of her game. She would not talk to him until she was ready, nor would she go quietly. He was at her mercy and the woman sitting in front of him was blatantly merciless. He must, must, win back control of himself and the situation. Play his own game.

"So what do you suggest, Francine? If, as you say, it's your word against mine, then you should know I'm a well-respected businessman here in Cork. Happily married for twenty-one years. No blemish on my record. I can guarantee that my word would carry more weight than yours."

"Really? But what about my witnesses? They saw my distress. They had to comfort me. I think they would give pretty compelling evidence."

"What in the fuck are you talking about now?"

"The porter, the delivery man. Remember? Friends of mine. They were a great comfort to me last night."

Francine focussed her steady gaze on him. That was when John Enright knew for certain that Francine Keyes had planned this moment. The porter and the delivery man could both testify that he was in her apartment last night. And doubtless to anything else she wanted them to say. She was a dangerous woman. She could, and John knew she would, play the victim, allege violation and psychological trauma. And worse still, she had no intention of letting him know now which course of action she intended taking. She would prolong his torture until she was ready to pounce. And doubtless enjoy every moment of his terror. Any offer he would make to her now would be construed as an admission of guilt. She had left him no option. He would have to control his awful fear and try to find the strength to fight her.

"We need to get some work done," he said with what he hoped was authority in his voice. Or at least a business-like attitude. Even vaguely professional would suffice until she got what she wanted. There was the question. What in the hell did Francine Keyes want from him?

★ ★ ★

By the time Meg reached Curtain Call, she had regained some of the optimism with which she had started the day. As she unlocked the door and flicked on lights she glanced around her, noticing the colours and textures, inhaling the scent of new fabric peculiar to the shop. The Fen Shui crystal she had hung up only last month twirled slowly in the breeze from the door, sparkling with the colours of the rainbow. Meg absorbed the aura of the beautiful things around her and drew strength and energy from them.

Lynn's arrival was late, even by her standards. Meg already had three customers served and the ordering done by the time Lynn rushed breathlessly in.

"Sorry I'm so late. I did too much salsa-dancing last night. What's the news about Carrie? Did she ring?"

A customer came in the door on Lynn's heels.

"I'll serve," Meg said. "Put on the kettle and I'll tell you over coffee."

The woman who had come in spent ten whole minutes choosing tasselled tiebacks. After going through every single tieback in stock she eventually settled for the first pair she had picked out. Meg clocked them in and wrapped them quickly in case the woman changed her mind again.

In the kitchenette Lynn was sitting on her high stool, coffee mug in hand. She blinked when she saw Meg, as if coming back from a long way off.

"I assume you've got good news," Lynn said. "You look chipper this morning."

"More than I can say for you. You must have worn out your dancing shoes last night. And yes. We heard from Carrie. Not a phone call though. It was a taped message."

"What! A tape? That sounds weird. Like a kidnapping."

Typical of Lynn to take the most dramatic interpretation. Meg ignored that comment and then explained everything as she made her own coffee.

"I don't know what to say," Lynn said doubtfully. "What does John think?"

"He's reasonably happy to wait until Friday to hear from Carrie. But he's going to have ILM and Karl Hemmings checked out by a friend of his in the Guards. By the way, he told me you called into EFAS last evening. Were you telling tales on me?"

Lynn got off her stool and, going over to the sink, began to rinse out her mug. She was silent for so long that Meg was puzzled.

"What's wrong, Lynn? Have you something to tell me? Something about John?"

The mug clattered onto the draining board as Lynn suddenly slammed it down. She turned to face Meg and her green eyes were huge in her face.

"No, it's not about John but I do have something to tell you. I need a break, Meg. Maybe it was the prick in the suit yesterday, I don't know, but suddenly I can't take much more of this lifestyle. I want to travel for a while. See new places and faces. And I don't mean a two-week holiday. That's not enough. I must get out of here."

"But why? I thought you had settled at last. What about

your apartment? What about the shop? Where are you going?"

The shop door opened. It was back to business. Anyway, Meg had her rescheduled appointment with Rhona Sheehan. They couldn't afford to mess up that job. Rhona Sheehan's new home had as many windows as four average homes. A nice little boost to profits.

"We'll talk more over lunch," Lynn said as she went out to the shop, "and we're going to the pub. I'm not letting The Suit get the better of me."

Meg frowned. She had assumed the man in the pub had been Lynn's problem. It seemed she was wrong. Whatever was troubling Lynn, it was far more than an insult from a rude stranger. What was she running away from? And why had she avoided discussing her visit to EFAS last night?

Meg and Lynn had a lot of talking to do.

★ ★ ★

Willy Feeney was away in London at a police conference.

"Is there someone else you would like to speak with?" the voice on the other end of the phone asked.

John hesitated. Anyone at the Garda Station could check out ILM and Karl Hemmings for him. But that would be getting the police officially involved. What would Carrie think? She seemed to be very close to Hemmings' son. She was a sensible girl. Good. She wouldn't have anything to do with him if he was in any way sinister. Besides it was not long to wait to hear from her. Only another day.

"No, thank you. This is a personal call. I'll catch up with Superintendent Feeney when he comes back."

Just as he put down the phone, Francine came into his office. She had her jacket on.

"I'm letting you know I'll be late back from lunch," she announced.

John had to take a deep breath. They had been polite to each other all morning. Like stags, testing each other's strengths. Even though Francine was the epitome of femininity, John saw now that there was a male quality to her iron will. The soft glances and sideways looks from underneath her blonde hair were gone. Her steely resolve was out in the open.

"How late?" he asked.

She shrugged. "I don't know. I'm meeting Patrick Morgan. We're arranging details for the video link-up with his nephew in New Zealand tonight. I assume you can make yourself available ?"

"You make a lot of assumptions, Francine."

"I make decisions, John. I haven't decided about you yet. Patrick might advise me."

The bitch! There were so many things John wanted to say to her but he knew instinctively the less said the better.

"Just let me know the time for the video-conference. I'll be here."

"So will I. See you later."

She turned then and walked out the door with an exaggerated sway to her hips.

Head in hands, John sat at his desk and reviewed his options. Fire Francine? A definite non-starter. Continue on as if nothing had happened and wait to see why she had manipulated him into this situation? This seemed to be the only reasonable course to take. And there was something else too. "No," he said out loud as he momentarily thought of telling Meg what had happened. That would take one of Francine's strengths away but it would also destroy Meg. Especially on top of this Hemmings problem with Carrie. Anyway, what could he say to his wife, how could he explain when he didn't know himself why he had so stupidly been led along by Francine?

He went back to the filing cabinet and got out the employment file on Francine he had abandoned that morning. His greatest weakness was that he knew very little about her.

Starting with her last employer, he jotted down the contact numbers. She had worked in London with a leisure club and an airline, then on her return to Ireland with a medical practice and her last job was as PA to a property developer.

There were a lot of questions he should have asked about Francine Keyes. He had allowed himself be blinded by her glamour but that was changed now. He intended finding out who this woman was, why she was in EFAS and what in the hell she wanted from him.

John picked up the phone and dialled the first number on the list he had made. Oakley Property Developers. He asked for Shane Richards, the name signed to Francine's reference. He was put on hold. As he listened to the tinkling music he read over the document again. It was full of superlatives. Just like the reference he would write for Francine now if only she would fuck off and leave him be.

"Shane Richards."

The voice was strong and energetic. The sound of a man who knew where he was going. John cleared his throat and tried to project the same sense of purpose. "Hello, Shane.

Thank you for taking my call. My name is John Enright, managing director of EFAS Storage."

"Yes, John. I've heard of your company. What can I do for you?"

"I'm ringing you about a reference you wrote for a Francine Keyes."

"Francine C Keyes?"

"That's right. What can you tell me about her?"

"Depends on what you want to know. Are you thinking of offering her a job?"

John hesitated. What could he say? It would seem very stupid to be checking a reference three months after employing her. Yet to lie directly would be equally stupid. The business circle in Cork was small in number but big on gossip. Compromise would be best.

"Actually, I have had her in temporary employment for the past three months. I'm considering offering her a permanent position."

"You should know her pretty well by now so. Why are you ringing me?"

"I was wondering why she stayed only a year with you. Or with any other company for that matter. Did you have any problems with her?"

Shane Richards laughed but there was no humour in the sound. "Three months you say Francine has been with you? You wouldn't be ringing me now unless you were the one having problems. You should have contacted me before you took her on, not three months later."

"Would you have advised me against employing her?"

"Wake up, John. You didn't choose her. She picked you."

"But you wrote her a good reference. You said things like

'indispensable' and 'super-efficient'. Are you telling me now that you lied?"

An impatient sigh reached John down the phone line. "All I'm saying, John, is that you left it a bit late to ring. You'll also write a good reference for her when she moves on. I must go now. I've a meeting in five minutes. Sorry I couldn't be of more help."

The line went dead. John put his arms on the desk and dropped his head on them. Shane Richards had said nothing and implied everything. And what had he meant by saying that Francine had chosen him? What in the name of God for?

For the second day running, John's head began to ache.

* * *

Patrick Morgan linked Francine's arm as they slowly made their way towards the restaurant. It had not been difficult for Francine to persuade him to come out to lunch. She knew he was grateful for the company.

"I don't think John's too happy about it," Patrick said.

"You mean about your nephew?"

"Yes. John Enright's a good man. A hard worker. But EFAS must move forward. The company needs new blood."

"Don't you worry about Mr Enright. I'll make sure he sees your point of view," Francine said, giving Patrick one of her gleaming smiles.

The old man smiled back at her. Francine knew then that everything was going to work out as she had planned.

CHAPTER 10

The rusty gate of Number 232 was opened back full. Tommy went to the door and knocked. As he stood waiting for an answer, he checked his phone again. No messages. He had assumed that Breeze had been busy with his new job today. Too busy to text. He knocked again, louder this time. The sound echoed hollowly. Walking through the high weeds he went to the window of the front room. There was no flicker of television from inside. Cupping his hands against the glass he peered in through the net curtains. Mrs Goodall's chair was still and unoccupied, the television off. Maybe she was in bed. Maybe Breeze was working late.

Kicking his way through the weeds, he returned to the front door. He raised his hand to knock and then hesitated. It could be that Breeze was inside and didn't want to answer. He had been pretty pissed off at not getting a job in EFAS. But then …

"No point in knocking. No one's home."

Tommy turned around to see an elderly man standing by

the gate. He had seen him before. He lived next door.

"Ellie's in hospital again."

"Ellie?"

"Ellie Goodall. Your pal's mother. He's gone in the ambulance with her."

"What hospital?"

"The University Hospital. It's the nearest. She's in a bad way this time."

Tommy walked up the path to the old man and thanked him. Then, head down, he started out towards the hospital. Thirty minutes' quick walk should get him there. Breeze was in trouble and Tommy was determined to be there for his friend.

* * *

Meg felt very tired this evening. Rhona Sheehan's huge house had taken forever to tour today. For once Meg had found it difficult to be enthusiastic about someone else's curtains. Her suggestions and advice had come automatically. But Rhona Sheehan hadn't seemed to notice. She had put in a big order. Big enough to keep Curtain Call busy for some time.

Thinking of work brought Meg's attention back to Lynn. From what conversation they had been able to have, it seemed Lynn was really serious about going away. And not to escape the Suit. He had not been in the pub today. Perhaps he had decided to stay at home with his wife or that the pub was no longer a proper place for him to lunch. Either way he was unlikely to be the cause of Lynn's sudden need to disappear. The old, restless Lynn was back with a vengeance. One minute she had been her usual vivacious self and the next she was planning an extended gallop around the globe without a care as to how Curtain Call was going to continue on without her. It had been fun in the past having Lynn send postcards from exotic places but they were both too old for that now.

Suddenly Meg felt too old for everything. For work, secretive daughters, defiant sons, preoccupied husbands and friends in crisis. She gave up on the book she had been trying to read.

Getting up from the armchair, she put her book on the coffee table and wandered into the kitchen. It was amazing how big this average-sized house seemed when she was alone in it. Tommy was out and John of course was in EFAS. He had rung earlier and said he was waiting for a video-conference from New Zealand with Patrick Morgan's nephew. Meg felt a little guilty at not having really listened when he told her about Patrick's plans for the future of EFAS. It was obviously worrying John a lot.

Restless, Meg left the kitchen and headed upstairs. She had been intending to tidy her wardrobe but as she passed Tommy's room she noticed the open door. The room was in chaos. Thin Lizzy posters plastered the walls and stuck in the middle of them was some half-naked pin-up girl. Shoes and clothes were scattered everywhere. The only tidy area was his desk. His computer was on. Meg was hypnotised by the swirling images on the screen saver. She walked to the desk and sat down, realising that she had overlooked something very basic. They all had. She logged onto the internet and got up the Google site. Then, fingers trembling, she typed in Inner Light Movement. The less than quarter second it took for the information to appear seemed like forever. When it did, she got five hundred and twenty thousand hits. Annoyed, she refined her search, adding Hemmings and Maine to the keywords.

There were fewer results this time. Scrolling through them, she scanned for the name Hemmings and opened the first site where she saw it. And there it was. The movement which was obviously influencing Carrie. **'All good things come from The Light and It is in you,'** the page proclaimed. There were photos. A group all holding hands, their eyes raised skyward. A smiling, dark-haired man. Karl Hemmings of Portland, Maine, founder of ILM! Meg put the cursor over his picture and clicked the mouse to enlarge. The face did not match the voice she had heard on the phone. His voice was strong and deep. The face was bland, the chin weak. A smile barely lifted the corners of his thin lips. Around his eyes the lids drooped under heavy brows and little puffs of flesh sat underneath. But the eyes were fascinating. They were dark. So dark that it was difficult to discern pupil from iris. His gaze had an intensity from which it was hard to look away. She clicked again and shrank his picture back but she could not take her attention away from his hypnotic eyes. The receding chin and hard mouth spoke of a cold man but the dark eyes held a promise of gentleness and understanding. His face was a contradiction. As was this web page. Had Karl Hemmings not said that technology was bad for the soul? Wasn't he the man who would not allow as much as a phone in the cabin where his son and Carrie were staying in Mount Desert Island? He must be happy to compromise his principles in order to spread the word. Obviously one rule for him and another for the members of his church or cult or whatever it was.

Meg began to read the text. She learned that twenty years ago Karl Hemmings had been working on an assembly line in Wixom Ford Motor Factory in Detroit. He worked and drank. Drank and worked. His life was a cycle of numbing routine and alcohol had been the anaesthetic. Until he lost his job to alcoholism and his wife to another man. He was left with a damaged liver, an empty bank account and a three-year-old son. Garth. Carrie's Garth.

Going back to his picture again, Meg examined Karl Hemmings' face for signs of his troubled past. They were there in the puffiness under his eyes and the deep furrows which guarded his thin mouth. More interested now she returned to his biography and read on with increasing disbelief. Karl Hemmings had had an epiphany. A full-blown revelation! The bank, it seemed, had reclaimed his Detroit home. As he packed what few belongings he could salvage, he was in despair. He had no home, no job, no one to turn to and a three-year-old child to support. When he stood for the last time at the front door of the home he had shared with his wife, his son's hand in his, he had cried for the first time in his adult life. He looked at his child and knew that he could not allow him live a life of poverty. A street child, a child of tenements and temporary lodgings. A child with no future. He thought of death. For both of them. Peace. Deliverance by the cutting wheels of a high-speed train or maybe he would buy a gun with what money he had left and shoot the boy first and then himself.

Holding his son's hand tightly, they walked together down the garden path and onto the sidewalk. Meg skimmed through the increasingly ridiculous script. Karl Hemmings had stood on the sidewalk, tears streaming down his face, and in an instant of utter despair he had raised his head skywards and cried out for help. It was then it happened. He had seen a blinding light and felt a warm, healing wave engulf him. In fact, he had a full-blown conversation with a spirit he referred to as The Light. This spirit apparently commanded him to get on a Greyhound bus and head for Maine. The story ended there. The Light had obviously set Karl Hemmings up in a thriving business. No wonder he was so keen to sing its praises.

Meg logged off but sat for a while at Tommy's desk thinking about what she had read. Karl Hemmings was either a fraud or a lunatic. Whichever category he fell into he was dangerous. And could his son be any less so? The worries about Carrie came tumbling back as bleak and despairing as they had been before the taped message from her. How could Carrie allow herself to be under the influence of a self-confessed drunkard, a man who had considered murdering his own son? A man who claimed to have talked to a beam of light? Where was her common sense gone, her intelligence? Could ILM have used mind-altering drugs or brainwashing techniques? And why only on Carrie? Her friends seemed unscathed. They had gone on to New York, leaving ILM, Karl Hemmings and Carrie behind to praise The Light to their heart's content.

Tommy's room began to close in around Meg. She got up and walked to the kitchen again. The only sound was the thermostat on the heating clicking on and off. Looking out through the window she saw that it was getting dark. The evenings were beginning to shorten in rehearsal for black winter nights. Meg shivered. She went to the lounge, turned on the television and then immediately turned it off again.

She paced some more before getting out her phone and dialling Lynn's number.

"Are you busy tonight?" she asked when Lynn answered.

"Well, I have a few parties and of course Richard Gere and Hugh Grant are calling over. The usual. Why?"

"I'm lonely, Lynn."

Meg was shocked. That was not what she had meant to say. What in the hell was she thinking? Sounding pathetic and weak. She should have said she was worried about Carrie. She was. She was worried about Tommy as well and John because he worked such long hours and looked so pale. And of course she was concerned also about Lynn and her renewed travel bug. But she had spoken the truth, hadn't she? She was worried but she was lonely too. A deep, gnawing, profound aloneness.

"Put on the kettle," Lynn said. "I'll be with you soon."

Meg walked over to the window and watched as the last of the day's light faded towards the west. Lynn had understood and for that she was very grateful. The trouble was Meg herself did not understand. Where had this great cold, empty space inside her come from? And why had it taken her so long to know that it was there?

Afraid of the answers to her questions, Meg busied herself getting supper ready for herself and Lynn.

* * *

Tommy looked around the hospital reception area, not sure which direction to take. Maybe he should go to Accident and Emergency. But then if Mrs Goodall had been brought in earlier this afternoon she could already be in a ward. He hesitated, not sure now that he should be here at all. If Breeze had wanted him to know, he would have rung or texted.

"Are you alright? Can I help you?"

Tommy turned towards the voice at the reception desk. A middle-aged woman behind the desk was watching him. He walked over towards her.

"I'm looking for a Mrs Goodall. Ellie Goodall. She was brought in here some time today."

The woman looked at her computer screen through her bifocals and then, raising her head, stared at Tommy over them.

"Well, she's up on Floor 3. In Intensive Care. You won't be allowed see her unless you're family."

"It's her son I want to see really. Is it okay if I go on up?"

"Lifts to your left at the end of the corridor," she recited in a bored voice, more interested now in answering the ringing phone.

Tommy shared the lift up with two nurses and a priest. The girls were young. Student nurses. He smiled at them and wondered what they were wearing underneath their uniforms. They ignored him and continued chatting together until they got off at the second floor. The priest and Tommy continued on to Floor 3. They did not make eye contact. Eyes downcast, the priest was clutching a little box with a cross etched on it. The lift doors opened on the third floor and Tommy sensed a different atmosphere the instant he set foot on the dimly lit corridor. There was a stillness here. No hustle and bustle, no visitors straggling towards wards, no nurses scurrying by, squeaking their rubber-soled shoes on the tiles. He saw a sign pointing to Intensive Care and headed towards it. So did the priest but he tapped on a door halfway along the corridor and went in while Tommy continued on to the desk at the very end. A nurse, senior by years and by the superior look on her face, sat at the desk and a group of men were seated on a bench alongside.

"Is Mrs Goodall here please? Ellie Goodall."

"Are you a relation?"

"No. I'm a friend of the family."

"I'm sorry. Relatives only allowed in."

"I need to speak with her son."

"I'm Ellie Goodall's son. Who's asking?" said a voice behind Tommy.

He turned around to see one of the men from the bench standing in front of him. He was in his late twenties, wearing a silk suit and a hand-painted silk tie. He looked like Breeze grown up, tanned and made over. Two younger men, more casually dressed, stood behind him, their arms held loosely by their sides as if ready to lash out. Tommy offered his hand to the man he assumed to be the older Goodall brother. Freddie Goodall. The drug dealer. Jesus!

"I'm Tommy. Breeze's friend. Are you his brother?"

"Why don't you mind your own business? Just get out of here."

Tommy's hand dropped to his side. The nurse stood up and walked around her desk. She planted herself between Tommy and the man in the expensive clothes. Tommy found himself rooted to the ground. The elder Goodall had the most terrifying glare he had ever seen. There was murder in his eyes.

"If you'd like to follow me, Mr Goodall, I'll bring you to your mother's room," the nurse said calmly.

Freddie ignored her, never taking his eyes off Tommy for

a second. "This is family business. You're not welcome. What're you doing here?"

Tommy was conscious now that the two stooges behind Freddie had come forward a step. Protecting their man. Against what? This man was crazy. Immediately Tommy remembered that Ellie Goodall was crazy too. Her eldest son must have inherited her demented gene.

"I just came to see if Breeze needed anything. I'd like to help if I could."

"We don't need any help. We look after our own," Freddie said, reminding Tommy of Breeze saying exactly the same thing.

One of the goons leaned towards Freddie and whispered something in his ear. Whatever he whispered caused Freddie to stare even more intensely at Tommy.

"Your name Enright?" he asked, the question sounding like an accusation.

Tommy nodded.

"Enough, Mr Goodall," the nurse said, stepping up to Freddie and taking his arm. "You've been made aware that your mother's time is very limited. Don't you think you should be spending it with her rather than bullying a young man?"

Freddie continued to stare. Suddenly he smiled. The flash of veneered teeth in the perma-tanned face had an even more terrifying quality than the glare. Tommy opened his mouth to ask how Freddie's goon knew his name but the nurse held up her hand to silence him.

"Go home, young man," she said.

Another look at Freddie Goodall and his two goons was enough to convince Tommy. He stepped back, afraid to take his eyes off them.

"Now you, Mr Goodall, have two choices," the nurse said to Freddie. "Either go into your mother's room or go away. I'll call security if you don't cooperate."

"I told you before, I'm not going in there while the padre is doing all that mumbo jumbo."

Tommy was still taking backward steps, the distance between himself and Freddie gradually increasing. He felt secure enough now to turn his back on the group around the desk. Just as he turned, a door opened to his right and the priest came out, the little box with the etched cross still clutched in his hand. Through the open door, Tommy saw a doctor standing at the end of the bed and a nurse on one side. On the other side of the bed Breeze was kneeling, his head resting on the pillow beside his mother's pallid face so that all Tommy could see of his friend was the glossy shock of black hair on his crown and the shoulders which were shaking with silent sobs. Even from a distance Tommy knew that Ellie Goodall was dead. Her perpetual rocking at last stilled. Ah, fuck! Poor Breeze.

As Tommy stood at the open door wondering if he should approach his friend, a little group headed by the priest walked towards him.

"I think it would be better to leave the family to grieve in privacy," the priest said, catching Tommy by the arm and nodding surreptitiously in the direction of Freddie Goodall who by now seemed rigid with anger.

"I'll tell your friend you were here," the nurse said to Tommy, glaring at Freddie and daring him to defy her.

With the priest still firmly holding onto his arm, Tommy muttered thanks and then turned his back on the Goodalls. He began to shake when he got into the lift.

"Are you alright, son?" the priest asked.

Tommy nodded. But he was far from alright. He knew, with certainty, that he had not seen the last of Freddie Goodall. He had felt the hatred from the elder Goodall bore into his back as he had walked down the corridor. And worst of all, he knew his father had been right. He should have stayed away from the Goodalls.

* * *

As John watched Francine's fingers fly over the keyboard he grudgingly admitted to himself that her work was more than good.

"This technology amazes me," Patrick Morgan remarked as he watched her set up the video link to New Zealand.

John nodded. Bloody great! Exactly what he needed now. An image of Patrick's long-lost nephew beaming from halfway around the world.

"You should remember meeting Yan before," said Patrick. "Twenty years ago."

John shook his head and wondered if the old man was beginning to lose his grip mentally as well as physically.

"You must remember, John. My sister brought him with her when she came home for our father's funeral. You had to have seen him. She insisted on bringing him to the church and the burial even though I asked her to leave him at home. Out of sight."

Hazy memories began to emerge now of a little boy, dark-haired, so shy that he never raised his head, clinging onto his mother's hand as his grandfather's coffin was lowered into the grave. Shit! Yan! John was the one losing his marbles He should have remembered! The only clear memory from then was of Patrick saying that he and his sister had rowed after the funeral. Something to do with their father's will. And that, as far as John had known until the past few days, had been the end of any contact between Patrick and the New Zealand branch of his family.

"Almost ready to link up now," Francine announced.

John leaned forward towards Patrick. There were so many questions he needed to ask, that he would have asked before now if he had not been so distracted by Carrie's mysterious silence and 'the incident' with Francine.

"When did you make this decision, Patrick? I understood that you had cut off all communication with your sister. You didn't even go to New Zealand when she died."

The old man's head bowed and Patrick noticed the scalp shine pinkly through the once-thick silver hair. His head seemed too big for the ever-shrinking body. A pathetic, sick old man. The big head rose up slowly and there was pain in his eyes as he looked at John.

"I was wrong, John. Stupid and stubborn and prejudiced and very wrong."

"Prejudiced? Why? That's one characteristic I would never have accused you of."

Patrick opened his mouth as if to answer but instead of words a stream of saliva slavered over his moist lips.

John looked away and turned his attention to the computer screen as he heard Francine talking.

"Good morning, Mr Gilmore. Francine Keyes of EFAS Ireland here. I wonder if you'd mind sitting a little closer to the webcam so that we can get a clearer view?"

John stood and walked to the desk. As he peered over

144

Francine's shoulder a face emerged from the shadows on the screen. It was a dark face. Brown-skinned, dark-eyed. He looked younger than his thirty years. Yan Gilmore had a vaguely Oriental look. A slant to the eyes. Could this be why Patrick had mentioned prejudice? Was his nephew of mixed race? John leaned forward to examine the face closely. He straightened up quickly when he noticed that Francine had split the screen and he saw an image of himself hanging over her shoulder gawping. Yan Gilmore must be looking at the same image and wondering what kind of a moron his uncle's partner was.

"Good morning, Francine. Or shouldn't I be saying good evening to you in Ireland?"

"Indeed. You're thirteen hours ahead of us."

"Is that John Enright I saw with you? Is my uncle there too?"

"I'm here, Yan," Patrick said, hauling himself up and shuffling closer to the desk. "You're on speaker so that we can all hear what you have to say."

"How are you, Uncle Pat? Has the new medication you got yesterday helped you any?"

John couldn't help raising an eyebrow. Obviously Patrick and his nephew were in constant contact. Well, why wouldn't they be? Yan was, after all, the heir to the throne and the incumbent was dying – quickly now. Patrick seemed to be getting more feeble by the day. Francine guided Patrick to the chair in front of the screen. She turned to John then.

"I'll be in reception if you need anything," she said, before giving him a smile and a brazen wink.

John tried to nod nonchalantly in her direction but the effect was ruined by the sudden flash of red he felt flood across his face. Francine's smile broadened at his discomfiture. She gave her hips an extra wriggle as she walked out the door.

Turning his attention back to the webcam, John saw that Patrick was leaning forward, closely examining the image of his nephew.

"I feel quite comfortable, thank you, Yan. But of course time is of the essence. You've seen that John Enright is here. I'm sure you and he have a lot to talk about so I'll hand you over to him now."

"Hello, John. Nice to talk to you."

The confident, cheery tone set John's teeth on edge like chalk scraping across the blackboard used to do when he was a schoolboy. He stooped down beside Patrick and adjusted the web cam until he saw his own image on the split screen. He smiled, trying to inject a friendliness he didn't feel into his voice.

"Good to talk to you too, Yan. I understand from Patrick that you've not been in Ireland since you were a young child."

"Ah, yes. A sad occasion that. My grandfather's funeral. I didn't know him very well of course but my mother had told me so much about him I felt close to him. I'm looking forward to going back to your beautiful island."

"I'm sure. I'd like to ask you a few questions if you don't mind?"

"Shoot."

"Patrick says you work in tourism? In what capacity?"

There was a pause. A delay in the phone link, a time-lapse as their voices were beamed across continents, over oceans and mountains, through storms and heat waves. When Yan finally answered, it wasn't the reply John had anticipated.

"I'd prefer to talk about EFAS, John. I'm anxious to find out as much as possible about the business before I arrive. Then we can both decide how best to go forward."

"That's why I asked the question about your experience. How relevant is it to the storage business here?"

"You tell me about EFAS and then I'll tell you how we can work together to develop the company."

John gripped the edge of the desk so tightly that his knuckles whitened. He was being screwed by Patrick Morgan and his vaguely Asian-looking nephew. This call wasn't about getting to know each other or making joint decisions. It was to inform John that, like it or lump it, he had a new boss. One who was patronising and insulting. What in the hell did he mean by 'develop the company'? Hadn't John already tripled EFAS business? Clever that. The hint, the implication that John was an ineffective manager, that he needed guidance. And while Yan Gilmore on first acquaintance seemed to be a cocky prick in his own right, it was obvious that he had been fed negative information about the current state of EFAS and its manager. Information that could only have come from Patrick Morgan. The man John had looked on as a surrogate father, the man whose approval he had always sought.

John glanced at Patrick and saw that the old man's head was bowed, his chin resting in the scraggy folds of his neck. His eyelids were closed. Maybe he was asleep. Maybe not. John cleared his throat and brought his eyes back to meet those of Yan Gilmore on the screen.

"This is difficult, Yan. I don't know how much Patrick has told you about EFAS. In fact until very recently I didn't even know that you and your uncle were in contact."

"You should have made it your business to know. Just proves that EFAS needs fresh ears and eyes to lead it into the future."

The delivery of the words was so sharp that John couldn't help but gasp. Retorts buzzed around in his head, all flying too fast to formulate let alone articulate. Gilmore was obviously trying to rile him. Fuck him! And fuck the devious old man too! John still owned forty percent of EFAS whether they liked it or not. He took a deep breath.

"When do you intend coming here?"

"Soon, John. Very soon. Just some odds and ends to tidy up here and of course the bureaucracy of immigration to deal with. Patrick has, of course, told me a lot about the business and has put me in contact with the company accountant. I've a fair idea where things stand at the moment with EFAS. I'd like your take though, John. Where you think we need to improve. Ideas for new business, that type of thing. It would be helpful if you'd have your secretary fax a report to me."

John gritted his teeth. 'Where we need to improve.' This prick was still thousands of miles away and he was issuing orders. Patrick had never done that. They had been a team. But that was bullshit, wasn't it? They never had parity and Patrick had just waited his opportunity to prove it. Seeing that the old man still had his eyes closed, John shot him a vengeful look.

"Is there a problem with that, John?"

"No, no. Sorry, Yan. I'll get that report together as soon as possible. Could you give me your fax number please?"

"Just give it to your secretary. She has all my contact

details. I wonder if you could put her back on to me, please? I look forward to meeting you and to us working together."

The door from reception into the office opened. Francine must have been listening on the outside.

John wished Yan Gilmore *"Bon Voyage"* and stood up.

Patrick muttered "Goodnight" to his nephew.

So, he had been awake.

"Hello again, Mr Gilmore. What can I do to help?"

Francine's voice had taken on a submissive, gentle tone as she spoke to Yan. John turned and walked out of the office, through reception and into the car park. By his car, he stood and looked back at EFAS. Security cameras stared at him and for a spilt second he felt they were looking inside his head, monitoring his thoughts. He scanned the span of the long, low building, the rows of roller-shutter doors, the tarmacadam car park and high wire fencing. He waited for the usual sense of pride and achievement to warm his soul. It didn't come. There was no space inside the flood of bitter thoughts. He had built this place up from the lock-up shed it had been to the state-of-the-art facility it now was and shit was his thanks. Yan bloody Gilmore would be the one to benefit from the endless hours of planning and hard work. What was he anyway, besides the lucky coincidence of being the nephew of a dying uncle? In the tourist business? What in the fuck did that mean?

"Everything alright, boss?"

John jumped as the night watchman tapped him on the shoulder. He turned and saw the respect on Ollie's face. How much longer would that be there? How would Ollie feel when he found out that the man he called boss had been railroaded into an arrangement that was dubious to say the least? Maybe he could yet buy Patrick out. Before it was too late. Make an offer he couldn't refuse. Unless papers had already been signed. John remembered Yan Gilmore's darkly handsome face and he was certain the prick would have assured his succession to his uncle's shares. John Enright had been the one who was slow off the mark.

"Everything's fine, Ollie. Thanks. Goodnight."

"'Night, boss."

John drove away quickly, for once glad to leave EFAS behind.

CHAPTER 11

For the first time ever there was a slight awkwardness between Meg and Lynn. Nothing that either could pinpoint. Just a wariness as they sat at the kitchen table in Meg's house.

"So what's all this about being lonely?" Lynn asked. "What's wrong, Meg?"

"How about all this running away again? What's wrong with *you*?"

"Maybe we're having mid-life crises," Lynn suggested.

They both laughed and that hint of tension dissipated as they continued to laugh, neither sure why.

"Okay. You first," Lynn said eventually.

Meg stood, walked to the patio door and looked up at the swollen harvest moon. Squeezing her eyes shut she sent a wish skyward onto the surface of the luminous planet. It was a wish for Carrie's safety. The earth would spin and wobble around its axis and Meg knew her wish would beam down on Carrie and keep her safe. Wherever she was.

"You're wishing on the moon, Meg Enright! Are you ever going to grow up?"

Meg turned around and smiled at her friend. Only Lynn could say something like that to her and not cause offence.

"Just sending a message to Carrie. She'll get it too. I know it. But what I really wanted to tell you about was Karl Hemmings. I looked him up on the internet. We should have thought of doing that long ago. I suppose we're all too upset to think straight."

"And?"

"He's a headbanger. A man who once considered murdering his son and then committing suicide. He even claims to have had a conversation with a spirit he calls The Light."

"By phone or in person?"

"Not funny, Lynn. He's obviously off the wall. In a clever way though. Somehow he's managed to get himself from being destitute to owning a whole string of cafés and being leader of this cult he calls Inner Light Movement."

"And the son he considered murdering – would he be the boy Carrie seems to have fallen for?"

"Garth. Yes. And I think it's great that Carrie has met someone special. I don't even care about ILM. Maybe they're right in their beliefs. Who knows? What really worries me is the fact that Carrie seems to have changed so much. She's secretive. Never a mention of Garth and from what I can gather they've been together since she arrived in the States. Even the fact that she went to this cabin in Mount Desert without letting us know is out of character. And deliberately leaving her phone behind. That's not Carrie. You know it's not."

Lynn sat at the table twisting her mug round and round in circles. Meg sat down opposite her.

"Stop fiddling with the mug, Lynn. Look at me. What is it you're trying not to say?"

Lynn raised her head and it was as if a mask had slipped. A Lynn with no jokes, no pithy comments to make.

"John says you don't want Carrie to grow up. That you can't cut the apron strings."

Meg's first reaction was anger. How dare Lynn and John discuss her behind her back! The anger quickly turned to resentment and then hurt.

"Why did you go to see him, Lynn? Was it to tell him his wife was completely losing it? Were you complaining about me? Why?"

"Actually I went to EFAS to tear strips off him. I could see what kind of pressure you were under and I noticed you weren't getting much support from your husband."

Meg took in a sharp breath and Lynn immediately raised her hand to silence any comment.

"I know. I know. None of my business. But I saw how quickly he cut you off when you rang him and for ages you've been hinting at the amount of time you spend alone while John's in EFAS. I didn't mean to interfere. Honest. Anyway, we three go back a long way, don't we? The Three Amigos?"

A wave of nostalgia swept over Meg. The Three Amigos! God, yes! How innocent and full of fun those days had been. Or had they? Hadn't John even then been intense and driven by ambition, Lynn restless and flighty. And Meg, how had she been? A daydreamer. Looking for answers to questions she did not yet understand. The big questions. The meaning of life, the reason for existence. And all the time being afraid. Afraid to live, to face the harshness of reality. Afraid of being alone.

"We haven't changed much, Lynn, have we? We're all still striving to reach our goals."

"Well, maybe that's a good thing. We'll know we've finally reached old age when we stop striving."

"You mean when John retires from EFAS, you settle down in one place and I stop worrying about everyone and everything?"

"Something like that. To be honest, there's a hint of truth in what John says. Your children are grown up now, Meg. You must let them fend for themselves. Having said that, I agree with you. Karl Hemmings sounds like a dodgy character. What has John found out about him?"

Meg blushed and this time it was embarrassment not anger which reddened her face.

"Nothing. He's been even more preoccupied since Patrick Morgan decided to give his majority shareholding in EFAS to his nephew from New Zealand. That's my husband's priority now."

"Did John expect to get EFAS lock, stock and barrel? Is his nose out of joint?"

"God damn it, yes! He obviously fooled himself into thinking that Patrick Morgan would leave him the lot. He's like a child whose lollipop has been taken away. I thought we had bonded as a family again. I believed for a small while that concern for Carrie was bringing us closer together. But here I am as usual. On my own. Wondering where in the hell he is. Afraid to ring EFAS in case he cuts me off. In case I'm being a nuisance. And then there's this new receptionist or secretary or whatever she is. She's drop-dead gorgeous and I don't trust her."

Meg stopped talking suddenly, her eyes wide with shock.

She had not meant to spill all that bile. Not to Lynn. Not to anybody. Jesus! What was she thinking? What must Lynn think?

"I'm … I'm sorry, Lynn. I didn't mean to go on like that. I didn't mean …"

Meg got up to get the coffee-pot. She couldn't say any more because she didn't know what she meant. Was she trying to say that her marriage was cold? Dead. How could she even think that after the passion she and John had shared last night? Her hands shook as she poured coffee. She knew, as she stood watching the dark liquid fill up in the white mugs, that what she and John had shared last night was a mutual worry about their daughter. It hadn't been a need for each other. It had been an instinctive reaching out for comfort.

"Are you saying you and John are having problems, Meg? You can't be serious. Not you and John."

Meg brought the mugs over to the table, sat down and then took a deep breath. "Yes, Lynn. That's exactly what I'm saying. I've only just realised it myself. We seem to be living parallel lives. That's all I can see ahead. Our two lives stretching into the distance and never, ever touching."

"Empty nest syndrome?"

Meg felt anger well up. That's exactly what John would say if she tried to broach the subject with him. She hadn't expected this reaction from Lynn. What had she expected? Sympathy? How could Lynn understand? She had no one else to worry about except herself. Her favourite subject. At that unfair thought, Meg added bitchiness to her arsenal of guilt. Not bad for one night. To find two qualities in abundance she had never known she possessed. Disloyalty and cynicism. She

155

smiled now, an attempt to atone for her quick judgement.

"Not that, Lynn. I'm happy for Carrie and Tommy to grow up and live their own lives. Anyway, enough about me. What about you? What brought on this latest bout of travel fever?"

Lynn shrugged her shoulders. "Just because."

"Not a good reason for upping sticks. Are you running away?"

Lynn was silent. She just sat and stared at Meg as if weighing up their years of friendship and measuring trust against them.

"Well?" Meg prompted at last. "What is it? You *are* running away, aren't you?"

"Isn't that my problem? I've nothing to run away *from,*" Lynn said, startling them both with her intensity.

"Don't be daft, Lynn! You have a great life. You've achieved so much."

"Like what? A business that can run very well without me, an apartment full of things and a life that is empty. Who'd notice if me and my single life disappeared down a big black hole? In a week people would be asking 'Lynn who'? That's my legacy. Lynn who? And I don't want it, Meg. I need someone in my life who cares that I don't like Tuesdays or Novembers, that I do like bread and jam with my boiled egg, that I still miss my gran even though she died twenty-two years ago. Someone who thinks I'm special. "

The kitchen clock ticked the passing seconds as Meg and Lynn sat silently and realised their lives were at a crossroads. They had come this far by keeping their heads down and plodding on day after day. Somehow they had reached this mid-stream viewing point together. Their young-girl dreams had flared and faded and the middle-age hopes seemed to lie on the other side of an unfordable torrent.

The sound of the key in the front door brought both women back from their moment of self-awareness.

"That'll be John," Meg said.

Lynn immediately got up and began to put on her jacket. But Meg was wrong. It was Tommy who came into the kitchen, his face so pale that he could have been a painted mime artist. As they looked at him, Meg and Lynn both knew that no matter how troubled they both felt, Tommy was more deeply upset than either of them.

* * *

The Enrights lived in a quiet cul-de-sac in the southern suburbs of Cork city. Detached four-bedroomed homes, neat lawns and large back gardens, most with decking. Sycamore Lawn was the kind of place where people seemed to follow the natural rhythm of the day. They rose with the sun, went to work and ended the day when the sun set. A mortgage-driven lifestyle.

As John drove towards his home, he glanced around and tried to remember the names of his neighbours. A few of them, like him, had bought back in the late eighties. That meant that he had lived beside these people for twenty years. Amazing! He didn't know who in the fuck half of them were. Trees planted back then had matured now, giving the area a settled feel. A wealthy aura. Collateral.

His stomach muscles tightened as the thought of remortgaging his home would not go away. How much was it worth now? What was left on the original mortgage? It couldn't be much. He should know. He should have known that Patrick Morgan would stab him in the back. He should have had a financial package together to buy Patrick out on his retirement. Was that the problem? Had Patrick been waiting for him to show initiative and ambition? And found him lacking. Incompetent.

Preoccupied as he was, John did not see the young man at the entrance to his house until he almost knocked him down. He jammed on the brakes inches from the man's legs. Definitely not a neighbour. He was a tough-looking guy. Small but muscular. Not the type you would like to annoy. John waved his hand in apology and the man walked on. As he eased the car more carefully onto the driveway, John noticed Lynn's car. Funny that. Until last night he hadn't seen Lynn for what seemed like ages and here she was again now. At least Meg might be more cheerful. Lynn was such a livewire. She had never lost her sense of fun, although she had been in a peculiar mood when she had called to EFAS last night.

Leaving his jacket and briefcase in the hall, John followed the sound of voices into the kitchen. Tommy was sitting at the table, the two women either side of him. They all looked up as John came in the door. Conversation stopped. The three faces turned towards him, Tommy's face pale and somehow older than it had been that morning. John's already fluttering stomach did a complete flip as fear hit him a cold smack.

"Carrie! Is she alright? Have ye heard something about her?"

Meg stood and came to his side. "No. We've heard nothing new, although we found out some things about Karl

Hemmings. Carrie's fine at the moment as far as we know. Tommy got a bit of a fright though. Sit down and let him tell you. I'll make supper while you talk."

Lynn got up from her seat at the table and hugged Tommy. "I'll be off now. You take care, young man," she said as she ruffled his hair.

"Don't go, Lynn. Stay for supper. Please. "

Lynn looked at the boy she had watched progress from baby to toddler to teenager and found it hard to refuse the plea in the hazel eyes. But she had to go. This was Enright business and none of hers. Her place was on the perimeter of this family circle. John had put her there all those years ago and there was no crossing the divide now.

"I'm sorry, Tommy. I must get my beauty sleep. Us oldies need more rest, you know."

"Would you stay if we gave you a boiled egg with bread and jam?" John asked.

Meg dropped a spoon she had in her hand. It made a loud clatter as it hit the granite stone worktop. She and Lynn looked at each other and they both laughed.

John looked bewildered. "Did I say something funny?"

"Just insightful," Lynn answered as she laid a hand on his shoulder. She should not have done that. Her fingers shook as they felt his muscles underneath the fabric of his shirt. For an instant she was possessed by a longing so strong to run her fingers over his back that her hand almost moved automatically. She pulled away as if she had been burned.

"I'll see you in the morning, Meg," she said and made for the front door.

"Thanks for coming over, Lynn, and …"

Lynn didn't hear the rest. She was hauling the front door

open and welcoming the blast of cool night air on her hot cheeks. Menopausal, she told herself. A hot flash. But she knew the blush was from embarrassment and guilt and shock at the strength of her reaction to her fleeting physical contact with John Enright. How had she managed all these years to bury a feeling so overwhelming?

Then, just as she put a foot on the doorstep, John came up behind her, his car keys in his hand.

"Sorry, Lynn. I parked behind you. I blocked you in. I'll pull out now and let you go."

Lynn tried not to look at him but her eyes turned towards him nonetheless. Wasn't that the story of her life? Blocked in. Unable to move. But it wasn't John Enright who would have to let her go. She would have to find her own way out of this impasse. As he brushed past her she felt the heat from his body, breathed in his clean, masculine smell. Lynn stood there watching as he got into his car and reversed down the driveway.

And she silently swore two solemn oaths. Tonight she would finish the chocolate sauce and ice cream she had abandoned last night in favour of salsa-dancing and tomorrow she would go to the travel agents and book a flight to the farthest-away place she could find.

* * *

John stood looking after Lynn as she drove away and for an instant he envied her. How nice it must be to have the freedom to make decisions and know, right or wrong, you have nobody to answer to but yourself. Nobody else's welfare to consider. He took his time locking up the car again. Whatever had happened to Tommy, at least he had survived it and John was in no mood to take on yet more problems. It would be nice if for once Meg dealt with a problem on her own.

But when he got back into the kitchen and saw the troubled faces of his wife and son, John felt guilty. He had forged out the role of head of the family for himself and now was not the time to reject that decision. He pushed aside the toasted sandwich Meg had made for him and smiled at Tommy.

"Right, Tom. Spill the beans. Have you got yourself into some sort of scrape?"

Tommy dropped his head.

Meg glared at her husband over the multi-coloured head of her son. "Just listen, John. Having a go at him isn't going to help now."

"Having a go? I only asked ..." John consciously tightened his mouth. What was the point in trying to justify himself? In Meg's eyes nobody could say boo to her precious son. Especially not his father. He nodded at Tommy to go ahead.

"I was at the hospital tonight. The University Hospital. Somebody followed me home."

"What were you doing at the hospital? Did you have an accident?"

"Breeze's mother was taken in there. I just went to see if I could help."

"She died," Meg added.

"I'm sorry to hear your friend has lost his mother but what has that got to do with somebody following you home?"

As Tommy related his story about meeting the infamous Freddie Goodall and his sidekicks, John had to bite his lip in order not to say 'I told you so'.

"You're certain it was one of Freddie Goodall's guys following you? And you're sure you were actually followed?"

"He came as far as the driveway. He didn't even try to hide the fact he was tailing me. He was just putting the frighteners on me. The prick succeeded."

John frowned as he drummed the table with his fingers, remembering now the man he had almost knocked down at the entrance to the house. "Was he a small, stocky guy? Leather jacket, greasy hair?"

"That's him!"

"He was still outside when I came home. I almost ran over him."

Despite Meg's warning, John felt his anger rise. Years ago, in fact almost eighteen years ago, he should have put his foot down with Tommy. If he had, this would never have happened. The end result of leaving Meg to manage the children was a daughter in a remote log cabin in the states and a son dragging the scum of society onto their doorstep.

"Why in the hell d'you insist on having anything to do with the Goodalls? They're trouble, Tommy. You've been told that. Bad enough putting your own future in jeopardy by hanging out with the wrong crowd but now you've brought them to our home and my business."

"Oh – your business! That's all you care about. Your poxy storage unit! And it's not even yours, is it? Patrick Morgan still pulls the strings there. Everyone knows that. Except you of course."

Meg knew these pair of stubborn males would soon be

roaring at each other and her head would be throbbing in pain. She was not going to allow that to happen.

"Shut up! Both of you!" Her voice was low but it crackled with anger. "For once, just for once, treat each other with a little respect!"

All three sat in silence. Meg looked at her husband and son and was gratified by their reaction. They were staring at her as if she had suddenly sprouted horns or ripped off all her clothes. She was ripping off layers alright. Layers and layers of self-delusion. Years of self-effacement, putting their needs first, even forgetting by now what her own needs were. But they were emerging again, the wants and needs of Meg Enright who used to be Meg Riordan. A shy, sensitive young girl who had somehow drifted towards middle-age without ever wondering where she was going. Following in the well-defined footsteps of her husband, lifting her children over the rough bits only to have them run ahead and never look back to see if she was alright. She had no footprints of her own, no defined path that was Meg Enright's imprint on life.

"Mom? Are you alright?"

Tommy's voice was plaintive. Quavering, like it used to be when he was small and wanted to get his own way. She had always given in then, touched by his vulnerability, driven by a need to protect him against sadness. Against reality. But the time for protecting had gone. Tommy would find his own strength now. Meg straightened up in her chair and smiled at her son.

"Yes, Tommy, I'm fine. Just worn out from this constant bickering and manipulating. Your father's a good man. He's worked hard to give you everything you need and you should respect him for that. And you, John," she said turning towards her husband, "should show equal respect for your son. He's a kind, generous person with loads of potential. He needs to find his own way. Don't try to bully him into your way of thinking. He's not John Enright Mark 2, he's his own man. And both of you should have some consideration for me. I've had enough of being the buffer between you."

Meg sat up even straighter. She felt proud of herself and she liked the feeling. It was the same as when she was driving fast. On the edge but in control. Exciting.

"Now, we must discuss the Goodalls," she went on. "Did this guy who followed you say anything to you, Tom, threaten you in any way?"

"Hanging around our house is threat enough," said John.

"I asked Tommy, not you. Let him speak for himself."

"That's rich coming from you! You never let him ..." John broke off and looked at Meg, his dark eyes puzzled. Then he waited silently for Tommy to continue.

"The guy said nothing. That was the creepiest thing. If I stopped, he stopped. When I hurried so did he but he never said a word."

"Why didn't you ring for one of us?"

"I didn't want to worry you, Mom – and I didn't want to explain to you, Dad. I don't need to hear the 'I told you so's'."

"So you led him to our door instead!" said John.

"It wasn't about finding out where I lived. Freddie Goodall knew who I was. He'd only have to open the phone book to work that out. Or ask Breeze."

"Bloody great! My son buddy-buddy with a criminal! A drug-pusher."

164

"That's not fair! Freddie's not my friend, Breeze is. And he's not a criminal."

"What's all this trailing around after you about then?" Meg asked. "A warning?"

They were quiet as they each tried to work out why Freddie Goodall would want to intimidate his young brother's friend. Meg thought of what Tommy had told her of Breeze's background. Tough, deprived, disadvantaged. Maybe that was the simple answer. It was resentment.

"I think Freddie Goodall is just a bully," she said. "He can't understand friendship, especially with someone he would consider very privileged. He must resent you, Tommy, and your relationship with Breeze. He was just frightening you off because he could."

Tommy thought about that. Breeze rarely mentioned his older brother but from what little he had said it was obvious there was bad feeling between them. Breeze would have nothing to do with drugs. The only time he had seen Breeze angry was the day Tommy had suggested they get some cannabis. Just one spliff. Breeze had gone ballistic. Maybe Freddie blamed Tommy for keeping his brother away from the family business. It was one explanation anyway.

"You could be right, Mom. Breeze will have nothing to do with whatever Freddie's involved in."

"Say it!" John said. "Drug-pushing. He's a dealer. Scum. Say it!"

"I'm not denying it, Dad. Freddie's all that but Breeze is not. Shit! Just look at the way Breeze is struggling while Freddie lives in the lap of luxury."

"How do you know that?"

"Breeze told me. Freddie has a big posh apartment somewhere. A penthouse. And three cars."

John leaned back in his chair and stretched his arms and legs. He was weary. Weak. Francine Keyes, Yan Gilmore, Karl Hemmings and now Freddie Goodall tap-danced around in his brain, sapping what little strength he had left. Could there be a connection between these people or was it just coincidence that they had all, just recently, wormed their way into the Enrights' lives ?

He looked across at his wife – slight, delicate, yet exuding a new vigour. It was as if she had absorbed his power by osmosis during their lovemaking last night. John Enright felt real fear. He was losing control and control was the lynchpin of his life.

"Well, I think you should stay away from Breeze for a while," Meg said to Tommy. "Let him cope with his mother's death and his problems with his brother. Don't get yourself involved in their family life. What do you think, John?"

John thought his spoiled brat of a son should have listened to him in the first place and stayed away from the Goodalls. None of this would have happened if he had. If, if, if! If he himself had not wanted so badly to touch Francine Keyes' tits, if he had bought Patrick Morgan's shares three years ago, if he had noticed that Carrie had not been in contact. If he had realised that Meg was dissatisfied – cross and impatient – a new element in the mix. He looked at her now and felt for a moment that she was asking his opinion out of courtesy, not respect. He blinked to clear that confusing image.

"Yes, I agree," he said. "Just cut all contact with this Breeze. Anyway you have school to think about. Get yourself cleaned up, Tommy. It's time for you to start taking responsibility for yourself."

Tommy stood up and walked to the kitchen door. He turned then to face his parents, one hand on the door.

"Okay. I'll go along with that. But I want you both to know that Breeze is not a bad person. He was a good friend to me. Probably one of the best I'll ever have."

He went then, trailing his black coat. John put his elbows on the table and leaned his head onto his hands.

"Did you get on to Willy Feeney?" Meg asked. "Do the police know anything about Karl Hemmings?"

John lifted his head slowly and looked at his wife. He saw anger in her beautiful hazel eyes. He flinched, imagining the hurt he would see there if she ever found out about Francine Keyes.

"He's in London. He won't be back 'til Monday."

"Didn't you ask someone else? Surely he has a deputy?"

"I didn't want to advertise our business. Willy Feeney would deal with it discreetly."

Meg too stood up. She walked over to stand beside John and looked down at him. She had been going to tell him not to bother, that she would contact the police herself, that he was never there for his family anyway. Never there for her. The bitter words remained unspoken. John was tired, the lines on his face deeper than she had noticed before, the expression in his eyes more haunted than she had ever seen.

"Did you talk to Patrick Morgan's nephew?"

"Yeah. He's on his way. Done deal. I've been thinking of trying to get money together. Going to the bank with a begging bowl. But I realise now I'm just kidding myself. I don't want that kind of debt for us and anyway Patrick

Morgan has not left me the choice."

Meg reached out her hand to touch John's face. To comfort him. But her hand would not go the distance. Her brain registered the fact that John was more deeply upset by the imminent arrival of Yan Gilmore than by the fact that the Enright family seemed to be in chaos.

She wished her husband goodnight and tried to quell the treacherous thought that goodbye would inevitably follow on.

CHAPTER 12

Carrie always liked Fridays but this one was tinged with sadness. As they took the ramp onto Route 1-95, she knew she should be looking out the window, noting all the details of the drive from Mount Desert Island back to Portland. She might never get the chance to come to Maine again.

With each passing mile the splendid isolation of the log cabin compound was becoming more of a fantasy and less the reality she had been living. She glanced at Garth. He was staring at the road ahead. He had one hand on the steering wheel while the other lay casually on his knee. Reaching across, Carrie laid her hand on his.

"Are you okay?" he asked.

She nodded and smiled at him, liking the way he always looked out for her. He made her feel so protected. So safe.

"I'm sad leaving Mount Desert behind," she said. "'Twas a great experience. Thank you, Garth."

"Don't thank me. It was my dad's suggestion to bring you there."

Carrie withdrew her hand from his and shuffled herself

into a more comfortable position in her seat. This was going to be a long journey, over one hundred and thirty miles. Almost the same distance as Cork to Dublin at home. Although the way the SUV was smoothly pushing ahead it might not seem too long. Her eyelids drooped, lulled by the heat and the quiet engine sounds.

"You don't like my father, do you?"

Carrie's eyes flew open. Why had Garth asked her that question? How did he know? She had been very careful not to let any of her misgivings show. Or she thought she had been.

"It's not that I don't like him, Garth. I don't know him."

"You've met him. You've joined him in prayer every evening."

"Well, yes. I always listen to his radio link and I had a few brief meetings with him."

"And you're judging him on those few meetings?"

"I'm not judging him. I'm just saying … It's just that I find him a little intimidating. A little bit intense."

As Carrie watched, Garth's lips pursed together into a tight line. His face was different now. Older. More closed.

"I'm sorry, Garth. I don't mean to be critical. Of course I admire what your father has done. And I respect the depth of his faith. Maybe I'm just in awe of him."

"There's no need to be. Anyway, I'm sure you'll change your mind this evening. We're having dinner with him in Prouts Neck."

Carrie kept her eyes on the vehicle ahead. A beat-up Chevrolet truck. They were gaining on it and would soon pass it by. She concentrated on the dented panels and the logs bumping around the truck bed until Garth guided the SUV past. Then all her mixed feelings clamoured for recognition.

At last! Garth was taking her to his home. She had heard about the house on Prouts Neck Penninsula from other people at the café but she had never been invited there. It was rumoured to be a mansion and Prouts Neck was the preserve of the elite. But why Karl Hemmings needed a home at all was a mystery. He seemed to spend his time floating between his cafés, dispensing blessings on his staff, broadcasting his evening prayer from wherever he happened to be. Collecting the profits. Plus the 10 percent of earnings ILM members donated towards the upkeep of the log cabin compounds. Besides Mount Desert, there were cabin compounds near Moosehead Lake in Piscataquis County and another in the area of Mount Katahdin. Plenty of space for disciples to reflect on the honour and glory of their leader. The Chosen One. And yet all these people, at least the ones Carrie had met, were educated and intelligent. Maybe not ditzy Joyanne. But even Joyanne, for all her silliness, had an unshakable faith in Karl Hemmings and appeared to have found purpose and peace through his teachings. Nobody else seemed to find his dark eyes manic, his thin mouth mean and cruel. Except of course Trina, who with her usual sense of drama, thought he was a "creepy perv".

"Was your mother blonde?" Carrie asked, needing to know that Garth had more of his mother than his father in him.

"Yes."

The terse answer told Carrie that here was another subject they would not discuss. They knew the minutiae of each other's lives, the likes and dislikes, favourite music, food, films. Even most embarrassing moments. But when it came to the big questions, the things that made them who they were and would guide what they would become, then there was a wall. Too high for Carrie to climb and obviously too comfortably protective for Garth to abandon. Suddenly Carrie badly needed to speak to her own mom. Gentle Meg. So supportive and understanding. What would she say about Garth? Probably advise her to trust her own instinct. Wasn't that the problem? Her instinct was telling her that Garth was the most beautiful person she had ever met and yet …

"I need to go by the café in Congress Street to pack for tomorrow and to get my phone. I must contact home before they send a posse looking for me. Your dad said my parents were very anxious, even after hearing my radio message. Is that alright with you, Garth?"

Garth nodded. Carrie closed her eyes again and settled down to sleep. When sleep did not come she kept her eyes closed anyway. It was easier that way.

* * *

From Maine Turnpike on Carrie had a surprising sense of homecoming. The further they drove onto the peninsula once named Machigonne by the native Wabanaki Indians, the more familiar everything became: the busy Portland waterfront area, beautiful Casco Bay, the stately Victorian buildings erected after a 4th of July fire devastated the city in 1866. Garth's encyclopaedic knowledge of his adopted homeland had given her an interest in its past but it was the beauty and vibrancy of the city which had made Portland such a special place for her. Trina and the rest of the gang had caught the bus out to the tourist area of Old Orchard Beach

172

every chance they could but Carrie had loved to wander the
cobbled sidewalks of The Old Port area or visit some of the
little arts and crafts shops and galleries dotted all around the
city.

When they arrived on Congress Street and pulled up
outside Haven Café, Carrie knew her holiday was over. It
had been a warm and dreamy summer full of discoveries but
it was goodbye time now. She glanced up at the three-story
red-brick building which had been the centre of her world
since she had arrived here three months ago. She had worked
in the café on the first floor, joined in the prayers in the
Communal Room on the second floor, slept with Trina in
an attic room on the third floor. It was here she had fallen in
love with Garth, with his gentleness and his goodness. With
his sexy body which he was so determined not to share.

"Pack all your things and do whatever you have to do,"
he said. "I'll pick you up later and take you out to Prouts
Neck."

Carrie felt sad at this little goodbye. They had spent all
their waking hours together this past week. How was she
going to cope with saying a permanent goodbye to him?

"I'll see you later then," she said as brightly as she could.

Garth lifted his hand and stroked her cheek. "Will you
stay over at my house tonight? On Prouts Neck? I'll drive
you to the Jetport in the morning."

Carrie hesitated. Sleeping in Garth's house was one thing.
Being under the same roof as Karl Hemmings was another.
She immediately felt ashamed. No matter what reservations
she had, the man was Garth's father. She smiled.

"I'd like that, Garth. Thank you."

She stood on the sidewalk and watched as the SUV drove

off down Congress Street. Garth hadn't said where he was going. She turned and went into the café. It seemed they were already going their separate ways.

The café was busy. It was a meeting place for the literati and those with a social conscience. Conversations here were always intense and meaningful and sometimes quite loud. Carrie continued on up the stairs and through the Communal Room onto the second flight. She was puffing by the time she landed her case on her narrow bed in the attic room.

The first thing she did when she got her breath was to go to the dressing table where she had left her phone on charge. Unplugging the charger she noticed it was quite hot. Maybe leaving it plugged in that long had not been the safest thing to do. Her eyes widened when she saw all her messages. She pulled her case onto the floor, flopped on the bed and began to plough through them. Mom, Dad, Tommy, Trina. Even one from Lynn. Then she listened to her voicemails, Mom's getting more and more frantic. What had she done? Oh, shit! She should have known when Karl Hemmings said her family had been trying to contact her. They must have thought she had been kidnapped. Or worse. How confusing must her radio message have been for them? But hell, she was twenty-one years of age! Couldn't she just have a little space without reporting her every move?

Carrie dropped her phone and, lowering her head, massaged her temples. It didn't help. It was as if she had suddenly been transported back home. She might physically be here in Portland but her mind was in Ireland. Trapped in that space between her mother and father, the space she had carved out for herself from the first time she realised that life in the Enright household was more bearable when Mom was not upset and Dad was not angry. Why had she taken on the responsibility of being their Kofi Annan? What had made her believe that it was her duty to smooth the Enright path to harmony? Tommy didn't give a toss and he was better off. At least he pretended he didn't care anyway.

Tension tightened around her head as she began to feel guilt and responsibility in equal measure. All Mom needed to know was that her daughter was safe. All Dad wanted was peace to get on with his work. It would only have taken a phone call. What had happened in Sycamore Lawn this past week? Had Mom been crying and Dad annoyed? Had Tommy gone on a bender to escape them? All because Carrie wanted to pretend she was independent. No! She was. It was her family who were dependent.

A sudden image of her mother flashed before Carrie. Petite, beautiful Meg, delicate features and tear-filled hazel eyes. So sensitive. So very fragile. Then Carrie knew she had been wrong, so wrong to upset her mother. Who would have comforted her? Not Dad. Too busy, too obsessed with EFAS. Not Tommy. Too involved in his own growing-up. Maybe Lynn. Flighty, lively Godmother Lynn. Carrie was overcome by a need to hold her mother in her arms, to protect her, to apologise.

Fingers shaking, she dialled Meg's mobile. It rang for a while. That must mean her mother was in Curtain Call and her phone was in the kitchenette behind the shop. Just when Carrie was worrying that the phone would ring out, she heard Meg's breathless voice.

"Carrie! Are you alright? Where are you? Oh, Carrie!"

"Hi, Mom. I'm well thanks. I'm in Portland. Just back from Mount Desert Island. How are you?"

"I'm great now that I've heard from you. Just great. Are you sure you're okay?"

"I'm fine. Really. You'd love Mount Desert, Mom. In fact you'd love Maine. It's so wild and beautiful. It inspires a lot of creativity. Just your type of place."

"You're coming home, Carr, aren't you?"

"Yes, of course! I'm not sure about college though. I've been thinking about it. We'll talk when I get back."

"And will we talk about Garth?"

Carrie hesitated. Was that a rebuke from Meg? Maybe she should have told them about Garth before now. Maybe not. It might yet turn out to be just another summer romance. "Yeah, sure. I'll talk about Garth. Tell you what, I'll send a photo of him to your phone now."

"Is he like his father?"

"How do you mean?"

"I saw his father's webpage. Inner Light Movement. I read all about it."

So! Meg had been trawling the Internet, Googling ILM. How desperate must she have been, how frightened?

"I'm sorry, Mom. I should have let you know where I was going. It was very thoughtless of me. I hope you weren't too worried."

"As long as you're safe now, everything's okay. Dad and Tommy will be relieved too."

"Tell them I was asking for them. I'll see you all soon. I'm flying to New York tomorrow to meet up with Trina and the others. I'll ring you from there. Everything going well, we'll be home Wednesday."

"I can't wait to see you. Love you, Carr."

"I love you too, Mom. Bye."

Carrie waited until Meg had cut the connection. Then she looked around her little room under the rafters. She would miss this room, this city, this state. Most of all she would miss Garth. Why did she have to fall for someone from another continent, another way of life? She hadn't realised until she heard her mother's voice just how much she had missed home while she'd been here. She had not allowed herself to think about Ireland. Not often anyway. But she really needed to see her dysfunctional family – her workaholic father, her confused brother and her gentle mother. To be in a place where she was truly loved.

Glancing at the dressing table Carrie saw the watch which she had taken off for her timeless time in Mount Desert. The evening was moving on. She wasn't sure when Garth would be here to pick her up but she must get to LLBean to buy a sweater for Dad and a jacket for Tommy before packing. Then she would have to dress for dinner with Karl Hemmings in Prouts Neck. Carrie grabbed her purse and ran back down the stairs before she had time to think about what the evening might bring.

* * *

As Carrie stood on the cliff and watched the sunset over the restless North Atlantic waters off Prouts Neck, she had a feeling of something she could only describe as connectivity. These were the same waters which ebbed and flowed in Cork Harbour, an umbilical cord between Portland and her home in Ireland. She could, on some lonely day in the future, stand on the cliffs in the Irish coastal town of Crosshaven and know that the breakers she saw crash onto the rocks at Roche's Point Lighthouse would eventually surge onto the jagged grey rocks of Prouts Neck shoreline. Maybe Garth would stand here and think of her, an ocean away.

Fog began to roll in, pink tinged on the horizon. Carrie shivered and pulled her cardigan more closely around her. Cropped and made from very fine wool, it was designed for style, not warmth. Garth took off his jacket and draped it around her shoulders.

"We'd better get to the house, he said. "Dad will be waiting."

Carrie gave a last look at Saco Bay and in the distance Old Orchard Beach and somewhere out there in the fast rolling fog, Stratten Island bird sanctuary. On impulse, shortly after arriving in Portland, she had bought a print of Winslow Homer's painting of Saco Bay. It captured the rugged beauty of the place where the nineteenth-century artist had lived and worked, the very place where Carrie now stood. She would hang it in her bedroom at home. More connectivity. She smiled at Garth.

"Better not keep your dad waiting," she said as she turned her back on the sea and faced towards Homer Winslow Road where they had parked.

"Wait," Garth said, standing in front of her and putting his hands on her shoulders. "I want to tell you something, Carrie. I want to say … I–I want you to know that …"

Carrie watched as the normally super-confident Garth stuttered and even blushed. Was this the big revelation? The 'it's not you, it's me'. The 'I'm gay' announcement? Hurt, confused, even angry, Carrie shook free of his hold and looked up at him, knowing and not caring that her anger was showing.

"For heaven's sake, Garth, stop bumbling. Is this about sex? Is it about the fact that we never got to first base, never had a shag?"

"Don't be crude, Carrie. It doesn't suit you."

"Oh, stop! Being patronising doesn't suit you either. You haven't made love to me, Garth. Even in Mount Desert, while the cabins around us were practically rocking with all the sex going on, you barely kissed me. You can't use ILM as an excuse. It's more liberal than the Catholic Church on the question of sex. I'll make it easy for you now. Are you gay?"

She watched in puzzlement as Garth laughed. A genuine, hearty laugh.

"Is that what you've been thinking?" he asked.

"Well, Trina said ..."

"Trina! She'd know, wouldn't she? She must qualify as a sex therapist by now."

"Don't you dare talk about my friend like that!"

"But you let her talk about me, didn't you?"

"She wasn't saying derogatory things, like you are. She just said you might be gay."

"And that's not derogatory?"

"Of course it's not! It's just what some people are. Or doesn't your father approve? Isn't there a place in ILM for gay people? Are all the love and blessings for straight, white, middle-class people?"

"I told you before, ILM's not racist or prejudiced in any way. Each human being is a creation of The Light. A minder of their individual share of The Light's power. It's just that some come under other influences."

Garth's eyes mirrored Carrie's anger now. At last they had peeled back layers of caution and were probing the sensitive depths beneath. They had reached the place where Garth was so sure of his beliefs and Carrie was still trying to make sense of her very existence. She hesitated for a moment. Would it be better to continue ignoring their differences for the short time they had left? Go to dinner with Karl, listen meekly to his pontificating, accept ILM's influence over Garth and then tomorrow kiss him goodbye at the airport and forget about him. She looked up into his blue eyes sparked with anger, at the tanned planes of his face, at his lips, so sensitive and full in comparison to his father's, at his sun-bleached blonde hair. A painful knot of need twisted in her stomach. This man was worth fighting for. Better to part with a passionate argument than passive acceptance of defeat.

"What are you trying to tell me, Garth? You're going around in circles. So, I take it you're not gay. But you haven't made love to me. Don't you find me attractive?"

"I think you're beautiful, Carrie. In every way. I love your laugh, your musical voice, your dark eyes, your gentleness. I want you so much. I don't ever want to be apart from you. I … I love you, Carrie."

Carrie closed her eyes. His words played over in her head while surf pounded, gulls screeched and somewhere a foghorn boomed. 'I love you, Carrie.' She had imagined this so many times but her imaginings had never factored in doubt and conditions to be met. She opened her eyes.

"I love you too, Garth, but there's more, isn't there? We can't be together unless I become a fully paid-up member of ILM. Is that it? Your father wouldn't approve."

"I don't like the way you said that. ILM isn't about money. It's about commitment to a way of life."

Carrie let that go. She could have said that Karl Hemmings' commitment to The Light had brought him a lot of financial blessings but she cared too deeply for Garth to hurt his feelings more than necessary.

"Okay. So you still haven't answered me. Do I have to make a full commitment to ILM in order to win your father's approval? And by default yours. You would never defy him, would you?"

"Inner Light Movement is part of what I am. I couldn't share my life with someone who didn't wholeheartedly support that. I wish with all my heart that you believe like I do but the decision must be yours."

Argument and counter argument battled in Carrie's mind. Would it matter if she threw her lot in with ILM? It wasn't as if she held any other strong beliefs. In fact, besides admitting that there probably was one supreme being who had created the Universe, she did not have any unshakable tenets of faith. Why couldn't that supreme being be The Light? Why should terminology matter when the basic principal was the same? She had been baptised into the Roman Catholic church but had only paid lip service to it ever since she learned to think for herself. All through her school years she had been a token Roman Catholic, keeping her concerns about teachings like the Virgin birth and Transubstantiation to herself. It was an inherited faith she had grown out of as she grew up. Her parents' faith. Well, her father's anyway. Mom was a free spirit, latching onto one idea after another to make sense of the senseless.

"I thought you believed in what ILM stands for," Garth said. "You pray with us. You give thanks and praise to The Light."

181

"Yes. That's all very nice, Garth. It's great when we all hold hands and praise The Light, when we sing together. Great for the morale. Your people, your ILM people, are all kind and considerate."

"Yet you've never said you'd like to join us. You've never asked my father's blessing."

Decision time. Is this where Carrie told Garth he was brainwashed by his father? What made someone as intelligent as Garth think that his father had the power to bestow a blessing on anyone, that the laying on of hands by Karl Hemmings had a spiritual significance?

The anger had left his eyes now. He looked vulnerable, standing there with the breeze tossing his blonde hair, an anxious, hurt expression on his face. How could she give him up when every cell in her body yearned for him? That was the reality. Maybe there was a spirit world. Maybe not. This could be all there was. This moment here on Winslow Homer Road with the fog rolling in off the sea and two young people who needed to be together. No matter what happened, tomorrow would be a goodbye anyway. She took a step towards him and lifted a hand to touch his face.

"I won't lie to you, Garth. I don't have the same belief in ILM as you do. But I'm willing to give it a try. I'll ask your father for his blessing. I'll become a consecrated member of ILM."

Garth put his arms around her and drew her towards him. Carrie closed her eyes and rested her face against his chest. She smiled contentedly as he ran his hands over her back, easing the tensions of their fraught conversation.

"Dad has something to tell you," he said. "Something special."

182

Carrie knew then the 'something special' had been dependent on her agreeing to become a member of ILM. She should have felt manipulated. Instead she just gloried in the freshness of the sea air, the coolness of the breeze, the tickling dampness of the fog and the warmth of Garth's body against hers. Who needed an ethereal heaven? This was it.

"We'd better go," Garth said, pulling away from her. "It's almost time for dinner."

Carrie put her hand in Garth's and together they walked back to the SUV. She felt strong now. Ready to face Karl Hemmings and the 'special something' he had waiting for her.

CHAPTER 13

Carrie lowered the sun visor and checked her hair and make-up in the mirror as they drove along Black Point Road.

"Is it only your father and us for dinner?" she asked "Will there be anyone else?"

"Just the staff."

Staff! Of course. What had made her think that The Light's chosen messenger would be peeling and chopping? Garth took a sharp left turn onto a roadway lined with pine trees. It twisted and turned for a quarter mile before it opened out into a beautifully landscaped lawn. They had arrived at the house and the rumours were true. It was a mansion. Carrie gaped at the sprawl of the elevated Colonial building. Garth parked in a gravelled area one level beneath the house. Carrie got out as he retrieved her overnight bag from her luggage. She looked up at the magnificent house and felt dwarfed.

"My God! How many windows does it have?" she asked in a whisper.

Garth laughed. "I don't know. Can't say I've ever counted them. I s'pose about fifty. Do you like it?"

Carrie gazed from the arches leading to the front door, to the balustrades on the first and second floors, right up to the heights of the slated hip roof. From the symmetrical wings on either side of the central block of the grey building to the intricate stone sculptures lurking under eaves and over arches. No, she didn't like it. It was cold and unwelcoming. Disdainful. Beautiful in a frigid kind of way.

"It's very impressive," she said truthfully. "When was it built?"

"It's not as old as it looks. It was only built in 1920. Colonial Revival rather than genuine Colonial. Dad's been careful though to keep everything as authentic as possible. C'mon, let's go inside."

Garth caught her hand and led her up the flight of steps leading to the front entrance. They walked under the arches and up to the ornate front door. Mahogany, Carrie guessed. Garth held the door open for her and waved her in ahead of him. The hall was vast. Acres of wooden floors glowing with the patina of age, a bow-legged hall table, a massive Wedgwood vase of flowers, a gilt framed mirror, oriental rugs, paintings of hunting and battle scenes. Rows of doors opening left and right off the central hallway. So many things. Too much to appreciate in one glance. Besides, the staircase stole all the attention. Painted white with intricate scrolling on the newels and balusters, it seemed to wend and weave skyward from the hall.

A door opened on the right-hand side towards the end of the hall. A plump, dark-skinned woman came towards them, wiping her hands on her apron as she walked.

"You're late," she said. "You know your father won't be none too pleased."

Garth walked up to her and threw his arm around her shoulders.

"Don't be cross, Pearl. Look, I've brought Carrie to meet you. You've been wanting to meet her for a long time, haven't you?"

Pearl turned luminous dark eyes on Carrie and regarded her solemnly. As Carrie looked back she saw the woman's eyes crinkle at the corners and her soft round face break into a smile. Pearl walked towards her and gently laid a hand on her shoulder.

"You're as beautiful as he said. I'm happy to meet you at last, Carrie."

Without knowing why, Carrie felt relief. Some instinct told her that Pearl's opinion carried weight with Garth. But why had he never mentioned her before?

"It's nice to meet you too, Pearl. Although I must say you and this house are a surprise. Garth never said that ... he never said ..."

"He never said that he lived in a great big house and was raised by a black woman? Is that what you're trying to say? It don't surprise me none. Garth was always a close one. He don't trust easy. Now come on, I'll show you to your room. Garth, your father's in the study. Go see him."

Pearl chatted all the way as Carrie followed her up the seemingly endless stairs, pointing out paintings on the walls and cornices on the ceiling. They were both puffing by the time they arrived on the landing of the first floor. The walls here were painted a rich cream on top and wood-panelled below. The floors, unlike downstairs, were carpeted. A long corridor ran from left and right of the landing. Pearl turned right and headed towards the end of the corridor, her round hips rolling as she walked.

"You're in the Rose Room," she said. "I thought from what Garth told me you'd like it."

"What did he tell you?"

Pearl stopped, her hand on the door knob of the last room and regarded Carrie again.

"He said you're a sensitive soul who's still searching for the truth. I pray you find the right answers. Garth needs you. Now come on in. Give me that bag you have and I'll unpack for you."

"No. It's alright, thanks. I can do that myself," Carrie said, clutching onto her battered overnight bag which seemed so out of place in all this luxury.

"I like independence," Pearl grinned as she held the door open. "See how you fancy this room."

Carrie gawped at the four-poster bed with the velvet canopy, the cherrywood floors and thick white rugs, the deep wine walls and white coving. Everywhere she looked there were exquisite artefacts and on the white bedside table a bowl of deep red roses.

"It's very beautiful," she said softly. "And so surprisingly warm and welcoming."

Pearl leaned towards her and whispered. "So you don' like the outside of the house neither. It's frightening. I'm always telling Karl to paint it but I do believe he likes the seriousness of all that grey stone. Your bathroom's here," she added, suddenly changing the subject and crossing the room to open a white painted door.

Carrie followed her and peeped into a room with a claw

bath on a raised platform and a walk-in shower placed discreetly in a screened area so that it did not spoil the sense of antiquity in the space. Carrie shook her head and smiled, wishing that Trina could see all this.

"There's more," Pearl said, opening yet another door to a walk-in wardrobe. A dressing room.

Carrie thought of the jeans and T-shirt she had packed for tomorrow and laughed out loud.

"I'll just need two hangers," she said.

"You freshen up and then come on down. I must get back to the kitchen. Dinner's in ten minutes. The dining room's through the first double doors on your right-hand side in the hall. D'you like turkey?"

"I do, thank you. Pearl, how long have you known Garth?"

"A long time. You've got a balcony too. Just open the door and walk out. You'll see then why this is called the Rose Room."

Pearl waddled busily out the door, leaving Carrie with a plethora of unanswered questions. What was Pearl's position here? Was she housekeeper, maid, mistress or was she wife? Karl Hemmings' dark secret? Why had Garth not mentioned her before? She was clearly an important person in his life. He had allowed Carrie accuse him and ILM of racism and all the while a black woman ran his home. She might even be his stepmother but then he would surely have said. So far, Pearl's status in the Hemmings household remained mysterious but obviously pivotal.

Dropping her overnight case on the floor, Carrie opened the balcony door and walked out. In front of her the tree-lined driveway she and Garth had just travelled wound into the foggy distance and below lay the smooth lawns, trimmed and luscious. Attracted by a beautiful scent, she leaned her arms on the stone balustrade and looked directly beneath her. Rose bushes, laden with fragrant blooms shone brightly in the fading light. Of course! The Rose Room was directly over the rose garden.

Feeling the damp in the air, Carrie went back into the room and closed the balcony door. The rose scent clung to the drapes, sweet and rich. Sweet and rich. That's what this house was. Like a succulent kernel encased in an ugly nut shell. And whoever Pearl was, whatever her role in this house, it was certain she was the source of the warmth and a figure of some authority. Carrie went about unpacking her meagre luggage, realising that she had a lot to learn about Garth Hemmings. The man she knew so well and yet not at all.

* * *

The dining room, just like the rest of the house, was warm, comfortable and not at all what Carrie would have expected when first she saw the grey exterior of Point House as she now knew the mansion was named. Silverware and crystal gleamed in the flickering candlelight as they sat at the oval table. Karl Hemmings was seated in a huge carver at the head while she and Garth sat at either side of him. Even Karl seemed less threatening, more approachable in the warm glow from the six candles in the magnificent silver candelabra. Pearl flitted over and back between the kitchen and the dining room, supervising the young Asian girl who was serving the food. The fresh salmon and prawn starter had been delicious and now Karl Hemmings was ceremoniously carving turkey crown.

Looking up from his task, he smiled at Carrie.

"What did you think of Mount Desert Island?" he asked.

"It was wonderful," she answered and thought how much better it could have been if only Garth had opened up to her.

"Everyone has the same reaction. It's not just a beautiful place. It beats to nature's rhythm. That's what I tried to explain to your parents. It's a respite from the pace of twenty-first century life. We all need a healing space, don't we?"

Carrie felt a blush begin to creep up her neck. What in the hell had gone on between her parents and Karl Hemmings? Dad had probably been hostile and Mom hysterical. Shit! What had they said? Knowing that it was her own fault for not keeping them informed didn't make her feel any more comfortable now as she watched Karl expertly carve the meat and felt the trail of embarrassment blaze its way onto her cheeks.

"Your parents love you very much, Carrie. That's a great blessing."

Seeing her discomfort, Garth reached across the table and squeezed her hand. She felt strength flow from him to her. She smiled at Karl.

"Yes, I know I'm lucky. I have a great family."

Pearl came back into the room, carrying a tray with bowls of vegetables.

"You eat up your dinner, girl," she said to Carrie. "Plenty of time to talk when you've had your fill."

"You going to join us, Pearl?" Karl asked.

"You know well I'm making your favourite apple pie for dessert. I must go see to it. Now eat while your food's hot."

She bustled off, leaving Carrie even more puzzled about Pearl's position in the household. She seemed to have an easy camaraderie with Karl Hemmings. More wife than employee. Whatever her status, she had a humanising effect on Karl. He was softer, more approachable. Even vulnerable.

Turkey carved and served, Karl sat down.

"Better do as we're told," he advised. "And a word of warning, Carrie. You'll have to clear your plate or else Pearl will want to know why. First we'll thank The Light for this plenty."

Having sat through the first grace-before-meal prayer, Carrie had thought the praying had been done and dusted. It looked like they were going to have to thank The Light at every course. Karl spread his arms wide and closed his eyes. His features were softened in the wavering candlelight. He was an imposing figure at the head of the table. His outstretched arms seemed to encompass Carrie and Garth.

Carrie closed her eyes too, breathing in the mixed aromas of roast turkey, the lingering rose scent on her clothes and hair and the warm, waxy smell of burning candles. In the silence she heard the wind whistle high around the chimney stacks, the creaks and clicks of settling timbers, the tiny sounds of clattering ware in the kitchen far down the corridor. Somehow it was right for her to also hold her arms spread wide.

"Carrie!" came Garth's voice softly as if from a great distance.

She slowly opened her eyes. The candles still flickered as before, the silver gleamed but yet every image was now imbued with a dream-like quality. Garth was reaching out a hand to her across the table. She clasped it. Closing her eyes again, she felt his father take her other hand. Their strength flowed through her.

Eyes closed, hands held, the three of them formed an invincible circle of friendship. And love.

Karl began to speak, his deep voice in perfect harmony with the peace of the moment.

"We thank you, Blessed Light, for this magnificent food. We thank you for bringing Carrie into our lives."

"Amen," Garth said as he squeezed Carrie's hand.

"Most of all we praise The Supreme Light for shining into Carrie's soul and for touching her heart with your love."

"Amen," said Carrie. Suddenly she felt lighter, warmer, almost as if she was floating in a thermal bath. Liking the sensation, she uttered the word again – "Amen!" – louder this time. The word dredged fervour from somewhere deep inside her and brought with it a flood of feeling so intense, so pure, that Carrie almost cried. It was as if, with that one word, she let go of skepticism and found trust in these two men. She kept her eyelids squeezed shut, not wanting the moment to end.

She felt them release her hands. A chair scraped on the timber floor and she heard Karl move towards her. There was no need to open her eyes to know he was beside her. She felt an energy flow from him and felt herself drawn towards it, needing to be immersed in his powerful presence.

"Give me your blessing, please," she whispered.

Both his hands gently touched her head, radiating heat and peace into her soul. For an instant, just one panicky micro-second, the old Carrie wondered what in the hell she was doing sitting here, eyes closed, being touched by a man who thought he had a hotline to a spirit. The moment passed as he spoke softly to her.

"Do you, Caroline Anne Enright, believe that as there can be no physical life on Earth without the sun, there can be no spiritual life without The Light?"

"I do."

"Do you promise to honour and praise The Light for the rest of your days?"

"I do."

"You have been touched by The Light, Carrie. You have looked into your heart and found the love and power of The Light there. It is now your life's work to spread that love to all the people you meet. You will honour the power of The Light and humbly accept your role as a disciple. The Light will bless your life and protect you from evil. You are now a member of Inner Light Movement."

"Amen!" the three of them chorused.

But Carrie's voice was weak. She was crying. Tears of pure joy. Behind her closed lids, a light shone inwards, into the core of her being. She felt strong, wise, safe in her inner glow. There were no dark corners now, no doubts or fears, no unanswered questions. And no going back. The Light was in her. She was The Light. Carrie had found her truth.

Opening her eyes, she saw Karl sit again at the head of the table, wisps of steam waft off the food, puffs of smoke drift up from the candles. Normal mundane things. But she knew, in her heart and the new-found depths of her soul, that nothing would ever be the same again.

★ ★ ★

Pearl's apple pie had the lightest pastry Carrie had ever tasted. She finished the last bite and sat back, replete. Satisfied as she had never been before.

Karl pushed his plate away and leaned forward, turning his black gaze directly on Carrie.

"Now, Carrie, Garth may have said that I have something to tell you."

Carrie nodded. "Yes, he said 'something special'."

"It is. It's The Light's work and that's always special."

The Asian girl came into the dining room carrying a tray with cups, saucers, sugar bowl and creamer. She was quickly followed by Pearl carrying the coffee pot. Karl sat back again and watched silently as they cleared the table of used ware and set out the cups and saucers.

"Your apple pie was delicious, thank you," Carrie said to Pearl.

The older woman smiled and patted her on the shoulder. "You need meat on them bones, girl," she said and then she left the room again, signalling to the young girl to follow on. Pearl obviously knew that Karl wanted to have a private conversation with Garth and Carrie.

"Tell me about your country," Karl said, turning his attention back to Carrie again.

Surprised by the question, Carrie hesitated for a moment. Where would she find the words to describe Ireland? An island of rugged coasts and fertile, incomparably green fields. A young nation, proudly taking its place in the European Union. A country of cities of the future and villages of the past. A race of Celts plagued by folk memories of famine and colonisation, driven forward by a need to create a modern, independent state. Ireland was all those things but it was mainly the people. The Irish. Those literate, musical, creative, humorous, ingenious people of Ireland.

"Ireland is its people," she announced. "The industrious, educated population. We're European leaders in technology, in the arts. Our economy is still the envy of Europe even though growth has slowed."

"Ah! Your economy," Karl said and then gazed at Carrie with increasing intensity.

She squirmed in her seat, knowing that for some reason she had said the wrong thing. She could not look away from him, hypnotised by his dark eyes.

"Let me tell you about your country," he said eventually. "Ireland's turning its back on spirituality. I have been told. In a vision. I heard the voice of The Light and it told me the Irish are worshipping at the altar of temporal success. They're rich in assets and poor in spirit. Old people are neglected, the poor are desperate, the uneducated worthless to a money-grabbing society."

"That's not really how …" Carrie began but a stern look from Karl silenced her.

"I sent one of my people, a member of ILM to Ireland on a fact-finding mission. What he told me when he returned pained me. Drug abuse, murder, drunkenness, immorality and a life style driven by greed. That's what your Ireland is now. Yes, there are still pockets of spirituality but Ireland is fast becoming a secular state with secular values."

His voice had risen on his last sentence and it seemed to echo around the room as the three of them sat in silence.

Carrie felt hurt and guilty, as if she were to blame for the modern Irish society which Karl Hemmings found so distasteful. She bowed her head and waited, not sure whether she was meant to answer or not. A deep sadness gripped her. Without knowing why, she wanted, she needed, Karl Hemmings' approval. She heard him get up from his chair again and walk towards her.

He put his hand on her bowed head and immediately she felt strength spread through her.

"That's why you were sent here, Carrie. Don't you see? It was meant to be. You and ILM. You and Garth. It's the will of The Light. Garth is to go to Ireland to spread the word and you are to be by Garth's side."

Carrie lifted her head and stared at Garth. He was smiling. "You're coming to Ireland? When? Why didn't you say?"

"He'll go when the time is right. And the time is right when The Light says so. I've already bought premises in your native city of Cork. We'll open our first café there which of course will incorporate our Communal Room. We'll bring The Light to the Irish people. Let us pray together now."

Carrie was shaking. Garth was coming to Ireland! This goodbye was just a temporary one. She would be able to introduce him to Mom and Dad, walk hand in hand with him on the banks of the River Lee, show him off to her friends. Be with him. Love him. Thank The Light! Oh, thank The Light!

"Amen!" Garth and Karl said at the conclusion of Karl's prayer and Carrie added her own heartfelt word of acceptance and faith. She still had questions but now she knew that the answers would come in their own time. In their own way.

* * *

"Does Pearl live here?" Carrie asked as she stopped walking and looked up at the lighted windows on the third floor of Point House.

"Most of the time," Garth answered.

"Why? Where else does she stay? Is she housekeeper here or … or something else?"

"You ask so many questions. You're very curious, aren't you?"

"Just interested. I'm interested in everything to do with you, Garth. You know that. But you can be very secretive."

It was cold now out on the front lawn. The breeze blew Carrie's hair back off her face and Garth raised his hand and gently touched her cheek.

"I'm not secretive. I don't ever want us to have secrets from each other."

"Then why didn't you tell me you were coming to Ireland?"

"You know why. It depended on your decision, and praise The Light, you made the right one. And before you ask me again, Pearl is housekeeper, friend and the heart of Point House. She raised me from the age of three. From when The Light first led my father to Portland. She lived down by The Old Port area then. She took us in, me and Dad, and trusted us to pay when Dad got work. That's why she'll always be with us."

"So she lives here too?"

"Pearl goes to the cabins or to the Communal Rooms around the state to talk to people. Most of the time she's here though."

"With your father?"

"Not in that way."

"I see."

They began to walk again, heading towards the upper terrace and the rose garden. Carrie felt tired. It had been a very emotional day, from leaving Mount Desert Island to learning that The Light had plans for herself and Garth. She breathed deeply, inhaling the perfume from the roses.

"This is such a beautiful garden. How long have you been living here?"

"Ever since old Mr Chapham died and left it to my father. Now, are you going to stop asking questions or am I going to have to silence you?"

"And how would you do that?"

Garth put his arms around Carrie and bent his head to hers. He kissed her, gently at first, then with increasing passion. They stepped closer to each other until their bodies were fitted together, hers slight and trembling, his strong and demanding. Garth moved away and caught her hand. She knew he was going to lead her to her beautiful bedroom and that he would come in there with her. She willingly took his hand and allowed herself to be led through the front door, the hall, up the stairs, along the corridor and into the Rose Room. The covers had been pulled back on the bed and the shimmery satin sheets were strewn with rose petals. Someone, probably Pearl, had prepared a fragrant nest for them.

Garth closed the door and kissed her again. Then he slowly and with the utmost gentleness undressed her, kissing each area of skin as it was exposed. When she finally stood there, naked and needy, he lifted her up and placed her on the rose-strewn sheets. Kneeling beside the bed, he touched her as if she were made from delicate porcelain, stroking her body from head to toe, until Carrie felt that she must drag him onto the bed with her. With shaking fingers she unbuttoned his shirt and pressed her face against his chest. He slipped out of the rest of his clothes and lay beside her. The velvet canopy enclosed them, the rose scent enveloped them, and as Garth entered her, Carrie knew in a moment of exquisite ecstasy that The Light was with them.

CHAPTER 14

Grey clouds and intermittent rain did not dull the sparkle of the day for Meg. It was homecoming day. The day she would again see Carrie, touch her, hear her, hold her in her arms. She checked her watch and the customer she was serving glared.

"I'm not rushing you," Meg smiled at the offended woman. "It's just that my daughter is coming home from the States today and I'm excited about seeing her."

A regular client in Curtain Call, the woman was surprised by Meg's garrulousness. In all her time coming here she had the curly, auburn-haired woman pegged as the chatty one and this dark-haired woman named Meg as the aloof, more stand-offish of the pair.

"How long has she been gone?" she asked.

"Too long," Meg answered. "The whole summer. It feels like for ever."

"They change, you know, when they go away. Don't expect her to be the same."

Meg leaned confidentially towards the woman with

whom she had previously exchanged only the minimum of conversation. "I don't care. Just as long as she's back on Irish soil and safe. Being able to see with my own eyes that she's alive and well is –"

She was interrupted by Lynn calling her to the phone.

"It's John! Take the call. I'll look after Mrs Duane here."

Before she had picked up the receiver, Meg knew what the call would be about. An apology. An excuse. Too busy to come to the airport. Knowing didn't make the hearing any easier.

"I'm sorry, Meg. Can't be helped. I'm meeting a potential client this afternoon. It could be a good contract. I can't afford to let it go."

"But you can afford not to welcome your daughter home. Where are your priorities, John?" Meg paused and before her husband had a chance to make more excuses she said goodbye to him. "I'll see you at home later. Bye."

She was still standing phone in hand when Lynn finally finished with Mrs Duane.

"I take it John's not going to Shannon Airport with you?"

Meg nodded and, only then realising she was still holding onto the phone, she put it firmly back on the cradle. It was twelve noon now. Twelve noon on the day Carrie would be home again. To hell with John and his stupid business, his coldness, his pre-occupation. To hell with John.

Lynn watched emotions ranging from hurt to anger cross Meg's face and she tried to understand what was going on with the Enrights. They were both turning into people she did not know. Or was it that she had been so blinded by her memories of the young John and Meg, of a beautiful couple so right together that she had idealised them? Accepted that their love was meant to be and embraced her own lovelessness as a punishment for not being Meg Riordan?

"Why don't you go off now, Meg?" she suggested. "Give yourself plenty of time to get ready. Maybe get your hair done. Is Tommy going with you?"

"He's back at school. He wouldn't be finished on time. The plane is due in at six. I want to leave early just in case traffic's heavy or something goes wrong."

"Do you want me to go with you?"

Meg shook her head. "Thanks, Lynn, but you'd better look after Curtain Call. Siobhán Farrell will be at the airport to meet Trina anyway. I won't be alone. And yes, I think it's a good idea to get my hair done. If it's okay with you I'll go now."

Lynn watched as Meg put on her jacket and got her bag. There was a firmness about her, a decisiveness in her movements totally alien to the person Meg had been, a woman so quiet and gentle that it was often easy to forget she was in the room, a wraith, a beautiful shadow. On impulse, Lynn walked over to her and hugged her.

"I'm sorry for the disruption," Meg said. "You seem to be getting the thin end of the wedge from the Enright family."

Lynn smiled but said nothing. What could she add? With those few words Meg had said it all.

* * *

John's footsteps echoed on the concrete floors as he walked the aisles of EFAS. Going from door to door, he checked against the spreadsheet in his hand. By shifting things around, he could free up two double units for Victor Collins, his prospective client. Collins had been a tough talker on the phone. John was not looking forward to meeting him. He seemed to be one of those defensive people who answered every question by asking another. Collins said he was manufacturing electronic components and that he needed secure storage. He had also made it clear that he was examining the feasibility of buying his own warehouse instead of paying EFAS for lock-up. Maybe he was bluffing. Looking for a better deal. All in all he was an awkward prick but John couldn't afford to let him get away. If this contract was in place for next week, then it would be a kick in the arse for Yan Gilmore. A nice welcome present. Putting down a marker. John Enright was the one who got contracts. The only one who could bring EFAS forward.

Folding up the spreadsheet, John walked back towards his office. Francine was at her desk, scribbling something on a notepad as she held the phone between her tilted head and her shoulder. She was smiling. Passing by, John heard her laugh softly. Bitch! She must be talking to Yan Gilmore. She now seemed to be reserving her 'girly' act exclusively for him. Hand on the door of his office, John glanced back at her. Wouldn't it be very, very nice if she turned her steely side on Gilmore. If she enticed and manipulated the New Zealander as she had him. Maybe he would quickly hightail it back to the South Pacific.

He had just sat down at his desk when Francine came into his office. She didn't bother knocking any more.

"Just letting you know I'm going to lunch now," she said. "I'll be late back. I'm bringing Patrick Morgan for a walk by the river after lunch."

"How kind of you. You're a regular saint, Francine."

Her eyes narrowed as she moved nearer to his desk and leaned towards him. "If you had the brains to look after Patrick Morgan yourself, you wouldn't be in the position you're in now. No forward planning, John. Bad move."

John just looked back at her and tried not to let his anger show. She was taunting him to get a reaction and he wasn't going to give her the satisfaction. That seemed to be her new tactic this week. Tease, insult and wait for a reaction. Why? Jesus, why? Despite his efforts he could not keep his silence.

"Why are you doing this? What do you want? I've nothing. Don't you know that? Just go away and leave me alone."

Francine straightened herself up and stood there, staring down at him. Her expression was suddenly, sad, demure. Innocent. "What can I do? As a victim of assault, I'm confused."

"Assault? Francine, you're crazy! You need treatment."

"So do you. At a sex offenders' unit."

John bowed his head, furious now that he hadn't kept his mouth shut. He had allowed her get her jibes in yet again. Had that man in Oakley Property Development Company gone through the same thing? Richards. That was it. Shane Richards. Had he too been lured and snared? Raising his head, John faced Francine.

"Is this what you did to Shane Richards? Is that how you ended up living in one of his plush Waterside Apartments? He doesn't seem to like you very much."

There was a momentary trace of shock on Francine's face. John had obviously guessed correctly. Oakleys were the developers of Waterside Apartments. He had been going to check but there was no need now. Francine's face confirmed it.

"Did you screw the property out of him or blackmail your way into it?"

She walked to the door, then turned towards him. Her face was now blank of expression. A beautiful blank canvas.

"You're in no position to cast aspersions, John. You're the offender here because I say so. And I'll continue to say so unless and until I decide otherwise."

She closed the door and left. But her perfume lingered on, as did the echo of her taunts and threats.

Taking out her employment records John began to read through them. He had been getting them out and putting them away again for the past few days, trying to decide what best to do. Richards had been the last boss for whom Francine had worked. Before that there had been her spell as secretary/receptionist in a medical practice. A consultant's practice in a private clinic. St Alban's Clinic. She would have fitted in well there. The reference from the clinic read almost identically to the one from the property developer. Francine C Keyes had been an asset. Efficient, reliable, responsible. It was signed by the consultant named on the headed notepaper. Professor Nigel Stagge. A neurologist with about a dozen letters after his name. So what had she got from him? A free medical check-up?

John reached out his hand to pick up the phone and then hesitated. It would be unlikely that he be put in direct contact with a high and mighty consultant. And it had been almost two years since Francine had been there.

As he was staring at it his phone rang. He considered not answering. It was probably Meg being sarcastic again just because he couldn't go to Shannon Airport with her to collect Carrie. It kept ringing, the shrill sound piercing his ears. Annoyed, he picked it up and snapped hello.

"Well, hello to you too, John. I see you haven't lost any of your charm. Willy Feeney here. I heard you were looking for me."

"Willy! Garda Superintendent Feeney now, I believe. Congratulations and sorry about the snappy hello. I'm under a bit of pressure here."

"I was in London when you called. Were you just catching up, John, or is there something I can do for you?"

Taking the lifeline offered, John said he'd just rung for a chat. What was the point in asking Willy about Karl Hemmings now that Carrie was on her way home? She'd soon forget all the religious nonsense.

"How about we meet up for a drink?" Willy suggested. "It's a long time since we reminisced about Hyde Street."

"Friday night around nine, The Wander Inn. Would that suit you?"

"See you then. I'm looking forward to talking over old times."

As John put down the phone it dawned on him that he might mention the Goodalls to Willy. The thug had not appeared at the house since the night he had followed Tommy home from the hospital last week and there had been no sign of that Breeze character hanging around EFAS since his mother had died but yet it wouldn't do any harm to ask Willy to keep an eye out. He could send a patrol car by EFAS at night just to make sure everything was okay. Without Ollie knowing of course. If Ollie knew his night-watchman skills were being monitored he'd be very insulted.

The more John thought about it, the more he realised how useful a contact Willy Feeney could turn out to be. There were a lot of things Willy could check out. Like Francine Keyes. Maybe she had a criminal record. Perhaps she was on file for a misdemeanour. Something, anything that would give him some leverage over her. There had to be a way of asking Willy to check out Francine without letting him know why. John was confident he could manage that. Bending the truth got easier with practice.

* * *

Francine had to look away a lot during lunch. The old man was drooling a river today. The housekeeper fussed over him, dabbing and patting and generally treating him like a child. He seemed annoyed by her fussiness and angry at his own need for her attention.

"I'm fine now, thank you," he said calmly enough but the frustration was apparent in the frowns which creased his forehead. "Could I have coffee please and one for Miss Keyes too?"

"You ate very little today, Patrick," the woman crooned. "Wouldn't you try another little bit? Just a morsel. I could liquidise it if that would make it easier for you to swallow."

"Two coffees please and close the door after you when you go out," Patrick said so firmly and with such authority that for a moment Francine regretted not having known him when he had been a fit and healthy man.

On first seeing him in the clinic over three years before she had thought him attractive despite his age. Admittedly most of the men who could afford to attend Professor

207

Stagge's clinic in St Alban's held a certain fascination for her. Money was a powerful aphrodisiac. She remembered feeling a tinge of regret as she had typed up his report, knowing that even the best medical care would not cure him. Maybe that was why she had secretly copied the report and made a point of chatting to him about his boring storage business as he waited his turn to go into the inner sanctum of Nigel Stagge's office. Or maybe that lucky chance had been down to her brilliant intuition. She was blessed with the gift of spotting opportunities even before they arose. She had managed to gloss over Patrick Morgan's hazy recollection of meeting her before. It was easy. He would never associate her with the clinic. She had been a flat-chested, large-nosed brunette when she had worked there. Until Professor Stagge had so kindly paid for her implants, rhinoplasty and a few more vital bits and pieces.

Francine frowned now as she remembered how lightly she had let Nigel Stagge off. She should have caught the prick for more. Veneers at least. He had paid the victim of his botched surgery a lot more to stay out of court than he had paid her to stay quiet. She had learned that lesson well. Shane Richards had not got away so cheaply.

She had forgotten about Patrick Morgan until later. Much later.

"Do you want to go for a walk today, Patrick? Do you feel up to it?"

The mood of frustration still hung over Patrick like a cloud. He narrowed his eyes and peered at Francine. "I can't understand why you're being so kind to me. Surely a young woman like you has better things to do with her lunch-time than baby-sit a dying old man?"

Francine sighed. Patrick could be quite acerbic at times. Not because of his illness. She guessed that sharpness and perhaps a touch of ruthlessness were core traits of his character. Sick and increasingly disabled as he was, Patrick Morgan was still a challenge.

"You heard me promise your nephew I'd spend some time with you, didn't you? I always keep my word."

"Isn't this EFAS time? John Enright can't be too pleased to have you playing nurse-maid."

"John has nothing to complain about. I make the time up and get my work done."

"I'm not criticising you, Francine. I'm giving you an out if you want it."

For a moment Francine wasn't sure how to play this scene. Hurt and upset, evoking his sympathy, or assertive and dismissive of his implied criticism? Probably the former. And it must be good. She worked on her facial expression now, managing to get a tremble on her lips and even a few tears in her eyes.

"Don't you want me to visit with you, Patrick? I do love our chats. Besides, the less time I have to spend in EFAS while John Enright is there the better."

"What do you mean? I thought you got on well with John."

"I-I used to think so too until … until …" Francine paused for a few sniffles and added a bowed head for effect.

"Until what? Tell me, Francine. Are you having problems with John Enright?"

She looked up slowly, a tear welling over and rolling down her cheek. "Don't say anything, please," she whimpered. "I need my job. I have a mortgage to pay. I'm sure he's sorry now."

"What happened? Answer me, Francine. Is he bullying you?"

Patrick reached out a shaking hand to her. She caught it and almost retched at the papery feel of his skin. Her stomach churned as his bony fingers seemed to tap out a Morse code message on her hand.

"I don't want to talk about it. I'm trying to forget. I shouldn't have said anything."

"Do you want me to talk to him for you?"

"No! I don't, thank you. That would only make things worse. Please don't ever mention this again, Patrick. It's too upsetting."

More lip-trembling. More glistening tears. More tapping of bony fingers on her hand. It was with relief that she heard the housekeeper come back into the room with the coffee.

"It's a damp old day, Patrick," the woman said, ignoring Francine as usual. "I don't think you should go out. You're a bit wheezy."

"I suppose you'd never stop nagging me if I did. Anyway I'd already decided not to."

The woman shot Francine a satisfied glance before leaving the room. Cow! thought Francine.

"Do you mind?" Patrick asked. "I enjoyed our few walks but it's getting too difficult now. I think it's time I gave in and got a wheelchair."

"Of course I don't mind. I'd like to just chat for a while. About anything except John Enright. Why don't you tell me again about when you were young. I like looking at your old photo album too. Will I get it?"

Patrick stared at her for a moment. His mouth was open as if to speak but maybe it was open because he was unable

210

to close it. She held her breath. She had thought she could handle this sick old man so easily. She had been wrong. Patrick Morgan was cautious. Too cautious. She wasn't sure that he had taken the bait about John Enright. In fact, nothing was as certain as she had hoped it would be at this stage.

Eventually he nodded his head. She took this as assent but maybe it had just been a twitch or a spasm. Before he could say otherwise, Francine went to the sideboard, opened the top drawer and lifted out the album with the tatty green velvet cover. She had a quick peep inside the drawer in case there was anything new there. One never knew when something interesting could turn up.

"Is there something in particular you're looking for?" Patrick asked.

So he was alert and aware. Francine put on her smile and turned to face him.

"Found it!" she said, holding up the grotty old album and pushing the drawer shut.

She shoved the cups and saucers aside, placed the album on the table and sat beside Patrick.

"Now tell me about your parents and your sister and about how you started your storage business from a lock-up garage at the side of your house. I love the story."

Patrick began to talk. Francine listened carefully, noting every word, closely examining the photographs. Every so often she smiled at him to encourage him. She stayed until the housekeeper finally insisted that Patrick needed some rest.

Satisfied for now, Francine made her way back to EFAS for some more mind games with the pompous ass John Enright.

* * *

Meg spotted Siobhán Farrell's people-carrier in the car park. Probably the whole Farrell tribe were here to welcome Trina home. Poor Carrie! She would have to do with a welcoming party of one. Glancing at her watch, Meg saw it was almost quarter to six. Just as well she had left Cork so early. There had been a stage while stuck in traffic outside Limerick city that she thought she would not make it here at all. Her last check on teletext before leaving home had told her that flight EI 106 from JFK was on schedule. Her legs felt wobbly now as she made her way towards the Arrivals area.

It was easy to find the Farrells in the crowd. They were the people underneath the waving *'Welcome Home'* helium balloon. All six of the family were here exuding a frightening amount of energy and excitement. No wonder Trina had such a bubbly personality. With a little start Meg realised the converse was true of Carrie. Her quiet intensity reflected the solemnity with which the Enrights lived their lives. Siobhán saw Meg and waved her over.

"Come and join us, Meg! They're nearly here. Can you believe it? Their time away flew, didn't it?"

Meg just smiled and nodded. Nobody wanted to hear about how she had counted the summer days and wondered why time had slowed and sometimes stopped altogether.

"Trina's bringing me an iPod," one the younger Farrell's piped up and was immediately challenged by a miniature version of Siobhán.

"No! I'm getting the iPod. You're getting a DVD player. Trina said."

Trina's dad moved to stand between his warring children. "And I'm saying any more arguing and nobody will get a present. Behave yourselves!"

Surprisingly the arguing immediately stopped and the children occupied themselves with waving the balloon and making faces behind their parents' backs. The public address system pinged. Meg strained her ears to hear over the volume of excited Farrells.

"Aer Lingus flight EI 106 from New York has landed ..."

Meg felt tears well in her eyes. Thank God! Thank Allah and Mohammad and Jesus and whatever other deity had conspired to bring Carrie safely home. Meg joined the children and pushed forward towards the front of the crowd.

"Take it easy. They'll be ages yet," Siobhán advised. "We were left waiting two hours for our luggage the last time we flew to London. Isn't that right, Barry?"

Her husband nodded agreement but continued to move forward anyway.

"And all this ridiculous security now," Siobhán grumbled. "I was searched. Can you believe that! Humiliating!"

"You look like a terrorist, Mom," one of the boys said and then skipped off before Siobhán could react.

The Farrell banter continued unabated around Meg but she didn't hear their words any more. All her senses were trained on the exit from the Arrivals Hall. Some stragglers from a previous flight came through, dragging wheeled luggage behind them, pushing trolleys loaded with baggage, carrying tired children and all turning expectantly towards the waiting crowd. There were hugs and kisses and some tears and then they were gone, back to their homes.

"How much longer? I want to see Trina," the mini-Siobhán demanded.

Before anyone could answer, the child had slipped under the rope barrier and was racing towards an approaching group, shouting as she ran. She leapt on a girl wearing a micro-skirt and a cropped top. With navel ring, spiky hair, purple shoes and a very loud laugh the girl could only be Trina Farrell. Just behind her, pushing her trolley, wearing jeans and a white T-shirt, Carrie seemed to move in isolated calm. She was with the group yet not one of them. Meg gazed at her daughter, at her slim figure, her long dark hair, her skin which was sun-kissed gold. En masse the Farrells galloped towards Trina but Meg could only stand and stare at her daughter, afraid to move in case this was a dream, afraid to blink in case Carrie disappeared. As she neared, Meg saw that Carrie was more beautiful than ever. More mature. She seemed to glow, her white T-shirt emphasising her tan. She was only yards away now. Convinced at last that Carrie was not a mirage, Meg moved to the end of the rope barrier and stood, arms open for her precious child. Her heart pounded as the daughter she had believed lost forever walked into her embrace. Meg tightened her arms around her and hugged her close.

"I missed you, Mom," Carrie whispered and she was again the little girl she had been. Meg stroked her shining black hair, touched her soft skin and gloried in the woman her little girl had become. Mother and daughter stood apart and looked at each other, finding each other again. Then they laughed. A bubbling up of overwhelming relief for Meg that everything was still the same and overwhelming joy for Carrie that everything in her life had changed.

CHAPTER 15

For the third time Tommy read through the list of instructions his mother had left for him. Most of it was done by now. The cooker was on and the lasagne was doing whatever it was that lasagnes did while they were in the oven. It smelled good anyway. He put the bread and butter pudding into the small oven at the lower temperature. Next he was to set the table in the dining room. Fuck! Taking the stuff his mother had prepared out of the fridge and putting it in the ovens had been one thing but setting the table was a step too far. And the old lady was fussy about cutlery and napkins and things like that. A take-away would have been fine. Just as long as Carrie was home, what did it matter?

Noticing that he still had his poxy school uniform on, Tommy went up to his room to change. He caught a glimpse of himself in the mirrored wardrobe door and did a double take. It was hard to get used to his short, monotoned hair. It felt more natural to have orange stripes. Just another year. One more year of boring school shite and then he'd be free to do whatever he liked.

Opening the door of his wardrobe, he slung his uniform over the top of the door. He might put it on a hanger later. Or maybe not. Finding his black T-shirt and jeans on the floor he shook them out and then put them on. As he was about to leave the room, he noticed his guitar standing in a corner against the wall. Silent, just like Breeze. He looked at his phone. Just to check. To be sure. No messages. No replies to any of his texts. Absolute silence from Breeze ever since his mother had died. A horrible feeling of self-disgust caught Tommy unawares. What had he expected? He claimed to be Breeze's friend and then he hadn't even had the balls to go to Ellie Goodall's funeral. Not because he didn't know when it was. He had read all the details in the death notice on the *Irish Examiner*. *'Deeply regretted by her sons Frederick and Jason.'* It was the Frederick part which had been the clincher. His fear of Freddie Goodall had been far stronger than his commitment to his friendship with Breeze. And of course he had promised his parents to stay away from the Goodalls. He could have lived with breaking that promise but not with the hatred he had felt from Freddie Goodall. Yellow, that's what Tommy Enright decided he was. A fucking chicken.

Quickly, while walking down the stairs, Tommy sent another text to Breeze. Just like all the others. **'How R U? C U L8R?'** He pressed SEND and then went to the dining room. Just as he was trying to figure out which way to arrange the cutlery on the table, his phone beeped. He grabbed it and opened the message. It was from Carrie. She and Mom were on the way home from Shannon Airport.

Suddenly Tommy felt a lot less troubled. Carrie would know what to do about Breeze. Carrie would know what to do about everything – about his future, what career he should be heading towards, where he should go backpacking, whether he should try the music business. She would listen and not judge, advise and not bully. It was only now, knowing that Carrie was less than an hour away, that Tommy admitted how much he had missed his sister's gentle influence during the summer.

He whistled as he placed knives and forks and spoons on the table. Then he stood back and examined his handiwork. It looked bloody fine. In fact everything was bloody fine now that Carrie was back. The Enrights would be a family again.

* * *

For someone who had flitted about so much and never really put down roots, Lynn had a lot of baggage in her apartment. Drawers and cupboards were packed with silly little mementos, pointless souvenirs, fading relics of a life half over but not yet lived. Feeling a knot of sadness in her throat, she began to energetically pull things out from their hiding places. She was annoyed with this new sensitive side to her nature or whatever it was that was causing her to look back rather than forward and was engulfing her in waves of inexplicable sadness.

She emptied drawers, cleared top shelves, opened boxes and bags and threw the contents on the floor of her bedroom. Then Lynn stood there surrounded by a gigantic mess. At her feet stood two huge cardboard boxes, one she had marked *'Keepers'* and the other *'Goners'*. Help! Where to start!

The estate agent told her she should remove everything

except basic furniture from her apartment. Tenants would want the storage space for their own clutter. She preferred not to think about those interlopers now. She hated the thought of strangers poking around her apartment, eating at her table, cooking in her kitchen, peeing in her loo for God's sake! But needs must. She couldn't afford to leave the place idle for the time she would be away. Six months. A year. Maybe for ever.

Taking a deep breath she began to tackle the rubbish piles. She picked up an orange sarong she had once thought chic and threw it in the *'Goners'* box. Next came a fluffy dressing gown with a big scorch mark at the back. She must have intended camouflaging the mark or maybe she had just forgotten to throw it out. Strings of beads, half empty perfume bottles, multi-coloured scarves, a woven straw donkey with a Mexican hat, oodles of handbags from her baggy phase, jeans flared and sequined, sweaters with appliqué flowers, all followed the sarong into the *'Goners'*. God, she was a magpie! It was as if she needed the evidence to remind herself that she had lived through all the fashions and phases represented by the piles of tat.

She smiled as she spotted the skirt of a navy suit. That had been from her power-dressing days when the get-up-and-go of the Thatcher era had inspired her to start a career in the insurance business. It had lasted six months before she had gone travelling again. She stooped down to pick up the skirt and then dropped it as she swooped on the pair of boots which had been hidden underneath. Clutching them to her chest, she walked to her bed and sat down.

Her Doc Marten boots! Closing her eyes she pictured herself twenty years younger, thin as a reed, auburn curls tumbling around her face, wearing a Laura Ashley dress and her big Doc Marten boots with the crepe soles and the black laces. The first time she had worn them had been that fateful night in the Grattan Club. The night she had first met John Enright. Or rather the first night John Enright had met Meg Riordan. Lynn had felt good in her flowery dress and oh-so-hip boots but Meg had been even more beautiful in her royal-blue sleeveless sheath dress, patterned tights and gold wedge-heeled sandals. "You could climb mountains in those boots," John had said and Lynn had not cared that it was not complimentary. He had spoken to her and that was all that had mattered. It was still all that mattered.

She ran her fingers over the leather. It was cracked and dry now, the laces were ravelled and the tongues were twisted and shrivelled. They looked sad, like tramps' boots abandoned on a municipal dump. Slowly, still clutching her Doc Martens to her chest, Lynn stood and walked to the box marked '*Goners*'. The sad knot was back. It rose hot and painful in her throat as she dropped her Doc Martens into the box, wishing that she could as easily throw away her sadness with them.

Knowing that the Laura Ashley dress must be somewhere in the jumble she began to sort through the piles. Just as she laid her hands on the white cotton with the little pink and lilac flowers, her phone rang. Taking a deep breath, she forced herself to smile. The caller would hear the smile in her voice and believe that Lynn Rooney was in her usual happy mood. Good old Lynn.

"Hello?"

"Hi! How's my favourite godmother?"

"Carrie! Are you home? How are you? Did you have a

good time? Oh, Carrie! It's great to hear your voice."

Carrie laughed, a lovely tinkling sound, and Lynn didn't have to pretend a smile any more.

"Good to hear you too, Lynn. I'm in the car with Mom and we're almost in Cork. I was wondering if you'd come over for dinner. I'd love to see you."

Lynn hesitated. She'd like to see Carrie too. Beautiful Carrie with her father's dark eyes and her mother's kind nature. She had loved the girl since first she had held her in her arms in the maternity hospital. But John was bound to be there too to welcome his daughter home. Of course he would. Lynn would again be the spinster friend. The outsider.

"I wouldn't like to intrude, Carrie. I know you'll want to talk to your mom and dad. Tommy too. I'll catch up with you tomorrow."

"Aw, come on, Lynn! Please? I brought you a present and Mom says to tell you there's a bread and butter pudding for dessert."

Lynn knew she would seem churlish now if she refused to go. She'd stay just for a little while and make sure she didn't look at John too much. And she would never make the mistake of touching him again.

"Okay," she agreed. "I've some tidying to finish here and I'll be over then."

"Cool. See you soon. Bye!"

Lynn put down the phone, went to the rubbish box, pulled out her Doc Martens and dropped them into the *'Keepers'* box. She would not get rid of them until she could think of John Enright without having her heart beat faster and her palms get sweaty. That calm and peaceful time was nowhere in sight. Not yet.

* * *

John was trying to concentrate on the costing for the Victor Collins contract but the fact that Francine was still in reception was disturbing him. With a perverse kind of honesty, she made up for the time she spent with Patrick Morgan by working late. She was on the phone now. Her voice, low and teasing, was barely audible through the closed office door. He was tempted to pick up his phone. He could, if he really wanted to, listen in on her conversation. He told himself he wouldn't stoop that low but the truth was that she would hear the click on the line and know that he was eavesdropping. Besides, he didn't have to listen in to know that she was talking to Yan Gilmore. She reserved her special little-girl tone for him. At least there was that satisfaction. Francine Keyes was working on destroying Yan Gilmore too.

Looking at the figures on his Excel sheet again, John decided he had cut as many corners as he could for Victor Collins. If he wouldn't accept this offer he could take a hike. Collins seemed to think that he would be doing EFAS a favour by allowing them to store his components. And he had so many demands. Twenty-four hour access, controlled temperature and humidity, and the use of the forklift to load containers when he had a batch ready for transport. Except that John needed this contract to shove in Gilmore's face, he'd tell Collins go to hell. And the funny thing was, his components were only for washing machines and dishwashers. It wasn't as if they were top secret weapons. Fucking washing machines and Collins carried on as if they were life or death. Maybe it would be better if Victor did indeed buy his own warehouse as he had said he might. The man was a pain in the arse.

John was just shutting down his computer when his mobile rang.

"Dad, Carrie and Mom will be here soon. Are you nearly ready to come home?"

"I'm on my way, Tommy. See you in ten minutes."

Switching off his phone, John felt relief that his son had rung him. He hadn't noticed how late it was getting. Meg would never forgive him if he wasn't at home to welcome Carrie. As he passed through reception Francine smiled at him but continued talking on the phone. He walked up to the desk.

"Make sure everything is shut down before you go," he said. "And let Ollie know when you're leaving."

She looked back at him but then laughed at something the caller said as if she hadn't even heard him. As if whatever he said was of no importance to her.

"No, no," she said into the phone. "It's just the cleaner. John Enright left early today to play golf. In fact he leaves early most days."

She stared at John and there was a challenge in her gaze. He could, of course, take the phone and tell Yan Gilmore that Francine was lying. If it was Gilmore she was talking to. Her look said that she would trade tale for tale. He could tell on her, but she would tell on him and she of course had the biggest tale to tell.

Francine won the battle of the stares. John turned his back and walked out the door. He had intended calling on Patrick Morgan tonight but it was too late now. He had to banish the thought that everything was too late. Out of control. Instead he thought about Carrie. So like the young Meg he had met and married. Quiet, caring. So very calm. For the first time in as long as he could remember, John was looking forward to going home.

* * *

When Tommy heard a car pull into the driveway, he ran to the hall. He was disappointed to see only his father come in the door.

"You'd better take off your jacket quick and look like you've been waiting," he advised.

John smiled at his son. "Thanks for the call, Tom. I hadn't noticed how late it was getting."

"You never do," Tommy answered and turned to go back into the kitchen. He had just reached the kitchen door when he heard another car pull up on the driveway. He raced back in time to hear two car doors slam. Two! Mom and Carrie! John, jacketless by now, opened the front door. Father and son stood there on the doorstep, suddenly shy.

Carrie seemed to glow as she walked up the driveway. She had jeans on but she carried herself as if she were gliding along a catwalk in a designer gown. Walking behind her, Meg basked in the light of her daughter. As John watched them both approach, he had an instant of self-loathing. How could he have done something to hurt these beautiful, precious women?

He took a deep breath and banished any thought of that slut Francine. Even thinking about her defiled his home. He opened his arms and Carrie walked into them. Warm, fragrant, fragile like her mother, his daughter leaned against him and whispered, " I love you, Dad." John kissed the top of her head and told her he loved her too.

Impatient, Tommy hopped from one foot to the other. Carrie stood back from her father and threw her arms around the boy who used to be her little brother but who towered over her now. Meg and John watched as brother and sister embraced.

"I missed you so much, Carr," Tommy said, his voice cracking. "I was worried that you'd never come back."

Meg slipped past them and went into the kitchen. It was filled with the warm smells of cooking. A glance into the dining room told her Tommy had made a reasonable job of setting the table. Then she opened the patio door and went out into the garden. It was an overcast night but high above she saw one bank of cloud glow brighter than the rest. She raised her face towards the watery light and imagined the moon, silver and watchful, stoically waiting for the clouds to pass. Just as she had waited for Carrie's return. From inside the house, Meg heard the excited voices of her children, the even tones of her husband, the sweet music as they all laughed together. "Thank you," Meg whispered to the corona of light in the sky. "Thank you to whoever or whatever brought Carrie home to us."

Satisfied that her thanksgiving would be. borne on moonbeams to where it belonged, Meg went back into the kitchen and into the arms of her reunited family.

* * *

Twice Lynn had changed her clothes before deciding on her favourite red dress. It had been hard to find anything in the mess her bedroom had become but the red dress had been the only choice in the end. A cherry-red, bias-cut jersey dress, it always gave her confidence. It clung in all the right places and more importantly it glanced over the lumps and bumps. If ever Lynn Rooney needed a confidence boost it was tonight.

As she approached Sycamore Lawn she saw that both cars were in the Enright driveway. Meg and Carrie were back from the airport. She would have to park behind Meg's car now and that would leave her near the road. Better for a quick getaway.

There was someone standing near the gateway as she swung in. A loutish-looking guy in a leather jacket. He began to walk on as he saw her approach. Lynn locked her car and waited until he had disappeared from view up the street. There was something threatening about the way he walked with his hands stuffed into his pockets and his chest puffed out that made Lynn remember Tommy being followed by a thug.

The moment Lynn pressed the doorbell, Tommy came barrelling out through the hallway and flung the door open. Lynn did a double take. His hair was cut short and dark brown. No orange streaks. No hoops, loops or studs. No visible ones anyway.

"I like your new look, Tom," she said as he led her towards the kitchen.

"It's not mine," he said over his shoulder. "This is the clone look. Designed by parents and teachers."

When Lynn stepped into the kitchen, it reminded her a little of the chaos she had left behind in her own bedroom. Except that this was a happy mess. Open suitcases littered the floor and bags were strewn on chairs and on the kitchen table. Meg was standing by the cooker, her eyes shining as she gazed at her family. Carrie was kneeling on the floor, poking through things in a case and John was sitting at the table, looking handsome in what was obviously a brand-new sweater.

"Found it!" Carrie said and stood up holding an eight by ten photograph in her hand. When she saw Lynn standing at the door she rushed to her and threw her arms around her. "Lynn! Thank you for coming round. It wouldn't have been a proper welcome home without you here!"

"You look stunning," Lynn said and she meant it. Over the course of the summer, Carrie Enright's natural beauty seemed to have blossomed. The golden hue of her skin emphasised her dark eyes. John's eyes. She seemed to glow with health and happiness.

"This is Garth," Carrie said as she held up the photograph in her hand.

They all crowded round, looking at the image of a blonde-haired, blue-eyed young man. Karl Hemmings' son. A stereotypical all-American boy. Lynn had seen many like him on her travels. Surfing, showing off their well-muscled bodies on the beaches, lounging in hotel lobbies, stretching their long legs across the aisles on planes. Confident, brash, sometimes loud and pushy.

"He's handsome, Carr. Would he be the reason you seem to have a glow about you?"

Carrie lowered her eyelids and blushed prettily. "You could be right, Lynn. I'll tell you all about him after dinner."

"He looks much more handsome there than in the phone picture you sent," Meg remarked.

Lynn caught a look of surprise cross John's face and she knew that he had not seen the camera-phone shot of Garth.

"Bet he never skipped school or said a fuck in his life," Tommy said sulkily and they all laughed at the words from the boy who looked like a man but still thought like a child.

"Your present, Lynn," Carrie said, handing her a bulky carrier bag. Lynn took out big furry slippers shaped like moose heads and, laughing, slipped out of her high heels and put on the fluffy moose heads with the felt antlers. They were warm and funny and very Lynn.

"Dinner's ready," Meg announced.

Together they all trooped into the dining room where candlelight cast a warm glow over the ebony table. Lynn sat with Carrie on her right-hand side and John on her left at the head of the table. Tommy was seated opposite her and Meg at the other end of the table. Melon starter decorated with mint sprigs sat in front of them. John picked up his spoon.

"*Bon appétit* to everyone and welcome home, Carrie! It's great to have you back."

"Let us praise The Light for the gift of food," Carrie said. "Join hands, please."

Carrie caught Meg's hand and Lynn's and stared at her father and Tommy until they too reached out their hands. Tommy's lips were moving as if to speak. Judging by the shape of his mouth whatever he wanted to say began with 'F'. Meg glared at him and his words remained unspoken. Lynn's fingers began to shake as John reached for her hand. Then his fingers were around hers, warm and strong, his head bowed as he listened to Carrie's soft voice.

"Thanks for this wonderful food and for giving me such

a loving family. All praise to The Light. Amen."

"Amen!" Lynn chorused and dragged her hand away from John's before he noticed that it was shaking. Before Meg noticed that she was breathing quickly. Elegant Meg in her well-cut cream blouse and brown pencil skirt. Crazy Lynn in the red dress that now felt vulgar and the big furry slippers. A replay of the Grattan Club. But this time there would be no endless days and nights of hoping, no tears at the rejection. This time Lynn would face the reality.

"I think I should tell you all my plans," she announced. "I'm going on a world tour. I've already talked to you about the idea, Meg, but I've arranged everything now. I'll be letting my apartment for six months. That'll cover my mortgage. I'll be off next week. Hong Kong, Dubai, Australia. The world's my oyster."

"Next week! But what about Curtain Call? Couldn't you wait until I get someone to replace you?"

Lynn looked at Meg's troubled face and she felt guilt. Of course it was thoughtless and selfish to spring this on her. It would be difficult with the shop. But what was she supposed to do? Stay here until the day she finally cracked and threw herself at John Enright? The way her body was trembling now and her hands longing to touch him, that day might not be too far away. No. Lynn must run. As far and as fast as possible.

" I have an announcement too," said Carrie. "I'm not going back to college."

Lynn heard John's sharp intake of breath. Tommy too was staring. Only Meg seemed to be oblivious to the import of Carrie's announcement.

"Have you left your common sense in Maine?" John

asked. "Of course you're going back to college. What else would you do?"

"I have plans. Big plans. A lot more important than a degree I don't really want."

Meg suddenly woke up from her euphoria. "You need a degree, Carrie. You can't get any work now without one. But this is no time for decision-making anyway."

"*I* have an announcement, " Tommy said. "I'm bloody starving!"

They all tucked into their food then but as Meg looked around the table at the people she loved most she knew instinctively that the announcing had only just begun.

CHAPTER 16

Dessert finished, Meg went to the kitchen to make coffee. As the percolator bubbled she stood with her back to the counter and watched her daughter through the open dining-room door. Carrie's face was animated as she showed a signed copy of Stephen King's 1974 novel *Carrie* to the others. Her expression was wistful as she told the story about her day in Bangor, Maine, where Stephen King had a home, and about how Garth had surprised her with this very special present. There was no doubt that Carrie Enright was in love.

"What's all this about Inner Light Movement?" Tommy asked, peering at the logo printed on Carrie's T-shirt.

"I've joined the movement. I'm a member now. Praise The Light."

"Electric light, is it? Or sunlight? Or maybe you're just a bit light-headed," Tommy sniggered trying to sound scathing but there was a hint of nervousness in his voice.

"I've pledged to spend my life giving honour and praise to The Light."

"For fuck's sake, Carr! You sound spaced out."

John and Lynn exchanged puzzled looks. They wouldn't have put it the same way as Tommy but they certainly both thought Carrie did sound strange.

"How do you mean you've joined the movement ?" John asked quietly. "Is this why you're talking about giving up college? What commitment have you made to Karl Hemmings?"

Carrie got up and came to stand by her father's side. For the first time Lynn detected a fanatical glow in Carrie's eyes and her stomach gave a nervous twist. Fragments of half-remembered cult stories floated in her head. All with horrible endings.

"My commitment was made to The Light. It's the life force, the power that creates us, that created the Universe. Each of us is born because The Light planned our existence and Its spirit is in each of us. Karl Hemmings has the special gift of communicating with The Light. I was blessed by Karl through the laying on of hands."

"You mean the old man touched you up?" said Tom.

"Be quiet, Tom!" John said impatiently. "You didn't answer me, Carrie. Are you giving up your education to follow this Hemmings person? Have you been forced into a decision?"

Meg sighed as she pushed herself away from the counter and walked towards the dining room. She sensed the beginnings of a family row. She could not allow that to happen tonight , no matter how strange Carrie's ideas seemed to have become. There should be nothing but joy on the night Carrie had come home to them.

"Who's for coffee?" she asked brightly but only Lynn and Tommy answered.

Carrie and John were still staring at each other, he angry and she intense.

"I wasn't forced into anything, Dad. I took the whole summer to think about it. I was sceptical, like you, for a long time until I was blessed. It was the best experience of my life. I felt peace like I'd never known before. ILM are good people. They're kind and —"

"And they're led by a man with a history of alcoholism who at one time planned to murder his son. And from what I can gather, he's making a nice living out of his Light scheme."

"Cool!" Tommy managed to say before John silenced him again with a glare.

"Coffee, John?" Meg asked and the tone of her voice carried a warning.

Lynn squirmed in her seat. She felt more uncomfortable than ever now. She was sitting here in her moose slippers and red dress at the heart of a family crisis. Her left side seemed to crackle with the electricity of John's anger. Or maybe it was fear that radiated from him. Lynn too felt fear for Carrie. Had the girl completely lost her reason over there in Maine? What was all this fanatical talk about and why was she giving up college? Lynn heard a shuddering sigh and she knew that John was letting go his anger.

"Yes. I'll have a coffee please, Meg," he said. "Sit down, Carrie. We'll talk about this another time. Not now."

As Carrie went back to her chair, Lynn's face reddened in embarrassment. John meant not in front of her. The family would discuss Carrie's religious turn of mind in private. When pathetic old hanger-on Lynn was gone. To hell with him! She stood up so quickly that her chair almost fell over.

"You'll all have to excuse me. I must go now."

She turned to Meg to thank her for the dinner but before she could say anything, Carrie was reaching for her hand, begging her to stay.

"No, Carr. I can't. I've loads to do. Besides, you've things to discuss as a family. I don't want to be in the way."

"Please stay, Lynn. Have a coffee anyway," Meg pleaded.

Lynn knew she was being used as a buffer between the besotted daughter and the angry father. And that she would not do. Not even for Carrie.

"Sorry. Must go. 'Night all."

As soon as she moved, the moose antlers on her left slipper tangled in the leg of her chair. John caught her arm in a firm grip to prevent her falling and then he kept his hand there, burning into her skin, sending tingles right through her.

"Please stay, Lynn. You're part of our family too. After all, I've known you for as long as I've known Meg and longer than I've known these two heroes I call my children. We'd all like you to finish dinner with us."

Lynn sat because her legs refused to hold her up. John smiled at her and for an instant she felt there was no one in the room except the two of them. Meg began to pour coffee and hand it around.

"Is The Light banned from the table so?" Tommy asked. "Are we switching it off?"

"You'd better not talk like that in front of Garth," Carrie warned.

Meg almost poured hot coffee over her hand. "Garth! Is he coming here? When?"

"When the time is right."

Meg relaxed. That was vague enough not to be worrying.

233

Now all she had to do was to change the topic. She turned to Lynn.

"So tell us about your trip. Where can we expect postcards from this time?"

While Lynn began to outline her hazy idea of where she wanted to visit, John went to get the globe the children used for geography lessons when they were in Primary School. They cleared the table of ware and then spun the world. From Alaska to Brazil to China they each suggested routes and places for Lynn to see. As John lowered his head beside hers to point out Tasmania on the globe, Lynn was glad that this time she had not run away.

* * *

It was almost midnight before Lynn finally took off her moose slippers and put on her shoes and jacket. Carrie and Tommy had gone upstairs. They had a whole summer of catching up to do. Meg and John walked out through the hall with Lynn. She tried not to let her envy show as the three of them stood near the front door. She had lulled herself into a sense of belonging for the past couple of hours but it was Meg who would stay, Meg who would curl her body around John's tonight.

"'Twas a lovely evening. Thanks for inviting me. I'm sorry for springing my trip on you so suddenly, Meg. But you know me."

"We've bigger problems to think about than staffing Curtain Call," John said, nodding his head in the direction of his son and daughter upstairs.

Lynn glanced at Meg's impassive face and for once she

felt annoyed by her friends' apparent equanimity. Couldn't she see that Tommy was borderline delinquent, Carrie in the throes of religious mania and her husband grey with worry? Then Lynn remembered Meg's concern for Carrie when she could not contact her in Maine and John's almost uncaring attitude. Even as they stood side by side now, Meg and John seemed isolated in their own worlds. Together yet apart. And why was she analysing their problems when she couldn't cope with her own?

She smiled at both of them and opened the front door. But the smile froze on her face when she glanced outside. Walking onto the step, she peered into the darkness, then dashed down the driveway.

It was gone.

"My car! It's been stolen!"

John and Meg followed her and together they looked helplessly at the space where Lynn's car had been parked.

"I locked it. I know I did. I double-checked because there was a creepy-looking guy hanging around the gateway when I drove in."

"Was he low-sized, muscular? Greasy hair."

"I don't know about his hair, John, but that description sounds about right. He was wearing a leather jacket. Why? Do you know him?"

"Tommy," John muttered through clenched teeth.

"You don't know that," Meg said defensively.

"For Christ's sake, Meg, wake up! This is serious."

"He hasn't been near Breeze since the night at the hospital. He's just going to school and keeping his head down. Will you give him a break for once! Next you'll be blaming him for global warming."

"He drew this Goodall crowd on us. Filth! I should have given him a clip across the ear long ago."

"You should've been here for him. Maybe then you'd realise your son's not a criminal!"

Lynn's head began to reel. She could not decide whether having her car stolen or witnessing the bitterness of the exchange between Meg and John was the bigger shock. As she was trying to decide, John suddenly dashed to the hall phone, his face pale. Lynn leaned against the gate pillar and wondered what was going on now.

"EFAS," Meg explained. "John's priority. He's ringing to make sure the same people haven't broken into his precious storage business. Heaven forbid that anyone interfere with a roller-shutter door. John can't let a customer down. He keeps his promises to them. It's only his family …" Meg stopped suddenly and walked over to Lynn. "I'm sorry, Lynn. This is so inconsiderate of us. You don't need a domestic incident on top of having your car taken. What had you in it? You've your phone and bag with you, don't you?"

John came down the steps again, seeming a little less anxious. "I've just been on to Ollie, the night-watchman. Everything's quiet at EFAS."

"Wonderful! What a relief!" Meg said sarcastically. "Now what are we going to do about Lynn's car?"

"Oh my God! Oh, no!"

"What is it?" Meg asked anxiously as she watched Lynn hold fistfuls of her auburn curls as she always did in times of crisis. "Was it something you left in the car. Money? Your credit cards?"

"The keys of the bloody shop. On the passenger seat

with Curtain Call and the address printed on the tag. Shit! I might as well have written an invitation."

"Well, at least there's not much to take there," John said and both women glared at him. Realising he had been too honest for comfort, John took Lynn by the arm.

"You've had a terrible shock. Come into the house. Will I ring the police for you?"

"What about Tommy?" Lynn asked hesitantly.

"What about him?"

"Well, the way you were talking … I mean I don't want to get him into trouble … not that I think he had anything to do with the car being stolen …"

"See! Look what you've done now!" Meg hissed at John. "Branded your son a car thief!"

"I didn't say that!" said Lynn. "It's just that he was followed from the hospital by … I only … I …"

Lynn stuttered to a halt. John was still holding her arm and glaring at Meg. Fuck them! Her car was gone. The car she had arranged to sell for spending money while she was away. She pulled her arm away from John's grasp and took her phone out of her bag.

"I'm phoning the Gardaí myself," she said.

Ten minutes later, Lynn had given all the details to the Garda on duty. He promised to pass them on to patrol cars and to let her know if her car was found or any sign of the tough-looking man in the leather jacket. She mentioned about the keys to Curtain Call too. "I'll radio the patrols," he promised. "Tell them keep an eye out. And don't forget to let your car insurance company know."

Meg came to the door to bring Lynn inside.

"The shop," Lynn said. "The police promised they would

keep an eye on it but don't you think we should check it out ourselves?"

"You're going nowhere until you've had a hot drink. You look ready to faint. Come in."

They heard raised voices from upstairs as they reached the hall. John and Tommy were arguing. Embarrassed, Meg brought Lynn into the kitchen and sat her down.

"That'll be about the boy Breeze," she explained, nodding her head in the direction of the raised voices.

"Jason Goodall? I thought Tommy agreed to stay away from the Goodalls after the fright he got. You said he hasn't seen him lately."

"He hasn't seen Breeze since his mother died. A pity. They were good friends."

Lynn still did not understand what was going on here. How could Meg think it a pity that her son had broken a dangerous link he never should have forged? Lynn knew she was treading on dangerous ground but she didn't give herself thinking time.

"How can you say it's a pity about Breeze? What are you thinking, Meg?"

"You sound just like John. Judgemental. Narrow-minded. Breeze is a good lad. He looked after his mother and plays his music. What's wrong with that?"

"Jason Goodall has a criminal brother and father. They've intimidated Tommy by following him and now they've probably stolen my car. I can't tell that to the police in case they implicate Tommy. This is getting very messy, Meg. You'll have to take a closer look at where your son is headed."

Meg placed a mug of hot chocolate in front of Lynn and sat down herself. She narrowed her hazel eyes and peered at Lynn.

"Let's face it, how could you know? You don't have children of your own so you've no right to judge my parenting. It's easy to say what should be done when you don't have to take the responsibility. You wouldn't be as critical if, for just once in your life, you had somebody else to worry about besides yourself!"

If Meg had slapped her across the face, Lynn could not have been more hurt. It was as if a well of resentment had been uncapped and was spewing its fetid contents on their friendship. So Meg thought she had no right to speak her mind, did she? That she was self-absorbed and uncaring? All the invitations to share family time and the please-stays had been bullshit.

"I care about Tommy," Lynn managed to say. "And Carrie too."

"You think I don't?"

"I don't know what to say, Meg. We're all a little bit tetchy. I need to go home."

"I can make up the spare bed for you. Why don't you stay?"

"No, thank you. Could you give me a lift please?"

"I'll drive you," John said from the doorway.

Lynn hadn't heard him come downstairs and wondered how much of the conversation he had overheard.

"We'll look in on Curtain Call too, just to be sure," he added.

"It's alarmed," Meg said. "We'd have been contacted if anyone had tried to break in."

"I'm tired of telling you to change that system on the shop. It's very basic. No challenge to a professional burglar. Especially if he also has the keys."

"Suit yourself." Meg shrugged and with that gesture seemed to dismiss them both.

Lynn stood and for the second time that night she walked out through the front door of the Enrights' house. As she looked back at a solemn-faced Meg framed in the doorway, Lynn wondered if she would ever be back there again.

* * *

They had reached the end of the South Link Motorway leading into Cork city before Lynn allowed the fact that she was alone with John to sink in. Up to then, she had been too preoccupied by her analysis of Meg's mood changes. The more she thought about their conversation, the more she saw Meg's point of view. Lynn had no right to criticise her. The way Meg reared her children was none of Lynn's business. But then there had been no need for Meg to be quite so nasty. Jumping in feet first was Lynn's domain but nastiness wasn't Meg's. At least it never had been before.

"Just as well to check on the shop," John said as they drove over Patrick's Bridge. "For peace of mind."

"Even though there's nothing worth taking?"

John grinned wryly at her. "Sorry about that. Thoughtless. It's just that, in comparison to the value of what's stored in EFAS, it seems small to me. "

"I wonder would you say that if we had to restock. Anyway, how are we going to check? I forgot to ask Meg for her keys."

They had pulled up outside the shop by now. John put his hand in his pocket and took out a bunch of keys. "I didn't

240

ask either. I just took them off the key hook in the hall. C'mon."

The instant they opened the door the alarm began to beep. "That's great," said John as he watched Lynn input the disarm code. "At least we know the alarm wasn't interfered with."

But even before they turned on the shop lights Lynn knew they were in trouble. She smelt cigarette smoke. There had been somebody here since she had locked up. The fact that she had anticipated the shock didn't lessen the impact. The shop had been vandalised. Some lunatic had run amok with a knife, slashing, ripping and tearing. Shards of fabric were strewn around in a manic riot of colour. Bolts of material had been opened out and shredded, cushions ripped, blinds broken. Even the kitchenette had not escaped. Ware was smashed and doors hung off the presses.

"Did you have the alarm code written down, Lynn? Somewhere in the car?"

Lynn tried to drag her eyes away from the devastation but she couldn't stop looking at the slash marks, at how deep the gouges were, how much hate and violence was evident in the destruction.

"Lynn! Did you have the code in the car?"

"Of course I didn't! We memorise it. It's not written anywhere. They must have come in from the yard. You know the back door's not alarmed. That key is on the ring too and clearly marked."

John took in a breath as if to start a tirade but then, without a word, let the breath go and strode through the kitchenette and onto the little corridor which led to the yard. The back door was open and the contents of the rubbish bins were strewn all around.

Lynn followed him and then stood still just inside the door. She began to shake. Jesus! What had she done? This was her fault. Why had she been so stupid as to leave the shop keys in the car? All she had been thinking about was running away. Her mind hadn't been working properly. Her mind was never working properly, always on the could-have-been and what-might-be instead of the here and now. She felt tears begin to well. Shit! In addition to upsetting Meg, having her car stolen and facilitating a break-in at the shop, she was now going to start crying. She walked back into the kitchenette and for some reason began to pick up shards of broken ware. Anything to stem the flood of tears which threatened to flow.

"Stop! Don't touch anything. There could be prints. Forensic evidence the police will want to use."

Lynn dropped the piece of pottery she had in her hand. It clattered onto the floor just as the tears spilled over. "I'm sorry, John. I'm so sorry," she sobbed. She didn't see John approach her because her eyes were blurred but she felt his arms come around her. Lynn laid her head on his shoulder and cried for all the mistakes she had made in her life, for all the chances missed, for all the lonely nights and pointlessly active days, for loving a man she had no right to love.

"It's okay, Lynn. It'll all be okay," he soothed.

"How? How in the hell can it ever be okay?" she asked, still locked in her own thoughts.

"Well, you're insured, aren't you?"

Lynn took a step back from John and laughed. He probably thought she was getting hysterical. Shocked. Maybe she was but the idea of being insured against falling in love with the wrong man was funny. So funny. A great business idea.

"We'd better ring the Gardaí again. And let Meg know too."

"I'll ring the police," Lynn offered. "They should know me by now. You ring Meg."

It meant starting all over again for Lynn. The duty officer had changed shifts and she had to go through all the name-giving and details. Except that this time they were going to send a patrol car to the shop.

When she had finished, she looked across the ruined shop at John.

"Is Meg coming in?"

"No. She had already gone to bed so I told her stay there. I didn't tell her the extent of the damage. No point in all of us losing sleep."

"There's no need for you to stay either. The Guards will be here soon. I can handle it. You go and get your rest."

"Stop, Lynn! As if I'd leave you here on your own. I wasn't complaining. Why are you so prickly?"

"I'm not. And even if I was, I think I'm entitled."

As they stood looking at each other, Lynn's stance defiant, John's defensive, the shop began to swirl with the reflected blue light from the patrol car which had screeched to a halt outside.

The detail-giving started over again. The search and research to ensure nothing had been stolen. It hadn't, not even the cash float in the till. This break-in had not been about theft.

"Do you have enemies that you know of?" the Garda

asked Lynn. "Anyone who would want to get back at you?"

She shook her head in denial. One advantage of her state of suspended animation. She might not have great love but there was no great enmity in her life either.

"And what about your partner? Meg Enright."

John laughed as he answered. "My wife wouldn't hurt a fly, Guard. She couldn't have an enemy."

"And yourself, sir? D'you think someone might be trying to get at you? Miss Rooney's car was stolen from outside your house, wasn't it?"

There was a beat, an infinitesimal moment when fear registered on John's face. It was there in the nerve that twitched briefly underneath his eye, the almost imperceptible raising of his eyebrows, the downturn of his pursed lips. Little signs that only a lover would notice or someone who had dreamt of that face for over twenty years. Someone like Lynn.

"No. Certainly not that I'm aware of," John said, his strong, self-assured tone belying the fear Lynn had seen in his face. "Isn't it possible that this is just a random act ?"

"Possible but not likely. The car theft and this break-in are obviously linked."

Lynn shivered, knowing now that someone must have been watching her, waiting for their chance to take her car and wreck her shop.

The guard looked at John and then wrote something on his report sheet. His partner, who had been out in the back yard, came in. "They came in over the back wall. Obviously used the keys. That back door should have been alarmed too because ...."

He stopped talking to answer the radio which had begun

to hiss and crackle in the pocket of his tunic.

"C'mon, Mick," he said to his partner. "Back-up needed urgently in the city centre."

Mick quickly put away his notebook and biro, told Lynn lock up and go home and even before he had finished telling them the fingerprint team would be here in the morning, he and his partner had left the shop.

John and Lynn looked helplessly at the ruined stock and then at each other.

"Is that it?" Lynn asked. "Lock up and wait until the morning?"

"Seems like it. Sounds good advice to me. There's nothing more we can do here. How about I drive you home?"

"I want a brandy. A large one."

"That's even better advice. What place would be open now?"

"I've a bottle back in my apartment. A Christmas present. I thought I'd keep it in case my car was stolen and the shop broken into."

They both laughed, tentatively at first, then with more gusto. It was a great release of pent-up shock and tension.

They locked the shop and drove to Lynn's apartment.

After her glass of brandy Lynn felt giddy and realised the alcohol had gone straight to her head. .

"I think I should have a coffee. Will you have one, John?"

"Please. I shouldn't have had the brandy when I'm driving. Two sugars and —"

"Plenty of milk. I know."

"How did you remember that?"

"How did you remember boiled egg with bread and jam?"

"I don't know. I just knew it."

Lynn's hands shook as she got out mugs, milk and sugar. She told herself it was a reaction to the night's events but she couldn't fool herself into believing that. The tremors had more to do with the fact that John Enright was in her apartment. She couldn't see him from here but as she waited for the kettle to boil she closed her eyes and imagined his face. So handsome and strong, dominated by his dark brown eyes, his chin stubbly now with beard that would feel prickly to the touch. There were lines too, little lines of worry around his mouth and on his forehead. Mentally her fingers traced the frowns, gently smoothing them away. The thermostat on the kettle clicked and Lynn started. Her car was gone, her shop thrashed, her travel plans in tatters and here she was fantasising like a silly young girl. Pathetic Lynn! She quickly made the coffee and brought it back to the living room.

"This is a nice apartment," John said as she put his mug on the table in front of him. "It's quite spacious, isn't it?"

"I like it anyway. Which is just as well since I'm going to have to stay here for another while now."

"How do you mean? I thought you were going away."

"I can't, can I? Not for a while. I couldn't leave Meg to cope alone with all this mess in the shop and anyway I had depended on selling the car for spending money. The insurance will probably take forever to come through."

"Maybe. Or maybe the police will find your car in perfect nick. What about your airline tickets?"

"Provisional bookings. I won't lose much. It wouldn't be fair of me to run out on Meg now."

John drummed his fingers on the table. His head was

246

bowed and Lynn admired the silver streaks through the black hair. His shoulders were slouched too, as if he was trying to physically make himself smaller. To disappear. He looked up suddenly and there was panic in his brown eyes.

"I wish *I* could run. As far and as fast as possible. Anywhere would do. Anywhere at all as long as it wasn't here."

"John! You're not the runner around here, I am. What's the matter?"

As soon as Lynn had asked the question she remembered his reaction to the Garda's question tonight. That fleeting reaction which told her that John knew who had destroyed the shop and probably knew why too.

"The man in the leather coat. You know who he is, don't you?"

"I'm pretty sure he's one of Goodall's heavy gang. I told Meg she should put her foot down with Tommy. How he got mixed up with that crowd of thugs is beyond me. But she won't listen. Not when it's about one of the kids." He paused. "I overheard what she said to you tonight."

Lynn felt the pain of Meg's sharp remark again. John was right. Meg was very defensive, and not in a good way, about Tommy and Carrie.

"She was right in what she said to me. I haven't learned yet to mind my own business. I don't blame her. But why would the Goodalls be trying to get at Tommy?"

"Shit, I don't know, Lynn. I don't know anything any more. I don't know why Tommy hates my guts and pals around with filth, I don't know why Carrie is gone off the rails with this Inner Light stuff and talking about leaving college, I don't know why Meg won't talk to me. I don't know why Patrick Morgan went over my head and brought his nephew in to run EFAS and I sure as hell don't know why Francine Keyes is trying to ruin me."

Lynn stood up and walked around the table to where John was sitting. She pulled out a chair and sat beside him. Close to him, she could see the nerve tick underneath his eye again and she could almost feel his fear.

"I think you need to talk, John. I'll listen for as long as it takes."

It took a long time. Lynn tried to listen without comment. To look wise and understanding and to just nod occasionally. Passiveness became more difficult as John told her how Meg was gradually cutting him out of her life and the children's too. How he had worked so hard in EFAS and then Patrick Morgan had stabbed him in the back. When he told her about Francine Keyes she could no longer stay quiet.

"My God, John! You walked yourself right into her trap. How far did it go? Did you ... did you ..."

"No! I didn't have sex with her if that's what you're asking. And that's not a Bill Clinton denial. I did nothing she hadn't wanted me to do. As it happens, the door bell rang just in time. Just before I – well, before I did something really inappropriate. Saved by a moussaka delivery man."

"But you obviously did enough for her to hold a threat over your head."

"This is it, Lynn. Don't you see? I don't know what she wants. She certainly wasn't interested in the money I offered her. It wasn't that big a sum but I don't have much anyway. What could she want from me?"

"Jesus! You offered her money! Are you mad? That's as good as admitting you have something to hide."

"I know. But I'd do anything to be rid of her. She keeps hinting and threatening. I considered telling Meg but now I think you understand why I can't. We're not strong enough to take it. Meg's not strong enough. She needs to be protected. That's all I ever wanted to do. To protect her. That's why I chose her over ..."

"That and the fact that she was pregnant with your baby when you married her – with Carrie, " Lynn said so bitterly that she surprised both of them.

John looked quizzically at her before answering.

"Well, yes, that. But Meg's vulnerability appealed to my male pride too. You're so strong and so independent."

Strong and independent was the last thing Lynn Rooney felt at this moment. She was flattered that John had confided in her, shocked at his confession about Francine, confused about his criticism of Meg, worried about Tommy and Carrie. But strong and independent? Shit, no! Besides, she was sitting too close to him. The heat from his body and the smell of his aftershave was making her feel dizzy. She got up and bringing the bottle of brandy back to the table, she held it over his glass. He nodded and she filled both their glasses with a hefty dollop of drink.

"You're sure Francine is threatening you? It's not just guilt making your imagination work overtime?"

"I'm very sure. I told you the things she's said! And I'm sure about her last employer. I'm certain she blackmailed her snazzy Waterside Apartment from him."

"So what are you going to do?"

"I'm damned if I know. I'm meeting an old buddy of mine on Friday. Willy Feeney. You might remember him from way back. He's a Superintendent in the Gardaí now.

I'm considering asking him to check out Francine Keyes."

"I mean about Tommy. Are you going to tell the police about his friendship with one of the Goodalls?"

"You didn't mention the Goodalls to the police either, did you? Probably for the same reasons I didn't. Meg would never talk to us again if we did. And maybe she's right. For me, it would be shopping my own son. I couldn't do it. But it's also true that a good dressing-down from the Gardaí now might be the best thing in the world for him. I'm screwed whichever way I turn."

They were both silent then. Sipping their brandy and thinking their thoughts. A quiet descended on the apartment. A peaceful oasis in the middle of all the chaos. Lynn filled the glasses again without asking. They didn't speak either as, glasses in hand, they walked to the couch, nor was any word spoken as John put his arm around Lynn and she lay her head on his shoulder. They finished their drinks and, arms around each other, drifted into sleep.

CHAPTER 17

Meg woke slowly, as if she had slept very deeply and had to swim through layers of sleep before finally awakening. First the Carrie layer. A smile curved Meg's lips as she remembered holding Carrie in the airport last night, feeling the warmth of her daughter in her arms. Carrie was home, alleluia! Tommy, for now at least, was behaving himself, conforming, head down and attending school. The Tommy layer was more penetrable and she floated through. Then Meg began to feel the panic of swimming in deep dark waters with no sign of light above or solid ground beneath.

She sat bolt upright in bed and forced her eyes to open. The sound of water splashing told her John was in the shower. It all began to come back to her then. The shop! Lynn's car!

Meg jumped out of bed and ran into the ensuite. John had his back turned to her, shampooing his hair.

Rapping loudly on the shower door, she called out to him. "The shop, John! What was taken?"

He didn't hear. She opened the door and reached in to turn off the water. John spun around to face her.

"What the …?"

"What about the shop? Why didn't you wake me when you came home? How much did they take?"

John just stood there, shampoo dribbling down his forehead, his eyes squinted against the rivulets of suds.

"Get breakfast started, would you? I'll be down and we'll talk then," he said.

"No! Just tell me. It can't be that bad, can it?"

He reached out a wet hand towards her and touched her arm. "I'm afraid it is, Meg. Your shop was vandalised. Sorry."

He closed the shower door and turned on the water. He counted to ten and then glanced over his shoulder. Meg had gone. Ducking his head underneath the flow he squeezed his eyes shut and replayed last night over again. Lynn's head had been on his shoulder when he had woken in her apartment at five o'clock this morning. His arm had been around her. In sleep, her face was relaxed, the little lines and wrinkles of an almost-forty woman ironed out. A hint of a smile had been playing around her lips.

John shook his head now as he remembered how strong the urge had been to kiss those lips. More finely chiselled than Meg's. Asleep in his arms, Lynn had again seemed like the young girl, so pretty, he had met all those years ago in The Grattan Club. The one he had rejected in favour of Meg.

Angry with himself, he turned off the water and got out of the shower. Maybe Francine Keyes was right. He was just a lecherous old fool. Not that he had done anything to Lynn. He had too much respect for her, and Meg. But God, he had wanted to. It had taken all his strength to ease away from her and then get a duvet from her messed-up bedroom and drape it over her on the couch. She had just sighed and snuggled into the duvet without waking. And he had been glad of that. How was he ever going to face Lynn again? What had possessed him to confess about Francine Keyes? Lynn and Meg were like sisters. Maybe she would tell Meg.

By the time John had dressed and combed his hair he had made up his mind to ring Lynn today and arrange to meet her. If Meg was going to be told, he should be the one to do it. Satisfied that he was at last behaving in a responsible way, John went down to the kitchen to talk to his wife about her vandalised shop.

* * *

Pain woke Lynn. Her neck was stiff and her right arm cramped. She threw back the duvet, sat up and for an instant wondered why in the hell she had slept on her couch. It had all begun to come back to her even before she saw the two brandy glasses on the table. She had fallen asleep in John Enright's arms. Slightly drunk, shocked after the theft of her car and the shop burglary, stunned by his confessions, confused by his closeness, she had cuddled up to him and fallen asleep. Jesus! How long had he been here? When had he put the duvet over her. Oh, fuck! Had they? They couldn't have!

Lynn ran to the bathroom mirror and closely examined her face. There were dark circles under her eyes, a pinched look about her mouth and her hair was flat on one side and sticking out on the other. Not the radiant face of one who had a night of sex with the man she had lusted after for almost a lifetime and certainly not the face of a woman who would tempt a man to cheat on his wife. Angrily Lynn turned her back on her image. How stupid! As if she would have to look in the mirror to know! She was still dressed, wasn't she ? In the clingy red dress that had looked so tarty beside Meg's tailored skirt and blouse. And now her tarty red dress smelt of John Enright's aftershave.

She sighed with relief and disappointment and went to the bedroom to find something to wear today. Something discreet. As she weaved her way through the mess there, her phone rang. The low volume told her it was still in her bag. She dashed back to the lounge and rooted to the bottom where her phone always seemed to end up. *Meg Calling* flashed on the screen. Lynn's hands began to shake. What in the hell was she supposed to say to her? What had John said? Hardly that he and Lynn had fallen asleep together on the couch, wound around each other. Undecided, her finger hovered over the Answer button. The phone stopped ringing.

Lynn flopped onto the couch. She felt guilty. Something must have happened last night. No. The guilt came from what she had wanted to happen. Her phone rang again and this time she answered it.

"Hi, Meg."

"Lynn, I hope I didn't wake you. John told me you were both in the shop until the small hours. I'm sorry I wasn't there to help. I didn't realise until this morning how much damage was done."

"No problem, Meg. There wasn't anything much you could have done last night anyway except wait for the police. They'll be in this morning to take fingerprints."

"That's why I'm ringing now. I'll go in to meet them. I'll get onto the insurance too. You take a rest. You must be exhausted. Carrie said she'll go with me. You come in when you've had a good sleep. Any news of your car?"

"I've heard nothing yet. Maybe that's good news. At least they haven't found a wreck. I must get on to my insurance company about hiring out a car until I hopefully get my own back. I'll take you up on the offer so, Meg. Thanks. I am tired. It was all a bit of a shock. I'll see you later then."

"Whenever you're ready. See you."

When Lynn closed her phone she wondered at how readily John had lied to Meg and how easily she herself had backed up his deceit. And that thought reminded her of John's confession last night about Francine Keyes. It seemed John Enright was becoming practiced in the art of deceit.

* * *

John was on autopilot as he drove to work. He couldn't allow himself conscious thought, laced as it was with deceit and threat. It wasn't until he almost mounted a kerb that he dragged his attention back to his driving. By then he was heading away from EFAS. Blast! Slowing down, he pulled onto the hard shoulder and, noticing the direction in which he was headed, changed his mind again. He was minutes from Patrick Morgan's house. The old man would probably still be in bed but it was worth a try anyway.

There was no sign of Patrick's car on the driveway. John guessed it must be safely stowed in the garage. It was sad that Patrick would never be able to drive himself again. A little Fiat Punto sat there instead. Presumably belonging to the housekeeper. As he parked, John was conscious of being watched from inside the house. A grey-haired woman opened the door to him on the first ring.

"Good morning. My name is John Enright. I'm Mr Morgan's business partner. I wonder if I could see him for a few minutes, please?"

Hands joined together, lips pursed, she examined John from head to toe and judging by her expression found him somewhat lacking.

"I don't think so, Mr Enright. Patrick's resting."

"I won't keep him long. I know he needs his rest."

Still doubtful, she opened the door back and asked him to step inside.

"Just wait here. I'll ask him if he's up to seeing you."

She headed off towards the back of the house.

At least Patrick was up, unless of course it was easier for him to sleep downstairs now. Maybe his study had been converted into a bedroom. A sick room. A place of dying.

While John waited, he glanced around the hall. The décor had not changed in years. Probably the same as when Patrick had been a boy. It was dark and very traditional. Hallstand, telephone table, some black and white family photos and a huge painting of a very young girl crowned by a glowing halo and holding a lamb in her arms. He recognised her as the fourth century Roman saint, Agnes. The virgin martyr. John shivered, remembering how stories of torture and persecution of Christian martyrs used to scare him when he was a child.

John heard low voices now, one male, one female. A door closed and the housekeeper came back along the hall.

"Would you come into the front room, please? Mr

Morgan will be with you soon. He said to ask you if you'd like a cup of tea."

John had to smother a smile. She had made it very clear that, left to her own devices, the last thing she would offer was hospitality.

"No, no. I'm fine, thank you. Just after my breakfast. I'm sorry, I don't know your name ..."

"Right. Follow me," she said, obviously deciding that John didn't need to know her name.

The instant John set foot in 'the front room', he smelt it. It was faint but unmistakable. Francine's perfume, the one he had thought sexy and alluring but which now suffocated with its sweetness. So this was where she spent her time. This was where she lunched with Patrick Morgan.

"Sit there," the housekeeper said, indicating an armchair.

John did as ordered. The woman hovered over him and then leaned close.

"You'd better not tire him out," she whispered. "He's going downhill fast. 'Tis late in the day you EFAS people thought of coming to see him, isn't it? That secretary woman is never off the doorstep these past few weeks. He's not able for ye now."

She straightened up just as Patrick appeared at the doorway. John stood and had to resist the urge to rush to the old man and help him. Patrick's body seemed to be dissolving, folding in on itself, held upright only by his walking stick, but the head was still high and independence shone in his eyes.

"This is a surprise," the old man said, shuffling across the room and standing in front of John.

"I was just passing and thought I'd call to say hello. I hope

I didn't get you out of bed."

"I don't sleep much these days. Just pass out every so often. Sit down, John."

The housekeeper was still standing there, hands folded, lips even more pursed.

Patrick turned to her. "That's all now, Anne. Thank you. Unless Mr Enright wants tea."

"He don't."

"Shut the door after you so, please."

She gave John a last disapproving look and went, closing the door with a solid little bang. Patrick smiled. "Not the easiest of women to handle but Anne has a heart of gold. Now John, why are you here?"

John began to fix the cushions behind his back in order to give himself some time to think. How could he answer that question without sounding desperate? Because I want to know why you're bringing your nephew in to run the business we built together, I want to know why you didn't at least give me first refusal, I want to know why you're so friendly with Francine Keyes? Because my life's in chaos. Because I want you to tell me what to do.

John raised his head slowly and looked into the steady gaze of the man he had come to think of as mentor and surrogate father. The man he had forgotten to thank and now it was too late.

"I'm sorry, Patrick," he said softly. "I should have known you were sick. I should have come to see you more often. Been there for you like you were for me."

"Water under the bridge now, lad. No point in fretting about it."

"Is that why you brought your nephew in over my head?

258

Without saying a word to me?"

Leaning heavily on his stick, Patrick eased himself down into the chair opposite John. It had extra cushions and was obviously Patrick's designated chair. Still leaning on his stick, he inclined his body towards John and stared long and hard at him.

"I have my reasons for acting the way I did. Some of them have to do with you but not all."

Patrick's mouth tightened and frowns played across his forehead. He closed his eyes. For a moment John thought the old man was going to cry. The room was deathly silent as Patrick struggled with his thoughts. Not sure whether to speak or not, John just sat and watched the other man struggle. He started when Patrick suddenly opened his eyes and spoke again.

"When I realised that my battle with this disease was a losing one, I looked back over my life. As you do when it's almost done. And I was full of regret, John. I did my sister such an injustice. I used a little loophole in Probate Law to ensure she didn't get any inheritance from my father. And it was prejudice. Pure small-minded, ignorant prejudice."

"How do you mean, Patrick? That's the second time you've mentioned prejudice. In what way? Is it because your nephew isn't ...because he appears to be of mixed race ?"

"Yes. My sister married a man of Chinese descent. His ancestors had come from Canton in China to The South Island of New Zealand in the 1860s. A lot of them came that time to work the goldmines around the Arrow River. After the goldmines were worked out, the family stayed in the town which had grown up around the Arrow and integrated into the community. They were market gardeners.

Hardworking people. Decent. And my sister married into them."

"You didn't approve?"

"No. God help me, I didn't. I felt she had let the family down. You'll have to remember that I was brought up in an age of racism. Sounds like an excuse now but my opinions were entrenched from a very young age. I was ashamed of my sister. Our parents never knew. They would have disowned her. I did it for them."

"So you decided to cut her out of your life?"

"Yes. Until I realised my own life was drawing to a close and that I'd have to answer to my Maker. That's when I knew I should contact my nephew. Try to make amends. That and the fact that Yan Gilmore's the only relation I have, so therefore legally my next-of-kin. I meant to track him down, to get in touch but it was easy to forget while I was still strong and independent."

"But how …?"

"In the end Yan made the decision for me. He contacted me."

"I see," John said but he didn't see at all. Patrick Morgan felt guilty about the way he had treated his sister. That was clear. But there was something not right about Yan contacting his long-lost uncle just as the old man was about to die. Or had they been in contact for a long time without John knowing anything?

"When did Yan get in touch? How long ago?"

Patrick peered at John and a shutter seemed to come down over his eyes. They were blank, either through exhaustion or a deliberate attempt to encourage John keep his nose out of family business.

"Some time ago," he said vaguely. "Will you have that cup of tea now, John?"

John nodded. It would give him time to think. To try to find the better side of his nature and say he was glad Patrick could now be reunited with his nephew and atone for the cruel way he had treated his sister. He could say it but he was damned if he meant it. Patrick picked up a little bell from the arm of his chair and rang it. The housekeeper put her head in the door and then toddled off with her order for two teas.

"So your decision had nothing to do with me really, had it, Patrick?"

"I wouldn't say that. I've watched you over these past three years since I retired. You've been efficient and competent. More than competent. You know how well you've continued to expand the business. But I also watched you allow EFAS to dominate your life. You're obsessed with it, John. You spend most of your waking hours there. I made that mistake too and look at me now. I don't want that for you."

"Shouldn't that have been my choice?"

"Maybe so. But I was thinking of Meg too and your children. And you're not getting any younger. EFAS needs energy to compete with all the new companies springing up. It needs a young man at the helm. Just as it did when I brought you on board. Besides, you gave me no indication that you wanted to own the whole company. You've never broached the subject in three years."

Anne came back into the room, cups and saucers rattling on a tray. She must have anticipated the order of tea for two she was back so quickly. She fussed about, pulling a coffee table between them and setting down milk, sugar and a plate of biscuits.

"You've an appointment with the specialist, Patrick. Don't forget," she said before she left.

"I think she's warning me not to stay long," John said when she had gone.

Patrick laughed. "She looks out for me. And I appreciate that. I want you to understand that's what I'm trying to do for you too. There's something else I need to talk to you about. Francine Keyes."

John's cup clinked as he dropped it quickly onto the saucer. What did the old man know? What in the bloody hell had Francine said?

"What about her?"

"She's dropping strong hints that she's afraid of you. That she prefers to go into the office when you're not there."

John bowed his head. Patrick's stare was too questioning, his gaze too sharp. How much had Francine said and how much should he confess to Patrick? It did, after all, seem to be confession time for past mistakes and misjudgements. But Patrick's prejudice, cruel as it had been, could be understood in the context of his age and the opinions which had been drilled into him as a boy growing up. John now believed his own behaviour with Francine was inexcusable in any context. He looked up and met Patrick's gaze.

"Francine Keyes isn't afraid of anyone. I misjudged her. I thought she was a very able receptionist and secretary. A boon to the company. In fact, work-wise, she is. But now I think there's more to her than meets the eye. I'm beginning to wonder why she sought out EFAS and why she wants to stay.

I'll admit we don't have a very comfortable working relationship."

"Has she something on you?

John had to lace his fingers together to keep them steady. Had Patrick asked this question because he didn't know the answer or because he wanted to force John into an admission? Fuck! The lies and the need for deceit were getting more complex by the day. John had a moment's longing to be with Lynn now, the only person with whom he could be totally honest.

"Well, John? What's going on?"

"I could ask the same. Why does she spend so much time here? Is there something going on between the two of you?"

Patrick threw back the head that was now too big for his body and gave a surprisingly hearty laugh. "I wouldn't have had a chance with a woman like that, even in my heyday," he said. "She's after something alright. But it surely isn't me!"

"What is it then? Money?"

Patrick made an attempt at a shrug and his body trembled all over. "Isn't everything about money these days? Sometimes I feel relieved that my time is almost up. When I look around me now, I don't like what I see."

"Why don't you tell her to leave you in peace?"

"I want to see where she's headed with all this visiting of the sick. Besides, I think I may –"

He paused, startled, as the housekeeper burst in the door. She was clapping her hands together and tut-tutting. "Now, Patrick, you've had enough. Time to rest before your doctor's appointment. Chop-chop!"

"You see what I have to put up with?" said Patrick but he was smiling. He put his hand on the head of his stick again and slowly hauled himself out of his chair. The housekeeper offered him her arm and he took it. "I'll have to go now, John. Anyway, I'm sure you want to get into work."

John watched as Anne helped Patrick move slowly towards him. Patrick raised a shaking hand and laid it on John's arm. His grip was still strong, if bony.

"It's very important you remember what I'm saying now. We've come a long way together and I only want the best for you. I want you to be very careful. Watch your back."

John embraced the shivering carcass that used to be Patrick Morgan . It was an unspoken apology. Afterwards John could analyse the words, worry about how much Patrick knew or guessed. For now, he just felt sympathy and a very deep sadness.

When John stepped back the housekeeper smiled at him. There was warmth in her eyes.

"Thanks for the tea, Anne."

"You're welcome. And don't tire Mr Morgan out like this the next time you visit."

John smiled back at her. Anne had invited him to call again! Praise indeed. He felt even more ashamed of himself as he drove away from Patrick Morgan's house. And more confused than ever.

CHAPTER 18

It was lunch-time before the police had finished dusting for
fingerprints in different areas of the shop, especially around
the back door. They weren't in the least hopeful of picking
up any incriminating prints but were making the effort
anyway, just in case.

"These guys would have worn gloves," the senior Guard
explained to Meg. "It's a professional job." They questioned
her again about any possible enemies she might have and
then they left saying they'd be in touch if they had any news.

Meg watched a passersby stop to read the *'Sorry. Closed
until further notice'* sign she had put in the window. She and
Carrie stood in the middle of the shop and looked helplessly
around at the destruction.

"Where do we start, Mom?"

Meg shivered. She felt hatred in every slash and rip. A sick
revenge. For what? A warning. Why?

"Did Tommy talk to you about the Goodalls?" she asked,
then quickly added, "I'm not asking you to break any
confidences. It's just that your father thinks they may be

behind this and I'm wondering if he could be right."

"He spoke about Breeze. And you can forget any idea that Breeze would ever do anything like this. I've met him. He's a terrific guy. Someone who has The Light in his heart."

"For heaven's sake, Carrie! Enough of The Light talk! Let's deal with one thing at a time. Tommy and the Goodalls first."

Carrie stepped in front of her mother and fixed her with a level gaze. Hazel eyes regarded dark brown.

"Mom! I'm disappointed to hear you say something like that. Everything comes from The Light. It's in our lives every step of the way, no matter what the circumstances. Instead of feeling angry now we should be praying. Asking The Light for help."

For the first time since meeting Carrie at the airport yesterday, Meg noticed radical changes in her daughter. Yes, she was still her little girl who had grown into a beautiful woman but there was something different in her eyes. A glow. A fanaticism. Last night she had thought it radiance. The special glow of a first real love. There was no doubt Carrie had fallen for Garth Hemmings. But this was different. More like an obsession. More like Karl Hemmings' influence than his son's. Meg remembered Karl's thin mouth and hypnotic eyes and shivered.

"Praying isn't going to tidy up this mess," she said, more abruptly than she had intended. "But praying will let us find happiness in the work we have to do," said Carrie. "Don't you understand, Mom?"

"Carrie! You're beginning to sound like an evangelist. A fanatic. Of course I respect your beliefs. I always encouraged both you and Tommy to question everything and form your own opinions but now you sound like – like as if you're quoting Karl Hemmings. Not your beliefs but his."

A defiant, defensive expression crossed Carrie's face and for an instant she could have been Tommy.

"Karl Hemmings has changed my life. Given it focus. I was drifting, Mom. Just like you have always done. Karl helped me to take control of my life by putting my faith in the absolute power of The Light. "

Annoyed by curious people staring in through the window at them, Meg walked towards the kitchenette and picked up the two stools which had been thrown to the floor. She sat and indicated to Carrie to do the same. They were silent, each recognising something different in the other. Meg remembered her own frantic prayers when she had thought she would never see Carrie again, the plea bargaining she had done with a power she had needed to believe in at that time of crisis. She had said, and meant it sincerely when she had said it, that she didn't care what condition Carrie came back in as long as she was home. Sitting here, listening to her daughter spout drivel, repeating mantras obviously planted by Karl Hemmings, was not a reality she was now prepared to accept. This wasn't right. And yet as John, Lynn and even Tommy had been so quick to point out, Carrie was twenty-one. An adult.

"I can't say I understand any of what you're saying, Carrie. It just sounds too fantastic. You were lukewarm to say the least about religion and now you seem obsessed with this God you call The Light. What does Inner Light Movement do – besides serving coffees and listening to Karl Hemmings on radio?"

"We pray. And by that I mean we join together to give

thanks and praise to our God. We are so strong when we join together with The Light. We help each other. We help those in trouble by praying with them. We change lives for the better. I really feel I belong."

Meg reached across and put her hand on her daughter's arm. "I'm not going to interfere with your religious beliefs, Carrie. I know I've no right to. But what about college? You're going into third year now. Are you really serious about giving up your Arts degree?"

"I only did Arts because I really didn't know what else to do. I love English literature and I like German too but I was just passing time. I had no particular aim. It was as if my whole life has been a waiting game until I found Inner Light Movement."

"But it's a belief system, not a goddamn career! How do you think you're going to support yourself? What do you intend doing? Praying full time? Giving out pamphlets on the streets?"

"You sound like Dad."

"I'm worried about you, Carrie. You've changed."

"Praise The Light for that."

Game, Set and Match to Carrie.

Meg decided it was time to change the subject.

"When is Garth coming here?"

Carrie's defiant expression softened. She smiled and her eyes took on a dreamy, more natural shine.

"I'm not sure. Whenever the time is right. What I *am* sure of is that my future is with him. He's so good, Mom. Kind and considerate and very handsome too. You saw that from his photo."

"Yes, he's a good-looking boy."

"He's much more than that. I told you his father has bought a premises in Cork. Just around the corner from us here. In McCurtain Street. Garth and I will be opening the first Irish Haven Café there. So you see, Mom, I will have a career. You don't have a college degree, do you, and you've your own successful business. Why should I be any different?"

Bitter thoughts Meg had believed long buried surfaced. Why should Carrie be different? Because Meg wanted, no, she *needed*, her daughter to have the opportunities she herself had never had. The opportunities she had given up so that she stay at home and mind the child of her unplanned-for pregnancy. The child born six months after she had married John Enright. The daughter for whom she had sacrificed her place in Art College. There had been no choice then. She had paid the price demanded by family honour and the social norms of the time.

Meg looked down at her tightly squeezed fists, ashamed of the way she felt. She had, of course, had fleeting regrets over the years for her lost opportunities but never before had she felt such a profound sense of loss. And, yes, resentment.

Guilty, she stood, walked over to Carrie and put her arms around her. "It's lunch time," she said. "Let's go get something to eat and you can show me Karl Hemmings' building on McCurtain Street. Lynn will be in after lunch and we'll get this place sorted in no time then."

"With the help of The Light," Carrie said, hugging her mother back.

Meg ignored the remark and decided that, for now, the best way to cope with Carrie's obsession was by ignoring it.

★ ★ ★

Head down, Tommy kicked a stone ahead of him as he walked up the road towards home. His brain was full of all the crap he had tried not to listen to in class today. Useless stuff like photosynthesis and Shakespeare. Plants would continue to do their green thing and Shakespeare would continue to hey-bloody-nonny-nonny his way through the centuries whether Tommy Enright memorised the lessons or not.

Catching up with the stone he had kicked ahead, he gave it a particularly clever tap with the side of his shoe and curled it around the corner leading to Sycamore Lawn. Pleased with his kicking skills, he lifted his head to follow the curved path of the stone. He stood still. There was somebody sitting on the low front wall of his house. Somebody with his dark hair shaved at the sides and a backpack on the ground at his feet. Breeze! Fuck! Had Breeze come here to confront him? To tell him what a prick he was not to have gone to Ellie Goodall's funeral? Excuses began to form in Tommy's head. They pushed and shoved. Freddie had warned him stay away. It was Freddie Goodall's fault. His parents had told him not to go. It was their fault.

Breeze saw him now and stood up. Tommy walked slowly towards him. The closer he got, the more he saw the changes in his friend. He was thinner, older-looking. He still emitted that same sense of contained energy but it was more focussed now and more intense for that.

"Hi, Breeze. I'm … I'm sorry about your mother. I … I …"

"Thanks, mate. The ward sister told me you called to the hospital the night my mam died."

Tommy looked down at his shoes and examined the scuff-marks left by the stone he had just been kicking. He couldn't make his excuses now. Not when Breeze was standing right in front of him, the grief of his mother's passing etched on his face.

"I came to tell you I'm going away."

Tommy's head shot up. "You're what? Where to? When?"

"Slow down, Enright, for fuck's sake! One question at a time."

"Look, come on in. There's nobody home in case you're worried about that."

"I'm not. Are you?"

"The fuck I am," Tommy said with bravado but glanced at his watch just to be sure that Meg and Carrie would be at the shop for another while. Satisfied that he had a good time buffer, Tommy led the way up the driveway and into the house. Breeze picked up his backpack and followed. In the kitchen, Tommy got out the soup and sandwiches Meg had left ready for him.

"Will you have some? There's plenty for both of us."

Breeze looked at the food in such a way that Tommy knew it had been a while since he had eaten.

"If you're sure. I don't want to take your lunch."

"My old lady makes enough to feed an army," Tommy said and then could have bitten his tongue off. Had Breeze's mother ever made a meal for him? Had there ever been a time when she hadn't been rocking and pissing?

Breeze sat himself down on a high stool at the breakfast counter as Tommy heated the soup and got out bowls and plates.

"So tell me. Where're you going?"

"London. Where else?"

"And what're you going to do there? Do you know someone?"

271

"D'you remember the job I told you about? The guy that took me on in the building?"

Tommy remembered the half-arsed builder and his promise of work for Breeze on an extension. He nodded.

"Well, he has a brother in the same game in London. In a bigger way though. He's going to take me on as a labourer."

"And where will you stay?"

"I'll find someplace."

"What about your house?"

"What about it? It belongs to the City Corpo. They can have it back."

Tommy dished out the soup and they were silent as they ate. Tommy knew his first impression had been right. Breeze was starving. When the last sandwich was gone, Breeze pushed back his plate and belched unashamedly. Tommy pretended not to notice, even though he was secretly glad that Meg was not here. She might have said something about manners.

"Thanks, mate," Breeze said and Tommy didn't care any more what Meg would say. Fuck them all. Breeze was his friend, manners or no manners, criminal family or not.

"Will we go up to my room? Put on some music?"

It was Breeze's turn to look at his watch now. "For a small while. I'm flying out this evening. I must mosey soon."

Together they walked upstairs, Breeze looking around him curiously.

"I'm going to own a place like this some day," he said.

Tommy ignored the comment. He didn't understand it. He went straight to his CD player and turned it on. The sound of Thin Lizzy and 'The Boys Are Back In Town'

272

blasted around the room. Tommy straightened out the duvet and they both sat on the bed, listening intently for a few minutes. Tommy glanced around surreptitiously at the chaos and for once he was ashamed. His clothes were draped everywhere except the wardrobe, shoes and books littered the floor. Breeze, the neat freak that he was, must be thinking that Tommy Enright was a dirty fucker. He squinted sideways at his friend and saw that Breeze had his eyes closed and was playing air guitar, totally absorbed in the music.

Suddenly Breeze opened his eyes and stopped jiggling about. He turned to fix Tommy with his intense gaze.

"I came here to warn you, Tom."

It seemed to Tommy that even Thin Lizzy fell silent. This was it. This was what his parents had been talking about. Surely not? Not Breeze! For fuck's sake! They were friends.

"What about?" Tommy asked quietly.

"My brother."

"Freddie?"

"Yeah. Prick! But not just that. He's a dangerous fucker and he's got the Enrights in his sights."

"But why? What did we ever do to him? I know he didn't want me at the hospital and he told me stay away from his family but Christ, we never did him any harm!"

"It's not about you. Even though, for some reason, he hates your guts. Thinks you have a bad influence on me. It's about your old man."

"Jesus! My old man! Why? What has he done?"

Breeze was quiet for an instant, squinting his eyes and peering ahead as if the answer to the question was off in the distance. Then he shrugged. "I'm not sure. I don't have the inside track with my brother but I did overhear something about your old man's business. Freddie plays dirty. Has there been any trouble at EFAS?"

"No. But my mom's shop has been totalled and her friend's car was stolen from outside the door here."

"That's it then. They're putting the frighteners on ye Enrights. Letting ye know they can get at ye any time they like."

"I was followed home from the hospital by one of Freddie's gang the night your mother — passed away. Lynn saw the same guy hanging around here last night too before her car was stolen."

"She won't ever get it back."

"Won't she?"

"No. It's over the border by now and will have new number plates and a paint job done."

"Jesus, can you call him off? Why in the fuck is he interested in EFAS? It's nothing only rows of lock-up garages full of shit. What does he think he's going to gain?"

"I dunno. Maybe protection money. Unless your old man's not afraid of being broken into."

"EFAS is tighter than Fort Knox. Cameras everywhere. And a security man."

Breeze laughed. A cynical sound, too weary and old for his years. "That's no challenge to my brother and father working together. They're an ace team. Especially if they have an inside contact."

"Fuck! Who?"

"Dunno. Don't know if they have. But that would be my bet. That's how they operate."

Tommy was shaking now. What was he supposed to do? Tell his old man that Breeze's family were out to destroy him? Tell his old lady that her shop was wrecked and Lynn's car taken because he was friendly with Breeze? They'd crucify him. And maybe have Breeze arrested. He might even be arrested himself. The fuzz often got it wrong, didn't they?

Breeze stood up. "I just wanted to warn you, Tommy. You were a good mate to me and I don't want to see your family done over. I'll be off now. I must collect my bag from the kitchen."

They walked downstairs together in silence. Breeze picked his bag off the kitchen floor and hoisted it onto his back. His worldly goods. Tommy remembered that he had a hundred euro upstairs in a drawer. His last wages from EFAS. He was about to offer it to Breeze when he recalled how proud and prickly Breeze could be. Offering him money would be an insult. They were as far as the hall when Tommy remembered something.

"One sec," he said and left Breeze to dash up the stairs. He came back carrying his guitar, brushing dust off the case. He held it out to Breeze.

"Here, take this. I'll never play it well. You will."

"No. No, I can't!"

"Take it. You might make more busking than you'd ever earn building. Or maybe you might get gigs. You know you can do it."

Tommy saw the struggle on Breeze's face. He wanted the guitar but he was battling his pride. He reached out his hand and touched the case.

"You'll have to tune it and get a new plectrum but won't it do until you can get an electric one? I'd really like you to have it, Breeze."

Breeze took the guitar and held it in both hands. He smiled at Tommy. "Thanks, man."

"Just give me a call when you form a group. I'll play drums. Or be the roadie."

Breeze slipped the strap over his shoulder and then held his hand palm up to Tommy. They high-fived awkwardly, each wanting to hug the other but reluctant to make the first move.

"Don't forget to warn your old man. He can take extra precautions or call the cops. Whatever."

Tommy nodded. "Thanks for telling me. You take care and keep in touch."

Everything he owned in his backpack, Tommy's guitar slung over his shoulder, Jason Goodall, also known as Breeze, turned and walked out of the Enrights' house, out of Cork city, out of his old life and into a future he hoped would hold the promise of a decent life. The life his mother had always wanted for him.

Tommy closed the door and stood with his back against it. What in the fuck was he going to do about Breeze's warning? His first instinct was to ask Carrie but from what he saw last night she would just tell him look into his heart and pray. Her trip to America had sent her into orbit. She had gone away sensible Carrie and come back a head-banger.

He would have to decide himself. Weigh up all the pros and cons. He imagined telling his father. the Fuehrer would rant and rave about unsuitable friends and wasted money on school fees. His mother would be upset and probably crying.

Tommy pushed himself away from the door and walked upstairs. By the time he reached his room he decided that he had thought enough about it. He would never repeat what Breeze had told him. He couldn't unless he wanted to risk ending up in the slammer himself. A trumped-up aiding and abetting charge. It was all bullshit anyway, dramatic talk about inside contacts and protection rackets. This was Cork, for God's sake! And why would anyone, especially Freddie Goodall, have an interest in boring EFAS? No. Breeze had got it wrong. Probably unhinged by his mother's death.

Tommy went back up to his room and turned up the volume on Thin Lizzie. The noise left no space for uncomfortable thinking.

* * *

Just because John wanted Francine out of the way, for once she seemed to be at her perch in reception all day. He thought about taking her employment files out but knew she could come in the door any minute without knocking. His conversation with Patrick Morgan this morning kept repeating over and over in his head. Even while Victor Collins had been here earlier, finally signing his contract, John had been tormented by the fact that Patrick had not thought him capable of running the company alone in the future. He was tortured too by Patrick's questions about Francine Keyes. How much did he know of what had gone on between John and Francine? Victor Collins must be laughing up his sleeve. He had got an incredibly good deal from EFAS for storage of his shitty washing machine components because John's energies and concentration had been scattered in so many different directions.

Getting up from his desk now, he opened the door to reception and looked out. Francine was still there and it was almost going home time. He walked towards her, drawn like a moth to flame.

"Not going to see Patrick today?" he asked. "Don't tell me he doesn't want your nursing services any more."

She smiled at him. A slow lazy smile. Mocking.

"Jealous, John? Maybe you need a little tender care too. Upset about your wife's shop and her friend's car, are you?"

John stared at her, a sick feeling in his stomach. "What do you know about that? Who told you?"

"I have my sources."

"Jesus! Don't tell me you had something to do with that. Are you crazy? Criminally insane?"

She smiled again but this time the steel glint was back in her eyes. "You're a fool! No wonder Patrick changed his will. How could he leave this company to you? You'd run it into the ground in no time. For your information, Dan Shorten told me about Meg's shop and Lynn's car. You blabbed it all to him, didn't you? His mouth is bigger than Cork Harbour."

"What are you talking about?" John asked, gripping her wrist. "How do you mean he changed his will? From what to what? Tell me."

She jerked her wrist away from him and an angry flush began to creep up her face.

"Don't touch me again. Ever. Unless you want a charge of assault and battery added to the charges I already have stacked up against you."

"Oh, for fuck's sake! Just tell me. Had I been named in Patrick's original will? Did he tell you?"

"Wouldn't you love to know!"

Francine looked very beautiful at that moment. Her eyes were glowing, her smile brilliant.

"You bitch!" John hissed and she laughed

He turned his back on her and returned to his office. His head was reeling now. Could it be true that Patrick Morgan had at one time intended leaving his 60 percent share to John, as John had always secretly hoped he would, or was Francine just winding him up? Turning the screw even tighter. Fuck her! And Yan Gilmore too.

Distraught, feeling more powerless than he had ever felt in his life, John took out his mobile and texted the only person in the world he could talk to without having to lie.

'Lynn, could we meet this evening? Your place or wherever you like. Need to talk. John.'

He pressed the Send button and then sat and waited for a reply.

* * *

Lynn sighed with relief as Carrie went out the door of the shop to get three take-out coffees. If she heard one more 'Praise The Light', she would scream. She flopped down on a stool in the kitchenette. Meg was still beavering away in the shop, checking ruined stock against the stocktaking list, labelling and packing or discarding damaged goods.

"You're doing the insurance company's job for them, Meg! Why don't you take a break?"

Putting her lists aside, Meg came into the kitchenette and pulled out the other stool.

"The better organised we are, the quicker it'll all be sorted. I think we'll be okay, do you?"

Lynn didn't know how to answer that question. It depended on what they were talking about, didn't it? Would Carrie be okay? Would she outgrow her new-found religious zeal? Would Tommy knuckle down, do a bit of study and get a career for himself? Stay away from undesirables? He was a clever lad. He could be anything he wanted. He just didn't seem to want anything much. The shop? Well, of course it would be okay. They'd get their insurance money, restock and open up again. It would take a while but their customer base was well established.

"Lynn? Did you hear me? Do you think we can get past this awful time and be alright again?"

Lynn looked over Meg's shoulder. Somewhere to the left. She couldn't look directly at her. Shit! She had slept with the woman's husband last night. They had not had sex of course but they had shared something which should only have been between husband and wife. Meg's husband. She beamed a smile in Meg's general direction now.

"Of course. It's just a glitch. The shop will soon be open again, glitzier than ever. I'll take off on my trip and Carrie will help out here. We have it all to look forward to."

Meg bowed her head. Copper strands gleamed in the dark hair, highlighted by the shine from the bare bulb overhead. Lynn made a mental note to claim a lightshade from the insurance. She had always meant to put one there.

"I'm sorry, Lynn."

Meg's head was still bowed and the words had been spoken very softly. Lynn reached out to touch her friend's hand.

"Don't be silly, Meg. It's not your fault. Anyway, I have wheels again. The insurance company have given me a car for the time being. Well, it's almost a car. A black and cream Smart car with a white roof-box bigger than the car itself. It's cute! And I know the shop will come back better than ever. Cheer up!"

"No. I mean about last night in Sycamore Lawn. I was horrible to you. Practically told you to mind your own business."

Lynn's mobile beeped. A text message.

"Get your message," Meg said. "It could be important."

It was. It was from John Enright. He wanted to see her tonight. Lynn looked at his wife and then back to her phone. **'See you in mine around eight,'** she keyed in and sent.

"Just someone from my salsa class," she said, putting her phone back into her bag.

"Oh, yes. Today's Thursday. I'm losing track with all the drama. I 'spose it's the last thing you want to do tonight."

Lynn smiled, amazed at how easily the lies came to her lips. "No, Meg, believe me. I'm really looking forward to my class. I'll dance all my problems away."

"Well, enjoy it. I must ring John now to make sure he comes home early for once. We have some serious talking to do with our two children."

Meg went to the shop to phone while Lynn sat on the stool and felt ashamed. And excited. And deliciously alive with anticipation. It was an altogether new feeling for Lynn Rooney.

CHAPTER 19

On her way home from the shop Meg stopped off at the artist's supply stores. She bought the biggest canvas they had in stock. Stretched on a frame. Not the best quality but she was more concerned with the size. She needed something to stick in the shop window to divert people's attention away from the chaos inside. Of course she could just blank out the window, smear the glass with opaque white, hang a blind, any type of temporary cover until they were again ready for business. The truth was she needed to paint. She needed the release and comfort of brush on canvas.

Meg noticed that Tommy was unusually quiet over the dinner he shared with herself and Carrie. He sulked while Carrie said grace before meals and then allowed himself to wallow in the sulk afterwards. Carrie waffled on endlessly about Garth's home in Maine. A big grey shell with a warm rose heart, according to her. Meg would have asked questions except that Carrie didn't draw breath long enough to allow her. Tommy interrupted the flow.

"Are you on something?" he asked his sister and Meg

waited with bated breath for the answer.

"I'm high on the goodness of The Light," she replied.

That was enough for Tommy. He excused himself and left the table.

"I hope you're not going out anywhere!" Meg called after him. "Remember I told you we're having a family meeting as soon as your father's home."

"I'm doing my homework," he muttered and went off to his room to turn on his music again.

"You too, Carr," Meg said. "You'll be here, won't you? We badly need to sit down together as a family and talk."

"Yes, I'll be here. I'm waiting for Garth to ring. I'll tidy up after dinner. I know you're anxious to start your painting."

Meg smiled her thanks at Carrie and hugged her. She felt a little thrill of excitement as she climbed up to the attic and found her easel and paints. The spattered jeans and sweat shirt she had worn during her last painting phase were there too. It took two trips up and down the steep folding stairs before she had everything she needed, then another two trips to drag it all downstairs and set up in the dining room. At last, dressed in her tatty jeans and sweat shirt, Meg was ready to prime the canvas. She stretched her fingers and flexed them, then with a contented little sigh began her work.

★ ★ ★

Francine Keyes tapped the steering wheel of her car impatiently. She had been sitting here for the past hour, waiting for John Enright to leave the apartment block across the road. Something told her, that sharp instinct which served her well, that she needed to know who John was visiting. It had been a lucky chance that she'd spotted his silver Ford Avensis turning in here while she had been driving back from the gym. Could it be possible that John Enright had a bit on the side? A secret lover?

Patience failing, Francine got out and locked her car. If worst came to worst and she bumped into John, she could make up some bullshit excuse. That would not be a problem. She crossed the road and entered the grounds of Oriel Rise Apartments, keeping her head bowed but all the time scanning ahead and around her. It was a fairly new build, four storey, lots of glass frontage and landscaped gardens. All the cars in the parking area were modern and mid-sized. Probably owned by business types halfway up the success ladder. It was that kind of place.

The lobby was spacious and too well lit for Francine's comfort. She walked over to the postboxes, not sure what she was looking for but knowing that she might find something there. And she had been right. As soon as she saw the name Lynn Rooney, Apartment 23B, on a postbox, she knew the wait had been worth while. Of course, Meg Enright could be there too. Unlikely since she hadn't been in the car with her husband but a phone call to Sycamore Road would soon clear that up.

Francine hurried back to her car and drove to EFAS. She would phone Enright's home number first and then she would put in a call to Queenstown with her interesting news. She would have to keep the man from New Zealand happy. For the time being at least.

* * *

Lynn felt more relaxed now. Earlier this evening had been a frantic rush to tidy up her apartment, especially the chaotic bedroom, get dinner on the go, and fit in time to shower and change. Deciding what to wear had been difficult. John was coming here to talk to her as a friend, so sexy would not be appropriate. She went for soft and feminine. A fluffy pale green sweater and her good cream skirt. She brushed her hair until the auburn curls were tamed and sleek and then sprayed on a splash of Red Door. Her favourite. Both she and the dinner of stuffed chicken breasts had been ready and waiting by the time John arrived.

Dinner finished, John sat back and smiled at Lynn.

"I could have sworn I wasn't hungry," he said. "That was lovely, Lynn. Thank you."

"You must eat, John. You can't let yourself get run down."

"Just like my mother used to say."

"Hannah. She was a strong lady, wasn't she?"

"That's one way of putting it. She had to be, of course."

Lynn nodded her agreement and kept her counsel. Nobody ever needed to be as tough as the hard-as-nails Hannah Enright had been. What would she think of the son she had reared now, sitting in another woman's apartment while his wife was at home? That was easy. She'd blame the two women, one for being too weak and the other for being too available.

"You said you wanted to talk, John. Shoot."

John picked up his teaspoon and began to tap it rhythmically against his saucer. The clinks seemed to be a countdown to an announcement. Eventually he looked directly at Lynn.

"I need to know if you're going to tell Meg about last night."

"Tell her what? There's nothing to tell, is there? Although I'll have to admit I was a bit uncomfortable going along with the story that we were in the shop all night."

"What else could I say? Who'd believe that we just fell asleep here?"

"Your mother?" Lynn asked and they both laughed.

"Lynn Rooney, you're an amazing woman. My life's a mess and yet you can make me laugh."

"I've learned to laugh at life. The alternative's too dreary. Why don't we get a drink, sit on the couch and talk about the mess you're in? We can always set the alarm in case we fall asleep again."

Lynn's alarm joke fell flat. She was too full of tension, too aware of the man across from her to fall asleep. And surprisingly, joyfully, she could feel the same tension from him. They looked at each other and tacitly agreed to stay sitting at the table. John leaned towards her, his face pale.

"Francine Keyes was particularly vile today."

"What did she do now? Tell me."

John told her the day's events, detail by detail.

"Does it sound to you like she knows about Patrick's will?" he asked anxiously when he'd finished.

Lynn shrugged. "Maybe. She's spending a lot of time with him, isn't she? Besides, I'd imagine she's not above prying into private papers."

"There's something very odd about the relationship between her and Patrick Morgan. He doesn't seem to either like or trust her and yet he allows her call to his house any time she pleases. But yet I'm certain now it was Francine he was referring to when he told me watch my back."

"You're very sure you never met her before? Could this

be revenge for something?"

"I'm positive. I never laid eyes on her before her first interview. I'd remember. So why in the hell is Francine Keyes torturing me?"

Lynn shook her head. John was right. He was in a mess and none of it made sense. Why was Francine Keyes out to destroy him?

Lynn got up and made coffee. She needed it to clear her head. When she came back, she was seeing things a little more logically. She handed John his cup and sat again.

"Right. As I see it, Francine Keyes holds all the cards at the moment. We must find out about her. Tell me what you know."

John told her all, from when he had first interviewed Francine to when he had spoken to her last employer.

"And the one before that?" Lynn asked.

"A clinic here in Cork. You know the one. St Alban's. Two hundred euro a visit."

"And what do they say about her?"

John shuffled his feet and squirmed on his seat. "I haven't really contacted them. I'm not sure what I could say."

"Leave it to me. I'll think of something. I'll go to the clinic for you. And ask that Garda Superintendent friend of yours when you meet him tomorrow night. He may know something about her. The more we find out about the bitch the better. And now I think you'd better go, John. Meg's expecting you back early tonight."

They stood at the same time. Lynn went around the table to walk John to the door. That had been the intention. But somehow their hands touched, they drifted towards the couch and Lynn's head was on John's shoulder and his arm around her before they had time to wonder what was happening. They leaned into each other, taking comfort from their closeness, excluding everything from their little circle except the beating of their hearts and the soothing feeling that each had found in the other an oasis of peace.

* * *

At times Meg was aware of the vibrations of Tommy's increasingly loud music and the sound of the television which Carrie had switched on. But they were just background. Nothing disturbed her concentration as she lost herself in her work until Carrie came to say somebody wanted her on the phone.

"A woman. I don't know who 'tis. She just asked for Mrs Enright."

Meg wiped her hands of paint and picked up the receiver in the hall. "Hello. Meg Enright here." There was silence and then a click on the other end of the line as the caller hung up. Meg frowned, disturbed by the eerie feeling that the caller was trying to frighten her. She shivered. Car thefts and shop break-ins were playing tricks on her mind. Of course it was just a wrong number or a prank caller. Going back into the dining room, she picked up her brush again. Her concentration was total. It was not until Carrie came to say goodnight that Meg realised John had not come home early as promised.

"We'll talk tomorrow, Mom. May The Light be with you."

Meg smiled at Carrie as she left the dining room. She began to tidy up. Suddenly her painting had lost its appeal. It was gone midnight and John had let her and the children down again. This time their need was greater and the letdown more hurtful than ever before.

He would not be at work. Not at this hour. She could ring EFAS and check. She could ring John and ask where the hell he was. But Meg did not want to know. It was enough to realise that wherever John was, whoever he was with, it was not his wife or family. And for Meg, still shocked from the vandalism in the shop, worried about Carrie's change in personality, frantic about Tommy's possible criminal links, perplexed by the coldness of her marriage, John's absence was a test too far.

Tired, confused, alone, Meg climbed the stairs and fell into a troubled sleep.

CHAPTER 20

Even before he drove in through the gates of EFAS the following morning, John noticed that Ollie was agitated. The old man was pacing over and back in front of the building, his hands behind his back, neck craned forward and eyes sweeping the area. He looked very old in the morning light, the sun shining through his wisps of sparse white hair. With sadness, John thought the day was close when he would have to ask his night-security man to leave.

"Morning, boss," Ollie said, leaping on John even before his car door was fully open.

"What's wrong, Ollie? You're up to ninety."

"It's those shagging trees over there. And we've no surveillance on them. There must have been a botched job done on camera five. It's on the blink again. There was someone hiding in the trees last night, I know it. Look!"

Ollie whipped a crumpled piece of paper out of his pocket, flattened it on the palm of his hand and held it towards John. A squashed cigarette butt nestled in the centre of the paper. John raised his eyebrows.

"A butt? That's what's troubling you?"

"Yes. I smelled cigarette smoke last night. Over there by the trees. I know I did. My nose is sensitive since I gave up the fags. I shone the torch all round. Into the trees and bushes. I saw nothing. I went right up to the fence and called."

John put his hand up then to stop the old man. "I warned you before, Ollie, not to put yourself at risk. You should have called me. Or the police. Suppose there had been someone there?"

"But there was! I found the butt this morning. It's fresh. You can see that. It was lashing yesterday but this butt never saw a drop of rain. They must have been up in the trees."

"Come on – coffee," John ordered, leading the way into his office.

Inside in the office, John could see the old man was getting annoyed.

"'Tis like you don't believe me. You can ask your receptionist if you want. She'll tell you!"

"What! Francine Keyes? Why should I ask her?"

"She was here, wasn't she? You told her to ring the boss in New Zealand or don't you remember? She said our night is the day in New Zealand so that's why she has to come in here late."

John nodded his head. He could hardly tell Ollie that Francine did what she liked in EFAS, when she liked. "What time was that?"

"Just after midnight. I do my full patrol of the perimeter fence on the hour. Miss Keyes even drove her car over to the trees and turned her headlights on to help me search. She smelled the smoke too and she thought she heard someone laugh."

John was taking more notice now. Of course Francine could have been winding the old man up but maybe not. Curtain Call had, after all, been vandalised and Lynn's car stolen. Why not an attempted break-in at EFAS?

"You checked everything else? There were no fences cut, no alarms going off?"

"Nothing else," Ollie muttered and put the piece of paper with the cigarette butt up on John's desk. "Look at it."

John stared at the segment of cigarette. Squashed. Ground out with the heel of a shoe or boot. It must have been stubbed out on the other side of the fence – in Jacuzzi and Hot Tub Land – and thrown into EFAS.

"If you're thinking it was thrown over the fence," Ollie said, "you're wrong. I've put a mark where I found it in our place. There are little bits of tobacco and filter squashed onto the ground."

John frowned. There had to be an explanation. "Any customers in last night? I know some of them need to access their units at odd times."

"Nobody except Miss Keyes and that new client you have. Mr Collins. He just went to his unit, dropped in a box and left. Never went near the trees. Anyway neither of them smoke."

"I see."

"I do too. You're thinking the old man is losing his marbles. Going ape over a cigarette butt that could be lying around for weeks or could have been tossed in here by kids just having a laugh. You're wrong, boss. I know every nook and cranny of this place, every stick and blade of grass in the yard. That butt wasn't there when I came on duty yesterday evening. Someone was lurking in those trees last night.

Looking in. Sizing up the place."

John ran his hands through his hair. Ollie was right. He *had* thought the old man was losing his marbles but now he wasn't so sure. He was annoyed too about camera five. He'd been charged a ransom by the engineer who'd called to fix it recently. It had been working yesterday afternoon. He'd checked it himself.

"When did you notice the camera wasn't working, Ollie?"

"When I came in yesterday evening."

Realising that Ollie wasn't about to make coffee, John got up and put on the kettle.

"I'll get on to the camera crowd this morning and give them a bollocking. And in future, Ollie, if you think there's anything suspicious going on just ring me."

"Will you talk to Miss Keyes? Ask her."

"Sure. Now will you stop fretting? We'll have that camera up and running tonight and I'm going to see about getting extra lighting over on the west side. Okay?"

Ollie stood up. "Herself will be wondering where I am. I'll be off."

John watched the old man as he went out the door, then he went to check on the perimeter fence, the lock-up units and every square inch of EFAS, including a futile search for traces of ground in tobacco. In reception he played back the tapes from the previous night. He saw Ollie patrol, Victor Collins and Francine Keyes come and go – everything that happened except what should have been recorded by camera five. He still did not know if EFAS security had been breached but he was chilled by suspicion that it could well have been.

* * *

The three women decided after just an hour in Curtain Call that staying for the day would be pointless. They had done as much tidying and organising as they could. It was just a matter of waiting for the newly ordered stock to come in. Another few days.

"We could all do with some time off anyway," Meg remarked as they locked up. "Any plans, Lynn? What are you going to do with your down-time?"

"Actually, I'm going to see the doctor."

"You do look tired," Carrie said. "Maybe he'll prescribe a holiday in the sun."

Lynn just smiled and said nothing more. Carrie and Meg believed, as she had intended, that she was going to see her GP. But Lynn hoped to be seeing a much more eminent doctor. A specialist in fact.

The irony was that Lynn had not felt as alive and well for a long time. Every cell in her body tingled with awareness of the sunlight, the puffy little clouds in the sky, the breeze against her face. Life! And love in the shape of her clandestine cuddles on the couch with John Enright.

Approaching St Alban's Clinic along the tree-lined avenue which led to the long, low sprawling building, Lynn began to wonder just what she was going to say. Even what in the hell she was doing here. Then she remembered John's troubled brown eyes. Her physical need of him, the tremors when he was near, the rapid heartbeats, the longing to feel his lips on hers, these things shamed her and emphasised her treachery towards Meg. But the urge to help him, to take his hand and tell him she was there for him was far more noble. Something she could do and not feel guilt. Or so she convinced herself.

The reception area was discreetly decorated with potted plants and abstract paintings. No sooner had she set foot in the door than she was approached by a well-groomed woman wearing a beautifully cut navy trouser suit.

"May I help you?" the woman asked in a very cultured accent.

"I'm looking for Professor Stagge's rooms, please."

"Do you have an appointment?"

"No. At least not with the Professor. I'm looking for a friend who works in his office. Francine Keyes. Do you know her?"

"Do you mean Frances?"

Lynn took a chance and nodded her head enthusiastically. "Of course. That's her name really but she sometimes like to call herself Francine. More sophisticated, she says. I'd like to surprise her. May I go to see her?"

The woman turned her clear intelligent gaze on Lynn. Her smile was gone.

"Frances no longer works here. Just how close a friend are you to her, Ms... ?"

"Murphy," Lynn said, spouting the first name that came into her head. "Helen Murphy." She held out her hand to the other woman who raised an eyebrow but took her hand anyway.

"Esther Canning."

"Nice to meet you, Esther. Francine, I mean Frances and I met in dancing class," Lynn explained, warming to her story. "There's an age gap of course. She's much younger than I but we got on well together. I'd like to catch up with her again."

"I think a lot of people would."

"What do you mean?"

The woman's lips tightened as if she realised she had been indiscreet and was not going to allow herself make the same mistake again. "I'm sorry I can't help you," she said. "Your friend left here over two years ago. Now if you'll excuse me, please, I'm busy."

"Do you know where she went after here?"

"No. I had no interest in contacting her after she left. Goodbye, Ms Murphy."

"Thank you for your time. It's a pity I can't find her. I'm getting married and I wanted her to be bridesmaid."

"Really? Isn't it more traditional to ask a person whose name you at least know?"

Lynn began to blush. The woman did not make it any easier by staring. Hot and red now, Lynn waved her thanks and turned quickly away. She had almost reached the door when someone tapped her shoulder. She turned to come face to face again with the elegant Esther Canning.

"It's obviously important to you to find Frances Keyes. I'll just warn you, if you did indeed know her two years ago, she's changed a lot since. Physically. She's had quite a lot of cosmetic surgery done. I'd imagine physically is the only way she has changed though."

"Did she leave or was she fired?"

"I can't answer that."

"What if I told you I was thinking of employing her?"

"Then I'd say you were telling me more lies. Now would you please leave?"

Lynn was left with no alternative but to go. Yet she was happy that the visit had not been wasted. She now knew that Francine might not always have been the super-model she appeared to be, nor indeed had she always been Francine.

As she walked back to her hire car, an elderly couple approached. The man was using a walking aid and the woman stepped slowly along beside him. They were obviously on their way in to attend a specialist on his condition. That's when Lynn realised that Professor Stagge was the leading specialist in Patrick Morgan's illness.

* * *

John was furious by the time he put the phone down from talking to the camera engineer. "No can do," was the only response he could get from the moron. Eventually, the best agreement John could reach was that the camera would be fixed by the next Wednesday. His mood didn't improve any when Francine and her cloud of perfume came into his office.

"Morning, John. You look tired. Late night last night? Out visiting maybe?"

"None of your business where I was. I need to talk to you about something."

"Snap! I'd like to have a chat about an apartment block over on the east-side. Oriel Rise. I'm thinking of buying there. The one where Lynn Rooney lives. 23B, isn't it? It's nice that both you and your wife are best friends with the same person."

John should have been shocked. Instead he absorbed the information without as much as a skipped heartbeat. He was saturated by shock now. So, the bitch knew he had been in

Lynn's apartment last night. She was staring at him, monitoring his reaction. Fuck her!

"Those apartments would be much too classy for you. Besides, you'd have to pay and that's not your style, is it? Now, I wanted to ask you about last night. I believe you were back here late. To ring Yan Gilmore."

A frown of annoyance creased Francine's forehead. Enright's reaction was so casual she wasn't sure now whether there was something going on between him and Lynn Rooney. She'd catch him though and probably with his trousers down. Dirty git! Playing his game, she smiled at him.

"Yes, I was here. And you should know that senile security man is a danger to himself and the unit. There was somebody, or several people, hiding in the trees over near the Jacuzzi factory and he was flapping about like a headless chicken. They were laughing at him."

"You're sure somebody was there?"

"I'm certain. Some secure unit you have. I don't think Yan is going to be too pleased when he hears."

Yan Gilmore's displeasure was at the bottom of John's list of concerns now. He was taken aback by Francine's account of last night's intrusion onto the premises. For once he felt Francine was telling the truth.

"Sounds like kids messing," he suggested. "There was no attempt made to come into the lock-ups."

"I don't think they were kids. They were playing with the old man. Showing him they could come in here any time they liked. It was probably a trial run. Victor Collins was not very pleased with your standard of security. He's on his way over to see you now."

Shit! Not the impression John wanted to give a new client

– even Victor Collins. Especially Victor Collins. John sighed and looked at Francine. She was smiling, enjoying all this.

"Yan will be furious," she gloated. "He has very definite ideas about how the company should be run. His plans don't include geriatric security men or incompetent management."

John's mobile rang. It was probably Meg, complaining about something but anything was preferable to listening to Francine. "That's all for now. Let me know when Victor Collins arrives."

She opened her mouth as if to say something else, then seemed to change her mind. He waited until she had closed the door before he answered the call. It wasn't his wife on the phone. It was Lynn and she had some very interesting news about her visit to St Alban's Clinic. And it could get even more interesting before the day was out because Lynn was now on her way to Oakley Property Developers. John smiled as he closed his mobile. If anyone could find a way through this maze it would be Lynn. His wife's best friend, and as John now realised, also the only friend he had.

* * *

Meg brought her easel closer to the patio doors and faced it towards the light. Already changed into her paint-stained sweat shirt and jeans, she was ready to start work again on her canvas. She frowned as brush touched canvas. She would have to vary pressures and shades very carefully in order to convey the delicate beauty and savage hate she intended for this picture. She worked ceaselessly until Carrie called her for lunch.

"I've made some salad, Mom. I knew you'd forget to eat."

Meg wiped off her hands and then went to the kitchen sink to wash them. "I hope to be finished by this evening. It would make such a difference to have the painting in the window for the weekend. Something for the curious to look at instead of peering into the devastated shop."

Carrie poured coffee for them both and then sat waiting for her mother to join her at the table. "Would you do a painting for our new Haven Café?" she asked.

"Yes, of course, if you want."

"I do and so does Karl. He's been on the phone while you were busy painting. He's arranged for the estate agent to give me the keys today. It's all happening quicker than I thought. All glory to The Light."

Meg looked up from her salad to see that Carrie's eyes were glowing. With excitement? With zeal? She could partly understand the excitement. Carrie had brought her to see the three-storey redbricked building on McCurtain Street yesterday. From the outside at least, it was magnificent. A Victorian structure, very similar to the Portland café she had worked in all summer according to Carrie. Inside, Meg knew the ceilings would be high, the rooms airy. It would probably need a lot of renovation though. Many businesses had come and gone from that particular building over the years. The upper floors had been let out as offices while the ground floor had traded as everything from a bicycle shop to a travel agency. And now it seemed it was destined to become a café and recruiting centre for Karl Hemmings' Inner Light Movement.

Meg felt a momentary flash of hatred for John. This is one of the things she had wanted the family to discuss last night. They needed to talk to Carrie, to find out how involved she had become with ILM, to let her know her family were there to support her if she was being put under undue pressure.

"Mom? Are you alright?"

Meg pushed her plate away from her and put her elbows on the table. She struggled for words. How was she going to warn Carrie, to protect her, without seeming to offend the beliefs she now appeared to hold so strongly? Nothing for it but to speak what was on her mind. Karl Hemmings had upped the ante by pushing things forward so quickly.

"I'm worried, Carr. You seem to be very influenced by Karl Hemmings. Meeting him has changed you a lot. You're not the same."

"I get the impression you think I've changed in a negative way. You're so wrong. I've never been happier. I have a mission in life now."

"Do you really believe all this – this extreme weirdness or are you just trotting out whatever Karl Hemmings has planted in your head?"

Hurt flashed in Carrie's hazel eyes and Meg immediately caught her daughter's hand.

"I'm sorry, Carr. That came out all wrong. I don't mean that you've been brainwashed. Well, not really…"

"Don't lie. That's exactly what you meant. Don't you see, lying has become a way of life for us? We deceive others and ourselves too. Be honest with me, Mom. Are you happy? Do you have fulfilment in your life. Purpose? Tell the truth."

Meg gazed at her daughter, wondering just how truthful she could afford to be. Carrie had touched on some very sensitive areas. But the new Carrie was no longer a child. She was a woman. An adult who needed adult honesty.

"I can't hide the fact that I feel my life is drifting by. But it's not because I haven't found your god. I'm worried about you and I won't apologise for that. Nor for being wary of Karl Hemmings. I believe he's making a very good living for himself exploiting other people's vulnerabilities."

"You've never even met him and you're judging him."

"I spoke to him on the phone. It was enough."

Carrie stood and, coming around to Meg's side of the table, she stooped down beside her.

"Mom, I don't want to argue with you but you must understand that my finding The Light has nothing much to do with Karl Hemmings. And if you believe he and ILM are such sinister brainwashers, why were Trina and the other girls not drawn into them too? Do you think they're strong and I'm weak-willed? Is that it?"

"You're sensitive, Carrie."

"Meaning you think I'm easily influenced."

"It's mainly intelligent, sensitive people who get caught up in cults like this."

Carrie stood up abruptly. She stared at Meg with frightening intensity.

"I'll pray for you, Mom. Now I'm going into town to meet the estate agent. Can I take the car? You won't need it this afternoon, will you?"

"Look, Carr…"

"I was going to ask you if Garth could stay here when he arrives but maybe now's not a good time. We'll talk later."

Carrie turned and walked out of the kitchen, leaving Meg floundering. One part of Meg felt she had handled this situation wrongly and the other questioned her right to have broached the subject at all. It was Carrie's life and she would have to live it as she saw fit. And for now there was no changing Carrie's mind that her life would be spent praising this god she called The Light and serving fair-trade coffees in Karl Hemmings Cork branch of Haven Café.

★ ★ ★

Victor Collins was very angry as he sat across the desk from John. Reasoning didn't seem to be making much impact on him. Maybe because John himself wasn't fully convinced by his own assurances. He had to concede that an attempted break-in to EFAS last night was at least a possibility. He tried a different tactic.

"Look, Victor," he said, standing up, "why don't we walk around the lock-ups again and I'll go through all our security features? You'll see that a few kids messing around outside, if they were indeed there at all, were no threat to the security of your lock-up. You have your own swipe card and code, for heaven's sake! Not even I could get into your unit now."

Victor Collins remained seated. His face was mottled with puce splotches and little beads of sweat had begun to form at his hairline. The man had either very high blood pressure or a filthy temper. Probably both. John was tempted to tell him and his grotty little electronic components to fuck off. Then he remembered Yan Gilmore. He smiled at the weasly man sitting in the chair and sat down again himself.

"We have a hundred percent record on security. How can I reassure you, Victor?"

"I want you to fire that doddering old man and put

proper night-time security in place."

"I beg your pardon? I value your custom, but I make decisions around here on personnel."

"Your choice. I'll take my goods now so."

"We do have a contract," John reminded him.

"Yes, we do. For the safe storage of my goods. You've broken it. I'll make sure your other customers know too. I'm familiar with quite a few of them."

John ran his hands through his hair. He dithered now on the edge of a decision. He had decided himself, hadn't he, that Ollie would have to go? Truth be told, Ollie should have retired at least two years ago but how in the hell could he be replaced? Nobody wanted to work the unsocial hours Ollie did. Not these days. He smiled, or tried to smile, at Victor Collins.

"It's not as easy as that, Victor. Ollie has been with us a long time. I agree with you that he may be too old for the job now but the major problem is replacing him. I prefer to use someone employed directly by us rather than subcontract the security. I have more control that way. But it's finding someone to work those hours is the difficulty."

Victor Collins sat forward and suddenly his puce colour seemed to fade to a lesser shade of purple. "I could help you there. I've two good blokes I use myself at my workshop. Two brothers. They're reliable and trustworthy."

John was slightly taken aback at Victor's sudden enthusiasm. It was as if he had been waiting for this moment and had pounced in case he lost the opportunity. For what? To get his own men here to guard the goods he was paying to lock up securely? What in the fuck was he making? Nuclear dishwashers? Collins was still leaning forward, staring, waiting anxiously for an answer. But John had a question.

"Do you mind if I ask, Victor, why you need us if you already have two security men of your own?"

"Space. I need space. My premises are small. For the time being anyway. I've got new contracts but I can't ship out until I have a container load. I thought I explained all that to you."

John nodded. He had indeed. It was just that events were making John suspicious of everyone and everything. His naturally cautious nature was becoming unnaturally distrusting. He made his decision now.

"I'll talk to Ollie. And maybe you'd ask these brothers to arrange an appointment. I'm not promising anything but I will speak to them. Is that alright with you?"

"I s'pose 'twill have to do for now," Collins said but his tone was a lot more conciliatory than it had been. "I'll tell the lads to ring you."

After he left the office John breathed a sigh of relief. Victor Collins was the type of person who seethed with tension and sucked everyone within reach into the vortex. Still, he was a new client to add to the already healthy client list. Yan Gilmore would yet be forced to admit that EFAS ran most efficiently with John Enright at the helm.

* * *

The building was one of the newest and most impressive in town. Rising seven stories high, plated with tinted glass, softly curved at the edges, it skirted the river edge near the city centre and stood side by side with the exclusive

Waterside Apartment block. Lynn had often noticed it in passing but had never been in this building before. The name plaques in the lobby had informed her that Oakley Property Developers had offices on the third floor. Needing to get her story straight in her head, she sat in one of the tub chairs which were placed discreetly around the lobby, each with a circular coffee table in front of it. She crossed her legs at the ankles, held her bag in her lap and tried to look as if she was waiting to meet somebody by appointment. It was a busy place. The lifts continuously took in and disgorged people and the automatic front doors were permanently swishing over and back.

The longer Lynn sat the less sure she was about how she should approach this problem. Even though she had come away from St Alban's with some new information about Francine, maybe she could have got more if she had been clever about it. Yet, try as she might, she could not come up with a scheme to pry the information she needed from Oakley Property Developers. Should she pretend to be from the Planning Office? They would know all the planning officials and see her instantly as a fraud. It was probably a criminal offence to impersonate a city official anyway. Scrap that. She could say Francine was a long-lost niece but then they wouldn't say anything negative about her and all Lynn wanted to hear about that particular lady was the negativity, the low-down, the dirt, anything to loosen her hold on John. Shit! She wasn't cut out for this pussyfooting around. Subterfuge had never been Lynn's way.

She stood up and walked over to the lifts. Maybe if she went to the third floor and looked at the offices of Oakley Developers some inspiration might come to her.

Getting out at level three, Lynn saw that the whole floor was taken by Oakley. A rest area near the lifts was beautifully laid out with couches at the windows overlooking the river. Time to sit and think again. Lynn was shaking now, all the bravado of her trip to the clinic deserting her. Glancing down at the river below she saw it was running quite high and wondered if the ground floor and basement of this building would flood in winter.

She picked up an Oakley brochure from the octagonal occasional table in front of the couch. It was glossy and very sophisticated, representing just the type of company where Francine would fit in. Flicking through it, her eye was caught by a full-page photograph. Mr Shane Richards MD. He was a silver-haired man. Very handsome. John said he had sounded like a confident man on the phone. Not the type to fall prey to Francine Keyes and yet it seemed he had. That's what he had hinted at anyway. Lynn put the brochure down and stood. She'd just have to wing it. Even try the same ruse as she had at the clinic.

Just as she walked away from the window, a man approached her from the right-hand corridor. He was tall, carrying a briefcase, silver-haired and even more handsome in person than in his photograph.

Lynn launched herself at Shane Richards without any clear idea what she should say to him.

"Excuse me, Mr Richards?"

"Yes? May I help you?"

He had a kind face. Tanned, the outdoor tan of a yachtsman, and his eyes were crinkled at the corners. Maybe it was truth time.

"Mr Richards, my name is Lynn Rooney. A very close

friend of mine is having problems with an ex-employee of yours. I'd like to ask you about her."

"Ah! Francine Keyes?"

Lynn nodded.

"And would your friend by any chance be MD of a storage company?"

Lynn nodded again. Shane Richards waved towards the window couches and Lynn walked ahead of him and sat.

He stood for a moment looking down on the river. "It's high," he remarked before seating himself beside Lynn. He looked at her with a clear blue, very perceptive gaze. "Now what do you think I can do for your friend? He spun me some yarn about the Keyes person being a temporary employee of his. I didn't believe him of course. "

"You gave her an excellent reference. Why?"

"Because she's an excellent worker. I'm sure your friend can't have any complaints with her work."

Lynn's hopes were fading. She had thought when Shane Richards had sat down with her that he was about to spill the beans on Francine. It seemed everywhere Francine had worked was happy to get rid of her but very reluctant to say why.

"Did you fire her?"

"In the first place I don't discuss my staff with strangers and in the second place it would be ridiculous to fire her and then give her a glowing reference. That should answer your question."

"It doesn't tell me why you told John – I mean my friend – that he should have rung you before he took Francine on. Would you have warned him against employing her?"

Shane Richards stooped down, picked up his briefcase and then stood.

"It was nice meeting you, Lynn Rooney. I'm sorry I couldn't be of more help. All I can tell you is that Francine Keyes worked here for a year and she was competent at her job. So competent in fact that she dealt with some very confidential files. Then she had herself a nice long holiday before starting work in the storage company."

"She lives in Waterside Apartments, doesn't she? One of your developments."

"So?"

Lynn stood now too and looked up at Shane Richards. He looked steadily back at her.

"Did you give her the apartment?" she asked directly.

He didn't flinch.

"I'm not accusing you of anything, Mr Richards," Lynn went on hurriedly, "or trying to interfere in your private business, but Francine is threatening my friend and he just doesn't know what to expect from her or what it would take to be rid of her."

Shane Richards took a step back from Lynn and brushed the lapel of his jacket as if subconsciously trying to brush away any memory of Francine Keyes.

"I'm sorry, I must go. I've an appointment. I hope everything works out well for your friend. He's a lucky man to have you on-side. It always helps to have someone to talk to. Francine will write her own terms, I'm afraid. Depends on what she wants. Maybe another long trip to New Zealand will fix it."

He turned and walked away towards the lift. He got in, waved at her just as the door was closing and then Shane Richards was gone, leaving Lynn with a feeling of failure. Not sure of what she had hoped to achieve by this visit, she knew she had not accomplished anything. The only new piece of information was that Francine was partial to holidays. What had he said? 'Maybe another long trip to New Zealand will fix it.'

Lynn glanced at the rising river again and then went to the lift. She was walking through the lobby when a thought struck her. She stood stock still. New Zealand! Wasn't Patrick Morgan's nephew from New Zealand? The man who was soon to be the new boss of EFAS. It couldn't be! Too much of a coincidence. New Zealand was vast. Four times bigger than Ireland. And yet, it would make sense.

"Are you alright, Mrs?"

Lynn smiled at the security man and walked on again. Yes, she was alright. Almost. She would be a lot better when she worked out just why Francine Keyes had chosen New Zealand for her long holiday, presumably paid for by Shane Richards. Had she gone just to visit Auckland, to bungee-jump, to see the Moeraki Boulders, to experience life on the Pacific edge? Not likely. It seemed that Francine Keyes always had a reason. A plan. All Lynn knew for now was that Francine's trip to New Zealand might possibly have a connection to her plan for John Enright and EFAS. Whatever that was.

CHAPTER 21

Meg ordered Indian takeaway to Sycamore Lawn. She had no time to cook dinner this evening. Her painting was almost finished and she would not stop until it was ready for display. When the doorbell rang, she waited for someone to answer. John was upstairs, getting ready for his meeting with Willy Feeney, Tommy was in his room, being deafened by music and Carrie was somewhere around the house. The bell rang again, more insistent this time. Sighing, Meg put down her brush and went to the door. The delivery boy handed over her order and went off happily with his tip.

"Dinner's here," she called up the stairs.

As she passed the lounge she saw Carrie, sitting on the couch, her arms stretched wide, eyes closed, face lifted towards the ceiling. Meg stood at the door and stared. Carrie appeared to be in a trance, like a painting of a visionary, someone under a mystical spell.

"Did you hear me, Carrie? Dinner's here."

Slowly, Carrie lowered her arms and opened her eyes. They glistened with tears. "Praise The Light," she whispered.

Meg shivered. She heard John rap on Tommy's bedroom door and then the sound of her husband's heavy tread as he came downstairs.

Clutching her carrier bag of Indian food, Meg went into the kitchen and got out plates. She was determined now. This family must talk. Tommy arrived, lured by the smell of food and Carrie floated into the kitchen last, her eyes still dreamy and unfocussed.

"Everyone okay?" Meg asked as they sat at the kitchen table.

"Thank The Light for this plenty," Carrie whispered.

"Thank New Deli Takeaway," Tommy answered.

"No squabbling! Just eat," John ordered as if his son and daughter were still children.

Carrie picked and Tommy wolfed. "Are you going to finish that?" he asked, staring at his sister's almost full plate. Carrie pushed the plate towards him and he tucked in again. Meg tried to catch John's eye. Could he not see that Carrie wasn't alright? John was staring out through the window, his eyes almost as vacant as Carrie's. Meg dropped her fork onto the table. Three heads turned in her direction.

"We have things to talk about," she said. "Family things."

John glanced at his watch. "I'm meeting Willy Feeney at nine. It had better be quick."

"What's more important, John? Seeing an old friend or your family?"

"Don't start, Meg. You know Lynn's car was taken from here, the shop was wrecked and now it seems someone tried to come into EFAS last night. Of course seeing Willy, who just happens to be a Superintendent in the Gardaí, takes precedence now."

"At least you can't blame Breeze for that," Tommy said. "He's in London."

"May The Light be with him," Carrie said softly.

It was a piety too far for Meg. She stood, leaning her hands palms down on the table, and glared at each of them in turn.

"John, forget EFAS for once. Your daughter is quitting college and opening up a café for a religious sect, your son spends his time listening to music and pretending to study for his Leaving Certificate and your wife is sick of taking all this worry on her own. Now do you think we should talk or would you prefer to run away again?"

Tommy stood. "This is between the two of you. I don't want to be involved in a domestic. I'm going to my room."

"Sit, Tommy! You just don't want to be involved, period. You're going to talk to your father and me whether you like it or not."

Tommy pouted his lips but he sat anyway. Carrie was looking from her mother to her father, more awareness now in her eyes than there had been.

"I can't believe your attitude, Mom," she said, looking at her mother with such hurt in her brown eyes that Meg felt like pulling her into her arms and explaining that she was only trying to protect her precious daughter. "You were always the one who was open to new experiences, who encouraged us to think for ourselves. Now that I've done just that you're insulting my intelligence and belittling my beliefs."

"I don't mean it that way ... I mean ..."

"I warned you that your lack of discipline with the children would come back to haunt you," John said so

313

emphatically that Meg knew he had been waiting to utter the words for a long time. "You always let them wind you around their little fingers. You'd never let me say boo to them, would you? No! Meg knew best. Well, this is the price. If they're irresponsible, it's your fault."

Meg thought of a thousand retorts to John's bitter comments. She could point out that she'd had to be mother and father, chauffeur and educator, everything, to the children. That he had never been there. But nothing either of them said now would change that. Meg pursed her lips and listened as Carrie spoke to her father.

"How can believing in God and honouring Him with your way of life be irresponsible, Dad? Are you being irresponsible when you trot off to Mass on Sunday mornings or go to Confession at Easter?"

"That's different."

"Why? Have you a better god than mine? Are Roman Catholic priests more holy than Karl Hemmings?"

"My priests are ordained men. They don't run cafés and recruit young girls."

"You're right, Dad," Tommy laughed. "They're more interested in –"

"Shut up, Tommy!"

Tommy shut up as ordered. Meg sat. From the look on Carrie's and John's faces, this could be a long discussion.

"Roman Catholicism is an established religion," John stated, as if longevity alone was justification for his faith. "It's not a business where people are brainwashed into working for nothing."

"You're not brainwashed? Really?" Carrie asked. "You haven't been filled with fear of hellfire if you don't confess your sins to a priest, a male priest by the way. Your church hasn't yet caught up with equal rights. You've never found the rituals of Mass and Sacraments hypnotic? Get real, Dad!"

"For heaven's sake, Carrie, where are your brains? Karl Hemmings hit on a good scam. A profitable one. He has combined cafés run on slave labour with all this Light babble and he's made a fortune from it."

"I don't know where you got that idea about ILM. The café staff are paid a decent wage. The going rate. They donate 10 percent to the upkeep of the community if they want to. It's voluntary. Everything's voluntary from contributing, to leaving if you feel you'd like to. And you won't find elitism in ILM. We recognise that everyone has The Light in their heart, even people who deny it. Every human being has the chance to be saved."

"Just join ILM. Is that the pathway to heaven?"

"It's a choice, Dad. Made by people who have reached the age of reason. We don't nab babies and baptise them like established religions do. You won't find any infant ILM members. We're all there because we want to be – not because our parents decided for us."

"God forbid that you'd listen to your parents. You'd much prefer to follow Karl Hemmings instead!" John shot back.

Seeing that the discussion was going in circles, Meg intervened. "What about college, Carrie? Are you sure about that decision? You could still study and be an ILM member if you really wanted."

Carrie turned to her mother and the dreamy look had left her eyes now. She was aware, responsive and for the first time, Meg recognised that her daughter was very sure of where she was going. "Garth and I will be setting up the café in McCurtain Street. We'll work there together, pray together and spend the rest of our lives with each other. We'll tell people who want to know about The Light. Guide them to look into their hearts, just like Garth and Karl guided me."

"You'll have baby saints who'll glow like 100-watt bulbs!" Tommy joked and was then immediately sorry he had said anything because John's attention turned to him..

"What's your mother's saying, Tom? Are you not studying?"

Tommy shrugged. "Believe what you want."

Meg sighed. John and Tommy always rubbed each other up the wrong way. This could end up in a full-blown fight.

"Tom, we're all adults here," she said. "Let's behave that way."

"Yeah! Let's do that. Why don't we respect each other? That would be a nice change."

Meg was shocked at the way Tommy spoke. He spat the words at them and his mouth sneered while his eyes began to fill with tears. Her heart ached for the man struggling for recognition inside the boy.

"Do you not think we show you respect, Tom?" she asked.

"Respect! You dis my best friend, my clothes, my music, even my bloody haircut! When I work at EFAS, Dad, you pay me less than anyone else and give me the shittiest jobs. And Mom, you've just accused me of not studying when you don't know the first thing about what I'm doing. That's not respect."

"Respect is something you earn, son," John said, pushing back his chair and standing up. "You've a deficit so far. You've dragged the scum of Cork city to our door and wasted your time and my money in that expensive school of yours. Don't you go criticising us until you've done something with your life."

"And you have? I hope when I'm your age I'm doing something more worthwhile than supervising lock-up garages!"

"Like what? Dealing drugs with your friends? Hanging around street corners? Tell us, Tom, where are you headed? Do you know?"

Any idea Tommy had of breaking his promise to himself and passing on Breeze's warning went out of his head now. If Freddie Goodall wanted to bust up EFAS, good on him! See how smart John Enright would be then. Tommy glared at his father and John glared back, waiting for an answer.

"Dad! Calm down! You're being unfair," Carrie said, lifting her hand to pat Tommy on the arm.

John walked to the kitchen door. He stood there, head bowed, and then turned to look at his family. The three faces were towards him. Three beautiful faces. His wife, her delicate features frozen in an expression of anger, his daughter with glowing dark eyes, his son, his wayward, stubborn son with hurt and hatred reflected equally. He felt like crying. He loved them all so much and yet he had not loved them enough.

"I'm sorry," he whispered. "I'm so very, very, sorry."

He quickly turned and walked away. Willy Feeney would be waiting.

* * *

The Wander Inn was in the centre of town. Glancing at his

317

watch John saw that he would not have time to call to Lynn now. He'd ring her later. Or text. Town was busy so he had to park two streets away from The Wander. He was puffing by the time he arrived in the pub. He spotted Willy Feeney immediately. Willy was six foot four and built to match. He was hard to miss. John sat beside him at the corner table Willy had found for them and lifted the pint of stout that was waiting for him.

"Thanks, Willy. Cheers. Here's to old times."

"Old times," Willy echoed, clinking his glass against John's. "Although," he added, "I wouldn't fancy going back, would you? They were tough times."

John swallowed a long draft of stout and thought about that. Times had been tough on Hyde Street. The poverty, the constant struggle to put food in bellies and clothes on backs had worn people down, none more so than the widow, Hannah Enright. Her struggle had been greater, the furrows on her face deeper, her bitterness more acid than anyone else's. John recognised now that his mother had missed out on the great compensations of the cash-deprived life they had lived on Hyde Street. The sharing, the warmth, the comfort of fighting a common cause. Hannah had kept her head high and her front door closed. She had shut out the joy. John shook his head to clear it of Hannah's shadow. He smiled at Willy.

"Tough but honest," he said. "More than I can say for now."

"No wonder you say that. I hear you've been having a few problems. What's going on, John?"

"I could ask you the same. I don't know if you remember Lynn Rooney?"

"Reddish curls? Flighty? I remember her alright. I met her at your wedding. Bridesmaid, wasn't she?"

"Jesus! You've a memory like an elephant. Yeah, Lynn and Meg were best friends. Still are. They run the curtain shop on Bridge Street together."

"The one that was vandalised? I read the reports. Sinister that."

"Lynn's car was stolen too the same night from outside our house. She'd left the shop keys in the car so maybe that's why they went there."

"Maybe. Or else she was deliberately targeted."

"Do you think so? She has no enemies that she's aware of. Nobody that would do something like that to her. What's the latest, do you know? Any sign of her car or anyone arrested for the break-in?"

Willy shook his head and looked at John through narrowed eyes. He was the policeman now and John began to feel uncomfortable.

"No. I checked before I met you. Suspects of course but that's not going to get us anywhere. You can't touch the bastards these days. They can hide behind the law. They'd have you in court for harassment in the blink of an eye."

"But you do have suspects?"

"We've been keeping an eye on a car-theft operation but nothing concrete at the moment. They're pretty good at what they do. Lynn Rooney has probably seen the last of her car. But the shop was different. Dangerous that. It has threat written all over it."

John squirmed in his seat, wondering what to do. He had changed his mind a hundred times on the way here. Should he mention the possible attempt to breach EFAS security?

Should he tell Willy about the Goodalls or not? The policeman's sharp eyes were gleaming as he stared at John. Willy almost certainly knew he was holding something back.

"Well, John. Could you shed any light on the break-in? We're at a standstill with the investigation. No prints, no witnesses. Have you any idea who might have done it? Could the target have been you? A warning?"

An image of Tommy's face, his eyes filled with childish tears, flashed before John. A fierce protective instinct gripped him so hard that his stomach muscles knotted. He could tell Willy about the Goodalls, about Breeze and Freddie and their thug who was hanging around the house on Sycamore Lawn, but that would be betraying his son. Telling the police that Tommy moved in criminal circles. Bringing him to their attention. No way! Whatever Tommy decided to do, when he finally grew up, he'd have to start with a clean sheet. No question marks against his name.

John looked back at Willy as steadily as possible now and lied to him. "I swear, Willy, I have no idea who could want to damage me or my family. You don't normally make enemies in the storage business. Now, it's my round. Same again?"

John took the time he spent ordering the drinks and waiting for them at the bar to calm himself down. He had felt flustered under Willy Feeney's penetrating gaze. Willy had become more policeman than old pal now. It must have come with the promotion. He felt better by the time he got back to their table but not yet steady enough to broach the subjects he really wanted to talk about. Not wanted. That was wrong. He didn't want to mention Karl Hemmings and

Francine Keyes any more than he wanted to mention Tommy's connection to the Goodalls but at this stage he didn't know what else to do.

He enquired after Nancy, Willy's wife, and their three children, half listening to the answers as he prepared himself to ask his question.

"I wonder if you could help me with a delicate matter, Willy?"

"If I can."

"It's about my daughter, Carrie. She was in the States for the summer."

"She's in college now, isn't she?"

John nodded, wondering if Willy Feeney knew everything about everyone. They hadn't seen each other for a long time and John didn't have a clue what Willie's children were up to. Willy always was a nosey fucker. But an influential one now. Maybe he already knew Tommy was associating with scum.

"Well, she was doing an Arts Degree. She's decided to leave now. None of this is official, is it? It's off the record?"

"Unless you're going to confess to a crime, Enright, my lips are sealed."

John smiled. Of all the things he could confess to – lies, neglect of his children and his wife – criminal activity wasn't one of them. Unless of course he counted the assault Francine was alleging. Bitch! He swallowed a mouthful of drink for courage before he spoke again.

"The thing is, Carrie got involved with a group when she was in Maine. She worked in one of their cafés in Portland. They're called Inner Light Movement. ILM for short. They're a religious cult. Their leader is a man named

Karl Hemmings. I was wondering if you could discreetly check them out for me, Willy. I'd appreciate it."

"Is she home?"

"Yes. But this Karl Hemmings has bought a premises on McCurtain Street. He's going to open one of his cafés there and Carrie intends running it. I think the catering is just a front for recruiting to ILM. Carrie seems to be unduly influenced by this man and his son Garth. I'm very concerned. She's changed so much."

Willy reached into his inside pocket, pulled out a notebook and began to write. John looked nervously around. Even though Willy was in civvies he looked every inch the cop and anyone watching would think John was being charged with something. Willy looked up.

"Karl and Garth Hemmings, Portland, Maine. Inner Light Movement. Right?"

John nodded. "The father, Karl, came to Maine from Detroit. I spoke to him on the phone and he gave me the creeps."

"I'll get onto the Interpol Office in Dublin. I've a friend there so he'll do a discreet check. I'll be able to tell you if he has any charges against him but his religious beliefs are another matter. You'll have to sort that one out with Carrie. Be careful. If you're too negative about the movement, it could drive her towards them."

"Isn't that the problem? She doesn't seem to be logical about it at all. She's found this god she calls The Light and Karl Hemmings has convinced her he's God's right-hand man."

"I'll get onto it Monday morning and give you a buzz as soon as I hear anything. There are support groups too who could help you. You should look them up."

Willy drained his pint and, just as John had primed himself to mention Francine Keyes, the tall man stood up.

"I'd like to stay and chat, John, but I'm afraid I've got to go now. Nancy's sister is fifty and they've organised a surprise party for her. I'll be in trouble if I don't show my face at it. You know the story."

Despite an opportunity lost, John felt relief. He had been let off the hook. He didn't have to try to broach the subject of Francine now. How could he when Willy was running away? He stood and shook the big man's hand. "It was good seeing you, Willy. And thanks for your help. We shouldn't leave it so long again before we meet up."

"Sure. I'll be in touch."

Willy walked away and John picked up his drink to finish it. As he put the glass down, Willy turned back from the door and returned to the table.

"I forgot to ask you about Francine Keyes," he said.

John was glad that he was sitting. His heart gave one violent thump and then seemed to stop.

"Wh–what about her?" he stuttered and knew his eyes were popping and his mouth slack.

"Did your company take her on? Your partner Patrick Morgan was on to us a couple of months ago to do a background check. Said ye were thinking of offering her a permanent job. Can't be too careful these days."

John was speechless. Patrick Morgan had checked up on Francine and said nothing about it. The fucker! The twisted old bollocks! Hadn't he hinted to John to check on her background? Willy was looking curiously at him now but John was finding it hard to hide the anger he was feeling.

"Patrick's sick, you know. Terminal. He's not got much time left."

"I'm sorry to hear that. I didn't know. He dealt with us by letter about the Keyes woman. Anyway she has a clean sheet. Did she get the job?"

"Yes, she's been with us a while now. Thanks again, Willy."

"I'd better run. Nancy will divorce me. Bye, John."

When John's heartbeat was under control again, he went to the bar and ordered a brandy. He was over the drink-driving limit now anyway so would have to call a taxi. The brandy trickled warm and bracing, down his throat and into his stomach but it brought no peace. There was only one place John knew he could find that peace. He took out his phone and did not ring a taxi company. He rang Lynn Rooney instead.

CHAPTER 22

Meg stood in front of her painting, moved her head from side to side, squinted her eyes and then opened them wide. "I think that's it!" she announced.

"It's cool, Mom," said Tommy.

"It's got soul," Carrie added.

Meg took the painting off the easel and began to tidy up. It was nearly midnight and she was exhausted, partly from the physical demands of being on her feet painting for so long but mostly from the trauma of the aborted family discussion. It wasn't John's attitude to the children which had upset her so much. That was par for the course. It was the look on his face as he had stood at the kitchen door and apologised to them. It had been a look of bewilderment, as if he only now saw that Carrie and Tommy were adults and that he had missed their growing years. Well, he had, hadn't he, and no amount of apologising would bring that time back.

"So what do you think, Mom? Will we do it?"

Meg turned to look at Tommy. He was smiling at her,

one eyebrow raised in the way his father did too. There was so much of John in his son. Even down to obsession. It just happened with John it was work and with Tommy music.

"I didn't catch the question. Will we do what?"

"Go into the shop and hang the picture now. We could have it in place for the morning. Give all the nosey fuckers something to gawp at."

"You'll really have to watch your language, Tom. It's a bit colourful. Anyway, it's too late."

"Come on, Mom. We'll both give you a hand," Carrie coaxed. "After all your hard work it should be on display for as long as possible. The new stock will be in by the middle of next week and you'll have to take it down then."

Meg looked at her painting again. It depicted all the delicate beauty of the stock in Curtain Call. Crisp cottons, fragile voiles, delicate embroidery and intricate handsewn appliqué. A cascade of beauty and creativity which she had highlighted by applying contrasting slashes of threatening blacks and blood reds. Angry, violent slashes through the pastels. Everything drew the eye towards the centre of the composition where an ethnic cushion bled its packing from a large gash in the cover. The knife which had destroyed it was still stuck into the guts of the cushion. The painting said today a cushion, tomorrow a human being.

Meg felt proud. Not of her work. That was rushed and on a cheap canvas. She was proud of the fact that her two children were supporting her, encouraging and praising, just as she had done with them for so long. Now was not the time to stop just because they were both walking in directions she would prefer they did not go. They were good people, her daughter and son. Wherever their exploratory journeys led them, it would not be towards evil. She smiled at them both now.

"Okay. C'mon! Let's put the masterpiece on display. Tom, would you bring the easel? And Meg would you run upstairs and get Granny Enright's sheets from the top of the hot press?"

Tommy whistled. "the Fuehrer will blow a fuse if he finds out you're using his old lady's precious linen sheets."

"I need a white backdrop. I'm sure Hannah wouldn't mind. Neither would your father. Not too much anyway."

"I don't know why he's kept them all these years. It's not as if we'd use them. Creepy."

"Granny Enright loved them. They were the only really good thing she owned."

"She was bloody laid out on them." Tommy shivered. "I was only four but I remember when she died. Her nails were all purple and she had a Rosary beads wound around her fingers. There was a long hair on the point of her chin and —"

"'Tommy!" cried Carrie. "I know you're going to say something cruel. Stop now while you're ahead. Just do as Mom asked and fold up the easel."

Tommy and Carrie continued to squabble but in a humorous way as they drove into town. It was eerie opening up the shop on Bridge Street at this hour of the morning. The street was quiet but anyone who did walk past seemed to be full of the carefree spirit of the weekend. Meg locked the door as soon as they were inside.

It took some time to fit a long brass rail across the window. When it was eventually done they draped Hannah's sheets across the rail. They made a perfect plain white background for the painting. Tommy stood the easel and then Meg lifted the picture onto it.

"Why don't you bless it, Carr?" Tommy joked. "You've a special line to the Man Above, haven't you?"

"Maybe you should," Meg said. "Hannah's probably cursing it at this minute."

Carrie stared at them both solemnly and for a moment Meg thought she was going to go on one of her 'Praise The Light' rants. Instead she burst out laughing.

"You're taking a big chance, Mom. I know we shouldn't keep secrets from Dad but if he knew Granny Enright's sheets were on display in town he'd have a hissy fit. So unless he asks, we won't say anything. Deal?"

Meg joined with Carrie and Tommy's high five and as her hand slammed against her daughter's elegant hand and her son's sturdy one, she felt a sense of unity between the three of them and knew that nothing would ever divide them. Not the Goodalls and not Inner Light Movement.

A group of young boys and girls passing stopped to stare at the three of them in the window.

"We'd better get out of here," Meg said, glancing at her watch and noticing that it was after one o'clock. "We're only drawing attention to the place. I don't know what we'd say to John if Hannah's sheets were stolen."

When they had locked up, they spent a minute outside looking in the window, admiring their handiwork. Meg was very pleased by the effect. It had impact and that is what she had intended.

As they drove back through the city centre Tommy spotted John's car parked on a side street.

"Dad must still be with his cop friend. I wonder where they've gone?"

"He should have left the car at home. They'll be drinking

pints and talking about Hyde Street. Nobody ever really leaves there. "

"Do you think so, Mum? Maybe he's talking about his delinquent son with the druggie friends. Asking the law for advice."

"Don't be so cynical, Tom," Carrie said. "You know Dad doesn't think you're a delinquent. He just worries about you. He worries about us all. He should pray more and then he'd have no need to worry."

"Carr! For feck's sake don't go back into Light mode. It's too late and we're all too knackered. And you should know your old man isn't everything he seems."

Meg looked sharply across at Tommy who was sitting beside her. He was staring straight ahead, his mouth pursed in a tight line. He always did that when he was angry and it made his chin stick out stubbornly. She thought of asking him to explain and then decided against it. Whatever Tommy meant it couldn't be what it sounded like. As if he suspected his father of – of something a teenage son considered awful. She turned her attention back to her driving. The three of them had shared a lovely night, or early morning as it was now, and Meg did not want to spoil it. They travelled the rest of the journey in silence.

Meg went to bed but not to sleep. She had been exhausted earlier on but the excitement of bringing her painting into the shop had renewed her energy. After almost an hour of tossing and turning she got up and went downstairs. She opened the back door and stepped into the garden. It was a cold night. She pulled her dressing gown more closely around her and stared up at the sky. It was beautiful. A black canopy hung with diamonds. Realising that she was probably getting pneumonia, she went back into the kitchen again and frowned as she saw the clock. It was quarter to three. Where in the hell had John and Willy Feeney gone? And with that question another nagging thought returned. What had Tommy meant by saying his father was not everything he seemed? John Enright was transparent. He was his work. EFAS was John Enright and John Enright was EFAS. Tommy should know that.

Needing to occupy her mind, Meg turned off the light in the kitchen and went into the lounge to get her crossword puzzle book. She had left it on the coffee table. Puzzles and pencil in hand, she went back upstairs.

About to climb back into bed, she heard a car come up Sycamore Road. She flicked off the overhead light and went to the window where she lifted a corner of the curtain and glanced out, expecting to see John in a taxi.

The car was pulling in to the side now, two doors up from the house. Meg frowned. The Nevins lived there and they were away on holiday in Portugal. Fearing that somebody was about to burgle the vacant house, Meg craned her neck and peered out. It was difficult to see clearly. Sycamore Road was not very well lit but, one thing was sure, the car was not a taxi. It was a compact little two-tone Smart car. Just like the one Lyn had on loan from her insurance company. As Meg watched, the car lights were switched off. Inside the car, she could make out two silhouettes. The passenger had a similar outline to John.

Meg dropped the curtain and tried to marshall her treacherous thoughts. Yes, that car looked like Lynn's but it couldn't be, could it? Why would she be parked outside Nevins'? And how could the passenger be John? He was with Willy Feeney. Just to reassure herself, she peeped again. That's when she noticed the odd-looking white roof-box glowing in the dim light. Lynn had laughed at that the first day she had been given the car. She had joked that the roof-box was bigger than the car.

What were the odds against more than one two-tone Smart cars with big white roof-boxes in Cork city? And that the second one was owned by Willy Feeney ? They must be pretty small. Suddenly Meg made a dash for the bed and jumped in. Christ! What was she thinking? How could she even consider that there might be anything going on between Lynn and John? She must be sick! An honest, loyal husband like John and a friend who was more like a sister!

Then she lay there. Waiting. As the minutes dragged by the urge to go to the window and spy got more intense. If it was Lynn and John, what in the hell were they talking about? Had Lynn had another disastrous encounter with a man and needed a shoulder to cry on? No. She would have told Meg if there was anyone special. Or anyone at all. Then what could she be doing with John at three o'clock in the morning? Maybe they were discussing their theory that Meg didn't want Carrie and Tommy to grow up. 'She can't cut the apron strings, blah, blah, blah!' And here was that niggling question again. What had Tommy meant by saying his father wasn't what he seemed?

It happened then, just when Meg had thought she couldn't bear the waiting another minute. A car door banged, an engine started. She heard footsteps walk down the street and approach her house. A key turned in the front door. It was John.

Meg rolled onto her left side and bent her knees. That's

the position in which she always slept. Feeling like a cheat, she closed her eyes and listened to John walk up the stairs and then go to the bathroom. He tiptoed into the bedroom, quickly took off his clothes and got into bed. Meg sniffed. Then she took a deeper breath. Red Door perfume. She knew it so well. She smelt it every day in the shop. It was Lynn's perfume, the one she always wore.

"Are you awake, Meg?"

What should she do now? He must have heard her sniffing. Meg straightened out her legs and turned towards him.

"Hmm. How did you get on with Willy Feeney?"

"Okay. He's going to check out Karl Hemmings for me. He's got some pal in Interpol."

"Don't say that to Carrie. She'll be furious. Where did you and Willy go?"

"To his house after The Wander Inn. We knocked back a fair bit of booze. My car's still in town. I had to get a taxi home."

"A taxi?"

"Yeah. It was either that or walk. I'm shattered now. Night, Meg."

"What taxi company did you use?"

"Jesus, Meg, I don't know who they were. Willy's wife called them. Nancy. Do you remember her?"

No. She didn't remember Nancy. Not much of Willy Feeney either. For all John's talk of friendship, he and Willy had seen very little of each other over the years. When it came to friends, the Enrights had only one real, genuine, lasting friendship. One true and loyal friend and Lynn Rooney was it. So why was John bullshitting about a taxi he didn't get and why was he awash in Red Door perfume?

"Sorry for waking you," John said. He kissed her on the cheek, a brush of lips like you might give a child, then turned his back.

Meg lay still, her mouth half open as if to say something. But the words would not come. She did not have the vocabulary to voice her fears of treachery, or the courage to ask why he was lying. Instead she lay beside him, feeling the heat from his body, listening to him breathe and within minutes he was breathing the deep even breaths of sleep.

Meg lay awake until dawn broke.

CHAPTER 23

Cork Airport was busy this Sunday evening. Francine glanced around her as she waited in the Arrivals area, just to be sure there was nobody who would recognise her. She didn't feel like going into explanations now. But of course, if she had to, she would. Francine Keyes always did what she had to do.

As people from the London flight began to trickle through, she felt a nervous flutter in her stomach.

She saw him as soon as he came through the doors. He was head and shoulders above everyone around him. Tall for a man of Chinese origin. That ancestry was way back in his bloodline. He was more New Zealand rugby player than Chinese, only the slight slant to his eyes betraying his oriental connections. His broad shoulders and well-muscled body fitted so beautifully into the dark suit he was wearing that, for an instant, Francine found herself remembering their passionate lovemaking. A hot flash seared through her body. Alleluia! They could do it all again now – all the thrusting, sometimes dangerous but always exciting things they had done to each other in New Zealand.

He smiled as he approached her, then stooped and kissed her on the cheek.

"Not here! Somebody might see us. You know I told Patrick Morgan you're not arriving until tomorrow. You'll have to learn about Irish curiosity."

"I've learned a lot about the Irish from you. You're an interesting bunch."

They both laughed and then headed towards the airport car park, chatting about his marathon flight from New Zealand along the way.

They were silent as they drove towards Francine's apartment, he with his eyes closed and she just happy that he was in the car beside her. As they approached Waterside Apartments, he opened his eyes.

"I can't wait to get into bed and have a good sleep," he said.

"Just sleep?" she asked coyly.

"Depends."

That's exactly what Francine had wanted to hear. Dependency. They were inter-dependent, she and Mike Choy from New Zealand. The man who for now would become Yan Gilmore, nephew and next-of-kin to Patrick Morgan. Lover and business partner to Francine Keyes.

"Has Patrick told you anything new since I was talking to you last?" she asked as they left the car in the parking lot and walked towards the apartment block.

"Only that he's looking forward to meeting me tomorrow. Not as much as I'm looking forward to meeting him though."

"Well, you and I have a lot of catching up to do first."

"You bet. Do you think we should start now?"

They were at the door of Francine's apartment by now. Smiling, he lifted her off her feet, carried her into her apartment and went straight to the bedroom as if he had been there a hundred times before.

As they made passionate love Francine forgot to plot and plan, forgot to work out an angle, an advantage she could take from the situation. Mike was the only man who had ever made her lose herself in the sensations he teased from her body, the only man who had ever drawn this intense, ecstatic response from her. The rest had all been like John Enright. Groping, pathetic idiots who aroused nothing more than her disgust.

She remembered now the first time she and Mike had made love in Queenstown. It had been after her bungee jump – the death-defying plunge she had booked through *Choy-Gilmore Sports*, the extreme-sports company Mike co-owned with Yan Gilmore. She had thought the leap from Kawarau Suspension Bridge was the ultimate thrill until he had later brought her to his apartment and slowly stripped her of her clothes and her steely control. She had allowed him to breach the defences it had taken her a lifetime to build. And he was doing it again here in Cork, in her own apartment. She was trembling, weak from his passion and the strength of her own response.

Feeling vulnerable, needing to regain some control, Francine got out of the bed they had almost dismantled with the energy of their lovemaking. She took her silk robe from the wardrobe and tied the sash tightly around her waist, knowing that this emphasised both her slimness and her enhanced breasts. He watched her lazily from the bed.

"So what are you planning now?" he asked.

"I'm planning on feeding us. You must be hungry after all that travelling."

"I'm not and you know that's not what I meant. Surely the woman who was clever enough to lure me halfway around the world has some scheme afoot to speed things up. I don't plan on staying here for long, you know."

"What do you suggest I do? Knock the old man off? I didn't know he was going to battle his disease this long, did I?"

"Well, you're the one who had access to his medical notes. You should know all his plans, living and dying . . ."

Francine turned and walked out to the kitchen. *He* was the one who knew all of Patrick's plans. He and the old man had been on the phone to each other almost daily for the past three months. He knew that he, in his role as Yan Gilmore, was going to get whatever Patrick Morgan had. Why else would he have made the journey?

She took the cold meat salad plates she had already prepared out of the fridge and opened a bottle of wine.

As she reached up to the shelf for glasses, he walked up behind her and put his arms around her. Lifting her hair, he covered the nape of her neck with soft kisses. She put down the glasses and turned to face him. Her breath caught in her throat. She was still stunned by his sheer flawlessness. He was wearing jeans but his chest was bare. His perfectly muscled torso, tanned and taut, just within her reach, was a dream she could not have dreamt before. Men like Mike Choy would not have looked twice at Frances Keyes. Not that big-nosed, flat-chested girl with the mousy hair and the bulky thighs that had needed so much liposuction. He put one hand on the small of her back, pulling her closer against his body while with the other he tilted her chin.

"It was a lucky day for me when you tracked me down in Queenstown," he said softly.

She tweaked his nipples playfully and laughed at him, though she wondered why he was bringing this topic up again now. "You know well I didn't track you down! It was just one of life's coincidences that I discovered the Gilmore in *Choy-Gilmore Sports* was none other than Yan, Patrick Morgan's nephew."

"And one of life's coincidences that you just happened to have met the terminally ill Patrick in St Alban's clinic and knew Yan was his next of kin?"

"Yes. Karma."

Francine was annoyed. It sounded as if he still didn't believe her. As she had told him before, his line of thinking was wrong. Odd as it seemed, it *had* all been fate that led her to Queenstown with nothing more on her mind than enjoying the holiday paid for by Oakley Developers. Her curiosity had been piqued when she saw the *Choy-Gilmore Sports* sign. It reminded her of Patrick Morgan and his nephew named Yan Gilmore. That's when coincidence had ended and deliberate planning had taken over. She had walked into their office, booked her bungee jump and chatted to the staff. The mouthy receptionist hadn't needed much encouragement to fill in the details. The Gilmore half of the company was owned by a man named Yan who did indeed have an Irish uncle named Patrick Morgan.

"Yan looks after the international safari and trekking part of the business. He's a nice man really but sometimes he gets a bit moody," the girl had confided. "He loves going off to very isolated places and staying there for months on end. He calls it research for the business but I think he just likes escaping."

"It would be nice to meet him," Francine said. "I know his Uncle Patrick."

"Yan's away at the moment actually – has been for the past six months. Somewhere in the Amazon jungle. He and a native guide are mapping out new treks for next season. Mike's getting a bit concerned. He hasn't heard from Yan for months. Mike's the other owner by the way – Mike Choy. You'll meet him when you're doing your jump."

It was his absence which had sparked Francine's idea to claim Yan's inheritance on his behalf. It had been merely a matter of putting the pieces together and realising that there could be a pot of gold there for the taking when Patrick Morgan died, as he soon must do. And Mike, after they had slept together a few times, had embraced the idea enthusiastically – though he had never quite believed that she had stumbled on Choy-Gilmore Sports by accident.

"What difference does it make how we met?" she asked him now. "You're here and until the old man dies and his will is read, you're the dutiful nephew. You won't be quibbling when you pocket your share of EFAS."

He narrowed his eyes and peered at her but he said nothing. She stared back and thought, not for the first time, that he was the one man she could not read. That's what made him so exciting. Mike Choy was a challenge. A game player. Just like Francine Keyes. They were a match made in the twisted alleys and cul-de-sacs of blind fate.

"Have you told John Enright yet that you want his forty percent share or else?" he suddenly asked.

"I haven't even told him he's going to meet you tomorrow. Yan Gilmore in EFAS will be a big surprise for him."

Francine moved away, filled the two glasses and handed one to him.

"You're not getting cold feet, are you?" she asked as they walked to the lounge.

He answered her with a cool glance.

Sitting on the couch, she slowly sipped her drink. He came and sat beside her. She smiled at him, tilting her head and allowing her long hair to fall over her shoulders in a way she knew was alluring to men. She felt like teasing him now because she knew their game always ended in bed. And there was one topic in particular guaranteed to rile Mike. She smiled at him and then casually swooped in for the kill.

"Have you heard anything from Yan yet?"

"No. I would have told you, wouldn't I?"

"I don't know. You're very silent about him and I don't understand your relationship. I was told you two were like brothers at one time — and now you're ready to swindle his inheritance. Why?"

"None of your business."

Francine found herself getting irritated again. "Everything to do with Yan Gilmore is my business! We can't afford to have any secrets at this stage. The old man may be sick but he's still as sharp as a needle. You won't be able to pull this off without my help and that means telling me everything you know about Yan."

"Oh, for God's sake!" he said peevishly. "Stop worrying about Yan Gilmore. He's in the middle of the Amazon jungle on one of his lunatic expeditions and likely to stay there. If by any chance he hears on the jungle drums that his uncle has died we'll be well gone before anyone here finds out about Yan — EFAS sold and our pockets full of money."

"Unless of course, somebody makes inquiries on Patrick Morgan's behalf. I'm amazed they haven't done so already."

"They have no reason to. Patrick is convinced I'm Yan. Besides, who could they ask? Yan's mother is dead, his father's gone back to China to trace his roots and my staff are instructed not to answer any questions about him should anyone inquire."

"Do you really believe your receptionist will keep her mouth shut?"

"I fired her. I meant to tell you. We're safe, Francine. And from now on I *am* Yan Gilmore and please stop calling me Mike."

Francine closed her eyes for a moment and thought about their future. She and Mike Choy and money. Heaven.

"Okay. Yan it is. And, yes, you will probably fool the old man into believing you're his nephew but you're not going to convince his solicitor without ID. Can I see what you brought with you?"

He got up from the couch and walked into the bedroom. Francine admired his long stride and the way his defined back muscles rippled when he moved. She was tempted to follow him and lure him back to bed.

He returned carrying what Francine thought was a small black notebook with gold lettering on it. He handed it to her.

"His passport. Good enough for you? I have his Birth Certificate too. What more do you need?"

"Who made them for you?"

"I know someone who is very, let's say – creative. They owed me a favour."

She flipped open Yan's passport to the photograph and

looked from the picture of Yan's face with the brown, slightly slanted eyes to the face of the man sitting beside her on the couch, marvelling once more at the resemblance between the two men.

"Is this really Yan's picture or did you have the photo altered?"

"It's Yan's. That's the only genuine bit."

"You're so alike! See? More coincidence! So you reckon the solicitor will be convinced by this?"

"Why not? He'll just check the details and they'll match. The number is valid too."

Francine took a deep breath and braced herself for her killer question – the one she had been wanting to ask him for some time.

"I know you hate Yan. Detest him with a passion. What did he do to you?"

She waited for him to answer but then she noticed that closed look on his face. The one that said she had gone far enough with her probing. Never mind. It might take time but she would, eventually, find out what had happened between Mike Choy and Yan Gilmore. If her instinct was right, and it had never let her down, there was a woman involved in the story.

"I'm very tired again," he said. "I may have to go back to bed." And the lopsided grin she so loved was on his face. He reached for the sash on her robe, untied it and holding the silky fabric open bent his head to her breasts.

Francine closed her eyes and ran her fingers through his sleek black hair as Mike Choy alias Yan Gilmore brought her to a place no man had ever brought her before.

Chapter 24

Meg sat and watched John as he slept in an armchair, the Sunday paper open across his knees. He looked so vulnerable in sleep that she felt guilty for the bitter thoughts she was harbouring. Getting up from her own chair she tip-toed across to where he was snoozing and leaning towards him, examined every detail of the face she had loved since she was seventeen years old. The nose, straight and large but not dominating, the eyebrows more arched on the right than the left-hand side, his mouth with a finely chiselled upper lip and fuller bottom lip. The sensitive mouth she had once kissed so passionately and so often.

His eyelids flickered and he woke. He looked up at her startled, and the newspaper fell from his knees onto the floor.

"Wh-what's wrong? What's going on?"

As she straightened up, Meg thought these were exactly the questions she should be asking. What in the hell was going on? Why had John lied to her about the taxi in the early hours of Friday morning? But she had not been able to ask and she wasn't going to now either. Maybe she didn't want to know the answer or perhaps she didn't want to hear more lies.

"Nothing," she said, going back to her own chair. "Will I switch on the television?"

He looked at his watch and then stooped to pick up the fallen paper. "If you want to. I have to go to EFAS."

"It's ten o'clock on Sunday night! Why do you need to go in?"

"I must check to see that Ollie's okay. I told you there were yobos playing ducks and drakes with him the other night. I'm afraid he'll have to go."

"Of course. He's used up, worn out, no good to you any more. Get rid of him."

John walked over and stood in front of her, an angry flush beginning to spread from his neck onto his cheeks. "What in the hell's wrong with you, Meg? You've hardly spoken two words to me all weekend and when you did they were only to criticise like now."

Meg bowed her head. She didn't want him to see the hurt in her eyes nor did she want to see the anger in his. How could she admit she had spied on him on Friday night? That she had been peeping from behind the curtains? That she knew he had lied to her. How could she say she now suspected he and Lynn might be having an affair? Maybe she should ask Lynn. There could be a logical explanation.

"Well, Meg?"

"Just tired," she muttered without lifting her head.

"Then why don't you go to bed? Where's Tommy?"

"At the cinema – and Carrie's over in Trina Farrell's house."

John dropped a kiss on the top of her head and then he was gone.

She listened until the noise of his car engine faded into the distance and then she allowed the tears to fall. They tracked down her face, dribbling over her chin and onto her good white sweater. Not caring, she let the tears flow, her breath coming in gulps.

Eventually she could cry no more. She hauled herself out of the chair and went to the bathroom mirror. Her image reflected exactly how she felt. Tragically comedic. A joke. The type that was cruel to laugh at but all the funnier for that. She washed her face and put on some eye lotion and moisturiser. She looked better now but still felt like a hurt child trapped in a woman's body.

Meg went to the kitchen and got a glass of water. Her head was aching and she needed some Paracetamol. The house was so quiet that her thoughts seemed loud. She couldn't forget the two-tone Smart car with the roof-box or the sweet scent of Red Door perfume on her husband. Who else could that have been but Lynn? Why had John lied and where was he gone now? To Lynn Rooney's taxi company again?

She swallowed her pills and then her rumbling stomach reminded her that she had eaten very little over the weekend. She normally hated fries and would never dream of having one so late at night but she had a longing now for sausages and rashers.

The fry was just cooked when Meg heard the front door opening.

Could John be back already? How was she going to explain her puffy eyes? The kitchen door opened and she turned to ask him if he wanted a fry too.

"Hi, Mum. That smells lovely. Can we share?"

Meg smiled at Carrie and tried not to let her

disappointment show. It was silly anyway. If John had gone to EFAS he couldn't be back that quickly. Not if he was chatting to Ollie. Firing him. "Of course. Will you have a fried egg?"

"Sit down, Mum. I'll do it. You look tired." Carrie peered more closely at her mother. "You weren't crying, were you?"

"Actually, I was. Just a silly film on TV but it was sad."

"Goose!" said Carrie as she broke an egg into the pan. "I don't know why you watch those weepy films. You always end up in floods of tears."

Carrie put a plate of fry in front of Meg and then went back to tending her egg.

"How's Trina settling back home after her summer in the States?" Meg asked.

"Madder than ever. She had the broadest brogue when we were in Maine and now that we're home she has a very impressive American drawl. She's such a drama queen. Still lecturing me about Inner Light Movement of course but I promised not to lecture her about hash if she said nothing more about Karl and Garth."

"She doesn't, does she?"

"Don't judge, Mum. None of us have the right."

Meg put down her knife and fork and looked at her daughter. Out of the mouths of babes. Meg didn't have the right to judge Trina, nor the right to judge John either. Or Lynn. "You're right, Carrie. You're so good."

"Everybody has some good and some bad in them. That's why we need The Light to help us find the good."

The front door opened again just as Carrie sat down with her plate of fry. "That's Tommy. I saw himself and his friends getting off the bus when Trina's mum was dropping me home. Eat up quick or he'll demolish your supper."

Meg laughed and cut a chunk of sausage. Just as she was about to put it in her mouth, Carrie asked where her dad was.

"He went to EFAS. Something he had to check on."

"I don't think so. I saw his car heading off in the other direction. He was going east."

Meg slowly lowered her fork. East. Towards Oriel Rise. Towards Lynn's apartment. Not west towards EFAS.

"Are you sure, Carrie?"

"Of course. Why wouldn't I know Dad's car with that awful EFAS sticker he insists on putting on the windscreen?"

Meg felt a surge of anger so strong that she almost gasped. Fuck him! And Lynn too. She jumped up from the table and dashed towards the kitchen door, almost colliding with Tommy on his way in.

"Hey! What's up? Is the kitchen on fire or something?"

Meg stopped for a moment and looked at her two children who were no longer children. But they weren't old enough to know what was wrong with her. Not yet. She tried to calm herself, to think about what she was doing. She was judging, being angry and spiteful and full of rage. Carrie's forehead was puckered with concern and her eyes were huge in her face.

"Pray for me, Carr," Meg whispered and then she turned and walked out into the hall, got her car keys and drove east after her husband. She didn't know yet what she would do when she got there. She just knew she must go.

* * *

Lynn and John were in what was quickly becoming their usual position when in her apartment. They were on the couch, his arm around her, her head on his shoulder, her eyes closed. It was their unspoken pact. They took comfort from the closeness but this was as intimate as they got. It was as if Meg was sitting between them, gazing solemnly at them both with her beautiful hazel eyes.

They had been discussing Lynn's discoveries about Francine – or Frances – Keyes.

John was staring straight ahead, a look of intense concentration on his face.

"So what do you think, John?" Lynn murmured, without opening her eyes. "About Francine's trip to New Zealand?"

"I'm still putting two and two together and trying not to come up with five. Francine is so friendly with Yan Gilmore on the phone I thought she was trying to reel him in too. To lure him until he took the bait like I did. But it could be that she's friendly because she already knows him. Why not? She's capable of anything."

"You could be right. If she met Patrick at St Alban's, she probably found out about his Kiwi nephew then. Which reminds me – her work reference from St Alban's – how did you not notice she was named Frances on that, not Francine?"

"But she wasn't. All the glowing references refer to her as *Francine* C Keyes. She probably wrote them herself."

"They were signed though, weren't they? By the employers, I mean."

John gave a mirthless laugh. "I'd let her write her own reference now too if she'd just go away and leave me alone."

Looking up at his troubled face, Lynn knew she would

348

have to wrap him in her arms or else move away from him. She stood.

"Will you have something, John? A drink? Tea? Coffee?"

"No, thanks. I must get home. I told Meg I was going to EFAS."

Lynn sat again but not beside John this time, choosing an armchair instead. She hated the lies. Hated deceiving Meg. It was as if she and John had something to hide when in fact they had done nothing. Nothing much. No kissing or pressing bodies close together. No shagging. But they were playing with fire.

"So you think Francine went to New Zealand and tracked down Patrick's nephew?" she said as calmly as possible. "And then what?"

"I haven't worked it out properly yet. Patrick said Yan rang him out of the blue. More coincidence, or was it that Francine had already found Yan in New Zealand and urged him on?"

"Hmm. Could be. But why?"

"Think like Francine. Try anyway, Lynn."

"Yan Gilmore is Patrick's nephew, his next-of-kin. He's legally and morally entitled to inherit from Patrick. Add 60 per cent of EFAS to the tourist business Yan's supposed to have in New Zealand and he'll be a wealthy man. A good catch for Francine. Which brings us back to the main question. What does Francine want from you? Why did she target *you*?"

John shrugged and looked at Lynn helplessly. "I'd better go," he said. "Meg's been in a mood all weekend. I don't want to make things worse."

Lynn looked down at her hands. Niggles of guilt resurged

at the mention of her best friend's name. She felt uneasy too at John's criticism of his wife. Meg had a right to be moody, hadn't she? Her husband had allowed himself to be seduced by one woman and was confiding in another. What did that leave for Meg? Not much, judging by the negative way she had been talking about her marriage last week. It seemed that the Enrights thought Lynn Rooney had nothing better to do than listen to their complaints about each other.

Suddenly, inexplicably, it was all too much. John just needed a confidante. Someone he could tell the things he was ashamed to tell his wife. Things like groping Francine Keyes in her apartment. But Lynn wanted more. So much more. The need made her edgy now. Sorry that she had cancelled her trip. Lynn Rooney wanted to run again.

John was standing up, getting his jacket and talking as he shrugged into it. "I think our best bet is to wait until Yan Gilmore arrives here. Some time next week according to Francine. Everything should be clearer by then. What do you think, Lynn?"

"I think you should go home to your wife. Talk to her. Tell her all the things you've told me. I know you want to protect Meg but she deserves the truth." Lynn was breathless, stunned by her flood of words but unable to stop them. "I can't do any more to help with the mess you've got yourself into, John. I can't go on talking to you behind Meg's back. It's not right."

John stood still, his hand on the jacket zip he had been just about to close. He stared at Lynn as if she had gone mad. "What's not right about us being friends? We've known each other for years, for God's sake!"

"So why are we lying to Meg?"

"She wouldn't understand …"

"For heaven's sake, don't give me that old line! My wife doesn't understand me! How do you know she wouldn't? You haven't told her any of this, have you? Are you waiting for Francine Keyes to tell her?"

John flinched as if she had struck him across the face. Lynn's anger was beginning to wane now and in its wake came a wave of overwhelming sadness. What in the fuck was she doing? Getting rid of the only man she had ever loved because of some sentimental loyalty to Meg Riordan. Had Meg thought of her friend when she waltzed John Enright up the aisle? When she had his children and washed his shirts and cuddled into him every night? Had she ever wondered why Lynn Rooney had never settled down, why she was restless and so often lonely? No, she had not.

"I don't understand" John said. "I thought we were friends."

Lynn looked at the confused man standing in front of her and for the first time saw him as he was. A weak man. Easy prey for Francine Keyes. A disloyal man, deceiving his wife, obsessed with his work, authoritarian with his children. A man so insensitive to other's feelings he could not see that Lynn was aching with love for him. Even now, even with the hazy veil of first love lifted, Lynn loved him more. He no longer fitted the ideals she had attributed to him but she could still see beyond the deceit and obsession to the warm-hearted, fun-loving man buried beneath. The man she had first met in The Grattan Club more than twenty years ago.

Frustrated, disgusted with herself, Lynn strode over to the hall door and turning to face him, held it wide open.

"Go home, John. Talk to Meg."

His face registered shock and Lynn felt a moment's satisfaction. His reaction restored pride to her battered ego. When the colour drained from his face she even stood a little taller. It was the staring eyes that began to worry her. She followed John's gaze to the corridor outside.

Meg was standing there, her hand raised as if to ring the bell. She too was ashen-faced, her beautiful eyes puffy from crying. They stood transfixed, the Three Amigos, each head thundering with words they could not speak.

Meg's hand dropped to her side and then she turned her back and walked stiffly away. Like a robot. A mechanical toy whose batteries were running down. Lynn heard a whoosh as John exhaled the breath he had been holding, then he too went down the corridor with the peculiar gait of someone shambling his way through a nightmare.

It was some time before Lynn got the strength to close the door.

* * *

Meg drove home on autopilot. She was parking in the driveway before anything began to register in her mind. Little things like the way John had been just about to close his jacket and how Lynn's cheeks had been flushed.

The light was on in the kitchen. Carrie was still up. She came into the hall to meet her mother.

"Where did you go, Mum? You gave me a fright rushing off like that."

"I- I ..."

Carrie peered at Meg and then took her by the arm and led her into the kitchen. She sat her down and then took her hand. "Is it Dad?" she asked. "You dashed off after I mentioned seeing him. Has something happened to him? An accident?"

Meg looked into her daughter's dark eyes. There would be no point in lying to her now. She'd have to know. Everyone would. Everyone probably already knew. Except Meg. Trusting, stupid Meg.

"Lynn," Meg whispered as if she was trying to speak the words so quietly that not even she would hear them. "He was in Lynn's apartment."

"So?"

"He told me he was going to work. He said he got a taxi on Friday night and she called to see him at work and they were discussing me ..."

"Mum! Slow down. You're not making any sense."

"But it makes perfect sense. I should have seen it before. She fancied him from the first day she saw him. I thought she had outgrown it though. I thought she was my friend."

"Surely you're not saying there's something going on between Dad and Lynn? Don't be daft, Mum! He just dropped in to ask about her car or something like that. What did he say?"

"I didn't wait to talk to him."

Carrie sat back and regarded her mother with a look that was so impatient yet loving that Meg felt like the child and her beautiful dark-eyed daughter the parent.

"Look at you! Look at the state you're in. Imagining all sorts of sordid things without even talking to Dad. Lynn is your best friend. Do you really believe that even if Dad wanted to mess around, he'd do it with your best friend?"

Meg heard the key in the front door. Her breath caught

in her throat. She wanted to see John, to look into his eyes and search for treachery there, to examine his lips for traces of someone else's kisses. And yet, with an equal intensity, she never wanted to see him again.

His footsteps were heavy and slow as he came through the hall. Eyes down, back to the door, Meg sensed his arrival into the kitchen. Carrie waved him over to sit at the table. Meg was engulfed in a wave of Red Door perfume. Lynn's. Bitch Lynn!

"Give me your hand, Dad," Carrie ordered and, like Meg, he recognised the adult in his child and did what he was told. "Now take Mum's."

John's hand came into Meg's line of vision. It was a strong hand, with well-shaped nails and soft black hairs on the back Meg used to love to stroke. When they used to hold hands. Before they both got too busy living their separate lives. John took her hand and she felt her skin shrivel at his touch as if it wanted to dissolve, as if physical contact with him was so repugnant that her hand would rather melt than latch onto his.

They were sitting now, the three of them, hands held, looking like they were ready to call up a ghost. The spectre of the Enrights' marriage. Meg raised her head to look at Carrie, to plead for her release from the circle which was threatening to choke her. Carrie's eyes were closed and her head bowed. She began to speak. Very softly at first but getting progressively stronger.

"I call on the healing Light to shine into John and Meg's hearts. Help them to see the love there. Praise The Light."

Meg felt her hand grow warm. The one Carrie was holding. Her other hand had lost its memory of sensation. It sat trapped in John's big hand, a prisoner to his strength. She clung on to her daughter and listened intently to the music in her voice. She didn't hear the words. They were all Karl Hemmings-type ramblings but she heard the sincerity, the faith, the hope.

"What in the hell's going on? Have ye all lost the plot?"

The circle was abruptly broken as the three at the table turned to look at Tommy.

"You look like shit, Mum. Were you crying?"

Tommy's eyes immediately turned to his father and he took a step forward.

Carrie stood and placed herself in front of her brother.

"Mum and Dad need some space, Tom. Let's go to the lounge."

"Why? What's going on? First Mum went running out of here like a scalded cat and now she's all upset. Is this your fault, Dad?"

Wearily, John lifted his head and spoke to his son. "It's just a misunderstanding. Do as Carrie says. I want to talk to your mother."

"A misunderstanding? How?"

Carrie caught Tommy by the arm and began to steer him towards the door but he pulled his arm away from her and walked back to his father.

"Stop treating me like this is none of my business," he said angrily to John. "Why is Mum upset? Look at her! She's like a zombie. What did you do to her?"

"Get out, Tommy! Go to your room."

"C'mon, Tom," Carrie encouraged but Tommy would not budge.

"No! You won't bully me this time. I'm not going until you tell me."

"It's private," Carrie explained. "It's about their relationship and nothing to do with us."

Tommy turned to Meg. "Mum? What have you to say? What happened to you?"

Meg heard the plea in her son's voice. She heard fear and a need to be respected. To be treated like an adult in an adult situation. She raised her head and looked at the long gangly figure that was her son. She saw the sparkle of anger in his eyes and the quiver of fear on his lips and decided he was not mature enough for the truth. Hell! She was not mature enough for this truth but they would all have to face it anyway. She took a deep breath.

"Carrie's right, Tom. This is about the relationship between your father and me. We have a lot of talking to do and I can't tell you yet what we'll decide."

"What you decide? Do you mean you might – that ye might …"

" I'm so sorry that you and Carrie have to go through this upset. Now, can you give us some time, please?"

When Tommy banged his fist on the table, Meg shrank back in fright at the rage she had unleashed in her son.

"You stupid old man!" He spat venomously at his father. "I warned you about that slut! She's just a cocktease. Everybody but you could see that. Even Dan Shorten saw it and he's as thick as two planks. Not John Enright though. She's nothing but a tarted-up tramp!"

"Tommy! Enough!" Carrie said in tones that for her were angry. "I know this is a terrible situation but you're making it worse. There could be, there probably is, a reasonable explanation for what happened tonight to upset Mum. That's for Dad and her to work out. But I think you should apologise for the disgusting names you've called Lynn."

Tommy stared at Carrie, mouth open. "Lynn? Lynn? I'm not talking about her. Why would I say anything like that about Lynn?"

"There's been a misunderstanding," John said again, his eyes darting about from one to the other. Like a trapped animal.

Meg and Carrie were silent, their quietness telling Tommy more than John's bluster. Now he knew. The old man had been knocking off Lynn Rooney. Had Meg caught them at it? Was that why she had gone dashing out tonight like someone possessed? The prick! The two-faced git!

Meg broke the silence. "Who were you talking about Tommy? Who is the 'tarted-up tramp' you and Dan Shorten discussed? The one you warned your father about?"

"Don't involve our son in this," John said quickly. "That's not fair, Meg. It's between us."

Meg turned briefly in her husband's direction. Just long enough to say "Shut up!". Then she looked at Tommy again. "Well, Tom? What else should I know?"

Tommy shook his head in bewilderment and for an instant Meg felt she had made a mistake. It was unfair to drag Tommy into the middle of this cesspit of deceit. But yet he had been adamant about 'the slut'. Meg was just working her way towards the answer when Tommy said the words.

"Francine Keyes. The receptionist in EFAS. I'm only saying he drools over her like an old fool. I'm not saying anything else, Mum. I shouldn't have mentioned it. Sorry. I've just made things worse. I'm going to my room. Are you coming, Carr?"

Meg felt as if she was outside herself, looking down on the sad tableau of a family in crisis. Husband exposed, shocked by being caught. Daughter, caring, holding desperately onto bonds which had held them together and were now snapping under the strain of the truth. Son, full of rage, resenting his father, protecting his mother. And the mother? Meg was floating, waiting, knowing that this peaceful quiet space she had found for herself was just a temporary respite.

The click of the kitchen door seemed loud as Carrie and Tommy closed it behind them. It shattered Meg's bubble of peace. John's mouth was working, preparing to make excuses, tell lies. Meg looked at him floundering and she felt strong. She smiled at him.

"Right, John. I want the truth. All of it. I want to hear about Lynn Rooney, Francine Keyes and any other affairs you may have had during our marriage."

His head was bowed and his shoulders slumped. Meg saw his body shake and realised he was crying. She felt glad. Elated that he too was feeling pain. The hot rush of vengeance swelled and ebbed, leaving Meg full of shame.

That's when Meg decided her self-respect was too big a price to pay. John Enright had already taken too much of what was good in Meg Riordan. He would get no more.

"I'll have the truth, John. Nothing less will do but I want you to know that anything you tell me will not have a bearing on the decision I've made. I want our marriage to end. It's over, and not because of tonight. It ended a long time ago. Maybe it never really began."

Tears clung to the long lashes framing John's dark brown eyes, his cheeks were pale, his eyebrows raised in shock. He found his voice. "You can't be serious Meg! You haven't even listened to what I have to say. Nothing happened with me and Lynn for Christ's sake! You can't end our marriage just like that. Without even talking about it!"

Meg looked away from his face. It was easier to hear his pain than to look at it. There was no space for weakness or sentiment now. Ending a long-standing marriage required determination and strength. Meg felt empowered by both. She was strong. She had heard, with pride, her own voice speak the words of release. John would never have spoken them. He was his mother's son, full of duty and obligation and resentment at the suffering those duties and obligations imposed. Just as he had married Meg out of duty, he would have stayed married to her until one of them had died, embittered and not loved enough. It would not matter now how John begged or pleaded or made excuses. The words had been spoken and they would no longer lie silently in wait.

"We've had the best we can offer each other, John. It's not enough."

"But I love you, Meg. You know I do."

She smiled at him and gently touched his hand. "I love you too, John. I always will. We've had some good times together and two beautiful children. But we're hurting each other now. Whatever we had together is cold and tinged with bitterness. It's time to end it before it destroys us."

He lifted her hand and pressed his lips to the long, artistic fingers which once drove him wild with passion. She stroked his hair and remembered how luxuriously black it had been before time and care had streaked it with silver.

"We must talk, John."

They did. Far into the night, they talked like they never had before. About Lynn Rooney and Francine Keyes. About hopes and dreams unfulfilled. About worries they had carried alone but never shared, loneliness that work and busy schedules never eased, expectations that were never fulfilled. When he asked how they could ever live without each other and she told him, he finally accepted that Meg would not change her mind.

"I'd like to stay in this house as long as the children need to be here," she said. "You can move out. We need to be separated for some time anyway before divorce."

They talked about maintenance and division of assets, of the minutiae of dismantling a marriage of over twenty years' duration. Then they cried for all the lost dreams and promises of eternal love which had proved impossible to keep. Exhausted, they turned off the kitchen lights and walked upstairs together.

"Do you think we can we still be friends?" John asked as they stood on the upstairs landing.

Meg shook her head. "Of course not. How can we? We have two children and a lifetime of sharing together. We'll always be more than just friends. What we were together will be the heart of what we will become apart."

"I'm so sorry, Meg. I never meant to hurt you."

Meg knew this was true. He had never meant for her to find out about Lynn or Francine Keyes either or ever give his marriage higher priority in his life over his precious work. But she said nothing now. All the talking had been done. Except for one thing.

"There's something I must tell you," she said, "and it will probably upset you a lot."

She heard his intake of breath and knew he was bracing himself.

"Your mother's sheets, her good white linens, are hanging in the window of Curtain Call. I used them as a backdrop for the painting I did."

She turned then and walked into their bedroom, closing the door firmly behind her. It was a few minutes before she heard the door to the guest bedroom open and then close. She imagined his face, pale and shocked, and she felt a deep sadness at knowing his biggest shock had been her announcement about Hannah Enright's goddamn sheets. Meg's biggest shock was the pleasure she had taken in making that announcement.

The grandeur of the forever wedding vows they had taken had finally faded. And Hannah Enright had been a glowering presence at the ignominious ending, just as she had been at the hopeful beginning.

CHAPTER 25

John sensed that he was in an unfamiliar place even before he opened his eyes. The morning light filtering through his closed lids was more intense, the smells were different. No trace of Meg's warm, flowery scent or of the lavender which pervaded their bedroom from the little bunches of the dried shrub Meg always hung in the wardrobe.

His eyes opened slowly and surveyed the neutrality of the spare bedroom. It was clean and bright. Like a room one could hire for the night in a medium-priced hotel. Along with the images of a bare dressing table and an empty wardrobe came the recollection of why he was in this room and the trail of events which had led him here. He saw Lynn holding the door of her apartment open for him to leave, Meg staring wide-eyed, Tommy red-faced with anger, Carrie's eyes glowing with fervour as she muttered words she believed could sort this mess, this nightmare so potent it refused to disperse in the daylight.

Throwing back the duvet, John got out of bed. Then he stood, not knowing what to do. Meg had been adamant last night. Her calmness had terrified him. There had been no shouting or hysterical tears. Just a coldness and a practicality John had never seen in his wife before. Those traits must have been there, along with her dissatisfaction and the sense of rejection she had spoken about. He had not seen them either.

Looking at his watch, John noted it was six o'clock in the morning. What in the fuck was he supposed to do now? Stay here and try talking to Meg again, beg her to change her mind? Go to EFAS and deal with part two of the nightmare there? Yan Gilmore would probably be here soon. John should know exactly when. He should have kept in touch with Yan instead of leaving that to Francine. That too was Francine's fault. If she hadn't been strutting around the place, sneering at him, threatening him, then he could have concentrated on the business of the new boss from down under. And maybe seen that Meg was dissatisfied and unhappy.

John felt a wave of anger so hot that it surged around his body, brought a red flush to his face and beads of sweat to his forehead. His breathing was ragged as he closed his eyes and imagined for an instant Francine tumbling head over heels down a rocky mountain and disappearing, screaming for help, limbs flailing, into a ravine. He tried to take comfort from the imagined scene but his eyes immediately opened. He didn't wish Francine harm. He just wished her gone. And with an intensity that shook his already shocked system, he wished he could be in Lynn's apartment now, sitting on her couch, Lynn's head on his shoulder. Being quietly together. Absorbing strength and support from the closeness. The one oasis of peace he had left in the turmoil his life had become.

Even that had been taken from him now. Meg had seen to that.

He tiptoed into the bedroom he had shared with Meg and knew they would never share it again. Standing beside the bed, he watched her sleeping, her dark hair spread out on the pillow, her full lips slightly parted. Even now, he was in awe of her delicate beauty. And with that thought came the realisation that her beauty alone had not been enough. He didn't understand this woman. He knew every inch of her body, every detail of her history but he did not know her. Nor did she know him. Had she ever understood how badly he had needed to succeed in business, how he had been driven by the instinct to protect his wife and children against the poverty he had known in childhood? Perhaps she had and he was the one who had not understood her need for sharing.

Turning away from the sleeping woman in the bed, John crept to the wardrobe and quietly took out what clothes he needed for the day. Later he would get the rest of his things, find some little bolthole where he could be alone. One of the legion of separated husbands who occupied bed-sits and pretended to revel in their enforced freedom. But first he must go to EFAS. Face Francine Keyes, the cause of all his problems, head-on. Life had been alright – the type of alright Meg was now rejecting but he had found comforting – before Francine imposed herself and her lethal breasts on him. He hadn't as much to lose now. He was hurting, humiliated, belittled in the eyes of his wife and children. However he managed it, the bitch Keyes would pay for that.

Showered, dressed and with a cup of coffee and a monumental anger inside him, John Enright headed for EFAS and a confrontation with Francine Keyes.

* * *

Lynn Rooney had been power-walking for fifteen minutes before the sun began to rise on a day she would prefer not to face. At some stage during the tear-filled night she had jumped in her car and driven towards the suburban town of Carrigaline, twelve kilometers south of Cork city. She didn't know why she had come here except that in her confused state of thinking, Carrigaline had seemed to offer an escape from her apartment where the very walls oozed accusations of treachery.

She had sniffed sea air on the wind when she got out of the car and had turned her face into the breeze to follow the ozone scent. The trail led her along the walkway linking Carrigaline to the coastal town of Crosshaven. She had been in Crosshaven many times before. When she had been young and full of hope and the expectation that life would be good and full of adventure. There had been a day, a very special Three Amigos day, when she and Meg and John had come to Crosshaven, swum in the cool Atlantic, stood near the old fort in Camden and gazed across the sparkling expanse of ocean at the cathedral town of Cobh, eaten chips wrapped in swathes of butchers' paper while sitting on the sea wall in the town and then, as the sun had set, they had gone to the amusement park and laughed and giggled as they crashed into each other in dodgems and whirled skyward in chair o'planes. They had been inseparable then, the Three Amigos.

As she strode along the walkway now, the Owenabue River on her left-hand side, the still blackness of forest on her right, Lynn knew that she could never escape the accusations because they were inside her head and were tramping along with her, pounding out the rhythm of her steps. Lynn Rooney husband thief, Lynn Rooney liar, Lynn Rooney cheat. Lynn Rooney destroyer of marriages.

She stopped walking. The eastern horizon was aflame with oranges and shimmering yellows. She had come to a widening in the Owenabue estuary and she remembered that this placid body of water was named Drake's Pool. According to legend, it was where in 1587, pursued by the Spanish fleet, Admiral Drake had led his five ships from the wide open spaces of Cork Harbour to shelter in this secluded spot until his enemies had given up the chase.

Exhausted, confused, she sat on one of the waterside benches and thought about Sir Francis Drake. Had his heart thumped painfully as he navigated his fleet towards the mouth of Cork Harbour? Had there been desperation in his voice as he urged his crew to greater efforts? Had he felt fear, imagined the agony of a cannon ball tearing through his gut or Atlantic brine flooding his lungs, sucking him and his crew to the silty floor of the ocean? Probably not. He would have stood on the prow of his galleon and calmly plotted his escape. Just as Lynn would have to do now.

The still waters of Drake's Pool were tinged with oranges and pinks. Anchored yachts began to emerge from the fading darkness. On the opposite side of the pool a cottage appeared, nestling in a backdrop of evergreens while the garden sloped down to the banks. A magic cottage, a safe place protected by water and wood, witness to reflected sunrise and sunset and maybe, just maybe, the ghostly image of Francis Drake's galleon as he protected his crew through the centuries.

Lynn felt a longing to be in that cottage now. Just in front of her, a rowing boat was moored. Suppose she slipped into it and rowed across to the slipway opposite, dipping her oars in the orange-tinged water, breaking the stillness, spreading ripples across the pool. She could walk up the slipway, through the garden and up to the safe little cottage. And then what? The owner would open the door and ask Lynn Rooney why she was here, tell her to go away and find her own safe place, her own husband, her own life.

The emergence of the new day was relentless. The sun rose and poked into the dark spaces. Feeling the chill of morning, Lynn left her seat and continued her arm-swinging, foot-pounding walk towards Crosshaven. There were deciduous trees now, mottled with the russets and golds of autumn. Such a rich season, full of the colour of life and the promise of rebirth in the spring. And in between the starkness of winter and death.

Lynn stopped walking again. Death. This was the thought which would not allow itself to be examined all night. It had lurked in the back of her mind, mocking her attempts at hope and reconciliation, disdainful of her hope for a future.

She turned to the river. It was moving faster here, surging towards the salty Atlantic waters. The river had nearly reached its goal. It was almost back to the sea. Home. Safe in the strong swells of the ocean below, the pull and push of the moon above. It had a purpose, a direction. It would be comforting to join with the purposeful river.

The fencing was low. Lynn climbed over and slipped and slid down the stony embankment until the water was lapping around her feet and she could see clumps of seaweed swirling beneath the surface. This was where brine and fresh water mingled and became one. A leaf, withered and brown, sailed past, tossed and tumbled by the race of the river towards its destiny. Lynn watched the leaf until she could see it no more and she felt an empathy with it. Had she not been as dependent on the course of the Enrights' relationship as the leaf was on the flow of the river? How many years had she stood on the edge of their lives, satisfied with the little access she had been allowed, loving them all, Meg and Carrie, Tommy and John with a passion which was futile and had now proved lethal?

That passion had destroyed them all. Lynn knew, standing here with the water lapping around her feet, that Meg would leave John. She had seen the devastation in Meg's beautiful face last night. And the same devastation had been reflected in John's. The Enrights' marriage was over. Carrie and Tommy would have to suffer the consequences of the breakdown of their parents' marriage. And it was all Lynn Rooney's fault. All because she had needed John to need her. Why had she not sent him home to Meg the first time he had wanted to confide in her? Telling her the things he wanted to spare Meg. The secret of his shameful visit to Francine Keyes apartment. What a fool John Enright was! An idiot to jeopardise everything for a quick thrill. A weak-willed, short-sighted, man.

And yet, Lynn loved him. She always would. Until the day she died. She had no control over the intensity of her passion for John Enright. Her love for him had been written in her DNA, ordained in her chromosomes. But she could control the duration. She could decide that today her destructive love would end. This could be the day when

Lynn Rooney would be no more. It would be so easy to float away in the path of the withered leaf, let the water wash over her humiliation, let the tide absorb her hurt. There would be nothing after her final struggle for air, her final gasp of pain. She knew that in the place deep inside where we all know our own truths. Death was a definitive ending. A nothingness. No deceitful John Enright, no accusing Meg, no guilty heartbeats and sweaty palms as she secretly pined for another woman's husband. No need to book another solo trip to a foreign country where she would wear her loneliness like a badge on her forehead, attracting those who preyed on needy, ageing women. Lynn knew all this with certainty. A step into the Owenabue River would take her towards oblivion. Ultimate peace.

The oranges and reds of sunrise had given way to the clear white light of day. The water sparkled now as it danced towards the sea. Lynn Rooney stood with her toes in the water and tried to decide if she had the strength to face Meg, to look John in the eye and say she never wanted to see him again, to apologise to Carrie and Tommy for her part in the break-up of their family, to run and run and see places that were garish and hot and not where she wanted to be. Or to take that final step towards the river. To end the turmoil in one quick, cold, choking gasp. These were the questions that Lynn asked the river, the trees, the rippling waves and the seagulls which swooped low over the surface of the water. The answers were not there. Then Lynn closed her eyes and looked inside her own head. That's where she found the answer she needed.

CHAPTER 26

As John approached EFAS storage unit he saw that Ollie was again fussing around the front of the building, his strides short and quick as he marched up and down. Either the yobs had been back last night, teasing the old security man, or Ollie was finally losing the plot. John made up his mind. This was it. The old man would have to go. He was a liability.

"Good morning, Ollie. Everything alright?"

"I want to talk to you," Ollie said abruptly in a most un-Ollie-like way. The energy John had assumed to be fussiness was more like anger now. There was no 'boss', no respect in the old man's steady gaze. Just fury and maybe contempt.

John sighed. So Ollie was joining in the get-John-Enright gang. Why not? Wordlessly, he signalled Ollie to follow him into the office. John put on the kettle and when the old man just sat there, making no effort to get out mugs and milk, John made the two coffees himself. The silence was dragging on as they sat on either side of the desk and it was getting on John's nerves.

"You wanted to talk to me, Ollie."

"Yes. I'll give you that courtesy. But you don't deserve it. Not after what you did."

John almost dropped the mugful of coffee from which he had been about to drink. Did the whole fucking world know every detail of his life? How dare this bothered old man sit here and judge him!

"I beg your pardon! What do you mean, Ollie? Since when is my private life any of your concern?"

"I don't give a toss about your private life. That's nothing to do with me and I have no interest in it anyway. I'm talking about work. I may have been low down on the ladder here. Just the night-security man. But I took my job seriously. I was conscientious, punctual and I believe good at my job. I deserve better than this."

"Ollie, what in the fuck are you talking about? You've lost me."

"Ah, stop, John! Don't make things worse. Victor Collins told me."

"Victor Collins! The guy with the washing-machine components he thinks are top priority? What about him? What did he say?"

"He told me what you hadn't the guts to say to my face. That you're getting rid of me and replacing me with some young fellows he knows. Starting this week. When were you going to tell me? On the phone, by letter? I never had you down as a coward. Until now, that is."

John put his elbows on the desk and lowered his head onto his hands. Jesus! Another knife in the back. Why in the fuck had Victor Collins stirred the shit like this? How much more could go wrong? A coward, Ollie had called him and that's exactly how John felt now. Cowardly. Cowering away from this life which seemed to be running out of control. There was outrage and hurt too in Ollie's watery eyes. John owed this dignified old man an explanation at the very least.

"The truth is, Ollie, that I was indeed considering asking you if you felt able to continue with this job. I wondered if the attempted break-in, or whatever it was that happened last week, had upset you too much. Victor Collins wasn't too happy about it and suggested I consider employing some people he knows for security here. But I did not, and you must believe this, Ollie, I did *not* make any arrangements to replace you. I don't know why Victor Collins said that."

"Maybe you should ask Francine Keyes. She seems to know Victor Collins better than you do."

"Francine knows Victor Collins well? Are you sure? What makes you think that?"

"I see them chatting a lot. They both have a habit of turning up here late at night. She rings the young boss in New Zealand. She says you told her to. Collins brings boxes in and out of his storage space. He's used it more in the short time he has it than most people do in a year. I don't trust him."

"He's kosher. He manufactures components and is just storing them until they're shipped. He's a prick though. An awkward bollocks."

"Anyway, John, Victor Collins is your problem now. And Francine Keyes too if I'm any judge of character. A sharp one that. You won't have to bother yourself firing me. I'm leaving."

"Ollie, I ..."

The old man raised his hand to silence John, a gesture which confirmed he, not his boss, was the one in charge. "I'm going immediately. I'm not leaving you in the lurch.

Collins' yobs are waiting to take my place. I don't want any more of this. It's too changed from when Patrick Morgan was here."

. Ollie stood and offered his hand to John. John took the calloused, wrinkled hand and felt sadness at yet another goodbye.

"Are you sure, Ollie? There's no need to go if you don't want to. I'm not firing you."

"Herself is worried since those brats tried to get in here. She told me leave."

"Well, that's that then," John said, relieved.

"She's a good woman. I owe her some time. You might send my paperwork out to me, please. My P45 and whatever monies are due. I doubt if I'll ever set foot in EFAS again."

Ollie turned then and walked out of the office where he and John had shared a morning cup of coffee for so many years. John had thought they had shared friendship too. He had been wrong. He had been wrong about so many things.

* * *

Francine gently stroked the smooth, brown skin of her lover's back, allowing her fingers trace each strong muscle, every curve and line of this perfect specimen of masculinity. She had been awake since dawn, lying in bed beside him, admiring him, thanking her lucky stars that out of a plethora of adventure sports companies in Queenstown, she had chosen this man's company. They were meant to be, she and Mike Choy. Their bodies fit like two parts of an intricately cut jigsaw and their minds were focused on the one aim. Their future.

He stirred and turned towards her, wrapping his arms and legs around her. She gently extricated herself from his embrace. Quickly, before she reached the stage where she could not say no.

"Good morning, Yan Gilmore," she said softly.

He opened his brown eyes, the unusual eyes slanted at the corners and as clear as mountain air. For an instant he looked puzzled. Just long enough for Francine to feel a little stab of pain. Then he smiled at her and she forgave him. She got out of bed and reached for her robe.

"Are you ready for today?" she asked.

He rolled onto his back again and put his arms behind his head. Francine tried not to look at his chest and what she could see of his flat stomach above the duvet. That was for later. Now was for introducing Patrick Morgan to his nephew. Re-introducing, she reminded herself. They had met when Yan was ten years old. At his grandfather's funeral.

"I'm nervous," Mike said and Francine was surprised.

"Why? You've spoken to him often enough on the phone, haven't you? Ye seem to get on fine. Why should it be any different in person?"

He shrugged and grinned at her. "No worries. You'll be with me, won't you?"

"All the way. I'm going into EFAS now. Today is the day I tell John Enright what I want from him. Pity you won't be there to see his reaction. I think he may even cry."

"You should have had that sorted before I arrived here."

"I was having fun," Francine said and put on her pouty face.

"Fun's over for now. This is the serious bit. I'll convince Patrick to sign his 60 per cent over to me immediately and you ensure John Enright's 40 per cent. Let's get this company sold as quickly as possible. Life is waiting to happen, Francine."

"I've another surprise for you," she said, sitting down on the bed beside him. She needed to be close to see his reaction. "I may have a buyer for EFAS."

"What! Already? We don't even own it yet. You're some tough cookie, Francine Keyes! Who?"

"A guy named Victor Collins. A new customer at EFAS. A fussy little prick. He manufactures some kind of components and he's obsessive about security. He's complaining since he signed the contract with EFAS."

"So why would he want to buy it if he's not satisfied?"

"Maybe he thinks he can run it better. Or maybe it would make business sense for him to own a secure facility instead of renting one."

"Could he afford six million or thereabouts? That's the valuation on EFAS according to the accountant."

Six million euro! Francine felt a thrill race through her body. She had estimated it would be in that region but it was nice to hear official confirmation. Three million of that would be hers. Francine Keyes, millionairess. She had always known she would make it some day. It was just icing on the cake that she was doing so with this gorgeous man by her side.

"Yes, I think Victor Collins can afford it. He didn't turn a hair when I mentioned what I thought the company was worth. And what's more I think he's definitely going to go for it. But not, I hope, until after the old man has signed over to you."

"That's my girl," Mike said and Francine felt a warm glow. She stood up reluctantly.

"I must get ready for work now. I'll go to EFAS to deal with John Enright first. Then I'll call to Patrick Morgan. Warn him that I'm on my way to the airport to collect his nephew. I'll call for you around eleven o'clock, okay? Make sure you're packed and ready when I arrive. And in character. Yan's character, that is."

"Yes, ma'am," he said, grinning as he gave her a mock salute.

Francine stooped and kissed him on the lips. A long, moist kiss.

"See you later, Yan Gilmore," she said as she managed to drag herself away from him. It was time to collect the dividends for all her plotting and planning. Francine sang as she got ready for work.

* * *

There was a new sound in Lynn's ears. Squelch, slap, squelch, slap as her wet shoes froze her feet and made walking back to the car park in Carrigaline a cold and heavy task.

At her car, she opened up the boot and wondered if she had always carried a spare pair of shoes in the car in preparation for today. Had she instinctively known that, one day, she would walk into a river meaning to float away, and then change her mind just as the water lapped around her calves. So obsessive was she about her spare shoes, that she had even put a pair into the lease car from the insurance company she was now driving. They were tan leather lace-ups, worn and encrusted with dried mud, but manna from heaven. Sitting in the driver's seat, facing out, Lynn took off her wet trainers and socks, dried her feet with tissues and pushed them into the tatty lace-ups.

376

Holding the sopping trainers in her hand she examined them curiously. Her suicide shoes. The footwear she would have been wearing when her body was recovered. If she had taken that extra step into the waiting water. Or maybe she would have disappeared without trace, swallowed up by sharks or nibbled into nothingness by crabs and creatures of the deep. By the ocean. Maybe one day, a child, searching a distant shoreline for treasure, would find a trainer, a suicide shoe, and wonder from where it had come. Just as Lynn wondered now from where the whole notion of ending it all, of opting out, had come. From guilt and shame for sure. But not her guilt or her shame. She had just loved too well, too quietly, for too long.

Holding the suicide shoes by the laces, Lynn walked over to the nearest litter bin. Feeling a ceremony would be appropriate, she swung the shoes in an arc over her head before dumping them. Then she laughed out loud with relief, with joy at the touch of warming sun on her face, with wonder at the luscious blackberries on the nearby brambles, with pleasure at the returning sensations in her freezing toes. Lynn laughed aloud as hope returned, a future loomed.

The laughing stopped abruptly when a jeep pulled into the car park. The joys of life were all very well but Lynn didn't want to be locked up in an asylum before she had a chance to live through the time she had almost rejected. Laughing into a litter bin was hardly the action of a sane, rational woman. The woman who would become the new Lynn Rooney.

The jeep stopped beside Lynn's car. A woman got out and was quickly followed by two golden Labradors. The dogs scampered across the grass, tails held high, sniffing at the things which interested dogs.

"Good morning," the woman greeted Lynn. "Isn't it beautiful now?"

"Good morning," Lynn answered. "It is indeed. I think it's going to be a magnificent day."

And Lynn Rooney truly believed what she said to the stranger in the car park in Carrigaline. It was going to be a magnificent day, week, year, life. And it would all begin as soon as she tidied up the loose ends of the life she was now going to leave behind.

CHAPTER 27

"Carr! Wake up, Carrie! What's going on? Do you know?"

Carrie woke to the sight of Tommy standing over her bed, his face puckered with worry. She squinted at him and then hauled herself up in bed.

"Shouldn't you be leaving for school now, Tom? You know you'll have to get the bus because Mum's not going into the shop until later."

"Fuck school! How can I go there when I don't know whether I have a home or not? The old man's gone. Is he just gone to EFAS or has he hightailed it to one of his other women? Pervy old git!"

"Tommy! None of this is going to be made any better by your attitude. You don't know what happened between Dad and Lynn and that Francine woman. I'm sure there's an explanation."

"Maybe about Lynn. I can't believe she'd hurt Mum like that. But Francine Keyes? I saw him, Carr. I knew there was something going on the way they were gawping at each other. Francine told Dan Shorten that Dad scared the shit out of her. That he was weird. I don't believe her though. The devil himself wouldn't scare her."

Carrie got out of bed. She liked to start the day with a quiet prayer but she just couldn't face Tommy's irreverent comments this morning. She smiled at him, noticing the dark circles under his eyes.

"Did you sleep at all last night?" she asked.

"For a while. I stayed awake as long as I could. I was listening for slamming doors or raised voices from the kitchen. There were none. The parents were very quiet, whatever they decided."

Carrie put on her dressing gown and then, seeing her brother's woebegone face, she hugged him.

"Everything will be alright, Tom. Just have faith."

"Don't mention The Light, Carr. I'll freak. There's enough insanity in this house already. Do you think they'll stay together?"

"I've no idea. We don't really know what happened to shock Mum so badly. C'mon downstairs. Have you had breakfast?"

"Couldn't eat. What'll happen to us if they split up? Where will we live?"

Carrie caught his hand. He looked so young, so vulnerable. A tender pawn in a tough game. She prayed. Silently, so that he could not be angry with her. She prayed that Garth would soon be with her, that Karl Hemmings would receive the sign he needed from The Light in order to send his son from Maine to Cork and to Carrie. She prayed for Meg and John, for Tommy and Lynn too. Poor lonely Lynn.

Squeezing Tommy's hand, Carrie tried to impart faith,

hope and calm in the touch.

"It's too early yet to decide anything. Relationships are complicated. We must give them space and wait for them to talk to us. Anyway, I thought you couldn't wait to get away from them. Now come on. Last down the stairs is a big girl's blouse!"

They raced down the stairs together, laughing and jostling each other.

Meg woke to the sound of their laughter. She smiled. Then she remembered the things sleep had blanked out. Meg cried.

* * *

Francine made no attempt at pseudo-respect this morning. She strode into John's office on particularly high heels and, standing with her hands on his desk, she sneered at him. There was no other way to describe the smile which curved her lips beautifully but lit her eyes with spite and disdain. It was an insult too far for John.

"Sit down, Francine. I need to talk to you about your continuing employment here. It's not viable. It can't continue."

She sat and slowly crossed her long legs so that John knew if the desk was not in the way he could probably see her pantics. Unless of course she wasn't wearing any. A possibility. She smiled coyly as if reading his thoughts. Fuck her!

"I've had enough of you and your threats, Francine. I admit I engaged in some inappropriate behavior. It was foolish but not criminal. You lured me into it. Initiated it.

Trapped me. I'll fight you every step of the way if you try to make a fuss. I should have thrown you out of here a long time ago."

Her smile had faded now but the disdain remained in her eyes, sharpened by a new glint of anger.

"You stupid man! You don't think I'd leave anything to chance, do you? I have witnesses who can place you at my apartment and testify to my upset after you left. And I have everything on video. If you knew anything at all about security you would have spotted the camera in my apartment. A professional would have."

John tried to keep his expression impassive but he knew his shock was apparent. Jesus! She had him on camera! In her apartment! Or had she? Was she telling yet more lies?

"I don't believe you," he said. "That's another one of your fantasies."

"Want to see it? It's beautifully edited. God! You look like an animal! A sex-starved gorilla, so repulsive, tearing at your secretary's robe, a big bulge in your trousers."

John's stomach muscles contracted so violently he had to swallow quickly to avoid vomiting. He struggled for a dismissive tone when he spoke. "You're nothing but a bluffer. Even your name is false, isn't it, Frances? Needed a more glamorous name to go with your silicon boobs, did you?"

Her head was still held high. In arrogance. But John thought he detected a slight intake of breath, a frown on her forehead when he had called her Frances. He must use the advantage now. "St Alban's Clinic had some interesting things to say about you. Esther Canning is certainly not a fan of yours."

"Hard-faced old cow! She's been secretly in love with that stuffed shirt Professor Stagge for years. It eats her up and makes her bitter."

"Funny thing is, Shane Richards doesn't have a good word to say for you either. And both he and the Professor gave you glowing references. Why's that? Did you do your slut act for them too?"

Francine threw her head back and laughed. Her long, smooth throat stretched and her blonde hair tumbled down her back as the tinkling sound of her laughter rippled around the room. Suddenly she stopped laughing, lowered her head and fixed John with an ice-blue gaze.

"You fool, John Enright. Both those men are sophisticated, intelligent men of the world. I'd never have caught them like I did you. With one it was a potential malpractice lawsuit, kept out of the court and the media by a secret payment. Or should I say, a payment that would have been very secret except that I just happened to witness it. With the other it was ubiquitous brown envelopes traveling secretly in the direction of government officials, easing the way to planning permissions. I'm sure even you can figure out which one was which. So you see, John, I wasn't the one who did wrong. I just charged a price for my silence."

"Silicon boobs and an apartment in Waterside?"

"Amongst other things, yes."

John sat back and took a deep breath. He picked up a pen from the desk and began to twirl it in his fingers. Anything to give himself time to calm down. The bitch had every last detail planned. Even a video tape and witnesses to a crime which had never been committed. He could take the chance. Defy her. Let her make a charge, take him to court.

He could get a sharp lawyer. Prove the claim was false. But she wouldn't have to go to court to win, would she? She probably had no intention of going down that route. She didn't have to. All she had to do to ruin John Enright was to make her allegations public. The more he'd deny, the more people would believe the beautiful blonde girl with the amazing blue eyes. Once the allegation had been made, how many people would believe John Enright was innocent? A pathetic, middle-aged lecher against a beautiful girl, so innocent, even virginal when she bowed her head shyly and gave that little smile she used to such effect.

The bitch couldn't affect his marriage any more. She'd already ruined that. Lynn might stand by him. Maybe not. What about Carrie and Tommy? Tommy thought little enough of his father now. And work, how would that play out in the face of notorious publicity? Patrick Morgan would be appalled. Francine would make sure he knew, even as he lay on his deathbed. Maybe she had already told him, confirming his opinion that John Enright was not capable of running EFAS, making him glad he had dragged Yan Gilmore halfway around the world to do the job. And there would be EFAS customers who would withdraw their support. There must be something she needed very badly.

John dropped the pen, sat forward again and stared at Francine as steadily as possible.

"What do you want, Francine?"

"That's more like it," she said, giving him a genuine smile now. "I want you to sign over your forty percent shareholding of EFAS to me."

It was John's turn to laugh. In disbelief. "Have you completely lost your mind? You're asking me to hand over almost two and a half a million euro to you? Like hell I will. I'll fight you through every court in the land. That might ruin me but I'd be happy to do it because it would destroy you also. You have too many murky secrets in your past. I'd make sure you did jail for your deals with Nigel Stagge and Shane Richards and for attempting to blackmail me. Do your worst, I'll never hand over what I've worked all my life to earn. Never!"

Francine sat there calmly, her legs crossed, her blonde hair shining. A vision of loveliness.

"Stop wasting time, John. You know damn well there's no evidence against me. Shane Richards and Nigel Stagge would testify on my behalf. You'd look pathetic. A rapist trying to justify himself. My testimony, my witnesses and the video would ruin what's left of your reputation. I don't have to go to court. I can just go public. Your punishment would be swifter and harsher then. Public opinion would find you guilty without trial."

"Tell me," he asked, "did you meet Patrick Morgan in St Alban's? Was Professor Stagge his specialist?"

"Well done! Yes. That's where I first became aware of EFAS. Patrick's 60 percent and your 40 percent share. And of course Patrick's next-of-kin, the intriguing Yan Gilmore."

"And did you meet Yan Gilmore on your trip to New Zealand curtsey of Shane Richards?"

Her surprise was more apparent this time. It took a nanosecond for her to wipe the sign of annoyance off her face.

"Why don't you ask him yourself? I'm going to the airport to collect him now."

John stopped speaking. He didn't want to give Francine

another chance to point out just how much he didn't know. If only he hadn't got his personal life into such a mess, he could have been on top of all the Yan Gilmore saga. If only, if only!

"I'll be bringing him to visit with his uncle first," Francine said, "but he'll be in EFAS this afternoon. You can chat to him then. Ask him whatever you like. The trouble is, I'd then feel free to tell him whatever I like. We get on very well, Yan Gilmore and I. I'm so looking forward to meeting him in person. He may have to fire you on his first day here. Patrick Morgan would be so upset. And probably angry with you. Dragging his business into disrepute."

John bowed his head. He felt dizzy. Sad. Stupid and inept. The Widow Enright would be so ashamed of her son. Rejected by his wife, entrapped by a trollop, about to lose everything for which he had worked.

He heard the swish of nylon on nylon and knew that Francine had uncrossed her long legs and was now standing up.

"I'll need your answer by tomorrow. All the necessary paperwork has been prepared. If you're sensible, I may not have to tell Yan and Patrick. I've already prepared Patrick. Dropped a hint here and there about how you scare me. He won't have any problem believing that you tried to rape me."

John saw a glimmer of hope. Just a little chink. He raised his head. "Who's being stupid now? Why would you stay here if that was the case? Shouldn't you be too terrified?"

"I've covered that, John. You must stop underestimating me. I've asked Dan Shorten to make sure he's within shouting distance every time I come into your office and I've informed Patrick I prefer to get my work done when you're off site. It's why I come in here so much at night. I told Patrick I have a mortgage to pay so every day I fight my distrust of you in order to come into work."

"So Shortie has his ear glued to the door now and is witness to all this conversation. Great! He can testify to your scams. The whole lot, St Albans and Oakley Developers."

"I warned you not to underestimate me. I told Dan that you have a camera trained on the door to monitor whoever comes into your office. He hides outside at my desk, where he thinks he can protect me and avoid detection by you. Far enough away not to hear a word of what's said in here. And in case you have any heroic ideas of exposing my arrangements with Nigel Stagge and Shane Richards, forget it. I told you they're professional, intelligent men. Everything's covered. Not a trace of evidence remains. You'd just end up looking like an even bigger fool. Maybe you'd get a reduced sentence on the grounds of diminished responsibility."

"Bitch!"

Francine did one of her catwalk swivels and then walked out the door, closing it softly after her. John imagined sneaky Dan Shorten, waiting patiently at the reception desk, hoping that Francine would need consolation which involved being comforted by him. Tommy had been right about Shortie. He was a slimeball. He had been right about Francine too. It seemed the son had more common sense than the father.

John took out his mobile phone. His need to talk to Lynn now overcame all caution. He dialled her number and listened in increasing despair as her phone rang out. Was she still asleep, exhausted from the traumas visited on her by the Enrights, or was she sitting listening to her phone ringing, watching his number flash up on the screen and deciding not to answer?

John dropped his head onto his hands and squeezed his eyelids shut as hot tears washed over his eyeballs and pooled at the corners of his eyes. He knew with a certainty as crushing as it was shocking, that the worst aspect of all the troubles destroying his life was the thought that he might never see Lynn Rooney again.

* * *

Meg was guiltily relieved when Carrie and Tommy left her to go to Karl Hemmings property in McCurtain Street. She had told them both the truth this morning. John and Meg Enright's marriage was no more. They had been tiptoeing around since, afraid to say anything which might upset her more. She had finally convinced them that she felt alright. Very, very sad, a little bit lost and frightened but over all – alright.

Meg stood alone now in the shop she and Lynn had run together. It had been cleared of all the devastation of the break-in but yet there remained a sense of violation about the bare shelves and empty display areas. The new stock would be delivered on Wednesday. Most of it anyway. And with the stock would come bills and the obligation to stay here and trade day after day, she and Lynn, side by side, selling their cushions and curtains, trying to pretend that they were still friends, that there was no hurt or betrayal between them.

Closing her eyes, Meg imagined the hours together when neither she nor Lynn would want to speak what was on their minds. The laughter and fun they had shared since they were children silenced by events which in retrospect seemed to have an inevitability about them. It was simple from this vantage point. The Widow Enright's son had chosen the wrong amigo as a life partner. How different would their lives have been had Meg not got pregnant with Carrie? If she and John had not been obliged to marry? If Hannah had not insisted, ordered them, to marry.

Meg opened her eyes, annoyed with herself for her pointless 'what if' thoughts. The fact was, she and John had married willingly. And they had made a mess of it. If Francine Keyes and secret trysts with Lynn Rooney had not happened, the time for John and Meg Enright to live separate lives had arrived anyway. The time for them both to end the emotional drought of their marriage.

Meg walked into the kitchenette, the place where she and Lynn had shared secrets. But not all of them. They would have to talk. Make decisions. And the sooner the better. Meg Enright was in the mood for decision-making. Getting out her phone, she began to tap in Lynn's number but then stopped when she heard a key rattle in the front door. It couldn't be John. He didn't have a set of keys to Curtain Call. Anyway, he would be in EFAS, firing Francine Keyes according to what he had said last night. Listening to his demeaning story of silky robes and breast-touching, Meg had known that John would not get rid of Francine that easily. He was probably trying to fire her and only now learning the cost of his ill-advised fall from the code of decent behavior.

It must be Lynn at the door then. Who else would have a key? Craning forward, Meg peered out into the shop. Lynn had opened the door and was stooping down to pick up an envelope off the floor. It must have been there when Meg came in earlier with Carrie and Tommy but they had missed it. Lynn stood for a moment, envelope in hand, looking around the shop, just as Meg had done. Lynn walked slowly towards the kitchenette in a most extraordinary pair of mucky lace-up shoes.

"I was hoping you'd be here," she said. "Can we talk, Meg?"

"We have to."

"I'm sorry. I'm so very, very sorry."

"Sorry because I found out, or sorry because you hadn't the decency to tell me yourself what had been going on?"

"Both. I should have insisted that John tell you about Francine Keyes. I should have sent him home to you."

"Why didn't you?"

Dropping the envelope on the counter behind her, Lynn pulled out the stools for both of them and they sat. They faced each other across the little kitchenette, just as they had done thousands of times before. But this time was different. There were no smiles, no easy camaraderie. Both women were wary, Lynn's wariness tinged with contrition and Meg's with anger. Lynn was the first to break the tense silence.

"I suppose this is crunch time. Nothing less than the truth will do now."

"Don't you think you owe me that much?"

Lynn nodded slowly and then seemed to brace herself by taking a big breath.

"You'll probably hate me even more, Meg, when you hear what I have to say. The truth is … the truth is I – I love John. I have done since the first night I spotted him walking in the door of the Grattan Club. All these years, all these long, lonely years, I've watched you have his babies and be by his side. When the hurt got too bad, I travelled. I went with other men but I've never loved anyone else the way I love John. When he told me how troubled he was, I couldn't turn him away. I knew he needed someone to listen to him and feel sympathy for him. Instead of sending him home, I felt very glad that it was me he chose as a sympathetic ear. So now you know."

Lynn, her green eyes huge, stared at the bowed head of the woman who used to be her best friend. Seconds lengthened into a minute of silence, then two. Eventually Meg lifted her head. Her eyes were filled with tears, her voice soft.

"I know, Lynn. I think I've always known."

"I told you often enough, didn't I? In the early days. Before he made his choice clear. I spotted him first as he came in the door of the club wearing that white shirt with the long lapels."

Meg laughed. "God! I'd forgotten that. What a horrible shirt! Do you remember it had buttons with a four-leafed clover stamped in the middle of them?"

"Yeah. His lucky shirt. But it wasn't lucky, was it? It's eventually led the three of us to this point. So what now, Meg? Can you ever understand how I've felt all these years? Can you forgive me for taking advantage when John was vulnerable, feeling low? Nothing happened, you know. There was no sex. Just talking about Francine Keyes and about how he wanted to protect you."

"That's what he told me too."

"And do you believe him?"

"How could I believe a man who was so idiotic and so

lacking in self-control that he would have, he almost did, have sex with his secretary, a woman who lured him to her apartment? Jesus, give me credit, Lynn!"

Lynn leaned forward, her gaze so intent that her eyes seemed to protrude. "I swear, Meg, I didn't. Not because I didn't want to, but because I couldn't do that to you. And to be fair to John, there was never any hint of sexuality in his visits. He was just desperate for someone to talk to."

Lynn stopped talking then. In an attempt to explain to Meg she had hurt her even more. Maybe a wife could understand and forgive her husband having sex with someone else but going to another woman for comfort and confidential chats – never! Lynn had usurped Meg's wifely role more surely than if she had spent her time with John making passionate love.

Lynn stood up. "Meg, I hope in time you'll accept my sincere apology. I never meant to hurt you. I hope you and John can work your way through this."

"No, we won't. We've agreed to separate. John's moving out today. I'm staying in the house until Tommy is finished school or college. Until both Carrie and he are independent. Then we'll sell the house. Our marriage is over."

Lynn flopped back onto the stool again. Jesus! Deep down she had known since last night that the Enrights' marriage was over but yet Meg's blunt announcement shocked her. Was that why John had been trying to ring her earlier? When she had decided she would never talk to him again, never again be a shoulder for him to cry on. She opened her mouth to speak but could find no words to express her deep pain. Maybe there were no words to express such regret, such awful guilt.

"It's not your fault, Lynn," Meg said softly. "This would have happened anyway. John seemed willing enough to let things run on as they were but I wasn't. For his sake too. He could have been so much happier with someone else. We both could."

Lynn examined Meg's face, the beautiful face she knew so well and had sometimes envied. The hazel eyes reflected sadness but there was no anger any more. Meg was hurt, disappointed. Yes. But her mouth was firm, her chin held high. She was damaged but not destroyed. For sure Meg Enright had not spent the morning with her feet in the estuary of the Owenabue River wondering if she should wade in or not. There was a calmness about her. As if she had a plan.

"What about the shop?" Lynn asked. "I came here to tell you I'm going away. For good this time. Will you be able to find a new partner or do you think you could run it on your own?"

Meg laughed. A hearty genuine laugh totally out of keeping with the mood of the morning. "That couldn't be better," she said. "I was just about to ring you to say I no longer wanted to continue on with this shop. The lease has only another month to run before renewal. Should we try to sell as a going concern?"

"We could cancel the stock orders and just leave the bloody place closed for the remainder of the lease. It wouldn't be worth much anyway with only a month to run. The landlord won't care. He'll have new tenants in no time. I don't think I ever want to see another curtain or cushion for as long as I live."

Meg reached her hand across and Lynn tentatively took the slim hand with the long fingers in hers.

"Deal!" they both said together.

Then there was a moment's awkward silence as they realised that Lynn Rooney and Meg Enright had no more reason to be together. Business done, confessions made, a reluctant absolution dispensed, why should they still be sitting here in the shop that had once meant so much to them? It was as if they knew their next goodbye would be their last and neither wanted to be the first to walk out on a friendship which had sustained them through the years.

"Any news from the Gardaí about the break-in?" Lynn asked.

Meg shook her head. "Not a word. John suspects the Goodalls had something to do with it but he said nothing to the police in case Tommy would be somehow implicated. But maybe you know that already."

Lynn let that little dig go, accepting that she deserved it. "Do Tommy and Carrie know about – about ..."

"Yes. They know exactly what's going on. Tommy's very angry and Carrie's trying bravely to pray her way out of the hurt. But they'll be alright in time. John and I will both be there for them."

"What are you going to do so, Meg? Are you going to look for a job?"

"Yeah. I'll have to. Anything to keep me going until September next year. I'm going to apply to the Art College and hope to be accepted as a mature student then. A bit late in the day, I know, but it's what I always wanted to do. What about you? Where are you off to?"

"I don't know yet. Just away. I'm going to see the estate agent now to rent my apartment out. I'm hoping the tenants he had lined up earlier may still be interested."

Meg was staring now, a puzzled look on her face, as if she was debating something with herself.

"I have an idea," she announced. "John is looking for a place to stay. How would you feel about renting your apartment to him? It would be a proper business arrangement of course but wouldn't it suit you both? Kill two birds with one stone."

Lynn was the puzzled one now. What an odd suggestion! How could Meg calmly suggest that her husband live in the very apartment where he and another woman had spent time together? The very place which had crystalised the problems in the Enrights' marriage and ultimately brought it to an end. Could it be Meg's way of forgiving them both or even more subtly, of punishing them, trapping them forever in the moment of awful discovery?

"I don't know, Meg. It would make sense but how do you think John would feel about it? I suppose if he's happy to rent, I would be to let. It would save having to pay the estate agent's fee. Suggest it to him."

"No, you do. It's your apartment, John's decision. Nothing to do with me. How soon are you going and for how long?"

Lynn picked up her bag and stood. How could she answer Meg when she herself hadn't even asked the questions yet let alone found the answers. She wasn't going to the sun. That was for sure. No more holiday resorts full of colour, noise and transient, seedy relationships. She needed quiet and subtle light to heal her wounds. It would appear Meg already had her own path marked out. How long had she been planning it, plotting every step along the way? Divorce, Art College and then probably a career in art.

Fulfillment. Fuck Meg Riordan! She always did get what she wanted. Lynn shrugged her shoulders now.

"I just don't know. I need some quiet. A place where I can stop running. I'd like to get back to sewing. It was my first love, even before John Enright. Not curtains though."

Lynn smiled as she recalled her early ambition to be a dress designer. Maybe she could think about that again, feel the thrill of putting scissors to fabric and cutting, stitching, tucking, embroidering, appliquéing until the inert material took on the shape of something beautiful. Or maybe not. There would be too many reminders of Curtain Call in the threads and fabrics.

"Where do you think Eileen Corkery will get her awful flowery drapes now?" Meg asked.

"Maybe she'll grow the fucking things," Lynn answered and, as they both laughed, they realised how much they would miss each other.

They stepped towards each other at the same moment and hugged awkwardly, a distance between them as if all that had happened in the past few days needed space for acknowledgement.

"We need time, Lynn. We'll be okay, won't we?"

"Maybe. Let's keep in touch. Good luck with your art, Meg."

"You too with whatever it is you decide to do. Don't worry about the wind-up of Curtain Call. I'll handle it and contact you if I need to."

Lynn lifted her head then, tossed her auburn curls and walked out of Curtain Call for the last time.

Meg sat in the silence and thought about how intertwined their lives had been. She felt sadness but not closure. She knew Lynn Rooney and Meg Enright had not yet finished their journey together.

Glancing at her watch, Meg noticed it was almost lunch-time. She had promised Carrie and Tommy she'd meet them for pizza. As she got off her stool, it toppled over. It lay abandoned on its side, cluttering up the little kitchenette, the scene of so many happy chats between Meg and Lynn.

Meg lifted her head, just as she had seen Lynn do, and walked out of the kitchenette. At the door she glanced back and caught sight of the envelope Lynn had picked up off the floor and left on the counter. Meg walked back to look at it. It was addressed to *The Proprietor, Curtain Call*. She hesitated, then picked it up. It was probably a bill, in which case the accountant could deal with it. Or maybe a complaint from an irate customer, demanding delivery of their blinds or curtains, in which case to hell with it.

She tore open the envelope. The one-page letter inside was typed on rich cream paper. Meg scanned through it and, with a smile spreading across her face, read it more carefully again. And again. Then laughing out loud, she tucked it into her bag and went to tell her news to Carrie and Tommy.

CHAPTER 28

As she opened the door to her apartment, Francine almost tripped over Mike's cases. He was all packed and ready to go. It had been so fabulous having him here, in secret, all to herself, even if only for one night. Tonight he would be sleeping in that old mausoleum of a house Patrick Morgan called home. She would miss Mike. But not for long. She'd soon organise special time together for them.

"Well, how do I look?" he asked. "Nephew-like?"

He was wearing his dark suit again, the one he had worn at the airport last night. A white shirt emphasised his tanned skin and the multicolored silk tie added an edge of sophistication.

"Very shaggable," Francine answered. "C'mon. We'd better go. Patrick has instructed that po-faced old housekeeper to have lunch ready for you. She'll be fussing about. Don't forget to mention her stodgy hotpot. We'd better not keep them waiting."

"How's Patrick this morning?"

"Actually, I thought he was even frailer than before the

weekend. His speech is quite slurred too. Difficult to understand."

"Poor bastard."

Francine didn't answer. Instead she began to roll the cases to the door. "You're sure of everything now, are you? The layout of the house, the grandparent's names and what they looked like, the –"

"Francine! Yan was ten years old when last he was here. He could hardly be expected to remember room plans and family histories."

"His mother would have told him and for sure Patrick will ask you questions."

"Don't you know he already has on the phone and I've obviously passed his tests. Thanks to your research. Now stop fretting. I'd say you've your knickers in a knot except that I know you're not wearing any."

Francine turned back towards him and gave him one of her sideways glances.

"And John Enright?" Mike asked. "Did you speak to him?"

"He almost peed in his pants with fright. He'll be no problem."

"Everything's good then."

Francine smiled. A warm, smug smile. How much better could life get? Patrick Morgan was getting ready to sign over his company to the man he believed to be his nephew, John Enright would bluster but would have to forfeit his forty percent share or face public disgrace, Victor Collins was gagging to buy EFAS and best of all, Mike Choy, the man of her dreams, was by her side. Mike, with his taciturn nature, was a challenge. A lifetime challenge, Francine hoped, as she checked the corridor outside to make sure it was empty. She waved Mike Choy aka Yan Gilmore out, and together they went to re-introduce Patrick Morgan to his long-lost nephew.

* * *

Answering the EFAS phones on top of trying to keep his panic in line was getting too much for John. He switched the phones over to a recorded message. To hell with them all. He couldn't cope.

He gripped his hands around his reeling head. What in the fuck had he done? Made himself and his family a laughing stock, put his business at risk and left himself vulnerable to a grabbing, lying, cheating bitch. No wonder Patrick Morgan had decided that taking a gamble on an unknown nephew was a better risk than entrusting the company to John Enright.

There was a knock on the office door. John smoothed his hair before calling "Come in!".

Victor Collins pushed his way in the door and sat without being invited.

"There's no one at the front desk," he said. "Where's Francine?"

"None of your business, Victor."

"You mean you don't know."

"I do actually but I'd like to remind you that you're a customer here. Not a member of staff."

"We could fix that too," Victor said with a sly grin. "I could have a chat with Patrick Morgan."

John looked at the sneering face and all his frustration and anger seemed to focus on the weasely features of Victor

Collins. He felt like thumping the pinched mouth and pointed nose until they were bruised and bloody.

"Look, Collins, I'm warning you, leave Patrick Morgan alone. The man is sick. If you've a problem, I'll deal with it."

"Like you dealt with the security? I heard Ollie walked out on you. I insist now on having my men here. When are you going to see them?"

Fuck! Yet another problem. Unless he patrolled the bloody place himself tonight, there would be no security. For the first time ever since he could remember, keeping EFAS safe was not John's priority.

"Put your men on, Collins. Starting tonight. Tell them call into the office here to discuss terms and conditions. Now if there's nothing else, I'm going to lunch."

"There's more but I want to speak to the boss. The real boss. The 60 percent man."

With that the weasel jumped up and scurried out of the office. John remained sitting, not knowing what to do next. He couldn't eat lunch. The thought of food disgusted him. He could go to an estate agent and start looking for a place to stay. That would be an admission that all hope of reconciliation with Meg was gone. It was. They'd both had enough of long boring silences and fraught conversations and each other.

He could walk around the unit, make sure everything was in order for Yan Gilmore's visit this afternoon. Fuck Gilmore!

The issue he didn't want to face could not be avoided any more. He would have to make a decision about Francine Keyes. There was only one person who could help him decide.

John rang Lynn Rooney's number. It rang and rang before the message minder clicked in. "I need to see you, Lynn," John said and then hesitated before adding "please". He cut the connection because he didn't trust himself not to start begging her to see him. He needed to keep the little bit of self-respect he had left.

* * *

Meg carried her bag clutched under her arm as if afraid it would be stolen during her short walk from Curtain Call to Karl Hemmings' building. The huge double door on the front of the building was ajar. Meg pushed it open and stepped inside. From high above she could hear Carrie and Tommy laughing and talking. She called out to them and then crossed her fingers as she heard them race down the two sets of stairs, their footsteps echoing in the empty building.

"Careful!" she warned, and then she realised, firstly, that they were no longer children and secondly, they were thankfully cheerful after all the upset last night.

"We've just discovered the coolest fireplace hidden behind a timber partition upstairs. We're going to open it up and make it a feature of the Communal Room," Tommy said.

"We? Are you going to be in the café too, Tom?"

"When I have time. Garth said they'd appreciate any help they could get."

"Garth said?"

Meg looked from Tommy to Carrie's radiant face and knew that she was not the only one with news. "What else had Garth to say?" she asked Carrie but she anticipated the answer even before Carrie blurted it out.

"They're coming here, Mum. Next week. Karl and Pearl and Garth. Can you believe it?"

No. Meg could *not* believe it. Karl Hemmings in Cork! She couldn't help the little shiver which ran down her spine.

"Why are Karl and Pearl coming? Are they going to make Cork their headquarters?"

"No. That will always be Portland. But Karl likes to oversee the opening of each new café. And of course he'll be officiating at our wedding."

Meg was lost for words. What could she say without offending Carrie? That the creepy Karl Hemmings had no legal or moral power to conduct a marriage service here? That it would be a farce? A pantomime. And yet she knew these things would have to be said. And soon by the sound of things. But not now. Not while Carrie was glowing with happiness.

"You'll love Garth, Mum. Tom likes him too, don't you?"

"He's cool."

Meg raised an eyebrow. Not many people got the ultimate 'cool' accolade from Tom. It seemed Garth Hemmings was making both her children happy. She smiled at Carrie now.

"You really love Garth, don't you?"

"With all my heart. He's kind and good and he has shown me The Light."

"For fecks's sake Carr! The religious stuff is bad enough but the soppy stuff is stomach-turning. I thought we were going for pizza?"

Carrie gave her brother a playful push and they both turned towards the door.

"Not so quick," Meg said "I have something to show you both."

She took her letter out of her bag and, opening up the envelope, read from the cream sheet of paper.

Dear Proprietor of Curtain Call,

Passing your premises I was greatly impressed by the piece of art work displayed in your window. I run an art gallery here in town and would very much like to negotiate the purchase of the work for my gallery.

If possible I would be interested in meeting the artist to discuss the possibility of exhibiting more of this original and talented work in Leeside Galleries. Do please contact me at the above number.

Sincerely,

Carrie and Tommy threw their arms around their mother.

"Well done, Mum! Brilliant!" cried Carrie. "And he wants more! What's his name?"

Meg glanced down at the bold signature. "*Girvan Cooper. Director, Leeside Art Gallery.*"

"How much is he going to pay?" Tommy asked. "That's the bottom line."

"No," Carrie interrupted her brother. "The bottom line is that we should be thanking The Light. For all —"

"For what, Carr? For the break-up of our family? Because Dad was knocking Lynn off? Or maybe the fact that he'll no longer be at home with us?"

Meg felt ashamed. She had been so excited about the letter from Girvan Cooper that she had momentarily forgotten her marriage was over. But Tommy hadn't. The boy's face was pinched with man-sized sadness. She reached out and laid her hand on his arm.

"I'm sorry, Tom. Do you want me to ring Dad and ask him to join us for lunch? We can still be a family, you know."

"The Fuehrer? Fuck, no!"

Tommy strode out the door ahead of them while Carrie and Meg laughed, relieved that the Tommy they knew and loved so well seemed set to survive.

* * *

To her surprise Francine found she was nervous as she and Mike Choy walked up to Patrick Morgan's front door.

"Ready?" she asked with her finger poised over the doorbell.

"As I'll ever be."

The housekeeper opened the door after the first ring. She must have been peeping out the window as they had arrived.

"Come in, Mr Gilmore. You're welcome," she said, managing to smile at Mike and glare at Francine at the same time. A feat only Anne could accomplish. "Mr Morgan is waiting for you in the front room."

She turned, leading them into the claustrophobic, musty old space she referred to as the front room. Patrick was sitting in his usual chair, surrounded by cushions, in exactly the same position he had been in when Francine had left him this morning. Even from the door Francine could hear his breath rattling in his chest. She felt a moment's panic. Suppose the old man died before the business was fixed up. What a cock-up that would be after all the planning! He was making a feeble attempt to stand now. Yan strode across the room to Patrick's chair. The old man held out his hand.

"Yan! You're welcome, lad. It's great to see you."

Ignoring the outstretched hand, Yan stooped down and embraced the bag of bones Patrick Morgan had become. "It's my pleasure to be here, Uncle Pat. I'm looking forward to us getting to know each other better."

"We've a lot of catching up to do and I'm afraid I don't have much time."

"You must be hungry, Mr Gilmore," Anne said. "I've a bit of lunch ready for you. Will I bring it in now?"

Yan turned his smile on the housekeeper and Francine could see the old woman's hard features soften. She wondered if there was a woman alive, no matter what age, who did not respond to that lopsided grin. "Actually I'm quite hungry, Anne," he said. "I heard you make a great hotpot. Have you cooked one for me?"

"I did indeed, Mr Gilmore. Just sit yourself down with your uncle and I'll be back shortly."

"Just call me Yan. We New Zealanders are not much for formalities."

Francine could have sworn the crabby old housekeeper giggled as she left the room.

"How was your flight?" Patrick asked.

"Tiring. It's a long haul. I'm looking forward to a good sleep tonight."

"Anne has your room ready. Maybe you'd like to rest after lunch. Give your body a chance to catch up with the changes in time zones."

Feeling ignored, Francine spoke to Yan. "You must go to EFAS this afternoon. John Enright's expecting you."

He turned to look at her, still standing inside the doorway since she had not been invited to sit.

"I need to talk to my uncle now, Francine. Thank you for collecting me at the airport. I'll call you later when I want to go to the storage unit."

Then, his back to Patrick, he winked and gave her a cheeky grin. She had to resist the temptation to grin back at him.

"Whatever you say, Yan. Just call me when you want to be driven to EFAS. If you need anything else, I'll be at the unit or else you can ring my mobile number."

She turned then and walked away, greatly pleased at how things were progressing. Mike Choy was good at playing the dutiful nephew.

In the hallway, Francine glared at the housekeeper who was holding a tray in her hands. It had cups, saucers and plates. Two of each. The old bitch had known that Francine would not be invited to stay.

"Not staying for lunch? What a pity."

"I don't have time, Anne. I've more important things to do."

"I'm sure!"

Francine was sure too. She had window-shopping to do. She would after all, shortly be a very wealthy woman.

CHAPTER 29

Lynn was amused by the fact that the estate agent kept looking down at her feet as she sat in his office.

"I was out walking. In the countryside," she explained.

He smiled at her. "I see. So what do you think of my suggestion? I don't want to push you but this client wants immediate occupancy."

Lynn looked at the stuffed suit sitting across from her, his expression a shade of funeral-director mournful. At the risk of making him cry, she asked him to repeat the proposal again.

"Your choice, Miss Rooney, is to rent out your apartment for whatever period would suit you. Or you could sell. If you opt for selling it just so happens I have a client on my books who is looking for an apartment in Oriel Rise. Yours is exactly the type he wants. But I don't want to pressurise you. The decision is yours. I'll certainly find tenants for you if that's what you want."

Wasn't that the trouble? What did she want? Certainly not to have John Enright in her apartment while she was off god knows where trying to forget him. That had been a devious suggestion by Meg. Nor did she want strangers in it either. But there was the mortgage to pay. It was a bloody millstone around her neck. Maybe the ultimate freedom would be to live mortgage free. Then she'd have no home. Wasn't it time to admit that Oriel Rise had never been home? Just a place to store the clutter of a sad life. Enough procrastination!

"I'll sell. Arrange a viewing with your client."

"Are you sure?"

Lynn stood. "I'm sure. I'm going away. Starting over." She scribbled a name and phone number on the desk pad. "This is my solicitor. Deal with him. Thank you."

"These clients will want vacant possession if they go ahead with the purchase. When do you intend leaving?"

"Now. I have a friend who runs a storage company. I'll arrange for him to store my furniture if the deal goes through. He owes me a favour."

"That sounds convenient."

"You have no idea how very inconvenient it has been," Lynn said. Then she smiled at the estate agent with the mournful face and clumped across his office in her walking shoes, depositing a dusting of dried mud on the pristine carpet.

Out on the street Lynn walked quickly to her car. Thinking time would be lethal now. She was on a roll. She had yet to collect her insurance check, hand back her lease car and pack whatever she was going to take with her to where ever the road would lead. Tomorrow was her deadline. By tomorrow Lynn Rooney would be on her way to a new, Enright-free life.

* * *

It was late afternoon before Mike Choy rang Francine.

"How is it going with the old man?" she asked.

"Very well, thank you," Mike said so formally that Francine knew Patrick must be nearby. "Would you collect me as soon as you can, please, Francine? I think it's time I saw EFAS and met John Enright."

"I'll be with you in thirty minutes, Mike. I mean Yan. Will you be able to get away for a little while tonight? Just an hour or so?"

"We'll schedule that, Francine. See you in thirty."

Francine switched off her phone and put back the piece of Louis Vuitton luggage she had been examining. "I'll think about it," she told the hovering sales assistant.

When she pulled up outside Patrick Morgan's house, the door opened immediately and Mike came out. From a distance he looked as imposing as ever but as he neared Francine noticed how tired he seemed.

"Everything alright?" she asked anxiously as he got into the car. "You look a bit frazzled."

He turned to stare at her, a frown drawing his dark eyebrows close together over his slanted eyes. "Francine, in the past forty-eight hours I've flown around the world, shagged you for a whole night and spent hours with a sick old man. How do you expect me to look?"

Without answering, she started the car and headed for EFAS. He was obviously in one of his moods and best left alone. Stopped at traffic lights, she glanced at him. His eyes were closed. Francine smiled. Poor lamb. He was exhausted.

She turned to wake him as they pulled up outside EFAS only to find that he was already awake and eagerly inspecting the layout of the storage unit.

"Pretty impressive," he said. "Very professional appearance. This must certainly inspire customer confidence."

"I suppose. Until you meet John Enright. I don't know why Patrick Morgan left him in charge for so long."

Mike didn't answer. Instead he got out of the car and began to stroll around the parking lot, examining fencing and looking up to see rooftop security cameras. Francine stood by the front door waiting for him until he came to her. He smiled at her.

"It's going great with Patrick. No glitches. He'll sign over within the next few days."

"Really? That soon. He has no doubts?"

"He thinks I have his sister's nose and chin. How good is that?"

"We'll have to see about a reward for you. Are you ready to go in now?"

He nodded, waving her in the door ahead of him. Francine led him through reception and straight over to the door of John Enright's office. She tapped on the door and walked in. John was sitting at his desk, his hair dishevelled, a haunted look in his dark eyes. Francine threw back her shoulders, pushed her breasts forward teasingly and beamed at him.

"John, I'm delighted to introduce you to Yan Gilmore from New Zealand. Patrick's nephew you have been so anxious to meet. Yan, meet John Enright."

John stood as the tall man behind Francine approached the desk, hand out in greeting.

411

"Nice to meet you in person, John. We didn't have much chance to talk over the phone. It'll be good to chat face to face."

John took the proffered hand and shook it. The New Zealander had a firm handshake.

"Welcome to Ireland, Yan. I'm sorry the circumstances are so sad for you because of your uncle's illness but I hope you'll be happy here. Sit down, please."

Yan sat down and stretched his long legs comfortably. John admired the man's confidence while at the same time resenting it. Yan Gilmore already seemed totally in charge. This opinion was confirmed when Yan turned to Francine and asked her to bring them two coffees.

"Or maybe you'd prefer tea, John?"

John shook his head and watched as Francine trotted off to do the new boss's bidding without as much as one objection.

"You've done a fair job running EFAS on your own, John. From the reports I've read I see that business is good. It could be better though. A lot of room for improvement."

John sat up straighter, more wary. The friendly greeting and warm handshake had been a sop to lull him into a false sense of security. The real Yan Gilmore was more apparent now.

"We're expanding all the time," John replied cautiously. "There's a lot of competition. It's a tough business."

"Patrick told me the company name, EFAS, was your idea."

John nodded agreement, remembering when he and Patrick had first progressed from the lock-up garages near Patrick's house to the industrial estate. They had decided then they needed a more sophisticated name than Morgan's Lock-up. It had been John who had come up with the simple idea of spelling 'safe' backwards. It had, at the time, seemed to encapsulate everything they wanted the new company to be. Safe whichever way you looked at it.

"Don't you like it, Yan? Are you suggesting that we change it?"

Yan didn't answer. Instead he stared at John with a disturbingly intense gaze. Just when John was beginning to find the scrutiny unbearable, Yan broke the silence.

"John. I need to talk to you about something important. Patrick wants to see you too. A sensitive issue. Would you be available in the morning to call out to his house? We could talk with more privacy there. Anne, Patrick's housekeeper says the best time for him is early morning. He's a bit stronger after a night's rest."

So! They were going to fire him. John didn't need the words spelled out for him. He read them in Yan's arrogant gaze, in his patronising attitude, in his criticisms. Nephew and uncle combining together to strike the final blow. 'Thank you for everything, John, and goodbye. Your services are no longer required.' Fuck them! He'd have a surprise for them too, wouldn't he? Maybe there would be some poetic justice in handing over his 40 per cent to Francine Keyes. Let the Morgan-Gilmore combination deal with the bitch.

"John?"

"Yes. Yes, of course, Yan. I'll call to the house. Around ten? I want to see Patrick anyway. How is he?"

A look of what appeared to be genuine sympathy crossed Yan's face. "He's very ill. Suffering a lot but not complaining. I'm really sorry I didn't get to know him earlier. He's a fascinating man. By the way, it's important that you don't mention this meeting to anybody else. Nobody at all. Understand?"

John nodded his agreement just as Francine came into the office with their coffees. She hovered.

"I'm sure you have work to catch up on," Yan said to her. "I'm sorry I've taken up so much of your time. John will show me around now. I'll give you a call when I need to be driven back to Patrick."

Francine hesitated before turning and leaving the room. Just long enough to throw John a vicious, threatening look. John glanced at Yan and for a moment, just a tiny instant, he was tempted to confess the mess he had allowed himself to get into with Ms Francine Keyes. It would be such a relief if everyone knew. If the fear of being found out was gone. The instant flashed past. How in the hell could he ever admit to this stranger to having made such a fool of himself? He had told Meg and she was divorcing him. He had told Lynn and now she wouldn't even answer the phone to him. Maybe she would never talk to him again.

"We'll do the grand tour as soon as you've finished your coffee, Yan. I'll introduce you to the rest of our staff."

"Great by me," Yan said. "We'll leave our serious talking until the morning."

And so, with his head spinning, a lump of sadness in his throat and despair in his heart, John Enright brought the heir apparent to EFAS on a conducted tour of the unit.

* * *

Meg's fingers shook as she sat at her kitchen table and dialled the number of Leeside Galleries. There was something very intimidating about talking to somebody whose name was Girvan and an Art gallery owner to boot. Carrie and Tommy were crowding around her offering advice, distracting her.

"Don't forget to ask him if Granny Enright's linen sheets are part of the deal," Tommy said.

Meg laughed just as a rich, plummy voice answered the phone. "Girvan Cooper speaking. How may I help?"

"My name is Meg Enright. I'm the owner of a shop in Bridge Street named Curtain Call. At least I was – I still am for a while…"

Carrie was frantically flapping her hands at Meg, urging her to calm down while Tommy was grinning at her discomfort. Girvan Cooper rescued Meg from her embarrassing waffle.

"Ah! You got my letter? Do tell me whose work you have displayed in your window. I pride myself on having an eye for all up and coming talent but that piece is unique and very different to any other I've seen."

"Go on! Tell him!" Carrie mouthed before dramatically spreading her arms and beginning to pray silently.

"Actually, Mr Cooper, I painted that picture. I'm not an artist, not really. Not yet. But I hope to go back to college soon as a mature student. And then –"

"And then you'd what? Learn techniques and methods? And maybe lose your beautiful originality and freshness? Your unique insight into colour and shape? No, no, Meg. Do you mind if I call you Meg? We must meet. Discuss a price for your painting if you're willing to sell. Discuss your future in the art world. Would you call to the gallery? You have the address."

"I know it, Mr Cooper. I've often been there."

"Girvan, please. Will you call tomorrow then? Around ten?"

"I'll look forward to that, Girvan. See you tomorrow."

As soon as Meg put down the phone Tommy began to hoop and holler. "Yes, Girvan. No, Girvan. Thank you, Girvan!"

Unperturbed, Carrie continued on with her praying until Tommy gave her a shake.

"Come back to us, Carr. Our old lady is going to be a famous artist. How about that for a miracle?"

Carrie lowered her hands and gazed solemnly at both of them. "I know. What do you think I was praying for? Praise The Light!"

"Maybe you should pray for the old man now too. the Fuehrer is knackered."

Meg stood up from the table and went to fill the kettle. Tommy was obviously deeply upset about his father. He was trying to hide the hurt behind his brashness but when it appeared it was sharp and damaging. As she plugged the kettle in, she looked at her son, all long legs and gangling arms which seemed to belong to someone else. Awkward, uncoordinated. Young. An almost man who needed his father.

She stared out the window at the shrubs and trees in the garden. Plants she and John had dug in when they had moved in here first, full of hope for the future and pride in their new home. The plants had rooted, grown, matured, survived through winter frost and summer drought. It was just the marriage which had failed to thrive. Why should Tommy pay the price for that? How could she deprive him of his father at this vital stage in his development? The father he pretended to hate but on whom he was clearly dependent. Turning away from the window she faced her son.

"How about we ask Dad to stay? Not to move out at all. Would that make you feel better, Tom?"

"Really? Even after — after everything?"

"Don't think John and I will ever get back together. We won't. We've discussed that and we both agree. But there's no need for him to go. Why should he live in some bed-sit? This is his home too. Will we ask him?"

Tommy shrugged. "If you want," but Meg knew it was exactly what Tommy wanted even though he would not admit it. Then she remembered the silly suggestion she had made to Lynn. Suppose John had already agreed to rent Lynn's apartment? Shit! She should have thought of that before she had said anything to Tommy.

"I'll have to ask John first. See what he thinks. I'm going to EFAS. I won't be long."

"I'll pray, Mom," Carrie said.

"I'm going to my room," Tommy said sulkily and made a point of storming out of the kitchen and tramping upstairs.

Carrie gave her mother a hug. "I'll look after him. He'll be fine."

As Meg drove to EFAS, she thought this had been one of the problems with their marriage. She had seldom gone to see John at work and he had never invited her to do so. EFAS had stood between them. A barrier John had built, a substitute for the lack of passion in his marriage. She had allowed him to do so because she had no passion to give him. It was all so clear looking back.

CHAPTER 30

Lynn's apartment looked a bit like a recycling centre to-night. Sorting through the left-over tatters of her life was easier this time around for her. Maybe the thought of selling her apartment had focused her mind. Rid it of self-delusion.

Her bits and bobs of outdated clothes and knick-knacks went into bin bags for the skip. Wherever she ended up, she was going to travel light, mentally as well as physically. The last items she needed to dump were her Doc Marten boots. She caught them by the laces and swung them over the bag, just as she had done with her suicide shoes in Carrigaline this morning. Then she smiled at the idea that footwear should have been so significant in the start and finish of her involvement with John Enright. Giving the boots an extra hard push she tucked them down into the bottom of the bag, sorry that she wouldn't be there to watch the big grinder on the back of the garbage truck chew them up, shred them, destroy them and finally cut all links to a love that never should have been.

Two by two, Lynn dragged the bin bags to the elevator

and then to the skip in the back yard of her apartment block. She was exhausted by the time the trekking up and down to the skip was finished but her apartment was beginning to look very organised. A bit like when she had first bought it, intending to settle here for the rest of her life.

Looking around now, she wondered why she didn't feel any sadness. She had been comfortable here, had enjoyed furnishing it and decorating. Buying all the accoutrements of homemaking. Except that it had never been a home. There had been no laughter here or noise or fuss, nobody to come home to, nobody for whom to care. Just sometimes tears and most times dry-eyed loneliness.

To hell with looking back! Lynn got out a bottle of wine. She hadn't packed her glasses yet. Pouring a glass full to the brim she brought it over to the hall mirror and examined her reflection. Her hair was still auburn, still curly. There were slight lines around her green eyes, slight double chin, slight spare tyre, slight tummy. Lynn Rooney was slightly old. She raised her glass. "Here's to slight happiness, old girl, and its companion slight sadness!"

She swallowed a big mouthful of the wine and then smiled at her reflection. Tilting her head she thought she looked younger when she smiled. Her teeth were good. Maybe she could think about having something done with the lines around her eyes before they etched her years on her face. With her free hand she pulled the skin by her left eye upwards. The lines were gone but she looked …

The door bell rang. Lynn started and some wine slopped over onto the floor. Going to the spy hole she peeped into the corridor. John Enright stood outside, head bowed, waiting for her to answer the door. Head bowed, Lynn stood inside the door. Impasse. What in the hell was she to do? Why was he here? To tell her how heartbroken he was at the ending of his marriage, to whine about the mess he got himself into with Francine Keyes? To hurt her again, to weaken her new-found resolve to move forward, away from him and towards life?

He rang again. Lynn could not move. All the strength she had found in herself on the banks of the Owenabue River this morning seemed to be seeping away. She should not blame John for that. She should be able to face him, to look into his dark brown, soulful eyes, to smell the clean just showered scent of him, and yet walk away. She owed that much to her self-respect.

"I know you're there, Lynn. I want to talk to you about your apartment."

Lynn smiled but this time her smile didn't make her look younger. It was a bitter little twisting of her lips, a self-depreciating sneer. She had fallen for it again. Imagining that John had called to pour his heart out to her. That he was here because he needed her and all the while he was patiently waiting in the corridor to discuss business. Pathetic Lynn Rooney.

Putting her glass on the hallstand Lynn opened the door and walked back into the lounge.

"I was just having a glass of wine, John. Would you like one?"

"No, thank you. I've got to go back to work."

Lynn collected her own glass and sat in an armchair. John sat opposite her in the other chair. The couch, scene of their clandestine cuddles, sat accusingly between them. He looked pale and tired, the circles dark under his eyes.

"Meg told me you're leaving," he said.

"She told me your marriage is over."

He flinched and Lynn regretted her impulse to make him suffer.

"I'm sorry, John. It's such a pity. It doesn't seem so long ago that the three of us were so full of hope and belief in ourselves."

"Meg is the one with all the self-belief now. She's really looking forward to her single life."

"Yes," Lynn agreed. "I saw a new side to Meg today. A determination I never noticed before. She'll be alright. And you?"

John threw himself back into his chair wearily. The man looked exhausted. Beaten.

"I don't know, Lynn. I've fucked up royally. Francine Keyes wants my 40 percent share of EFAS or else she's going to accuse me of attempted rape. I think Patrick Morgan and his nephew want me out of EFAS. Carrie is going to open up a café-cum-recruiting centre with the Hemmings and Tommy is a surly brat with the potential to become a lay-about. Where did it all go wrong?"

"In Francine Keyes' apartment?"

"That was below the belt but maybe I deserved it. I don't know any more. Everything is just gone beyond my control."

John closed his eyes and laid his head against the back rest. Lynn took another sip of her wine and firmly gripped the glass with both hands. She was almost overcome by the urge to run over to him, run her fingers through his hair, smooth the frowns on his forehead, kiss the sadness away. Almost. She reminded herself that he had not yet asked her how she was. How she was coping with last night's visit by

Meg. Why should she care at all when he cared so little? His eyes flickered open. He smiled at her.

"I'm sorry, Lynn. There I go again, pouring out all my troubles to you. What about you? I tried to ring you several times today but I got no reply. Where are you going? For how long?"

He must have read her mind. Maybe she was being unfair expecting consideration from him. He was under horrific pressure. He was entitled to a modicum of self-pity.

"I haven't decided where yet. Just away from here. Not on a holiday and then back to the same old ding dong. I'm going for good. I'm selling this apartment."

"Really? Meg said something to me about me renting it from you."

"You can buy it if you want. A nice bachelor pad."

"There's been a change of plan. I'll be staying at home. It seems Tommy is upset at the prospect of me leaving so Meg and I agreed to stay at the house together."

Jesus! Had they not just been talking about Meg's single life? And now he was telling her they were getting back together. Bloody Enrights! They deserved each other. She drained her glass. "I'm having another. Are you sure you don't want one?"

"No, I won't thanks. I'd better get back to work."

"You do that, John. Back to work. Back to your wife."

"What do you mean? Meg and I will just be sharing the house. A temporary arrangement until Tommy is more comfortable with our new situation. Meg has no interest in reconciliation."

"Have you?"

"To be honest, I don't know how I feel about anything

422

at the moment. I've never been so frightened in my life. Everything I worked for and depended on is being taken away from me. But I know one thing for sure. I'll miss you, Lynn. Will you keep in touch, let me know where you are and how you're getting on?"

It would be so easy now for Lynn to agree. To phone him, email, maybe write letters to him. Keep the memory of him alive, keep the hope alive. What would be the point in going then? She'd still be the outsider, the friend from his youth, the one he hadn't married. And what if he and Meg did get together again, or if he met someone new? Good old Lynn couldn't take being bridesmaid second time around. No way!

"I'll be in contact with Meg from time to time. She'll tell you how I am. I'd like you to arrange storage for my furniture, please. My estate agent will be in contact with you."

She stood and began to walk towards the door. Shades of last night when she opened the door to allow Meg see her husband in another woman's apartment. Other women's apartments seemed to be an unfortunate habit of John Enright's. Why had Lynn wasted so much of her life and all of her love on this man? Hand on the latch, she turned at the door to find he was standing just behind her. Up close his face showed even more of his desperation. His eyes were haunted by fear.

"I hope everything works out well for you, John," she said, meaning her words as a farewell.

He stooped and kissed her on the lips. A gentle brush of his lips on hers, the tenderest of kisses. A fire raced through Lynn, from the top of her head right down to her toes. She closed her eyes and allowed the fire to burn. His arms came around her and she leaned against his body. They were a perfect fit, her head lying snugly against his shoulder. He rocked her in his arms, a slow dance of love that could have been, passion that should have been. They clung together and Lynn mourned what they never had while John discovered what they could have shared. It was all too late.

Lynn pulled away from him and opened the door. "Goodbye, John. Take care."

"It could have been so different," he said.

He looked at her with those dark brown eyes she loved so much, opened his mouth to say something else but instead just gently touched his fingers to her face as if trying to memorise her features through touch. He brushed her eyes, her cheeks, her nose, her lips. Then silently, sadly, shoulders hunched and head bowed, John Enright walked out of Lynn Rooney's life.

* * *

John parked his car on the road at the entrance to the industrial estate. He'd walk to EFAS from here. A good brisk pace. He needed the cold night air on his face and the solid ground underneath his feet. He needed the quiet and dark. His head was dizzy, his heart thumping and a hot lump of sadness sat in his throat, almost choking him.

His lips still tasted of Lynn, a wine-flavored sweetness, his body still felt the warm weight of her against him. Jesus, how had he not seen it? How had he not known? This was not the gentle passion aroused by Meg's fragile body or the wild flood of hormones released by Francine's blatant sexuality. A warmth, a longing, a need to be with Lynn accompanied him every step of the way. But stronger still was the terrible sadness, the realisation that he had discovered the completeness of Lynn and him too late. It was as if their lips had fanned a dormant fire, one that he had not known was smouldering quietly for so many years.

John stopped walking. Ahead he could see the lights of EFAS. Why was he thinking about Lynn Rooney, torturing himself with might-have-beens? Lynn was off to make a new life for herself while he would have to concentrate on salvaging what he could of his old life. He began to walk again, more quickly. He must see this new security man Victor Collins had imposed on him and then get home. Tommy seemed to need reassurance and he must talk to Carrie about Garth Hemmings. Find out how serious she was about him. Then he would go to bed in the guest room and begin his life as a single man.

There were three cars in the car park. One belonged to the maintenance man. John knew he was doing overtime tonight to finish up some rewiring that had been dragging on and on. Victor Collins' car was there too and one other he didn't recognise. Probably belonged to the new security man.

John began to walk again, a more measured pace now. He went in through the gates and across the car park to the entrance door which was open. No sign of a security person anywhere. If Ollie had been here, he would have been out patrolling the grounds, watching, challenging, protecting EFAS. Inside, Victor Collins was standing by the desk in reception and beside him stood a low-sized, squat man in a snazzy security guards' uniform. Navy jacket and pants, blue shirt, navy tie with embossed logo, even a hat. Very professional looking, so what in the hell was he doing standing here in reception while anybody could walk into the place.

"Good night," John said. "Any harm in asking what's going on here? The gate and front door are open."

"We were watching you on CCTV," Victor Collins answered. "We had you well spotted. John, this is Barry Mahony. He and his brother Finn will share the night-security duties here from now on. I'm just giving him a rundown on the surveillance system."

John glared at Victor Collins, wanting to ask him why he thought he had a right to interfere like this but then he reconsidered. As a customer, Collins had a right to twenty-four hour access to the unit where his property was stored and, besides, John had already agreed to allow this new security man start tonight. John offered his hand to Barry Mahony, examining him closely as he did so. There was something very familiar about the set of the thick neck on the broad shoulders.

"Nice to meet ye, boss," the man said in an accent as thick as his neck, taking John's hand in a bearlike grip.

"You look familiar, Barry. Have I met you before?"

"Naw. Don't think so."

John turned back to Victor Collins. "Have you told Barry about camera five being down? It won't be repaired until Wednesday. The west side on the boundary near the Jacuzzi Company is very vulnerable."

They all glanced at the blank screen of camera five.

"Don't worry, John. We've everything under control. Just keep a sharp eye out there, Barry. In fact, you could check now."

The new security man gave a mock salute to Collins and, without saying a word, turned and walked out through reception. As John watched him cross reception and head towards the entrance a cold shiver ran down his spine. It was the gait he recognised, the ape-like way the arms hung loosely by the man's sides. He was certain he had seen him before. He had almost knocked him down. Outside the house in Sycamore Lawn, at the front gate the night Tommy said he had been followed home from the hospital by one of Freddie Goodall's goons. And he matched the description of the thug Lynn had seen hanging around the house the night her car was stolen and the shop wrecked. He could not be certain of course but nevertheless the hairs on the back of his neck were bristling.

"Where did you dig him up? What company does he work for? What's the logo on the tie?"

Collins laughed. "Company? None. Just him and his brother. The uniform is pantomime. They like their bling, himself and Finn. They're good though. You'd be foolish to cross them."

"They're violent? That's not what we want here."

"We want protection, don't we? I want to sleep easy knowing my stock is safe. I can do that with Barry and Finn Mahony in charge. Now, I'm going home. You should too. You look done in."

"Is there any possibility these people work for a person named Goodall? Freddie Goodall?"

Victor Collins shuffled from one foot to the other, squinting his eyes so that his features took on an even more feral appearance. His teeth were pointed and bared in a grimace. John feared for an instant that Victor Collins would bite him and infect him with rabies.

427

"I don't know who you're taking about, Enright, but I don't like the tone of your voice. I won't deal with you any more. You're only the stooge here anyway. I prefer to deal with the real boss."

Victor Collins turned then and scurried out the front door. John stood where he was, hearing the weasel man's words echo in his head. "You're only the stooge here." Collins' animal instincts were so right. Cruel but true. John Enright was a stooge. The patsy who had built up EFAS storage so that Yan Gilmore could swan in from New Zealand and take over a thriving business. He had sacrificed everything to make this business a success. Put it before everything else. His marriage, his children, his life for fuck's sake! And for what? To stand here and have a piece of shit like Victor Collins call him a stooge? To allow Yan Gilmore order him about, call him to early morning meetings? He should have taken what he could. Paid himself more – much more. How idiotic he had been ploughing back every euro he possibly could into the company. He should have lined his own pockets. Looked after his family instead of Patrick Morgan's business. He would have been better off and more thanked.

Standing in front of the bank of monitors, John watched Victor Collins walk to his car, the security man loping towards him, arms dangling. John was certain then. This was the man whom he had almost knocked down at the driveway of Sycamore Lawn. The man Tommy said had trailed him from the hospital. The man who was one of Freddie Goodall's thugs.

Barry Mahony and Victor Collins had their heads close

together now. John could imagine Collins' eyes squinting and his pinched little mouth spitting out words. He frowned, trying to figure out why Collins had manipulated events so that Freddie Goodall's thug was employed by EFAS. Collins was a lot of disgusting things but a drug dealer he was not. His business was legitimate if not as high profile as Collins implied. John had checked it out. The weasel did indeed manufacture electronic components for washing machines and dishwashers. Over on the north side of the city. The area from which Freddie Goodall and his brother Breeze originated. Tommy's bosom buddy.

John ran his hands through his hair. Jesus! Criminals infiltrating the business which had been his life? A blackmailing slut and a drug-pusher's thug. Slowly, John dropped his hands to his side as realisation dawned. A smile began to spread across his tired face. How perfect! What poetic justice! Tomorrow he would have to sign his 40 percent share over to Francine. She had left him no other viable option. The price of her silence. Yan Gilmore was probably set to fire him from his job. But now he didn't give a fuck! They could have it, criminals and all. Let Yan Gilmore deal with Francine Keyes and her lethal breasts, with Victor Collins and his lethal friends. They deserved each other.

Collins was driving away now and his sidekick was sloping off into the shadows. He was probably a very efficient security man. He appeared capable of killing if he had to. Or even just for pleasure. John turned his back on the monitors and walked to his car, certain now that Freddie Goodall had a toe-hold in EFAS. Trailing Tommy, stealing Lynn's car, vandalising the shop, had just been warning shots.

Hints that Freddie Goodall was not to be thwarted. John got satisfaction too in figuring out that Goodall must have an even bigger hold over the weasel. His front man. Victor Collins.

CHAPTER 31

Lynn had not slept at all last night. She had worked through the dark hours, packing, cleaning, organising her get-away. The new day had dawned before the two suitcases she was allowing herself were packed and waiting in the hall.

Exhausted now, she refused to sit down. She could not afford thinking time. She checked her passport – in date. Her credit cards – clear. Her bank card – healthy because of the insurance check. Flight ticket – one way to London. She had booked it on-line last night. A few days in London doing the tourist thing. Hyde Park, London's Eye, Tate Gallery, Buckingham Palace. She loved London. She could lose herself in the throngs and draw energy from this most vibrant of cities before traveling on to a destination yet to be decided. Maybe France. Her French was just about good enough for her to manage to work there.

She phoned for a taxi. "In thirty minutes, please," she said. The tight schedule meant she had to dash into the shower, throw on some clothes, forget about make-up until later. As the thirty minutes ticked away Lynn rushed around her apartment, turning off switches, making sure she had dumped all perishables, checking taps to ensure they were off. When the intercom sounded, she knew she had cut the time too tight.

"Taxi for Rooney," the voice on the other end said.

"Two minutes," Lynn promised.

She ran around again, double checking. Sure that she had eliminated all danger of flood or fire she picked up her cases and gave a last look at her apartment. There were still so many details to be arranged before she finally sold it but they could all be handled long-distance through her solicitor and the estate agent. But only she could say goodbye to her apartment, to the place where she and John Enright had at last connected in the way they should have over twenty years ago. The place where she and John Enright had said their last goodbye. Pushing her cases ahead of her out into the hall, Lynn closed the door. The slam was loud in the morning quiet. Final. She dropped her keys into her bag. A souvenir. The estate agent had a duplicate set. Maybe she would set up home somewhere else again and start another sorry collection of memorabilia. These keys could start the new collection.

The taxi driver was drumming his fingers impatiently on the steering wheel when she reached him. He got out reluctantly to help with her cases.

"Where to, ma'am?" he asked.

"The airport," Lynn said abruptly, hating being called by a title as sedate as 'ma'am'.

The taxi driver laughed. "You'll be lucky. I hope you're not in a hurry to get away. Haven't you seen the weather?"

It was only then that Lynn noticed the thick fog. One of the worst she had seen. It swirled in gauzy sheets, blanketing

Cork in an eerie half-light. Even the sounds of the waking city were muffled.

"Maybe it's better at the airport," Lynn said hopefully. "That's much higher up."

The taxi man shrugged and looked at her as if she was a bit crazy. He got back in the car.

"Well, do you want to go or not?"

"I must. I have to be in London today."

Lynn sat in beside him and peered through the windscreen as they drove along. It was as if they were traveling through an alien land of swirling mists, the only colour coming from the foglights of approaching cars. She had hoped to see the clock face on the Shandon Steeple, the grand sweep of Patrick Street, the deep and winding river Lee and magnificent Trinity Church with its Gothic spire. Landmarks of Cork city. A place she loved and might never see again.

"Good luck," the man said to her at the airport as he handed her the two cases. "I hope you don't have to wait too long."

He drove away and Lynn looked around her as far as she could see. It wasn't far enough. If anything, the fog was thicker here. When she stepped inside the airport her fears were confirmed. People were crowded around the monitors and every screen had the words *'Delayed'* or *'Cancelled'* against the flight times. Incoming flights were being diverted to Dublin or Shannon but the outgoing were just on hold or not going at all. Her London flight was on the cancelled list. Shit!

Lynn sat down, her cases on the ground by her feet. She could join the long queue at the information desk but what was the point in that? 'Sorry. Beyond our control. We'll let you know as soon as possible.' Bollocks to that!

Dragging her cases along, too impatient to go find a trolley, Lynn marched up to the first car-hire desk she could find. In twenty minutes it was all arranged. Lynn Rooney had a car, her cases were in the boot and she was heading slowly and carefully out of Cork airport. It wasn't until she came to the roundabout at the entrance to the airport that Lynn seriously thought about where she was going. Left back into the city and then to Dublin, Donegal, Belfast. Straight ahead to Carrigaline, the scene of her despair. A right turn would take her towards West Cork, picturesque, wild in places, lush and fertile in others.

Another driver hooted impatiently behind her. Lynn indicated to turn right. Wild and lush it would be.

The fog seemed to get worse as Lynn drove. But instead of feeling threatened by the rolling mist, she felt safe. On and on she traveled through her grey-white, silent tunnel, every mile making her more confident in her future. She knew now it didn't matter where she went. How far away or how near. She would have to find her own safe place, her own John Enright free space in her head. Then, and only then, could Lynn Rooney find peace.

* * *

As John Enright drew the curtains in the guest bedroom of his house, he thought the morning weather was appropriate to his mood. It was foggy and grey, sunlight struggling to filter through the thick mist. He hadn't slept much. This bed was narrow and uncomfortable and he missed Meg. He had

434

lain beside her for twenty-one years and he missed her warmth and the comfort of knowing that he wasn't alone during the dark hours.

He made coffee and toast and sat at the kitchen table. It was seven o'clock now. He should have a strategy planned for his meeting with Patrick Morgan and Yan Gilmore. He should know how he was going to handle today's confrontation with Francine Keyes. All the tossing and turning last night had brought him no nearer definitive answers. Should he wait until Patrick and Yan fired him or should he beat them to it? Jump before being pushed? Simply hand over his shares to Francine. Admit defeat. How could he be sure that this would buy her silence? How had Shane Richards and Nigel Stagge guaranteed that one pay-off was all she'd get? Or had they?

His thoughts were no clearer in the morning light. The coffee went cold and butter congealed on his toast as his thinking went around in circles. Suddenly it was seven thirty and John was not yet showered, had no strategy, no plan and no way forward. But now thankfully, he had no more time to think.

* * *

Meg had waited to get up until after she heard John leave the house. It was more comfortable that way. For both of them. Glancing at her watch as she pulled on her sweater, she saw it was after nine o'clock. John's meeting with Patrick Morgan and Yan Gilmore was only an hour away. His fate would be sealed. All their futures decided.

Carrie was already eating breakfast when Meg came

downstairs. "How are you, Mum? You look more rested this morning."

"Hi, Carr. I feel well thanks. Tommy gone to school?"

"Yeah. Do you know he was awake at six this morning studying?"

Meg laughed. "My God! Who stole our Tommy and left a student there instead?"

"No, Mum. Don't laugh at him He needs encouragement now. You know he can do it if he wants. He's very clever. He'll get the points in his Leaving Cert if he gets down to work."

When Meg had her orange juice and muesli ready she sat down opposite Carrie.

"It's not that I don't want to encourage him," she explained, "but this sudden interest in architecture started just because he discovered the hidden fireplace in Karl Hemmings' building. Hardly a basis for choosing a career. He could change his mind again by tomorrow. You know what he's like."

"I do indeed know what my brother's like. He's clever and funny and very determined when he wants something. In his own way he has seen The Light. We all serve in different ways." She got up from the table. "I'm off to McCurtain Street. I'm trying to get as much organised as I possibly can before Garth gets here. I can't believe he'll be in Cork so soon. Tommy's calling to give me a hand after school so don't expect him home until tea-time. And don't be late for your date with Mr Girvan Cooper."

"It's not a date! You cheeky monkey! You know it's a business meeting. I'm a proper artist."

Carrie laughed as she walked out to the hall to collect

her jacket. She called back over her shoulder. "Ask a fair price for your work! Don't go selling it for half nothing. I'll say a prayer."

Meg heard the front door bang and then she was alone in the house that had once meant so much to her. It still did, full of memories as it was. She remembered the new smell of it when she and John and baby Carrie had first moved in. Fresh paint, fresh plaster, fresh start. It had seemed so big after the cramped space of the flat in which they had been living. They never could have bought this house except that Patrick Morgan had so generously increased John's pay when he got married. It seemed that John had not repaid that generosity very well.

Their bed, their king-sized bed, had been the first piece of furniture they bought for their new home. It had been so exciting waiting for the delivery and then tearing swathes of plastic wrapping off the mattress and carefully dressing the bed with new sheets and that sickly lemon, nylon quilted spread Meg had thought very chic at the time. How many times had she and John made love in that bed? Tommy had been conceived there. When had they begun to move to their own side of the bed, to sleep together but apart?

Annoyed with herself, Meg got up to make coffee. If she spent any longer reminiscing, she would think herself into depression and she'd had enough sadness in the past few days to last her a lifetime. In that short space of time she had lost her husband and her best friend. She still hurt. She probably would for a long time to come.

Mug of coffee in hand, Meg wandered out onto the patio. It was a damp and very foggy day. Bleak. Shivering, she walked back inside and went upstairs. She would have to choose what to wear for her meeting with Girvan Cooper and more importantly she would have to decide what price she was going to put on her work. Her art was her hope for the future now. How much was Meg Enright's future worth?

* * *

Leeside Art Gallery was aptly named. It was housed in a converted granary store on the banks of the River Lee. The building itself had a striking exterior, granite stone and deep-set windows with blue-painted frames and a double door, the timber painted the same azure as the window frames. A comfortable blend of imposing and welcoming.

Meg was nervous as she walked through the double doors and unsure if she should have brought her painting with her. She had decided against doing that. Suppose Girvan Cooper had changed his mind? How foolish would she look then with her picture under her arm, slinking away in failure?

She stood inside the doors and felt more alone than she had ever felt in her life. Meg hesitated, one part of her wanting to confidently walk across the old oak flooring of the gallery while the other part, the shyer, timid part, wanted to run to the arms of the people she so loved. To find again her place as wife, mother, friend, and forget about independence and fulfillment. And her clothes weren't right. What had possessed her to wear jeans and high heels with her navy jacket? Why hadn't she worn a skirt, gone for sophistication? She could do smart too…

"May I help you? You seem a bit lost."

Meg started as she recognised the voice from the phone

call. She had not seen Girvan Cooper approach, engrossed as she had been in self-doubt. He was tall, tanned, blonde-haired. Probably fortyish. A very handsome man with azure eyes which matched the window frames and door of his gallery. She smiled at him.

"Girvan? I'm Meg Enright. We spoke on the phone."

"Meg! How nice to meet you in person. Come into my office please. We'll be more comfortable chatting there."

He led her through the main gallery, past the area where sculptures were displayed and through a heavy door with cast iron latches and door knob. He saw her admiring glance at the door as he held it open for her. "Reclaimed," he said. "Sort of. I found it in a skip."

"It's beautiful. It would have been a shame to destroy it."

He waved her to a seat and sat himself behind the walnut bureau. "Now," he said, pushing some paperwork aside and then clasping both hands together on the desk top, "I think we should get business out of the way first. Then we can chat. I assume you understand I want to buy the painting you have on display in Curtain Call. I would like it for my own personal collection. You're willing to sell?"

Meg nodded, afraid to say anything in case she gave away how very naïve she was in art dealing.

"Well, let's try to reach an agreement then without spilling any blood. Suppose we both write down how much we think your painting's worth and then we'll try to reach a middle ground."

He pushed a sheet of paper and pen towards Meg and then quickly wrote on a page himself, folded it and held it up in his hand. Meg sat, her pen poised over her page, remembering Carrie's words not to sell her work too cheaply. Maybe one hundred euro. No, too cheap. To hell with it! She'd chance two hundred. She could always backtrack. She wrote her figure, folded it as she had seen him do with his and held it up.

"Ready? Swop."

They exchanged papers. Meg's hands were shaking as she opened his page. She looked and then looked again to be sure. Six hundred euro! Tommy could be right. Girvan Cooper must want Hannah Enright's linen sheets thrown into the deal. Six hundred euro!

Girvan looked up from his page and smiled at Meg.

"Lesson one. Know your worth. I offered you the money I did because I know neither the canvas nor paints are of good quality but the painting itself, your work, will some day be very valuable."

"Thank you. Thank you very much. I've always sketched and painted. I never wanted to do anything else really."

"Can we make a deal?" he asked. "I'll take all your future work and put it on display here. When you sell, which you will, I'll take 20 per cent of whatever price you charge. And of course I'd like you to complete another painting as soon as possible because I want the Curtain Call shop painting for my private collection as I told you. What's the title, by the way?"

"Inside Out," Meg replied without even having to think. What else could it be called when all their lives had been turned inside out over the past few weeks, exposing tender, sensitive parts to the coldness of reality. Carrie's soul. She wore it on the outside now, always pandering to its demands for prayer and understanding and forgiveness. Unrelenting goodness. Tommy's struggle to lose the child inside and live

440

comfortably with the man he had almost become. John's secret trysts with Francine Keyes and Lynn Rooney, exposed. Turned inside out. Lynn's secret passion for her best friend's husband no longer an inside secret but an outside shame. And Meg? Inner, hidden grumblings of dissatisfaction, dragged from their hiding place. Inside out.

"I'd like to know the inspiration behind it." Girvan said. "What inspired the passionate, angry strokes juxtaposed with your delicate brushwork, Meg?"

"A long story."

"How about we exchange stories over coffee? You tell me about Inside Out and I'll tell you about the plans I have for Leeside Art Gallery."

Meg looked at the handsome man sitting across from her, at the kind eyes with the laughter lines at the corners, at his blonde hair and his strong chin. She smiled at him.

"I'd like that, Girvan. I'd like that very much, thank you."

Girvan served coffee in Spode cups with delicately crafted matching saucers. By the time they were on their second coffee Meg knew Girvan was originally from England but that he had moved to Ireland as a child when his father had inherited an estate in Cork County.

"Carnlee House. Do you know it?" he asked. "It's east of Cork City. Fifteen kilometers or so."

Meg shook her head. She didn't know the house but now she knew the origin of Girvan's posh accent. English and gentry. Made for very proper pronunciation.

"It's a millstone, you know, the house. It was built in 1750 and it has seemed to need re-building every second year since. It's a huge responsibility as far as maintenance is concerned. It's not very grand but historically it's interesting and well worth the effort of preserving it."

Meg heard the pride in his voice and saw the passion in his eyes. It was obvious that Girvan Cooper loved every stone of Carnlee House.

"Do you farm the estate?"

"Good lord, no! I'm afraid the days when the Carnlee Coopers were landed gentry are well and truly gone. We've sold off practically all of the land over the years to pay duties and taxes and other such vulgarities. Twenty acres around the house is what's left of our once two-thousand acre estate. Most of that twenty is woodland. It's very beautiful. You must come to see it some day."

"That would be nice. I love woods. And streams. Do you have a stream?"

"My very own babbling brook. My wife used to love it. She used to say ..." He stopped talking and looked away into the distance.

Meg saw pain in his blue eyes. Suddenly he blinked and brought his attention back to her.

"Sorry. Unfortunately my wife died two years ago. I miss her very much. But that's enough about me. What about you, Meg? Any deep, dark secrets I should know about the newest artist in Leeside Art Gallery?"

Meg laughed. Secrets! My God! How about a husband who might soon be penniless because he couldn't resist his secretary, a best friend who had run away because she loved him, a daughter in a religious sect and a son – well, Tommy was Tommy.

"Don't we all have secrets?" she asked. "My painting, or rather my ambition to be a painter has always been my secret."

442

"You have children?"

"A boy and girl. I should say a man and woman. They're aged twenty-one and almost eighteen now. Grown up."

"Time for Meg to bring her secret ambitions into the open then. Your husband must be very proud of your talent."

It was Meg's turn now to stare into the distance. What should she say about John? He's not my husband any more? What a cruel denial that would be of all they had shared together, their children, the home they had built. And yet, had they ever been husband and wife? Boyfriend and girlfriend in the beginning. Mother and father then. But husband and wife? A real, grown-up, mutually supportive relationship – no.

She shifted her gaze to the owner of Leeside Art Gallery. Girvan Cooper was a stranger to her. John Enright was part of who she was. She smiled at Girvan.

"Yes, he's very proud and supportive."

"Good. Well then, I've some suggestions to put to you as to how we might further your artistic career. I know some of our more established artists would be happy to take you under their wing and guide you along. Also, if you'd consider it, I have a vacancy at the gallery for a part-time assistant. Cataloguing, invoicing, that type of thing. Just a few days a week but it would help you get to know the art business. "

Meg knew she was getting herself into a knot here. She should go now. She wasn't in a position to take Girvan's offer of part-time work or spend enthralling hours painting. Not until she knew what was happening with John. She wanted this job. How she wanted it. To be around other artists, to be immersed in the beauty of Leeside Art Gallery, lost in the creativity of her work. But none of that would pay the bills or send Tommy to college if John was out of work and broke. She stood and offered her hand to Girvan.

"Thank you for the offer, Girvan. If you don't mind, I'll take a little while to think about it. Talk it over with my husband."

Girvan took her outstretched hand and smiled at her. "Of course, Meg. Take whatever time you need."

The fog was rolling off the river in diaphanous sheets when Meg went outside. Leaving her car where she had parked it, she strolled along the quayside, over St Patrick's Bridge spanning the River Lee since 1861 when it replaced the original toll bridge destroyed in the great flood of 1853, down busy Patrick's Street and then headed in the direction of the park. She walked and thought and sometimes prayed. Eventually she sat on a secluded park bench and cried. Meg Enright was hostage to her husband's fate and there was nothing she could do but wait.

CHAPTER 32

At two minutes to ten John parked outside Patrick Morgan's house. At least it was a break from EFAS where he had spent the past hours watching and waiting in vain for Francine Keyes to turn up. The woman was mistress of exquisite torture.

John noticed that the window on the lounge, or the front room as the housekeeper Anne called it, was open so he knew Patrick was already up and waiting. The old man always insisted on having the window open when he was in the room and obviously this damp and foggy morning was no exception.

Surprisingly, Anne didn't answer until the second ring. When she opened the door to John she seemed unusually flustered.

"He's in the front room, waiting for you, but I told Yan and I'm warning you now too, don't go upsetting him with business. He's not well this morning. Not well at all."

When John saw Patrick, child-like in his big chair surrounded by cushions, his skin so pale and delicate that a purple network of veins shone through, his breath rasping, he understood Anne's concerns. Yan was sitting in a chair across from his uncle, an expression of completely false concern on his face. How could he care about this sick old man he had met briefly as a child and with whom he just yesterday renewed his acquaintance?

"Come in, John," said Yan. "Sit down. Coffee?"

John nodded to Yan and sat as invited. Yan Gilmore seemed to have mastered the art of taking charge of his surroundings. He appeared to be the one in authority here too. EFAS wasn't enough for him. Anne went off presumably to get coffee and John leaned towards the old man.

"How are you feeling, Patrick?" he asked, not knowing what else to say. What do you ask someone who's obviously in pain, visibly suffering? Blatantly dying.

Patrick coughed and both younger men leaned forward anxiously as he seemed to struggle for breath.

Anne appeared, patted Patrick's back firmly and settled him into his cushions again.

"If I hear that cough once more, you're going on your oxygen and I don't care how proud you are," she said sternly.

Patrick smiled at her and there was a shadow of his old grin. "Anne, aren't you late for Mass? Why are you still here?"

"I must get Mr Enright's coffee. And I'm not sure about leaving you."

Yan stood up and walking across to Anne caught her by the elbow. "Tell you what," he said, "I'll get coffee, you go to Mass and pray for us all. Deal?"

Anne looked up at Yan and John could have sworn he saw adoration in her eyes. "Well … if you're sure. I haven't missed morning Mass in forty years."

"You won't this morning either," said Yan, leading Anne out the door.

The front room was very quiet when they had gone except for the sound of Patrick's laboured breathing.

"Thank you for coming here to see me, John," he gasped. "This is my best time of day and as I'm sure you notice, it's not up to much. There are things to be discussed and it's now or never for me."

John opened his mouth to utter encouraging sounds, to say maybe this is a bad patch and tomorrow you'll feel better, that there may be a drug, a miracle cure. Such mumblings would have been an affront to the old man's intelligence.

"No problem, Patrick. You know I'm an early bird anyway."

"I thought I knew you very well. Everything about you. We never really know another person though, do we? Not really."

Patrick's head suddenly dropped onto his chest. John half stood, his mouth open to call Anne back. Then Patrick raised his head, a stream of mucousy spittle dribbling out of the corner of his mouth. "I've done some things, John, that you may find hard to accept. I apologise in advance and hope you understand. If you don't mind now, I'll just have a little rest before our meeting starts."

The head, too heavy for the shrunken body, dropped again but this time John stayed sitting as he was. So that was it. Patrick was definitely going to fire him. Not Yan Gilmore. Patrick himself was going to do the dirt. Doubtless at Yan's instigation. Were they going to make an offer for his shares? Was that it? Yan wanted 100 percent control. Maybe he should just tell them stuff their job and announce that he was giving his shares to Francine Keyes. That they had a new partner. Patrick gasped, a distressed heave to get air into his lungs. John bowed his head and felt shame. How could he think of upsetting this man to whom he owed so much and who now was suffering more than anyone ever should?

The front door banged. John stood and looked out the window. He could see Anne's red headscarf bob along between the high hedges which bordered the pathway. In fact the whole front garden was a mass of overgrown shrubs and hedges. A natural habitat for birds Patrick used to claim although John had always suspected he just couldn't be bothered with the garden and there was no woman in his life to nag him into cutting and trimming and planting flower beds.

Yan Gilmore came into the room, two mugs of coffee in his hands, and gave one to John.

"I made yours strong, John. You'll need it."

"Really?"

Yan went over to Patrick and shook him gently. "Are you up to having the meeting now, Pat? If you like you can just rest and we'll carry on."

"No. I'll be alright." Patrick heaved himself up in the chair with surprising strength. "Right, John. First things first. You and Francine Keyes."

About to swallow a mouthful of coffee, John almost choked. "Wh-what?"

"Shut up, John. There's no time for bullshit. Francine Keyes set you up. She's blackmailing you."

Patrick was peering at John now and there was no trace of weakness or incapacity in his eyes. John felt a shiver go through his body. But it wasn't fear. Or shock. It was relief.

A glorious letting go of secrecy and the dread of being discovered, of having his stupidity and naivety exposed. Patrick and Yan knew. Soon everyone would know. They'd laugh and snigger but the world wouldn't stop. Or change. The tides would still turn, the deserts burn. Nothing of importance, worth or beauty would have been lost. Just John Enright's pride. He looked from Patrick to Yan and lifted his head a little higher, spoke a little stronger.

"She wants me to sign over my 40 percent holding of EFAS to her or else she'll bring proceedings against me for attempted rape. I did nothing to her. She seduced —"

"We know," Yan interrupted. "We know everything about Francine Keyes. Her past history including St Alban's Clinic and Oakley Developers. Her future plans for EFAS."

"But how …? Why didn't you warn me?"

"I tried to, lad," said Patrick, "as much as I could. We had to let her hang herself. I'm sorry you had to go through this. Although you'll have to admit you brought a lot of it on yourself."

John's newfound feeling of relief was fast dissipating. How in the hell could Patrick have done this to him? The answer to that must be Yan Gilmore. The bloody New Zealander wanted a clear pitch. He wanted everything to himself, even John's 40 per cent.

"You were just a part of Francine's plan," Yan said. "She had much bigger ambitions. She wanted the whole company."

"So she tried to get to you too, did she? I found out that she went on a visit to New Zealand before she joined EFAS. Is that where you met her? Did she go there to track down Patrick Morgan's nephew?"

449

John noticed Patrick and Yan exchange glances. They were surprised that he knew about her New Zealand trip, were they? They must think him a complete and utter fool.

Patrick cleared his throat with a harsh rattling sound.

"My nephew, Yan Gilmore, is dead," he announced.

Outside John heard the muffled sound of traffic as it drove through the stillness of fog ... in the distance a siren sounded ... a bird warbled sweetly in the garden ... while in the front room Patrick continued his noisy battle for breath. John himself inhaled a huge gulp of air and tried to talk but no words came out.

Patrick was speaking to him, gently, his words interspersed with rattles. "Unfortunately Yan died before I had a chance to make amends for my years of neglect. I wasn't lying, John, when I said how bitterly I regret that now."

John turned his eyes on the man from New Zealand, sitting there so quietly, just watching John squirm and Patrick gasp.

"If Yan is dead, who the fuck are you?"

The tall man stood and offered his hand to John. "Mike Choy. Yan Gilmore's partner in business and his best friend. Yan died in the Amazon jungle. We got official confirmation two months ago. I still can't believe he's gone. Dead."

John saw pain in the clear brown eyes. Real pain. He had obviously loved and respected Yan Gilmore. John shook the hand he offered.

"I'm sorry about Yan," he said, "but why are you here and why were you pretending to be him?"

"I'm here because Francine Keyes needs to be stopped and because Yan Gilmore left behind a wife and three small children. I'm just protecting them from Francine. And I'm trying to protect his uncle too."

John stood and began to pace. This was too confusing. Yan Gilmore wasn't here. He was dead. So what about Francine?

"Does Francine think you're Yan?"

"No. The whole impersonation thing was her idea."

John stopped pacing. It all began to make sense now. A real Francine plan. Trick a dying old man out of his company shares and blackmail his fool of a partner for the rest.

"Clever," John muttered. "Very clever."

"Not really," Mike said. "She's not as smart as she thinks. She doesn't know Yan is dead. I never told her. She believes he's still in the Amazon."

"Why did you not tell her?"

"Because she'd probably go after his wife and children then. They're next in line to inherit. I promised Yan that I'd look out for them if he – if he wasn't around to do it himself. Francine is still under the impression she and I are going to sail off into the sunset with the profits from the sale of EFAS."

"She never figured on decency," Patrick said. "Mike rang me and told me about her plan. I've known since first she suggested it to him in Queenstown. I asked him to play along. We've watched her every step of the way. I want her caught good and proper. She's abused her trust and hurt people for the last time."

"And I want her caught too," John said with heartfelt sincerity, "but how are you going to do that? She could make a case against me if she wanted to unless she gets her shares and I'm sure she has contingency plans for you also. Francine will get her way."

"Francine Keyes will get what she deserves and Yan Gilmore's widow will get what's due to her," Mike said angrily. "We're calling in the police. We wanted to talk to you first."

John's heart constricted in his chest. Jesus! The very thing he had been trying to avoid. Police, publicity, maybe being questioned by Willy Feeney. He felt sweat break out on his forehead. He felt faint, as if he needed a whiff of Patrick's oxygen.

"Don't worry about the attempted rape story," Mike said. "She won't go ahead with that. She told me exactly what happened and how much she paid the delivery man and porter to lie. I'll testify to that. And there was no camera in her apartment. Forget it. She'll have bigger problems to worry about. Besides, you didn't miss anything. She's not much in the sack."

This was all too sudden for John. There were too many extremes of emotion. Yan Gilmore was dead. Mike Choy had pretended to be Yan Gilmore. Mike and Patrick had entrapped the entrapper. Francine would get her comeuppance. And they had all played John Enright for a fool.

"You should have told me," he accused Patrick.

"How could I? You might have told her. I couldn't take that chance."

"Do you honestly think I'd have protected her if I'd known the truth?"

"We've grown apart over the past few years, John. I wasn't sure what you would do."

Touché! John Enright had reaped the rewards of his neglect of Patrick Morgan.

"I'm going into a nursing home soon," Patrick said now. "It's time. You should know, John, that I've named Yan's widow as beneficiary of my estate. At least I can help her look after his children. This house I'm leaving to my housekeeper Anne. She'll care for it. But everything else to Yan's widow. I've had an offer for EFAS. A good one. Would you be willing to sell your shares too?"

John bowed his head. Could he let EFAS go? The challenge, the pride. The achievement. The bottomless well into which he had thrown his youth, his marriage, his children's growing-up years. The life-sapping, soul-scarring smallness of it all. He thought of Patrick Morgan. An old man, dying alone. A statistic. An EFAS victim. John looked again into the EFAS well. It had become a cesspit, a burial ground for what could have been. His decision made, he lifted his head.

"Yes, I'd like to sell."

Yan laughed. "You'll enjoy this, John. The funny thing is that Francine set up the sale. You know Victor Collins?"

John nodded. Victor Collins. Suddenly the weasel's proprietorial air in EFAS made sense. The little prick felt he owned it already.

"I want the deal done and dusted. You can see how little time I have left for bargaining," said Patrick. "He's offered six million for the lot. One hundred percent ownership. How would that suit you, John?"

Forty percent of six million would suit John bloody fine. And Francine behind bars. Just great. But how could he allow Patrick go ahead, suspecting what he did now? He couldn't.

"I don't think we should sell to Collins. He may have

criminal connections. I'm pretty sure that the security people he uses are employed by a well-known drug dealer. You've probably heard of him. Freddie Goodall. I'm afraid I've allowed Collins bring them to EFAS too but I'll get rid of them today."

Patrick put up a hand to stop John. The remnants of a hand. It was more bone and sinew wrapped in translucent skin now. "Collins' business is legitimate. That's our only concern. He's made an offer, is willing to put his money up front and sign on the dotted line today."

"Today? Jesus! That's quick!"

"We pushed him. And if you're asking, John, if I trust Victor Collins – no, I don't. He's shifty and can't look you straight in the eye. But he hasn't the balls to be a small-time criminal let alone a pusher. He may be fronting for someone though. Someone who's bankrolling him for the purchase. He says he's using his components business as loan collateral but I don't believe him. Someone needs EFAS for their own purpose and is using Collins to get it. But I don't give a damn. Nor does Mike. You shouldn't either."

"But what if it's bought with – say drug money – what kind of shit would we end up in then?"

"Our solicitor has drawn up papers. So has Collins' solicitor. It's up to those guys to advise us and their advice to date is that everything is above board. We're ready to swap contracts on your say-so, John. What do you think?"

John thought Freddie Goodall was buying EFAS as a delivery and distribution centre for his drugs. The perfect cover. Lock the contraband safely away from prying eyes until he needed it. Protect it with his own security under the guise of running a legitimate business. Goodall obviously had something on Collins. Some bit of information valuable to Goodall and a nightmare to Collins. For the first time, John felt some empathy with the weasel man.

There was a possibility too that John was wrong. He hadn't shown great judgment lately, had he? Maybe Collins was just a despicable little prick with money to spare. And why shouldn't Yan Gilmore's widow and John Enright have some of that?

"Well, John?"

"What are you getting out of this, Mike? What's your cut?"

"I'm getting justice for Yan Gilmore and keeping my word to him that I'd look after his family. And of course I got a trip to Ireland and a chance to meet Patrick, old rogue that he is!"

"I want Mike to take payment but he won't. He's going back to his crazy extreme sports business. He could almost be my real nephew he's so stubborn."

John smiled at Patrick and then nodded his agreement to the deal. It seemed that Victor Collins was about to buy himself a storage business.

Mike Choy stood. "Do you want me to make the calls now, Pat? The solicitor and the police."

"Solicitor first, please. Let's get that one out of the way. He'll need my signature. Ask him to call soon. I'm getting too tired for all this."

Mike went out to the hall to make the call. John watched as Patrick Morgan's head fell onto his chest again. He felt pity and a deep sorrow at the man's suffering, at the unfairness of it. Walking on tiptoe across the room, he stooped down beside the old man and held the paper-dry hand in his. Patrick shakily lifted his other hand, touched John on the shoulder and then tiredly raised his head. Both men regarded each other with affection and the sadness of goodbye. They forgave each other for the things they'd had to do to survive.

* * *

Outside in the rambling garden, underneath the windowsill of Patrick Morgan's front room, Francine Keyes was stiff and cramped. And shocked. And very, very angry. Maybe the worst thing of all was hearing Mike Choy say so casually that she was 'not much in the sack'. Pig! Traitor!

A thrush was singing its stupid head off in the wilderness of the garden. Francine wished she could throw a stone at it. Or better yet if she had a gun she could shut the creature up for good and then turn the weapon into the disgustingly musty old room on the other side of the window and spray the wheezy, dribbling old man, the fumbling John Enright and the beautiful, deceitful Mike Choy with a hail of bullets and watch them squirm and twist and bleed and cry out in pain.

Knowing that the old bag Anne would shortly be back from Mass, Francine began to make her way out of the garden in the same way as she had come in, creeping between shrubs and bushes, keeping low until she reached the perimeter wall. Glancing up and down along the footpath and back at the house she saw that the coast was clear. She slid over the low wall and crept along until she had reached the bend in the road. Then she straightened up and raced towards her car which she had parked in a cul-de-sac three streets away.

Fuck Mike Choy! Damn him to hell! What a narrow escape she'd had. She'd been so lucky that Dan Shorten had been eavesdropping yesterday when Mike and John Enright were talking about meeting this morning in Patrick Morgan's house. Dan had told her what he overheard. Enough to make her curious and determined to investigate for herself. She still couldn't believe that Mike had deceived her so thoroughly. The intuition on which she relied so heavily had let her down. Francine had been thinking true love and even wedding bells. He'd pay for this. He'd pay dearly. He'd wish he was as dead as Yan Gilmore. She knew where to find him. Mike would never leave his precious Extreme Sport Company in Queenstown. He was a boy in a man's body. But what a body! What a shame.

Traffic was crawling in the thick fog. Francine knew now she was dealing with a very clever enemy so the sooner she was organised and on her way the better. She would have to get back to her apartment, collect cash and passport. Her credit cards she would leave behind. Too traceable. She'd soon pick up more. The apartment she didn't give a toss about. It belonged to Shane Richards anyway. He had just allowed her to stay there rent free for as long as she chose. He'd be glad to be rid of her. As she stopped at traffic lights she tried to decide whether to take the time to sell her car or not. She would be unlikely to get an instant cash buyer. Not worth the risk. Anyway she had plenty of cash put by from various little scams and grateful, or scared, ex-boyfriends. Enough to set up somewhere else. She had always liked cash in the hand. Real money.

In the apartment at Waterside, Francine packed make-up, jewellery, two changes of clothes, two pairs of shoes and underwear. Then she opened her wall safe and took out her cash and her passports. What a clever girl she was! Who did she want to be? Not Francine Keyes any more, so she shredded that passport. Catherine Dunne? No. She didn't like her photo. She fed that to the shredder too and picked up the next one. Elizabeth Austin. Nice. Classy. Satisfied, she popped it in her bag with the cash. The one remaining passport had Frances Keyes written on it and an ugly, dark-haired, big-nosed photo. It was the only authentic passport she had, valid for another two years. She left it in a top drawer of her dressing table in case anybody, maybe the police, maybe Mike Choy, would check to see if she had left the country. Idiots!

Essentials packed and carrying the contents of the shredder in a carrier bag, Francine took the elevator down to the lobby and walked out onto the street. It was only ten minutes' walk from Waterside to the railway station. There she bought her one-way ticket and found a litter bin in which to dump her shredded counterfeit passports. Just to be sure. She made the Cork-Dublin Intercity Express train with five minutes to spare. In two and a half hours she would be in Dublin. She would fly on from there. London, New York, maybe Dubai. Some oil money would be nice. She smiled as she planned her future. A future full of plans and schemes and loads of money. Much, much more than a measly three million. It was only when she thought of Mike Choy that her smile faded. She would never, ever, again, work with someone else. Never get emotionally involved with a man. Alone, she was unbeatable. But she would not forget Mike Choy and what he had meant to her. Nor would she ever rest until she had wreaked her revenge on him.

* * *

A tramp, stinking of alcohol and cradling a brown paper bag, came to sit on the park bench beside Meg. Nervous, she stood and began to pace up and down, wishing that she could talk to Lynn. Wishing the past few weeks into oblivion.

Her thoughts were interrupted by the muffled sound of her phone ringing in her bag.

She opened her bag and saw that it was John calling. She hesitated. He must be ringing to say he had paid Francine Keyes off and that Patrick Morgan had fired him. That they were penniless. The phone rang out. Immediately it began to ring again. She took a deep breath and tried to keep her frustration and resentment out of her voice.

"Yes, John ?"

"Meg. I thought you'd never answer. Wait until you hear what happened at Patrick Morgan's house this morning!"

Meg listened and then began to smile, the smile getting broader with each revelation.

"So it will be all settled within a week?" she asked, hardly daring to believe the news John was telling her about the sale of EFAS.

"And Francine, what about her?"

Meg's smile got even more radiant as she heard that the manipulator had been out-manipulated. The hobo was watching her curiously, gathering himself and his paper bag up as if to follow her.

"Thanks for letting me know, John. I've got to go now. I'm busy. "

She switched off her phone without waiting for John's reply. He had done that to her often enough. For one vengeful moment, she hoped he was feeling hurt and bewildered by the fact that she was too busy to talk to him. She headed back in the direction from which she had come but this time her step was light and her head held high.

* * *

Girvan, sitting at his walnut bureau in Leeside Art Gallery, watched Meg with a slightly puzzled expression, waiting for her to open the conversation.

"About that part-time job in the gallery," she said . "I'd like to take you up on the offer, please."

Girvan's face lit up. "I'm delighted, Meg. Welcome on board! I know you'll be a great asset to Leeside Art Gallery." He held out his hand to her and they shook on the deal.

"I hope you'll enjoy working with us."

"There's just one thing, Girvan. My daughter's fiancé is arriving from the States next week. Would it be alright if I didn't start until the week after ?"

"No problem at all. Family must come first. Just let us know when you're ready."

Meg smiled at Girvan Cooper. She knew, with every instinct of her sensitive nature, that her association with Leeside Art Gallery and this blonde-haired, blue-eyed owner of a babbling brook was going to be a very happy one.

CHAPTER 33

There was no sign of Tommy. He had locked himself into his room. Taking his example, John had escaped to the garden shed. Carrie and Meg were setting his teeth on edge with all their fussing. They were in a welter of excitement about the arrival this evening of the Hemmings. They were cooking, polishing, hoovering, arranging and rearranging the house. He had been in their way. In fact, in the week since he had left EFAS, John felt that he was in everybody's way.

He emptied a box of odds and ends onto his work bench and searched for a screw that might fit the coffee table he was trying to fix. A job he had started four years ago and had never got around to finishing.

His phone rang . He dug frantically into the pocket of his overalls. Lynn – it might be Lynn.

The name that flashed on the screen was not Lynn Rooney. It was Willy Feeney and he had some very interesting news about his research into Karl Hemmings and Inner Light Movement. John listened intently. Then he went to find Meg.

* * *

Meg checked her watch and then popped the roast into the oven.

"I think we're done here, Carr. We'd best get ourselves ready now."

Carrie looked up from the napkins she was folding and smiled at her mother. "Thanks for going to this trouble, Mom. I know Karl said we could all meet at their hotel but this is a lot more personal, isn't it ?"

Meg went to Carrie and hugged her close. "Anything for you, Carr."

"You're going to love Garth. And he you."

"I'm sure. I'll finish that for you. Go make yourself glamorous for your boyfriend."

Carrie didn't need telling a second time. She scurried away just as John came in the back door in his overalls, trailing sawdust as he went.

"The floor, John! I've just washed it!"

"Never mind the bloody floor. Where's Carrie?"

"Gone upstairs to get ready. Why?"

John went and closed the connecting door between the kitchen and the hall, then came to stand in front of Meg.

"Willy Feeney rang," he said.

"Oh! Have they caught Francine Keyes? Or was it about Lynn's car?"

"No."

"Why am I not surprised?" Meg said sarcastically. She got the dustpan and brush and began to sweep up the sawdust.

"Stop!" John caught her by the elbow and turned her to

462

face him. A nerve ticked underneath his right eye. Meg knew then he was very angry. And afraid. There were so many things, so many tiny, intimate details they knew about each other.

"What's wrong? Something Willy Feeney said, is it?" A fearful suspicion chilled her. "You asked him to find out about ILM, didn't you?"

"Yes, and he did. ILM's crazy but not sinister. The FBI did a thorough investigation. It seems Carrie could leave any time she likes and nobody would try to stop her."

"Well then, what's all the drama about?"

"Karl Hemmings. And Pearl."

"Pearl? Why? Carrie has nothing but good to say of her. She practically reared Garth."

"She's a – a – prostitute."

Meg laughed. "God! Willy Feeney told you this? He must be winding you up. For one thing Pearl is devoutly spiritual and for another she's sixty for heaven's sake!"

"Alright so. I should have said she *was* a prostitute. This is serious, Meg. Willy got the information from Interpol. Our future son-in-law was reared by a common tart. She ran what Karl Hemmings likes to call the 'boarding house' where he stayed when first he went to Portland. It was, in fact, a brothel in which Pearl entertained her clients. The police were called in when someone complained about a child living there."

"Garth?"

"Yes. He was only three. Some start for a child. What kind of father could do that to his own son?"

Meg sat at the kitchen table. She felt tears well in her eyes. Poor Garth! A little three-year-old in a brothel.

"What else?" she asked. "How did they start off in a brothel and end up in the mansion on Prouts Neck?"

"Karl and Pearl teamed up and somewhere along the line dreamed up the epiphany story. They looked after the old man who owned the Prouts Neck house. He left the mansion to them. They probably conned it out of him. Garth's mother didn't run away with another man either. That's another lie. She committed suicide."

"Suicide!" Meg struggled to absorb this traumatic news. She was afraid to ask the next question. "What about Garth? Was there anything about him?"

John shook his head. "No. Not on record at least."

"Well then, none of this has anything to do with him and Carrie."

John flopped onto a chair opposite her, puffing more sawdust around the kitchen.

"Are you serious, Meg? Are you going to let her marry into this family with a cheat and liar as a father-in-law and a prostitute as a surrogate mother-in-law?"

"I'm certainly not having Willy Feeney make my decision for me."

"Well, I'm going to tell Karl Hemmings exactly what I think of him. And I really don't want that Pearl woman in my house."

"Our house."

"Maybe we should draw a line down the middle then! Prostitutes and fraudsters on your side —"

"And Francine Keyes on yours! She'd make the perfect balance."

The door to the hall opened and Tommy came in. He looked from his mother's teary eyes to his father's flushed face.

"Ye're not at it again, are ye? I thought all the arguing was done and dusted."

"It is." Meg stood and handed the dustpan and brush to John. "I'm going to change. Let me know if you're staying for dinner."

Then she went to get ready to greet her American guests.

* * *

Meg picked up her glass and took a sip of wine. Not because she needed a drink but she wanted to feel the wetness and tang of it, the smoothness and weight of the glass, see the reflection of candlelight on the cut-glass planes. In this surreal situation she was soothed by the reassurance of familiar things.

She looked from face to face around the dining table and took another sip. Karl Hemmings dominated the whole room by dint of his physical size and his extraordinarily black, hypnotic eyes. He was a huge man, at least six foot five. Garth was tall too but otherwise had no resemblance to his father. He was blonde and blue-eyed. A very handsome boy with an open face and a ready smile. A smile matched by Carrie's who couldn't keep her eyes off him. Tommy, all neat and tidy in a shirt and jeans, was behaving. John was a glowering presence at the head of the table, poised to break the fragile peace.

"How's your hotel?" Meg asked Karl.

"Very good. It's quite near the new café so that will be convenient. I believe you've agreed to do a painting for the café?"

"I'd be delighted to. When do you hope to open?"

"It usually takes two months to get a Haven Café up and running," said Garth. "Cork will take longer though because we don't have the infra-structure set up here yet."

"Do you intend hanging around Cork until the café opens?" John asked brusquely, staring at Karl.

Meg gripped the stem of her glass more tightly. She knew John was ready to launch an attack. She tried to catch his eye, to send him a warning glance but he deliberately avoided looking in her direction.

"I'll stay for two weeks," Karl answered calmly, "and then I have more work to do around Europe. I'll be back for the opening though and to bless the marriage of Carrie and Garth."

John took a deep breath and Meg knew it was too late to stop him. She swallowed a huge gulp of wine.

"What makes you think you have any right or power to bless my daughter's marriage?"

Meg caught a glimpse of the hurt on Carrie's face. She hurriedly stood up. "Excuse me. I must see if Pearl needs a hand. John, would you help too, please?"

As if on cue, Pearl came bustling into the room, pushing the hostess trolley laden with plates of roast beef and potatoes and serving dishes.

"Sit down, Meg," she said. "Pearl don't need no help. No wonder you're so skinny. Always fretting. And John's right. It won't be Karl Hemmings blessing the marriage of our Garth and Carrie. All blessings are from The Light."

"Are you sure you wouldn't like me to help, Pearl?" Meg asked.

"She's really enjoying this," Garth explained. "We had a job keeping her out of hotel kitchens while we were traveling. Pearl likes looking after people."

"Looking after people's what I know," said Pearl, putting two plates down in front of Carrie and Garth. "Giving them what they need. I used to be a prostitute."

Having made her announcement she returned to her serving, leaving John and Tommy open-mouthed. Meg glanced at the fond smile on Carrie's face and knew that Pearl's past was no revelation to her. Another secret she had kept from her family. Her Enright family. There was something different, something deep about the way she seemed to have been absorbed into the Hemmings. They had a closeness, an acceptance of each other.

"We can only be at peace with the present when we reconcile our past. Just as Pearl has," said Karl.

"And you're reconciled to your past, are you? All of it?"

Meg cringed. John was off again. For the first time Meg noticed the tight line of Karl's mouth. The thin lips she had noted on his website. They were pursed now. His eyes glittered as he looked at his son.

"I've done some things that make me ashamed now but nothing happens without a purpose. My past is what brought me to where I am today. Praise The Light. I wouldn't change any of it, even if I could. And you, John ? Are you at peace with yourself?"

John bowed his head. An image of Francine Keyes holding her silk robe open, exposing her naked body, flashed before his eyes. He felt shame. Yes, he would change that episode in his life if he could. Then he imagined Lynn with her auburn curls and infectious smile. Sitting on Lynn's couch, her head on his shoulder, had been the only real peace he had ever known. Or would ever know. He raised his head and looked at the man who was probably a fraud but spoke wisely nonetheless.

"No, Karl, I'm not at peace. Not yet."

Karl turned his black eyes on Meg. "And you?"

"That's it now," Pearl said, having placed the gravy jug and vegetable dishes on the table. "We'd better say Grace. Our food will be going cold."

She sat herself down beside Karl and caught his hand.

Everyone joined hands then. Karl Hemmings' deep voice boomed around the dining-room, invoking The Light, thanking his god for the blessing of his son and his new daughter, for leading him to the Enright family, for bringing joy and hope into their lives.

Meg looked at her husband, head bowed, and knew that he had a long, lonely path to travel before he found his peace, at Carrie and Garth and their love so strong that it seemed to shine, at Tommy, casting curious sideways glances at Pearl, trying to look bored but still touched by the sacredness of this special candlelit moment.

Prayer over, everyone picked up their knives and forks.

Meg looked at Karl. Past the receding chin and thin lips, into his kind and very wise black eyes.

"I can answer your question now, Karl. Yes. I am at peace with myself."

"Praise The Light."

Meg Enright smiled. As mother and wife her job was done. She was just beginning her journey towards Meg Enright artist and woman. She was at peace with that.

EPILOGUE

2 YEARS LATER

Even through the heavy door of Girvan's office, Meg could hear the buzz of conversation. There must be several hundred people in the gallery and they were all here to see her. The page in her hand was shaking so much, she couldn't read the words she had written. She threw it onto the desk and turned to Girvan, tears welling in her eyes.

"I can't do it. I'm going home. Make my excuses."

He took a step towards her, so close now she could see the faint green flecks in his azure eyes. He lifted his hand and gently stroked her cheek.

"You can do it. And you're not going home. Not yet. Your public is waiting."

"I'm an artist, not a public speaker. I cannot, I repeat *cannot*, go into that room full of people and talk to them. Let them buy my art or not. That's up to them. I'm not going to be a performing monkey for them."

Girvan's lips twitched and his eyes twinkled.

"You're laughing at me!" Meg accused. "Don't you realise the press people out there are just waiting for me to say something stupid. They'd love it. They built me up when I won my art awards and now they're waiting to pull me down."

Girvan stepped back from her. The twinkle in his eyes faded and he regarded her seriously.

"Your family's out there. Carrie and Garth. I saw John come in too. Your patrons, your clients are also here, people who have helped you along the way. They're all waiting to see you and to maybe hear you thank them for the assistance they've given you. This isn't just about you, Meg."

Ashamed, Meg bowed her head. Of course Girvan was right. She was a recognised and feted artist now. In two short years she had come from anonymity to having her work on display in the Hoffman Gallery in New York. She had grown as an artist. It was time that she grew as a person too.

"I'm sorry, Girvan. Of course you're right. I can't let people down. Just give me five minutes to go over my notes and catch my breath. I'll face the music then."

"I wouldn't push, Meg except I know it's the right thing for you. I could launch the exhibition, make your excuses but I don't think you'd excuse yourself. You're not one to turn down a challenge. Not any more."

Meg smiled at him. How well he knew her. Sometimes better than she knew herself. If there was anybody she should thank more than others, it would have to be Girvan Cooper.

He left then, the noise of the crowd outside getting louder as he opened the door and dimming again as it swung shut behind him. Meg picked up her notes and tried to read them. The lines of writing still blurred. God! What was she going to do? She couldn't stand in front of the microphone and talk to those hundreds of people, no matter what she had promised Girvan. Her paintings would have to do the talking for her.

Going over to the little cloakroom, she looked in the mirror to check her make-up. She was pale, her hazel eyes seeming huge in her face. Her dress was classic. A cream silk strapless gown which showed off the pearls Girvan had given her to perfection. This necklace was a family heirloom, worn by generations of Cooper women. Meg frowned at her reflection. She had yet to decide whether she would become one of that illustrious line or not. She loved Girvan, of that she was sure. She loved the fun, the laughter, the kindness he brought into her life, their shared passion for art and Carnlee House. The way he made her feel special and loved and safe. But marriage? Meg Enright had been hurt by forever promises.

A tap on the door interrupted her thoughts. It must be time. She stepped back into the office expecting to see Girvan. Instead John was standing there, darkly handsome in a charcoal grey suit and white shirt. He had lost some weight and looked healthier than he had done for a long time.

"I thought you should know that Carrie and Garth are attracting some attention outside. They've decided to hold a prayer meeting."

Meg laughed, imagining the scene as her daughter and son-in-law stood with outstretched arms, singing their praises to The Light. No surprise to the people of Cork City at this stage. The Haven Café in McCurtain street had become the most popular meeting place in town and Inner Light meetings were well attended. The new cafés in Limerick and Dublin cities were following suit and their log cabin retreat near Owenahincha Woods was always occupied. Karl Hemmings had been right. Ireland was ready for a new type of spirituality.

"Any sign of Tommy?"

"He arrived just minutes ago, all fluster and panic," John said. "His flight from Dublin was delayed. He got the results of his summer exams by the way. First class honours. In another two years we'll have an architect as well as an artist in the family."

Meg crossed her fingers. Taking control of her own life had done nothing to lessen her superstition. Tommy deserved success. He worked hard but life wasn't always fair. The only way she could protect her children from harsh reality now was to tip the favour in their balance by her superstitious little rituals.

"Did he mention Breeze?" Meg asked. "Any news from London?"

"Yes. He's got his recording contract. Tommy is more excited about that than his own exam results."

"I'm glad," Meg said and meant it. Jason Goodall deserved success and happiness.

John walked towards her and for an instant she was Meg Riordan again, watching the handsome young John Enright approach across the crowded dance floor of the Grattan Club.

He put his hand on her arm and smiled at her. "I'm so proud of you, Meg. I always have been."

"I know. Thank you, John. Thank you for all the happy times we had and sorry that it had to end the way it did."

"We won't talk about endings. Too sad. It's all about new beginnings now. Can you believe we'll be grandparents in just three months' time?"

472

Meg shook her head, still stunned at the prospect of her little Carrie becoming a mother. Yet more confounding was the prospect of becoming Granny Enright the Second. Maybe it was time.

John had not lost the ability to read her thoughts. "You and Girvan? It's serious, isn't it? Will we see a new lady of Carnlee House?"

"He's asked me to marry him, yes. And I do love him very much."

"But?"

"But nothing. I'll talk to you after I've spoken to him. And you? How's Lynn?"

John's soulful brown eyes glowed with a warm light Meg knew she had never inspired. His face lit up as he spoke about Lynn. "She's in great form. Talking about getting another dog. A companion for Enwrong."

Meg laughed as she always did when she heard the name Lynn had christened the little mongrel she'd rescued from the animal shelter. Only Lynn could turn an Enright into an Enwrong.

"Obviously living in West Cork and walking the dog suits you, John. You look very trim. How's your business going?"

"Well enough. It's a very small unit in comparison to EFAS but I've learned at last to put work in perspective. Unfortunately, I learned the hard way."

They were silent, each thinking just how much they had learned about themselves in the past two years and how difficult the learning process had been. There had been hectic days and lonely nights. Days when John wondered if he should have stayed in EFAS and worked for Victor Collins instead of trying to set up his own business, when Meg wondered if she should have kept Curtain Call instead of struggling with her creative demons. Nights when John and Meg had lain in their separate beds, in their separate houses, their bodies aching for the comfort of each other.

"It was fate, wasn't it?" Meg asked now. "The fog which kept Lynn from leaving the country and the break-in at Curtain Call that led to Girvan buying my painting."

"That was all down to my mother's sheets," John laughed but then his expression changed, became more serious. "You're right, Meg. It was all meant to be. Even the bad days of Francine Keyes. I often think it was Carrie's prayers which led me to West Cork and to Lynn."

"Any news about Ms Keyes? Is she still on the run?"

"Yes, probably with a new name, a new appearance and new victims. Mike Choy knows she'll turn up in New Zealand eventually, all set to get her revenge on him. He's ready for her though. At least she's out of our lives. We didn't do too badly, did we? The years we shared together gave us Carrie and Tommy. And memories."

"And Girvan. And Lynn. And the future," Meg added.

"Praise The Light, as Carrie might say!"

They laughed and then they kissed. Not the demanding kiss of lovers but a warm exchange of affection between friends. Just as John closed the door, Meg remembered something she should have told him. A rumour. Gossip around the city. People saying that something very peculiar was happening in EFAS. A lot of police activity there, things being removed from lock-up units in sealed forensic bags. Then maybe John didn't need to know. EFAS was their past. It belonged in sealed forensic bags.

Meg reapplied her lip gloss. Then she opened the heavy door, reclaimed from a skip, and entered the gallery. A ripple of applause went around the cavernous room, growing and swelling, until it thundered in her ears.

She saw Carrie and Tommy, side by side, clapping enthusiastically. Garth Hemmings stood behind them, watching out for them both. Beside them John and Lynn, so close together that they seemed like one. Girvan walked forward and caught her hand, leading her towards the dais set up at the centre of room.

"Ready?" he whispered.

He smiled and she read the encouragement in his blue eyes. She took the microphone and faced her family, her public. All eyes were on her, watching, waiting, listening.

Silence fell on the Leeside Art Gallery. Outside, traffic passed along the quay, the evening sun slanted towards the west, the sound of a woman's laugh drifted through an open window. In here, surrounded by those she loved and those who wished her well, Meg felt safe. Loved. Protected.

She folded up her notes, then lifted her head and spoke from her heart.

Meg Enright, woman and artist, had come of age.

The End

If you enjoyed *Inside Out*, don't miss out on
Ebb & Flow, also published by Poolbeg.

Here is a sneak preview of Chapter One . . .

Ebb and Flow

Mary
O'Sullivan

CHAPTER 1

Ella knew what he was going to say long before he voiced the words. The whole scene had an inevitability, as if it had been waiting for this moment in the silences and unspoken tensions of their relationship.

He was holding his head, pacing the room, struggling for control. She sat still, wedged into her chair between cushions of guilt and hopelessness. She would have reached out to him, would have put her arms around him and held him close to her, laughed in the way she used to do, made him smile, kissed away his anger. She would have. But she could not.

"You're making no effort, Ella," he said. "There's nothing really wrong with you. Haven't you been listening to your doctor? Have you been listening to anyone else at all? Would you just snap out of it, for Christ's sake!"

Walking over to where she was sitting he stooped down and took her hands in his, the gentleness of his touch a contrast to the anger of his words. She looked into the familiar blue eyes, noticed the dark stubble on his chin, the stray threads of white in his thick, black hair. She examined his features and waited for some stirring of emotion, some vestige of feeling for this man who was pleading with her to respond. He was good-looking in a sophisticated way. A generic handsomeness, born of good breeding and careful grooming. She felt nothing but regret and pity.

"I'm sorry, Andrew," she whispered.

Dropping her hands, he straightened up. He walked to the door and then turned back to face her.

"I give up," he said. "Bury yourself here if that's what you want. But you can stop using your accident as an excuse. That was almost a year ago and you're fully recovered now. You're just being selfish."

He slammed the door shut.

Ella closed her eyes and listened to the sounds of her husband getting ready for the party she was refusing to attend. She shivered at the thought of the noisy, meaningless jumble of prescribed chitchat which passed for party conversation. The type of social occasion she used to love. Maybe she should go. Everyone would compliment her on how well she was looking, acknowledging the level of social acceptability Ella and Andrew Ford had attained, how successful their business had become. Nobody would mention the accident. That would be impolite. A party pooper.

Ella heard the rattle of car keys as Andrew picked them up from the hall table. He banged the front door on his way out. She relaxed and sank further into the blackness, into the only place where her mind would allow her to go.

* * *

480

Andrew mingled. He was good at that. The noise and vibrancy of the party was such a welcome relief from the silent blackness of Ella that he launched himself into the spirit of it with gusto. 'Resting. Just a little tired,' was his stock reply to the questions on Ella's whereabouts. There were fewer people asking now. An unaccompanied Andrew Ford on the social circuit was getting to be the norm.

He grabbed a drink from a passing waiter. The Cox brothers were not sparing anything in celebrating the completion of their latest apartment block. The wine and champagne were flowing. And so well they might. Andrew had handled the sale of the old brewery to the Coxes. They had bought the derelict building for a song and had converted it into an apartment block. It was all sold now, from the bijou one-bedroom flats to the penthouse suite. At exorbitant prices. This party was in effect an advertising campaign for their next project. Another old building at a knockdown price was due to get the Cox treatment. This time Andrew had found them a disused warehouse and the Coxes would soon transform the grotty building into *the* place to live, *the* address to have. Andrew raised his glass in a silent toast to the enterprising brothers. Being the estate agents for them meant that every time the Coxes made money, so did Andrew and Ella Ford.

"That's a very smug smile, Andrew."

Maxine Doran was standing in front of him, smiling. She looked stunning, her golden skin testament to the fact that she was just back from holiday in some exotic location. Or more likely a shoot. She was one of the more sought-after models.

"Just enjoying my champagne, Maxine. You look wonderful. Is the tan from holiday or work?"

"A bit of both actually. I was in The Seychelles. Where's Ella?"

"She's resting. She still gets very tired."

Maxine nodded in sympathy. "It will take her a long time to get over that awful accident. She was so lucky to survive. I believe she's back at work?"

Andrew nodded. That was one of the most puzzling aspects of Ella's painfully slow recovery. She had been back in the office even before getting medical clearance. And she seemed to have lost none of her business acumen. She had been, and still was, one of the most astute business people Andrew had ever worked with.

"So what do you think about this new warehouse development?" Maxine asked. "Would you advise someone to invest? In, say, a two-bed apartment with maybe a roof garden?"

"Are you interested? I've a copy of the plans in the office. If you call in, I can show them to you. You would want to move quickly though. Interest is brisk already."

Maxine laughed. "Ever the estate agent, aren't you? I'll call to your office if you promise to have a drink with me afterwards."

Andrew held out his hand to her. "Deal. Just ring to let me know and we'll take it from there."

Maxine took his hand, leaned towards him and kissed him on the cheek. Her softness, her perfume, the gentle touch of her lips, all reminded Andrew how much he missed intimacy with Ellen. How much he missed the warmth and sharing they used to have. He pushed the thought out of his mind and smiled at the beautiful woman in front of him.

"Where are you living now?" he asked. "You have a downtown apartment, don't you?"

Maxine signalled to a passing waiter and took another glass of champagne from the tray. Raising her glass, she took a sip and then slowly licked her lips. Andrew stared at the tip of her pink tongue. He felt his breath quicken.

"Why not come to see my apartment now, Andrew? Carry out a valuation. You're at the cutting edge of all this property business. You could let me know where I stand. Financially, that is."

Andrew's blood began to course through his veins. He was not naïve. He knew that Maxine Doran's invitation had nothing to do with valuing her property. He was flattered. And surprised. He and Ella knew the model socially. They usually ended up on the same invitation lists. Of course, he had always admired Maxine but she had never before shown any interest in him. She was usually on the arm of some powerbroker. Even though Ford Auctioneers was growing, it was not yet in the Maxine Doran super-league. He thought again of his wife, of Ella. Poor, sad, depressed Ella. Cold, unresponsive Ella. He took Maxine's champagne glass and placed it on a table.

"Let's say our goodbyes. I'll meet you in the car park in ten minutes. You can lead the way."

She lowered her eyelids and looked up at him through her long, curling lashes.

"I hope you like where I'm going to lead you, Andrew."

Game on. Andrew knew he was going to be very good at playing follow the leader.

* * *

Ella was still sitting in the same position as she had been when Andrew left for the Cox brothers' party. She was held there by the weight of her tiredness, by the heavy pall of guilt, by the replaying over and over in her mind of those few horrific seconds of slaughter and destruction. The accident. Post Traumatic Stress Disorder was the latest official title given to her despair. Selfishness, Andrew called it. They were all wrong. This depression was far deeper and more disabling than reaction or introspection. It was starting again now, the whole scene playing over in her head. She could not outrun, outwit or obliterate the images. Ella closed her eyes and frame by frame, relived the accident.

* * *

It had been raining all that evening. She never liked showing prospective clients around a property on a gloomy grey day. Bad weather always had a negative effect on moods and perceptions. She was sure as she led the way around the five-bedroom house that her clients felt as cold and miserable as she did. She stood on the landing and looked out into the garden. It seemed desolate and bare. Ella frowned. The garden should be one of the best features of this property, the focal point of the beautiful bay windows. Anyway, her instinct told her that these particular clients were not serious buyers. She waited for them as they poked and prodded at everything, leaving no corner unexplored and no door unopened. Glancing at her watch she noticed that it was almost six o'clock. She would have to call back to the office before going home. Getting ready for the dinner party would be a rush. Damn! Time to bring this pointless inspection to an end. She excused herself, allowing the couple time to formulate a polite refusal and giving her a chance to ring Andrew.

"Hi, Andy. Just reminding you that we have dinner with the Mahers tonight."

"Shit! I completely forgot."

Ella laughed. "How did I know you'd say that? I must be psychic!"

"I don't know what I'd do without you. Will you be back soon or will I head home and meet you there?"

"I'm out at The Orchards. I'll see you at home as soon as possible."

"Any good?" he asked.

"WOTS," Ella said, using their code for waste-of-time clients.

"See you soon then. Take care. The traffic will be heavy in this rain."

She had switched off her phone and gone to find her clients who were now opening each and every kitchen press. They all went through the motions of pretending that this was a serious viewing of the property. When they parted company at the front door they knew they would not be meeting again.

It was raining so heavily by now that Ella got drenched when she left the car to lock the gates behind her. The clock on the dash told her it was already twenty minutes past six. Blast! It was all right out here but she knew traffic would be chaotic nearer the city. Maybe she could skip the office and go straight home. But she was waiting on a close-of-deal call and had forgotten to give the prospective buyer her mobile number. If she rang him now, she would seem over-anxious and pushy. It was potentially a huge opportunity. An American with a tenuous Irish ancestry and a fortune in dot.com money to invest in Irish property. It was one call she could not afford to miss. Nothing for it but to wait in the office. Anyway, there was a seven o'clock deadline on the call and these Americans were usually as punctual as they were wealthy.

Ella was seeing the road ahead through wavering rivulets of rain. The windscreen wipers were walloping over and back but were fighting a losing battle with the torrents of water. The channels at the side of the narrow road were beginning to overflow. The sooner she got off the miserable soon-to-be-flooded little strip of tarmac the better. She pressed her foot on the accelerator. The car aquaplaned. One second she was driving forward and the next she was being borne helplessly towards the ditch on the opposite side of the road. Her hands were glued rigidly to the steering wheel, her breath stuck somewhere between lungs and mouth. Then she felt the tyres grip. She turned the steering wheel and the car responded. Control returned as quickly as it had been lost. Her breath gushed out and the blood she had not realised had left her face rushed back.

"Fuck!" she said softly, the profanity a mixture of relief and fear.

Back on her own side of the road, she slowed down to a crawling pace. There was a hairpin bend ahead and besides she was shaking with fright. That had been so close. Too close. This was her last coherent thought. The four-wheel drive lunged at her from around the bend, looming huge and menacing and already out of control. Ella knew then that the skid had only given her a scare, a forerunner of the terror which gripped her now. It filled her with the knowledge that she might never see Andrew again, never hear him laugh, never see another sunrise or feel the wind on her face.

The woman at the wheel of the Land Cruiser was screaming, her mouth open wide, her eyes staring. She had one hand reaching behind her towards the back seat and Ella realised there must be a child or children there. Real time stopped. Sound and vision were swept into a maelstrom of intense, slow-moving emotion. Fear was the overriding feeling but it was tempered with fascination. Minute details burned onto Ella's brain, as if her senses were grabbing at the last smells, sights and sounds they would ever perceive. She smelt the scent of her perfume mixed with perspiration and knew it was the smell of fear, heard the thunderous crunch of metal on metal as the two vehicles crashed, saw an intricate spider-web pattern creep across the windscreen of the 4x4 as the woman's blonde head hit it with force. Ella struggled for breath as her airbag pushed her back and the impetus of the motor pushed her forward. Her car began to spin out of control. The Land Cruiser was heading for the opposite ditch. When the 4x4 mounted the stone wall, Ella was turned in that direction. A child's face was glued to the back window. A beautiful child. A little boy, blonde-haired like his mother. He was crying, calling out for help. Ella's car spun again and this time it landed in the deep roadside channel. It had overturned. The rest of Ella's nightmare was viewed from this upside-down perspective, until finally, mercifully, when the hell became too much, she lost consciousness.

* * *

Ella shook her head now and stood up. Why was this happening? Why did she have to relive this nightmare over and over? It had not been her fault. The inquest had said so. Andrew had said so. The man who was the husband of the woman and father of the little boy had said so. Why couldn't she forgive herself? And why was she sitting here, full of self-pity, when she should be at the Cox brothers' party? By her husband's side. She looked at her watch. It was twelve fifteen. Where had the night gone? She must have slept without realising it. Too late to go out now. "Too late," Ella muttered out loud as she thought of the person she had been before that horrible day. Sometimes she imagined that the bright, ambitious, fun-loving Ella had died in the crash and was replaced by this manic-depressive zombie who was also named Ella. Maybe she was just plain exhausted. Sleep was now just a series of hellish re-enactments of the accident.

She went to the medicine cabinet and took out two of the sleeping tablets the doctor had prescribed for her. Two little nuggets of oblivion. She swallowed them with a glass of water and then went to bed. She fell into a drug-induced, gloriously dreamless sleep.

* * *

Maxine's apartment was just what Andrew would have expected her to have. It was chic, spacious and tasteful. He examined the artwork on the walls with interest.

"You have quite an eye for up-and-coming talent, haven't you?" he remarked.

"My talent lies in knowing the right people. It pays to know who to talk to."

Andrew looked sharply at her, surprised and a bit disappointed at the crass comment. She laughed at him. "C'mon, Andrew! Don't be a hypocrite. You haven't built up your business without kissing some bottoms. You might like to call it networking but it's the same thing. How many of your clients, the big ones, the money-spinners, do you actually like?"

Taking the drink she offered him, Andrew sat down on the cream leather sofa. She was right. He had to deal on a daily basis with gobshites but he smiled at them and agreed with their points of view and went to their parties. With few exceptions he had learned that the bigger the account, the more obnoxious the account-holder. He shrugged.

"You're spot on, Max. If kissing arse pays, why not do it? Let's drink to that!"

They touched glasses and then she sat down at the opposite end of the couch. Kicking off her shoes, she settled cushions behind her back and gracefully put her long legs up onto the soft leather. Andrew held tightly onto his glass. His fingers needed something solid to hold, something to distract them from following in the direction his mind was already travelling. He imagined how soft her skin would feel. Smooth and cool. She was unpinning her hair now, shaking her head as the blonde shining tresses came loose and tumbled around her face and shoulders.

"Comfortable?" she asked, stretching out one leg towards him and touching the side of his thigh with her perfectly shaped, tanned foot.

He gripped his glass even tighter. He was hypnotised by the slow movements of the model's red-varnished toenails as her foot stroked his thigh. Blood-red varnish. Blood. Like he had seen pour from Ella's head. He shivered, remembering his wife after the accident, her waxen face, her bruised and swollen eyes, remembering how he had prayed for her survival, bargained with any god who might listen.

"It must be a year now since Ella's accident," said Maxine, almost as if she knew what he was thinking.

Andrew nodded. It would be exactly a year next week. Twelve months of absorbing the horror of the crash, the deaths of the young mother and her child, the seemingly endless wait for Ella to come out of her coma, the joy when she opened her eyes. Then the inquests, the therapy and the pain of realising that the Ella he had known and loved was gone forever.

"Do you think Ella has changed? Events like that can alter people's personalities."

"I don't want to talk about my wife," Andrew said abruptly.

Maxine swung her legs down from the couch and, smiling, took his hand. "Of course you don't. You want to value my apartment. Come with me and I'll show you around. There are only two bedrooms but the master bedroom is big and has a Jacuzzi. Maybe you'd like to see it?"

Andrew put his glass down and cleared his mind of all Ella thoughts. He was not really being unfaithful to her. Twelve months of celibacy was all he could take. He needed sex and obviously his wife did not. He needed this beautiful woman who was leading him by the hand into her bedroom. It was just a fuck.

"I may need to try the bed too," he said to Maxine.

"Of course," she smiled. "Nothing quite like hands-on experience, is there?"

Her smile and her words freed Andrew. He took Maxine

with all the hunger and passion of a man deprived of sex for a year. Then he took her again with the tenderness of a man making love to a beautiful woman.

* * *

As Andrew dressed, Maxine noticed in the dim light that she had left a scratch on his back. She felt sated, totally satisfied, as she had never been before. This had not been part of the plan. She had meant to be the one in control. And she had been for a while. The man had been desperate for her. For any woman. It seemed like stuck-up Ella Ford was holding out on her husband. Not surprising maybe after the trauma of that fatal accident. Silly bitch. She could have found rehabilitation in her husband's arms. Maxine stretched and put her hands behind her head, knowing that she was showing off her breasts to their best advantage. She smiled at Andrew.

"Funny, isn't it, that we have known each other socially for so long and yet we never got together before now?"

"I'm married," he answered sharply.

And guilty, Maxine thought. Better let him work that one out for himself. She was not worried. Andrew Ford would be back. Of that she was sure.

In conversation with

MARY O'SULLIVAN

1. Is writing a new discovery for you?

The glorious thing about writing is that it's a discovery every time you sit down to create a new character or story. My love of reading and the escape it provided from everyday life led me to pen my first tentative words – angst-filled poetry and rambling school essays. I wrote about the sea, nature, my teenage passions and insecurities. I'm glad to say not much has changed. I still write about the power and beauty of the sea, the grandeur of nature and the vagaries of life well past the teens but still passionate and insecure.

2. Tell us about your writing process; where do you write? When? Are you a planner or "ride-the-wave" writer?

There's a little room in our house. It measures approximately eight by ten and just about accommodates a desk, computer, bookshelves, CD rack and a filing cabinet. This is where I come to write. My space – filled with my treasures and unbounded by its diminutive size. A heap of stones surround the base of the monitor. Not just any old pebbles. I pick up a stone in every new place I visit so each holds a special meaning and memory. Family photos, a world map and a poster of Martin Luther King decorate the walls.

Currently writing my sixth book, I have developed a routine. First a crossword to limber the brain. Then I put on a CD. Music, to me, is an essential element in my writing. A book, like music, reflects moods, has varying tempos and evokes memories. For instance, my first book, *Parting Company* was written to the strains of Andrea Bocelli's *Romanza* CD. Con Te Partirò (Time To Say Goodbye) in which he and Sarah Brightman sing together really captures the heartbreak of goodbyes and parting company.

Next step is to boot up the computer and say good morning to my characters. Ah! The writer's life! There's none like it.

3. Your first novel *Parting Company* was published in 2006, followed by your second, *As Easy as That* in 2007, and third, *Ebb and Flow*, in January 2008 – has your life changed much?

My life has changed immeasurably since becoming a published author. Writing is my full-time occupation now but I would never regard it as a job. The very word job implies time constraints, rules and regulations and dragging yourself into work on days when you would rather curl up and sleep. My alarm clock has become redundant since my first book was published. I get up earlier and go to bed later because each day has too few writing hours.

Yes, there are publishers' deadlines, certain guidelines to follow and standards to be met. Writing is challenging. It can be frustrating and tiring but it is also interesting and fulfilling. It is a way of life and one that I consider myself very fortunate to live.

4. Do you have a favourite character in *Inside Out*?

I love all my characters, even the baddies. Maybe especially the baddies as they have such devious personalities.

In *Inside Out* Meg Enright is very close to my heart. Mother, wife and successful business-woman, Meg should be happy. As I got to know her it became apparent that Meg, surrounded by people, was lonely. She's a shy woman, sensitive, intelligent and attractive. Yet there is something wistful about her. She was a very interesting character to develop and to accompany as she coped with a missing daughter, an unfaithful husband and her own unfulfilled ambitions. I admire her most of all for the courageous way in which she resolved all the issues in her life.

5. What character & scene in *Inside Out* was most difficult to write?

No hesitation here in saying the scene in which Lynn Rooney walked by the banks of the Owenabue River in the early hours of the morning. What made the writing difficult was the fact that Lynn was contemplating suicide. I had to mentally walk every step of that traumatic journey with her, think her thoughts and feel her despair. I don't presume to know what depth of hurt and lack of hope could drive a person to consider death as their only viable option but I do know as Lynn took those last few steps into the river, she saw nothingness as preferable to living with her guilt.

6. In *Inside Out* Meg's daughter Carrie disappears and joins the Inner Light Movement (ILM), a quasi-religious cult in America – you often write about people on the fringes of society searching for something more. How do you create such strong characters?

The answer to that is I create the situations and they in turn, spawn the characters. I always write on a topic which interests me or appeals to my curiosity. For example in *Parting Company*, I wrote about research into a cancer cure because my family, like so many others, has been affected by the disease. In *As Easy As That*, I touched on off-shore accounts, infertility and alcoholism. *Ebb and Flow* dealt with post traumatic stress disorder and the tantalising possibility that ghosts may in fact exist.

Given those situations and the various crises which arise, the characters need to be strong to come through to the last page! Like all of us, they dig deep and find hidden strength when they most need it.

7. Your previous books also deal with interesting issues. *Parting Company* discusses a cure for cancer, *As Easy as That* sees the main character influenced by

deception and fraud and in *Ebb & Flow* the theme of the other world and mental health are developed. Research seems to be a big part of your novels. How do you research for your books?

The Internet – what a resource! Whatever you need to know in seconds. Of course reading and talking to experts in specific areas is also invaluable.

Research can be one of the most absorbing aspects of writing a novel. I find I quite easily get side-tracked while researching a topic. One thing leads to another and I can end up reading reams on the lesser spotted catshark when I set out to look up rainfall in Maine! That's the fun part and often inspires an idea for the next novel.

Personal experience is also very useful, although I would disagree with those who say you should write only about things you are familiar with. All our life-experiences are necessarily limited whereas imagination is limitless.

8. How would you describe your novels? What or who influences your distinct writing style?

I would describe myself as a story teller and my novels as a peep into the worlds of ordinary people at extraordinary times in their lives.

My writing style is the cumulative effect of many influences. Firstly my parents, both of whom loved to write satirical poetry and had a great love of language; the educational system which introduced me to grammar and the rigors of proper sentence structure; reading, from an early age – Enid Blyton and Hans Christian Andersen's Fairy Tales – right up to the present day when reading is one of the great pleasures in my life.

I am of course, influenced by the many writers I admire but I am also of the belief that each of us, whether we put our stories in print or not, have a special story to tell and a unique way of telling it.

9. Who are your favourite authors and what are your favourite novels?

John Irving – I love John Irving's writing for his quirky characters, his attention to detail and the warmth of the relationships he portrays. *The World According To Garp* is one of my all time favourite novels

Irene Dische – I've just recently discovered this American writer and I was enthralled by her novel *The Empress of Weehawken*. Her prose is powerful and sweeps confidently from scene to scene. The Empress is a grumpy, selfish character but Dische's writing skills lure you into caring about the old lady's fate.

Jodi Picoult – Jodi's research, fluidity of writing and great plots are always entertaining. I really enjoyed her latest novel *Change Of Heart*

Beatrice Coogan – author of another favourite novel of mine. *The Big Wind*, set in nineteenth century Ireland, deals with the lives and loves of a generation during that complex and turbulent period in Irish history. The book opens just as the worst storm ever to cross Ireland (6th Jan

1839) lashes its fury on rich and poor alike.

Marian Keyes – Marian's great talent is to take life's tragedies and find the humour which always lurks, even in the darkest moments. *Watermelon* had me laughing out loud and cheering Claire on.

Melissa Hill – Melissa is mistress of the 'twist in the tail'. She keeps you guessing right up to the last page. *Never Say Never* is a particular favourite.

10. We want to get a sneak preview – tell us a bit about your next book – have you started writing it yet?!

The first draft is complete but there's many a re-write between now and the final book.

It has the working title *Under the Rainbow* and deals with friendship and loss. The main character, Adele, a primary school teacher on a year's leave from her job, has become almost like a sister to me because I wrote this book in the first person. Writing 'I' instead of 'she' brought the character that much closer.

Adele returns to her home place with the romantic notion of stepping back in time and being as carefree as when last she lived there. She had forgotten that she had grown-up, as had her best friends Carla and Jodi. Tensions arise between the friends, between Adele and her mother and between Adele and the new arrival in town, Eoin Ahearn. With the tension comes the need for honesty and with tragedy the need for healing.

Also published by Poolbeg

Parting Company

MARY O'SULLIVAN

On the surface Claire Hearn has lived a charmed life
with success at work and at home. But now
everything she holds dear is starting to fall apart.

Just why is her ambitious husband Brendan flying off
to a secret meeting in Bonn? And how come his
boss, Claire's father Frank Dawson who is valiantly
fighting to keep the family business afloat, has no
idea what Brendan is up to?

As her marriage disintegrates before her eyes, Claire
channels all her passion into her research which is on
the brink of an important breakthrough. But little does
she know that powerful people have set their sights on
this discovery and want it for themselves.

With tragedy and heartbreak threatening to engulf her
world, Claire will need to keep her wits about her as
she comes up against the glamorous and dangerous
Yvette Previn and the multinational she represents.

But as the web of intrigue starts to unravel Claire
must remember to protect the most vulnerable thing
of all . . . her heart.

ISBN 978-1-84223-255-2

Also published by Poolbeg

As Easy as That

MARY O'SULLIVAN

Kate Lucas is happy. She's married to businessman Fred
and works as P.A. to the leading trial lawyer in the
country. A member of the smart set, Kate believes that
having a baby is all she needs now for total fulfilment.

That is until a tragic accident reveals her friends in a
new and shocking light. As proof of immoral and illegal
behaviour unfolds, Kate is forced to find answers to
some very difficult questions. Her quest for the truth
leads her from Ireland to Budapest.

Along the way her relationship with her husband
weakens while that with her boss grows into something
far more than just loyalty to her employer.

Has Kate's chance of complete happiness slipped
away from her, never to be recaptured?

From the bestselling author of *Parting Company*

ISBN 978-1-84223-270-5